About the

Elizabeth Beacon has a passion for history and storytelling and, with the English West Country on her doorstep, never lacks a glorious setting for her books. Elizabeth tried horticulture, higher education as a mature student, and briefly taught English and worked in an office, before finally turning her daydreams about dashing, piratical heroes and their stubborn and independent heroines into her dream job – writing Regency romances for Mills & Boon.

Regency Rebels

Regency Rebels:

Second Chance

ELIZABETH BEACON

MILLS & BOON

First Published in Great Britain 2024
By Mills & Boon, an imprint of HarperCollins*Publishers* Ltd,
1 London Bridge Street, London, SE1 9GF

www.harpercollins.co.uk

HarperCollins*Publishers*
Macken House, 39/40 Mayor Street Upper,
Dublin 1, D01 C9W8, Ireland

ISBN: 978-0-263-32328-3

UNSUITABLE BRIDE
FOR A VISCOUNT

Chapter One

Viscount Stratford hardly noticed the rain-sodden countryside he was riding through or the cloud-veiled hills slowly emerging from the gloom.

Confounded storm, Alaric thought briefly as urgency drove him relentlessly on.

Finding his niece was all that mattered and last night's rain had cost him precious hours. He spent the time pacing a wayside barn impatient for even a glimmer of light and how could he sleep when his niece was missing in a deluge? At this time of year nights were short, and the rain had finally stopped, but at this very moment Juno could be wandering alone and lost and soaked to the skin in the hills—even if she had been taken in by strangers would they be kind to her or use her to make money? He shook his head to try and shake off an image of his naive niece held for ransom by hardy rogues, or lying hurt and feverish somewhere and needing him. So badly it hurt to think that he had failed her yet again.

How had he ever managed to persuade himself it was a good idea to leave Juno in his mother's care while he went to Paris to try and be useful to the Duke of Wellington in his new role as British Ambassador to France? The Royalists and even some former Bonapartists might fawn on the Duke, but it was Bonaparte's former capital, for goodness' sake. It beat Alaric how anyone thought it a good notion to put one of the defeated emperor's foes in such a post, but never mind that now. Juno was all that mattered and thank goodness his London agent had sent warning all was not well so he was already on his way home when she ran away.

And who can blame her when her life was intolerable and you were busy being self-important elsewhere, Stratford? What a fine guardian you have proved to be.

No wonder his orphaned niece had run away to find her former governess, who was now living in the still-sleeping town just visible in the distance. What comfort had Juno ever got from him or his mother?

None at all, the relentless voice of his conscience condemned him once again.

Even thinking about the Dowager Lady Stratford made the weariness of his days on the road between here and Paris lie heavy on his shoulders and he tried to shake it off. But now that Juno had run away from the only family she had left he could not escape the truth any longer. Since he inherited this wretched title he had neglected his niece and driven himself to places he did not really want to go and done things he had no need to do just so he did not have to think about the dratted woman and all the cold places she had left in his life. Which made him a coward, he concluded as he eyed the sleepy Herefordshire town up ahead.

Even if she was not so fond of Miss Grantham, he could see why Juno would set out for this quiet and out-of-the-way place so far from fashionable Mayfair. His mother would sooner walk barefoot down New Bond Street in rags than come here to make her granddaughter return to Stratford House and do as she was bid. So of course Miss Grantham had looked like Juno's best ally in a crisis. The lady had taught, guided and cared for the girl for four years and he had not. His own niece did not feel she could ask him for help when his mother decided to ignore Juno's objections and marry her off against her will to a rich middle-aged peer who was willing to pay the Dowager Lady Stratford handsomely for a young wife and the prospect of an heir as soon as he could get one on her.

'Over my dead body,' Alaric vowed as impatience and guilt made the distance between here and Broadley seem endless.

His horse had to pick its way past ruts and potholes full of floodwater and it would be reckless and cruel to try and spur him on. How dare two selfish aristocrats try to impose such a repellent match on such a young and diffident girl? And what a fool he was to think it would do his shy niece good to meet people her own age who would teach her to take life less seriously. He had only ever wanted her to make a few friends and see that under all the show and sparkle, the polite world was made up of human beings with all the faults, virtues and foibles of their kind. It was never his intention to marry her off so young and especially not against her wishes.

He thought he had made that very clear to his mother when he financed an extravagant new wardrobe for her and Juno and told his staff to make Stratford House ready to launch his niece in style. It was a rite of passage, he had reasoned, an experience Juno would have to go through sooner or later, so she might as well get it out of the way rather than build it up into a dreaded ordeal. And society would expect the only child of the last Viscount Stratford to make her curtsy the moment she was old enough. Alaric did not want whispers there was something wrong with the girl and her family were keeping her close to make her debut seem even more daunting if they put it off until she was older.

He knew Juno was a bright girl who could talk happily enough when she felt at ease with her company because he had heard her laughing and chattering to Miss Grantham on their walks around the park and pleasure gardens at Stratford Park. He even got past her wariness and shyness himself now and again, but they were not close enough to be easy together very often. He had to blame himself for that, as well as so many other things that had gone wrong with Juno's life while he was not looking.

There now, he was on the outskirts of the town he

had been aiming for ever since he grimly ordered a fresh horse and set out from Stratford House. At least the place was small enough for him to find the centre easily so he rode his weary and very muddy horse as fast as he dared into the stable yard of the posting inn and tipped a sleepy groom to tend to the animal as it deserved after such stalwart service.

'Do you know of a Milton Cottage?' he asked as the groom yawned, stared sleepily at such a filthy gentleman and scratched his head as if he had never seen the like of him before.

'Aye.'

'Where is it then, man?' Alaric demanded, impatience and terror making him sound harsh. It was either that or fall into the nearest haystack and sleep for a week, but he could not do that until he knew Juno was safe and sound.

'Up yonder.' The man pointed at an area of more prosperous-looking houses to the east of the town and backing on to yet more hills and heath.

'What street?' Alaric demanded, not wanting to waste time wandering about in the sleepy streets looking at every house along the way.

'Hill side of Silver Square—see them little houses almost out of the town by the Big House beyond, governor?' Alaric nodded. 'About in the middle is Milton Cottage.'

'My thanks,' Alaric said and tossed the man another coin before striding off as fast as he could go. The sun was nearly up at last so that would have to do. He could not wait for a respectable hour to find out if Juno was safely with her former governess.

It was hardly a square at all by London or Bath standards. The only house worth a second glance was the large one taking up the whole of the south side of the so-called square with one row of cottages at a right angle to it and another one ranged opposite. The rest was open to the view of the western plain and he could see a hint of distant hills and thought it was probably a fine prospect on a clear day. Today only the odd shaft of sunlight managed to peer past the hurrying clouds left over from last night's downpour. Alaric frowned against the brilliance of one of those bright rays of light as he knocked on the highly polished brass knocker loudly enough to tell whoever was supposed to answer it to get out of bed and do their duty.

He was lifting his hand to do it again and never mind the respectable ladies sleeping within who had a right to sleep for several hours yet, he had to know if Juno had got here safely. At last he heard movement inside and bolts being drawn back, then a key turning in the lock. About time, he huffed to himself, and glared into the narrow crack of space at the stranger warily peering back at him.

Alaric blinked to make sure he was not seeing wonders conjured up by his weary mind instead of a much plainer truth. No, she was still there, staring back at him as if he was about the worst thing she could imagine opening a door to at any time of day, let alone this one. Ye gods, what ailed him? He had never been the sort of low and lusty fool to ogle and squeeze the maids whenever he managed to catch one alone in a dark corner. He despised masters who preyed on local girls and left a trail of little bastards and ruined lives behind them. Yet even as he was ordering himself to look away and think why he was here and how urgent it was to find Juno his eyes were eating the woman up as if she was the best thing they had ever seen and they could not get enough of her.

A shaft of that curious sunlight darted into the corridor through an open door behind her and added a shine of gold to her honey-coloured hair. She had eyes of a clear, light blue he refused to call forget-me-not because it would be a cliché and there was nothing weary or shopworn about them. Still, he could not think of a better description, so it would have to do for a worn-out fool like him. It was not as if he was going to write poems to a housemaid, so it hardly mattered what colour he called her fascinating blue gaze. Still, his mind would not let go of the delightful picture of this tall and slender female blinking back at him in the early morning light.

She must have slept in her dark-coloured gown and her hair was tumbling down her back and made him want to reach out and find out for himself if it was as softly full of life and as silkily touchable as the brown-and-gold mass looked from here. Her face was a nearly perfect oval and she had finely cut features and a haughty nose, but it was her mouth—generous and still half-asleep and unwary as if it had not yet caught up with the rest of her—that did the most damage. It drew his gaze like a magnet and made him yearn for things he had no right to yearn for. He tried to dismiss the idea of kissing her unguarded lips properly awake as he wondered how such a definite, determined-looking female managed to take orders and skivvy for her so-called betters. And how *would* it feel to kiss that soft and sleepy mouth until the differences between lord and maidservant faded away and he felt as if he had come home at last to a place he was made for and fitted perfectly.

Stiff and still half-asleep, Marianne Turner was woken by hammering on the door and stumbled to open it before whoever was out there could knock again. On her way here hope won over weariness for a heady moment, then reason told her if this was the lost girl she had a very heavy hand with a door knocker. Marianne sighed with tiredness and disappointment as she drew back the bolts and unlocked the door as quietly as she could. The impatience of whoever was out there had made her fumble, which said a lot about impatience and people who used it as a weapon to get their own way.

'About time,' a deep masculine voice grumbled as soon as she had the door open a cautious few inches to eye up the stranger on the doorstep and shake her head in disbelief. He made it sound as if she was incompetent for not coming sooner when he was being rude and demanding at an outrageous hour of the morning.

'What do you mean by thundering on a lady's

door at cockcrow? You will wake up half the street.' She blinked at the unshaven, mud-spattered and very male idiot standing on the doorstep as if he had every right to go where he chose and wake up anyone he wanted to and never mind the time. She glared at him and, goodness, there was an awful lot of him to glare at, wasn't there? 'You must have heard me trying to get the door open—have you no manners at all?' she demanded.

'Not with incompetent bunglers. Now hurry up and let me in, then go and tell Miss Grantham I need to speak to her,' he demanded as if she should scurry about at his bidding and curtsy as if her life depended on it all the while and she was not doing that either.

'No,' Marianne said grumpily and refused to be awed by his height and powerful build.

Luckily, he could have no idea Fliss Grantham was not upstairs fast asleep in her maidenly bed. In fact, Fliss had been marooned up in the Broadley Hills by last night's storm and at least Miss Donne's maid had told Marianne's brother, Darius, about a shepherds' hut up there where they could take shelter from the deluge. Secretly Marianne had been delighted that the stubborn pair would now have to admit the powerful attraction between them that had been so obvious from the start. They would have to marry after a night alone in the hills so that was one reason to be cheerful this morning, now she came to think of it. Except this ill-mannered, unshaven and travel-worn stranger had thrust his very muddy boot in the door while she was busy thinking about Fliss and Darius, so now she could not slam it in his face.

Oh, and Fliss's former pupil, Juno Defford, was still missing after a night of heavy rain. She had far more important things to do than wonder how it might feel if this arrogantly masculine fool was clean, had shaved and was as fascinated by her as she was in danger of being by him, if she did not wake up properly and get back to real life.

'Go away and take a bath and shave, then come back at a civilised hour,' she ordered the man impatiently. 'But only if you intend to ask civil questions when you get here, mind. Throwing demands about as if the rest of us cannot wait to obey you sets people's backs up and we have enough to worry about already.'

She glared down at his intrusive foot in the hope he would remove it. No such luck; the man had neither manners nor regard for a lady's peace and privacy. She tried not to blink in the face of his eagle-eyed scrutiny, but he was tall and she was not used to looking up that far at a man. It felt as if a force of nature was glowering back at her and it was far too early in the morning to deal with one of those when she had so many other things to worry about. She eyed the powerful masculine form under his dirt-spattered and travel-worn clothing and wrinkled her nose fastidiously to tell him what she thought of his disreputable state.

Behind several days' growth of beard his features were clean-cut and patrician and she supposed he would look stern and impatient even without the whiskers. With them he looked like a pirate, or a very dirty duellist who was all hard eyes and dangerous edges. Something deep inside her whispered he looked like a warrior rather than the idle gentleman of means his accent and the quality of his clothes under all that dirt argued he must be. She almost preferred him this way if he had to be here at all. The set of smooth-shaven and immaculate gentlemen of fashion he probably belonged to when he was clean and decent and not trying to intimidate his way into strange houses made her inner radical stir and shake her fist at the luxury they took for granted while so many people in this unfair world had nothing but the rags on their backs.

'I must speak with Miss Grantham immediately,' he argued like a king in disguise.

A pretty heavy disguise, she argued silently and stayed where she was.

'On personal business,' he added in the deep and growling voice that secretly sent a shiver of awareness down her spine. 'Kindly let me in without more ado, then go and tell Miss Grantham I have arrived. Never mind if she is dressed or no, it is urgent,' he added as if his outrageous demand would remove her from his path like magic.

'Absolutely not,' she replied, folding her arms across her body to make it very clear she was going nowhere.

She could stand here until half the townsfolk were wide awake if she had to and she had no intention of telling this grim and arrogant stranger that Fliss had been out all night with a man she would now have to marry if she wanted to save her good name. Even if Marianne had wanted to tell him that tale, it was not hers to tell. The man glared at her again and looked determined to stay in the way until he got what he wanted. She felt a treacherous stir of pity for the dark shadows under his hard blue eyes and the lines of exhaustion so stark around his mouth. He looked as if he had been screwing up his face against the elements and physical weariness most of the way here. He was not wet enough to have been out in the worst of the storm, but he did not look as if he'd spent much of last night sleeping either. In fact he looked as if he had spent days of hard effort and not much sleep to get here with the dawn.

For a fleeting moment he reminded her sharply of her husband Daniel after too many hard days on the march. But this was not the time to weaken or grieve for what she had lost and this man did not need her pity. Her memory of how exhausted she had felt after days in the tail of the Peninsular Army would not help her be sternly objective about him either. And this bossy autocrat had nothing in common with gallant and kind Sergeant Daniel Turner and his beloved but sometimes very weary wife. She reminded herself this man's filthy clothes had once been of the finest quality and no amount of money could buy him a right to stand on a lady's doorstep issuing brusque orders at dawn. He needed taking down a peg or two if he thought it should.

'Go to the local inn and get some sleep,' she told him brusquely. 'If you fall down on their doorstep, at least the grooms and ostlers can carry you to the barn to sleep off your journey. If you collapse out there, we will just have to leave you lying there until you wake up again.'

'I dare say you think you are a good girl protecting your employer's privacy, but a young woman's life could depend on you doing as you are bid, my girl, and you are confoundedly in the way,' he informed her with exaggerated patience, as if she was the last straw he was trying hard not to sweep aside like an annoying fly.

'I am not the maid, you stupid man. Nor am I a girl,' she told him with a sneaky little worm of temper writhing away inside her. He must have taken one look at her slept-in clothes and unkempt hair and decided she was of no account.

'Who are you, then?' he barked impatiently.

'A friend of Miss Grantham's and of her own former governess, Miss Donne—whose privacy you are violating by calling at her house at such an unearthly hour and demanding the company of a lady living under her roof.'

'Privacy be damned,' he said with an exasperated sigh, as if he was still thinking of pushing past her to rouse the household and maybe even opening every door he came across until he found Fliss behind one of them. And all he would find was an empty room and neatly made bed so she could not allow that.

'Do tell me where you live, sir, so I can organise an early morning invasion of your house and see how *you* like it,' she said and did her best not to blink when he stared back as if daring her to do her worst.

'Stratford Park,' he snapped impatiently.

Oh, no, he must be Viscount Stratford, then— Juno Defford's uncle and guardian and Fliss's former employer. How could she not have realised he was the only autocrat likely to turn up in Broadley demanding Fliss's presence at this ridiculous hour of the day and throwing his weight about when she did not jump to obey his orders? He was supposed to be in Paris annoying the French, but here he was on Miss Donne's doorstep, annoying Marianne instead.

'So *you* are the idiot who caused this unholy mess in the first place,' she said with a glare to let him know what she thought of him for neglecting a girl he should be honour bound to care for.

'Maybe,' he said wearily. He took off a fine and filthy riding glove to rub a hand over his eyes.

'I suppose you really are Lord Stratford?' she said with haughtily raised brows to let him know his title cut no ice with her.

'Yes, and you are still in my way. Whoever you are, you seem to know a great deal about me and mine although we have never set eyes on one another until this very moment, so you must also know how urgent my mission is and I must suppose you are being rude and obstructive on purpose.'

'Think what you please, I am not rousing the household when they had so little sleep and so much worry yesterday because of what you did to your unfortunate ward.'

'Is Juno here, then—is she safe?'

Chapter Two

At last, there was a gruff but almost painful anxiety for the lost girl in his voice and Marianne had been accusing him of not caring about her ever since she heard Juno Defford's sad story from a panicked Fliss yesterday morning. He had treated the poor child like an unwanted package he could hand over to his mother to be rid of however she chose and look how the wretched woman had chosen to do it. The very idea of such an April and December marriage for the girl had made *her* shudder with revulsion, so goodness knew how alone and desperate such a young woman must have felt when she realised what was being planned for her. Taking a deeper breath to calm her temper and trying to remind herself there were two sides to every story, Marianne struggled to be fair to him, although it really was a struggle.

'No,' she said starkly. She could not give him false hope. There had been no sign of the girl yesterday and no late-night knock on the door to usher in a soaked and exhausted Juno.

'God help us, then,' he murmured wearily, as if hope his ward was here was all that had kept him riding on for what looked like days and the loss of it meant he might collapse after all. 'What must I do to find her?' he added despairingly.

Marianne knew he was not speaking to her when he shut his eyes and swayed as if her *No* was a felling blow. She watched him battle exhaustion and despair and her temper calmed at such signs he really did care about that lonely little rich girl whose only refuge in a storm was her former governess, but something told her sympathy would only revolt such a proud man so she had best not risk it for both their sakes.

'We looked all the way from here to Worcester yesterday and searched every hiding place we could think of on the way back,' she explained curtly. 'The rain was so heavy in the end we could only see a few steps in front of us, so we were forced to give up the search for the night. It will begin again as soon as all the searchers are awake after their long and weary day yesterday.'

'I would not have stopped,' he muttered almost accusingly.

She felt fury flare again and was glad it stopped her having to feel sorry for his lordly arrogance. 'Then you would be no use to anyone now, would you? I told you we could not see for the force of the rain. If you had been out looking for her in it with no idea of the local terrain, we would now be put to the trouble of rescuing you as well as finding your niece.'

'You were out in it as well, then?' he asked incredulously.

'Of course I was. Did you expect me to sit at home sewing while a young woman was lost and alone and with all that brooding cloud about to warn us that a heavy storm was on the way?'

'I expect nothing, ma'am. You are a stranger to me and still in my way.'

His hard expression and stony look of indifference made her temper flare, hot and invigorating this time, and there was no reason to hold back now he had made it so obvious her opinion did not matter a jot. 'Then *expect* me to be furious about a girl's lonely and probably terrifying journey from London to Worcester on the stage. She must have been easy prey for a petty thief and thank God she met with nothing worse than robbery, unschooled as she must be in the ways of rogues and con men. I dare say she has never even travelled by post before, let alone on a public stagecoach, and I admire her for getting as far as she did.

'So you can *expect* me to admire her courage in walking into an unfamiliar countryside when all her money was stolen and I doubt she is used to much more than a leisurely stroll in the Park. And *expect* me to pity a lonely, put-upon girl who felt the only person she could flee to for protection was her former governess. But please *don't* expect me to think *you* care a snap of your fingers for your niece and ward, my lord. I cannot believe you can possibly do so when you left her so alone and friendless under your noble London roof that she felt she had to come all this way on her own to find sanctuary with the one person who would love and support her come what may.'

'I expect nothing of you. I do not even know who you are,' he replied shortly.

She might have felt her temper hitch even higher if not for the flat weariness in his blue eyes as he stared back at her as if he could hardly see who she was for utter weariness and worry. 'Just as well,' she said grumpily because she did not want to feel compassion for him. Loathing for the haughty and indifferent family who gave a shy girl no choice but to run away from home had powered her through anxiety, fatigue and the threatening storm all day yesterday. She did not want to be fair to him until Juno Defford was safe and she was still very tired herself. She had fallen asleep waiting up for Juno to knock on Miss Donne's door and walk in out of the endless rain. Obviously she needed to be angry with someone to keep on doing whatever had to be done to find the missing girl and he would do very well.

'Who is it, Marianne?' Miss Donne's sleepy voice demanded from the top of the stairs and Marianne could hear the painful anxiety in it.

Lord Stratford used the momentary distraction to move her out of his way as if she weighed nothing. He was inside the house before she could protest or counter his sneaky move. Oh, drat the man! She cursed him under her breath. She should never have lowered her guard for even a second and now he was sure to get in the way of the search for his niece. He would throw orders out left, right and centre and he had no idea of the shape of the countryside or any of the places where a girl might seek shelter from a storm. Marianne shut the door behind him with an outraged sniff and glared at his lordly back. She had been right about his arrogance and bad manners all along then. How stupid of her to feel even an iota of pity for the man when he obviously did not deserve any.

'Viscount Stratford,' she called out to warn Miss Donne exactly who had broken into her house at an outrageous hour of the morning. Yet her shoulders still felt the echo of his leashed strength under that fleeting touch. She refused to let that be because awareness of him as a man had shot through her when he put her aside as if she was weightless.

'Oh.' Miss Donne's voice gave away her horror at such a visitor arriving at her door at dawn with Fliss not here to greet him.

A few moments of tense silence stretched out and Marianne hoped His Lordship was squirming with discomfort as the wrongness of forcing his way into a lady's residence at such a ridiculous hour of the day finally hit home. No, of course he was not, she decided as his impatient frown stayed firmly in place. He was not capable of examining his own actions and could only pick holes in all they had done yesterday to find his unfortunate niece.

'Then of course you must let His Lordship in,

Marianne, dear. Ask him to wait in the front parlour while I dress. I will come down and explain what little we know of his niece's movements as soon as I am fit to be seen.'

Miss Donne's voice faded as she went back to her room and shut the door behind her and Marianne was left eyeing the filthy viscount dubiously. She raised an eyebrow to tell him he was not fit for a lady's parlour, particularly not one as neat and clean as Miss Donne's. 'You could always come back when you are cleaner and more civilised and in a better temper,' she suggested coldly.

'Where is the kitchen?' he barked as if she had not spoken.

'Of course, silly me. You are not humble or polite enough to go away to bathe, shave and change out of your riding clothes and come back later, are you? How could I be so stupid as to think you might act like a gentleman instead of an aristocrat?' she carped as he shot her an impatient glance, then strode down the corridor leading to the cheerful best kitchen Miss Donne and Fliss used as a dining and sitting room when they did not have company. She had left the door open when she stumbled towards the front door still half-asleep to stop his rattle on the front door. Silly of her, she reflected now, as he spotted the obvious place for a filthy and travel-worn gentleman and Marianne had to tag on behind like a sheepdog keeping a wary eye on a fox.

'All I care about is my niece, everything else can

wait,' he told her and looked around the sunny room as if they might be hiding Juno in a corner.

Now she had to admit to herself he really was desperate to find his niece and he seemed so much safer when she could fool herself he was heartless. He sighed when he realised he was wrong about Juno perhaps being hidden in here from the likes of him, then he frowned down at the last faint glow of last night's fire as if he had never seen one before. That traitor pity for his desperate state of mind and body turned her heart over; followed by embarrassment when she realised her own nest of cushions and covers was still lying on a Windsor chair like a discarded shell and betraying her own largely sleepless night.

She hastily folded the quilt Miss Donne's maid had found for her when Marianne insisted on waiting up just in case the missing girl found her way to Miss Donne's house despite the downpour and nobody heard her knocking. She might as well have accepted the guest bedroom Miss Donne offered her. Then at least she would not have woken with a crick in her neck and half her wits missing when this man hammered on the front door and startled her out of the rest of them. Marianne plumped up the cushions that had shaped themselves around her while she slept and would have knelt to rekindle the dying fire if he had not got there first.

Silence stretched between them like fine wire this time as he concentrated on reviving the fire and ignored her as best he could. Who would have thought he even knew how, let alone be considerate enough to sweep up the cold ashes on the stone slab to save them spilling out into the room? He looked at the brass shovel full of them when he had gathered them as neatly as he could as if he did not know what to do with them. She was glad of something to look disapproving about as she took it off him without a word, then went outside to add them to the neat ash pile by the back-garden gate. She paused out in the fresh air to frown at a new pall of cloud trying to blot out the early morning sun.

'I really hope it is not going to rain again,' she observed as she re-entered the room. He seemed taller and darker without the sun to lighten the place with a little hope.

He frowned as if it might be her fault it had gone in. 'Where the devil can Juno be?' he barked and glared at her as if she should know. Apparently their brief truce was over now he had got the fire burning nicely and Miss Donne would be down shortly for him to be a lot more polite to.

'If I knew that I would not have been out looking for her most of yesterday,' Marianne snapped because she had only had a couple of hours' uneasy sleep as well and she did not see why she should play the perfect lady when he was being such a poor gentleman.

'If you truly want to help my ward, then tell me everything you know about her journey and the search so far.'

'I doubt if I know much more than you do.'

'All I know is my ward has been missing in the wilds of Herefordshire for far too long. I rode to

Worcester, expecting to find out she had taken the Leominster stage to get here at last only to discover some cur took every penny she had so she could not buy a seat. If only I had got to her a few hours earlier I could have saved her the ordeal of wandering penniless and alone through a strange countryside. If only I had left Paris even a day before I did I could have made sure she got here safe and well or that she need not flee in the first place. Because I failed to find her in time my niece is probably lost and frightened half out of her wits at this very moment and even if she has not fallen into the hands of a villain she could be soaked to the skin and in a high fever.'

She had wanted him to show some sign of emotion and now he had she was not quite sure she knew what to do with it all. 'Stop imagining the worst,' she told him briskly. 'For either of us to be of any use in this search we must believe your niece had the good sense to find shelter last night. After having her pocket picked she is sure to be wary of being seen walking alone, so even not finding sight or sound of her is a good thing when you think about it rationally.'

'Where is she, then?' he asked starkly.

All she could do was shake her head in reply because she was tired as well and the girl had seemed to vanish from the face of the earth from the moment she walked across the New Bridge at Worcester and out into the countryside. It was probably as well brisk footsteps on the stone-flagged floor announced Miss Donne's arrival and stopped them both imagining

Juno in all sorts of terrible situations now he had put them back into her head.

'Have you brought us good news of Miss Defford, my lord?' Miss Donne asked rather breathlessly.

Marianne marvelled hope could blind such a shrewd lady to Lord Stratford's grim expression and weary eyes.

'Only that she is still lost, ma'am. I hoped to find my niece when I got here and I was bitterly disappointed,' he said wearily.

'Indeed?' Miss Donne said with a sigh as if a heavy weight was back on her shoulders. 'Then we must begin searching once again,' she said resolutely and looked at Marianne as if she would know where to start.

'Miss Defford may be walking into town after sheltering from the storm as we speak,' she made herself say bracingly.

Chapter Three

Alaric stared down at the fire and tried to do as Marianne said and put the worst of his terrors out of his head. He could not call her anything else because he had no idea who she was and where she fitted into brisk little Miss Donne's household and perhaps Miss Grantham's life as well. Speaking of whom, where the devil was the woman? He glared at the door between this cosy room and the rest of the oddly silent and empty-feeling house and sensed yet another mystery on the other side of it. A pity his brain seemed so slow and dazed with lack of sleep since he really needed it smartly aware and on parade with its buttons polished and boots blacked.

It was lack of sleep that made him puzzled and foggy about the unfamiliar new world he seemed to have been wandering in ever since he had reached Stratford House—however long ago that now was— and found out Juno was missing. He would probably find a genuine housemaid, dazzling and quick-witted and even a little bit compassionate towards such a bumbling idiot right now. And wholly delicious and so very unconscious of her own attractions. Tall and slender and just the right height for a lofty lord like him as well, his inner idiot pointed out as he tried to pretend he was as unaware of her as a woman as she seemed of him as a man.

Marianne seemed to be doing her best to pretend he was not even here as she bent cautiously to push the already-filled kettle hanging on its iron arm over the fire without coming anywhere near him. She swiftly stepped back and away as if he might be contagious and he knew he was filthy and smelt of horse and mud and whatever had been in the barn before he took shelter in it last night. He was lucky both ladies had much better manners or a lot more compassion than his mother.

He only had to imagine the Dowager Lady Stratford's hard grey eyes icing over with contempt at even a glimpse, or a whiff, of him right now and he felt all the coldness of his childhood at his back like a January wind from the Arctic ice caps. Shivering in his boots despite the fire and the calendar telling them it was high summer, he tried to gauge whatever it was they were being so careful not to tell him about Miss Grantham's prolonged absence.

He had told himself all the way to Paris and back it was sensible for him to marry kind, well-bred and beautiful Miss Grantham so he could provide a much better home for Juno and a loving mother to his children when they came along. At least he knew enough about bleak and unloving childhoods to want better for his sons and daughters than the one he endured. Yet now he was here and Miss Grantham might have decided to accept his sensible offer of marriage, he felt as if he had left something crucial out of his calculations. Surely he could not have felt as if Marianne was all the warmth and impulsiveness and loyalty he had ever wanted at first glance if there was any more than polite friendship between him and Juno's former governess? How could he have thought common interests and civility were enough, that instant of surprised and horrified recognition had whispered, as he had stared at a very different female when she had opened the door? He wanted her until his bones ached and a lot more besides he had best not even think about now.

'Tea, my lord?' Miss Donne asked and it felt as if he had to come a long way back to the now sunny-again kitchen to look at her as if he had never even heard of the stuff.

'Hmm?' he heard himself say like a looby.

'A beverage made with leaves from the tea plant and imported from China at great expense,' Marianne pointed out impatiently and with a wave at the fat brown kitchen teapot on the scrubbed table as if he might not have seen one before.

'I do vaguely recall the idea,' he said with a smile of apology for Miss Donne and a wary glance at Marianne in case she had any idea why he had been lost in his thoughts. From the frown of impatience knitting her slender honey-and-brown brows almost together, he imagined to her he was just being an annoying sort of lord again instead of a lustful and predatory one. So at least he had been excused the shame and indignity of being rejected by Marianne Whoever-She-Was before he could do more than stare at her like a mooncalf. That was one horror to cross off his list, then. He did not know if he could face another furious lady telling him how hateful he was and how bitterly she wished he had never been born after his mother did just that when he found out what she had done to Juno and challenged her selfishness and lack of feeling. 'The French seem to prefer coffee,' he added, 'or drink chocolate at breakfast time.'

'You can hardly expect us to roast and grind coffee beans or ask our closest wealthy neighbour to lend us cocoa beans and her chocolate pot when you have turned up on the doorstep with the dawn uninvited, Lord Stratford.'

'Now then, Marianne, that is hardly polite and invitations are unimportant at a time of crisis,' Miss Donne said and Alaric could have hugged her, except he liked her too much already to engulf her in the reek of sweaty man and the less savoury smells of the road.

'Thank you, Miss Donne. Miss...' he let his voice tail off because he could hardly call her Marianne.

'Mrs,' she snapped crossly, and he suspected her tiredness was almost as huge as his when she seemed to repent her brusque impatience with a sigh. 'My name is Mrs Turner,' she admitted as she avoided both their gazes and poured tea into all three breakfast teacups without waiting for any more foolish arguments from him.

Just as well since jealousy and acute hatred of the lucky Mr Turner shot through him in a hot arrow of frustration. He was too late, he let himself mourn silently as the absurdity of being too late for a woman he had not even met an hour ago tried to snap him back to sanity. She obviously did not like him, so that made his feral longing for another man's wife feel even worse.

'I am a widow,' she told him almost defiantly and with no idea she had just freed him from a fire he had never wanted to burn on. He did not have to want another man's wife so unmercifully he was having trouble keeping hold of the elusive thread of this not quite a conversation as well as his dignity.

'I am sorry for your loss,' he lied.

'Thank you,' she said as if that was the last she wanted to hear on the subject. 'Do not let your tea get cold,' she advised him. 'It might not be coffee or chocolate, but it is hot and you look as if you need reviving, my lord.'

'Well, really, my dear,' Miss Donne chided, as if personal comments mattered at a time like this, 'this is not the time for picking at one another with Miss Defford still to find and time a-wasting.'

'No, you are right,' Mrs Turner admitted. 'We need to eat and be out and ready for the search as soon as the others are awake,' she added.

Alaric could only nod his agreement and drink his tea. Both ladies were right, they did need to eat and drink so they would have strength for the resumed search for Juno. His niece was all that mattered and never mind his foolish obsession with a honey-haired widow with dreamy blue eyes and a mouth a man would ride a hundred miles to kiss, if only those eyes were dreamy for him and her mouth half-asleep still after a night of hot and heady loving in his bed.

When Miss Donne's Bet came downstairs, tying her apron and struggling with her cap, she blurted out the story of Fliss walking off into the hills in the pouring rain last night to look for Miss Defford before she even noticed the travel-worn lord lurking in front of the kitchen fire. So then Miss Donne had to tell His Lordship Marianne's brother, Darius, had gone after Fliss and neither of them had returned yet. Lord Stratford had tersely demanded directions and marched out of the back door as soon as Bet could gasp them out. By the time Marianne put her damp shoes on and stumbled after him, the viscount was almost out of sight and obviously in a fine temper. She had been forced to pant after him up the winding lane out of town and even then she only just managed to keep him in sight.

She scurried into earshot just in time to hear why he was in such a hurry. Apparently Darius had compromised Fliss before Lord Stratford could marry her himself. From the dreamy way Fliss was looking at Darius, Lord Stratford would not have got his way even if he had got here in time to keep them apart last night. Then the viscount said Fliss had recently inherited a fortune and accused Darius of being a fortune hunter. How ironic when Darius had tried so hard to resist his attraction to Fliss because she was a poor governess and he thought he should marry money. If Juno's disappearance was not so sharp in all their minds, Marianne might have been amused by the sight of Lord Stratford frustrated of a rich and suitable viscountess.

She did smile now as she recalled the look on Fliss and Darius's faces while they faced His Lordship on a sodden hillside track. Every look and gesture screamed they were lovers and Fliss did not look in the least bit sorry to turn her back on His Lordship's flattering offer. Then they all remembered Juno was still missing and never mind who would marry whom.

Lord Stratford was the girl's guardian and he had said they should all forget worrying about gossip. If the whole world knew she had gone missing, they just needed to find her—so now half the neighbourhood were out looking for the missing girl. Finding waiting for news at Miss Donne's more wearing than actively looking for Juno, Marianne was glad when Darius asked her to come back to Owlet Manor with his orders for the men today so he could stay in Broadley.

All these hours on, Marianne shook her head at her vivid mental image of Lord Stratford when she should be worrying about the still-missing Juno. In her shoes Marianne knew she would have bolted as well, however worrying it was not to have found the girl so many hours after she set out to walk the last stage of her long journey. Indeed, she *had* run away to marry Daniel, but that was a glorious adventure with him at the end of it. Marianne felt the bleakness of Daniel's death at the bloody siege of Badajoz more than two years ago threaten and there was always this hollow in her heart now. No Daniel to tease and quarrel and laugh with or to love with every breath in her body. How fiercely he would argue with her about that empty heart if he could hear her! He would insist she must live life to the full and love again, even if the best part of her was cut away the night he died.

Marianne shook her head at the bereft and gloomy place her tired mind had taken her when she was not paying attention. Things were better now. She was free of the suffocating respectability of genteel Bath society and her parents' compact new home. Darius inheriting Owlet Manor had rescued her from her mother and the condemnation of the Bath tabbies. She would rather scrub floors than go back there, so it was best to live in the moment and worry about the future when it got here.

And now the tall and fancifully twisted brick chimneys of Owlet Manor were visible above the sheltering trees at last and she was nearly home. A slender, dark-haired girl stepped out from behind the largest tree of all next to the grand gates of Owlet Manor nobody had shut for at least half a century. Marianne drew rein sharply and made Robin snort and shake his head in protest as she stared down at the girl and paid no attention to her horse this once. If she had not seen Lord Stratford first she might wonder if there was more than one girl wandering the countryside today, since this one was in quite the wrong place, but if there was a Defford stamp this girl had it. She was as dark haired as the viscount and her eyes the same clear bright blue.

Juno shot Marianne a wary look, her white teeth worrying at her lower lip like a child who knew she had not learned her lesson well enough. Marianne recalled Fliss worrying about the girl's painful shyness with strangers and bit back the rebuke for all the trouble she had caused that was trembling on her lips. The girl would bolt into the woods if Marianne was not careful and she had proved very good at being invisible when she chose, so goodness knew when they would manage to find her again.

'Good afternoon, Miss Defford,' she managed to say calmly. 'Would you like a seat in the gig for the last bit of the way to my brother's house?'

Juno shook her head, shot a frightened look towards the bustle and noise of the farmyards where the men must be thatching ricks and seemed to be on the edge of doing that bolt Marianne was so worried about. The men were doing whatever it was with so much shouting and laughter Marianne guessed they had taken advantage of Darius's absence to drink a lot more cider than they should have this morning. She hoped the hay was dry under the tarpaulins before they began again or the wet grass could overheat and catch fire and that was the last thing Darius needed.

'Will you promise me not to run away again

while I have Robin stabled and rubbed down? Miss Grantham has chewed her nails to the quick worrying about you and you must love her if you have come all this way to see her. I hope you will not let her suffer such painful anxiety for much longer by running away yet again.'

Juno looked shamefaced and shook her head, but that was not enough for Marianne. 'Promise me out loud that you will not bolt as soon as my back is turned,' she insisted with a stern look to say she would know if the girl lied.

'I promise,' she whispered and even managed to look Marianne in the eye so she supposed she would have to trust her.

'Very well, then. If you do not wish to be seen, follow the path over there. It winds around the house by the side of the lake and nobody in the stable yard or on the other side of the farm will be able to see you. There is a garden door round there and a bench where you can wait while I see to Robin and get the men working as they should be. I will have to get them to see the error of their ways while I am about it, so do not be surprised if it takes longer than either of us want it to.'

Juno surprised her with a shy smile and another shake of the head at the notion of Marianne ordering the farm workers about and them doing as she said.

'Having dealt with soldiers of most ranks and temperaments when I was with the army, those rogues are child's play,' she told the girl with a nod towards the noisy rickyard before she smiled back with mischief in her eyes. 'It is just a matter of learning how to handle them,' she added.

Juno shook her head again and looked dubious about the notion of even trying to understand what made most men tick.

'I will try not to be long,' Marianne promised with one last look at the diffident but determined girl who was already slipping into the unkempt gardens like a wraith. Marianne shook the reins to persuade patient Robin to move on and tried not to look back as she fervently hoped Juno Defford was a girl of her word.

After handing out brusque orders to the farm servants and a crushing rebuke to make them see the error of their ways, Marianne made sure Robin was spoiled after his gruelling day yesterday. She let herself into the manor house by the back door as if in no particular hurry lest any of the men were watching her go, but as soon as it was shut behind her she dashed across the hall to let the girl in. Juno rose from the sun-warmed bench and Marianne gave a sigh of relief.

'What the deuce are you doing here, young lady?' she asked with all the effort and worry of the last day making her sound brusque and irritated.

'Miss Grantham told me about you and your brother and this poor old house in her letters,' Juno replied with a half-defiant, half-apologetic look that said there might be more of her uncle's fire in her than appearances suggested.

'Walking on past Broadley for the sake of curiosity would be cruel, so I hope you have a better reason for doing it. Miss Grantham is beside herself with worry.'

'I should never have sent that message. Nobody would have known I was here if I had not scribbled it in panic after I was robbed,' the girl said sulkily.

'And that would make everything all right, would it? You sound very young and foolish when you spout such rubbish and you put us through hours of worry today for no good reason. Can you even imagine what horrors Miss Grantham is dreading as the hours tick by with no sign of you?'

'I—' The girl broke off whatever she was going to say and Marianne saw her throat work as if she was fighting a sob. 'I will not go back to London and I will *not* marry that man. I would rather die.'

'Stop being such a tragedienne. Of course you must not marry a man who is so much older than you, especially if you do not even like him.'

Juno shook her head as if she could hardly believe someone was agreeing with her. She burst into over-wrought tears as the strain and hardship of the last days and weeks caught up with her and Marianne drew the sobbing girl into her arms.

'I am a crotchety old woman to rip up at you like that when you have been having such a dreadful time, but we have been so worried about you,' she said to the top of the girl's head. 'And now I have made you cry when there are so many things we could be busy doing.'

'I am so sorry,' the girl managed to gasp out be-tween sobs.

Marianne urged her back towards the ancient oak bench. 'Here, sit down and cry it all out,' she said and had to guide Juno's steps as she could not see for tears. Trying to will comfort into the weary and woebegone girl, Marianne recalled her little sister crying as bitterly seven years ago when Marianne had told Viola she was leaving home to find Daniel. If anything could have kept Marianne away from him, it would have been her sister's tears, but she had loved him too much to be swayed even by Viola's heartbreak. So she had gone anyway and the close bond between her and Viola had broken that night and the gap had never truly healed.

Her little sister had not written back when Marianne sent letters to tell her about her adventures as an army wife and tried to bridge the gulf between peaceful England and the war-torn lands where she had spent most of her married life. When she had come back, she was too full of pain and grief to reach out to her aloof and preoccupied teacher sister.

Then Viola had taken her current post as governess to Sir Harry Marbeck's wards and moved fifty miles from Bath and their parents' cramped house and it was too late. A few stiff letters since had not mended things and Marianne did not feel far from tears herself now. She smoothed Juno's tangled dark hair. 'Better?' she asked at a pause between sobs.

'Yes,' Juno said with a sigh that sounded as if it came from her boots and a hiccupping sob. 'Have you a handkerchief? I lost mine.'

Marianne dug in her unfashionable but convenient

pocket and Juno wiped her eyes, then blew her nose a few times and held out the handkerchief. Marianne shook her head and was pleased when Juno managed a small chuckle. 'Not very appealing, is it?' she said.

'It can be washed. Speaking of washing—after you have done so, brushed your hair and eaten something, I expect you will feel much more ready to face the world again.'

'I am not sure I want to.'

'No? Well, I will have to send word to Miss Grantham you are safe and well and here with me so that she can call off the search and stop worrying about you.'

'Does Uncle Alaric have to know?'

'Alaric?' Marianne frowned and searched her memory for one of those. Oh, of course, the girl must mean Lord Stratford. 'Is that His Lordship's name?' Juno nodded. 'It suits him,' Marianne said unwarily.

'The first one was King of the Visigoths who sacked Rome. Uncle Alaric is not a barbarian.'

He had certainly looked like one when he had been filthy from the road, unshaven and tired half to death, her inner Marianne argued silently, and that reminded respectable Mrs Turner how much trouble she had had with her inner siren this morning. Her silly fantasy of a pirate lover had been ridiculous, especially when he had turned out to be a viscount and way above her touch. 'Then why did you walk past Broadley and not let His Lordship and Miss Grantham know you are safe and well?'

'Because he might make me go back and I truly

cannot live with Grandmama ever again after some of the things she said and did while we were in London, Mrs Turner. She told me she would lock me in my room until I agreed to marry Lord…' Juno paused as if she could not even bring herself to say the man's name. 'Anyway, I ran away before she could actually do it, but then I got to Worcester and…' Juno's voice tailed off as she remembered the disaster of being robbed and Marianne expected more distraught tears.

'I suppose you were right to run away—' she began to say.

'I *knew* you would understand,' Juno interrupted impulsively and gave a gusty sigh of relief.

'If there was no other way to make your feelings plain to your suitor and your family, but it was very wrong of you to leave Miss Grantham and your uncle frantically searching for you today when you are quite safe. His Lordship must have ridden after you as if the devil himself was on his heels and I doubt from the look of him that the poor man has had much sleep since he left France.'

'I saw him. I hid behind a hedge when I heard a horseman coming and nearly stepped out when I saw it was Uncle Alaric, but he looked so grim and stern I did not dare. Maybe he is furious with me and has come to fetch me back and make me marry that horrid man and Grandmama was right all along and he did approve of the match. So that is why I came here to beg you to hide me, then get word to Miss Grantham, but ask her not to tell my family where I am because I would rather die than wed that—that man…' Juno paused as if she did not have words in her to describe how much she hated the lord her grandmother had been so determined to make her wed.

Marianne wondered what they had done between them to make Juno so revolted by the very idea of him she could not even say his name. From the almost childlike appeal in the girl's blue eyes she really hoped it had not been the ultimate in forced persuasion to make her agree she would have to marry a man who had ravished her. Heaven forbid, Marianne decided with a shudder. Sooner or later Fliss or Lord Stratford or maybe even Mrs Marianne Turner would have to try and persuade Juno to talk about what had happened to make the terrible risks of running away from all she knew to get here and escape that terrible situation seem worthwhile.

'I promise I will make myself useful and I would much sooner scrub floors and clean windows for the rest of my life than marry that awful old man. I know you work very hard because Miss Grantham said so in her letters and I am sure you could do with some help,' Juno said earnestly and that proved she was still more child than woman, did it not? To think she would just stay here and pretend the frantic search for her would die away and leave her in peace with Lord Stratford ransacking half the Welsh Marches for her was a world away from reality.

'Hiring yourself out as a housemaid until you are of age could never work. Lord Stratford nearly collapsed from shock and exhaustion when he found out you had not got to Broadley ahead of him, so we simply have to tell him you are safe, Juno. It would be cruel not to and you do not seem a heartless person to me.'

'No, I am not,' Juno said, her extreme youth obvious in her pout and refusal to meet Marianne's eyes and admit she was wrong to panic and come here instead of simply walking on into the town and saving herself and everyone else the extra trouble and effort of coming all the way out here. 'I suppose you are right,' she said at last.

'Can I trust you not to run away again while I write to tell Miss Grantham you are here and ask her to pass the news on to your uncle?'

'I did promise I would not,' Juno said and sounded so sulky and misused that Marianne nearly laughed. She resisted the urge as the girl was obviously in a fragile state and might take offence and flounce off if she did, promise or no.

'Good, then I will write a hasty letter and get our stable lad to deliver it before I come and find you again. Thank goodness the lad had enough sense to stay sober so he is in a fit state to ride Robin's brother Swift to Broadley.'

'I must hope he is not, then,' Juno said. 'Swift,' she explained when Marianne raised her eyebrows.

Chapter Four

Alaric knew it was a mistake to come, but he could not stay away. Even after the bath and shave Miss Donne had insisted on before he set out and the change of clothes he had needed for so long, he was not fit to do much more than sleep. But he had to see Juno with his own eyes and reassure himself she was safe, however foolish it was not to rest first and let her do so as well. At least every time his vision blurred and his brain threatened to shut down, his abiding sense of shame jerked him back to life again and urged him relentlessly on.

This was all his fault; he should have stayed in England and never mind his mother's open dislike of her only surviving child. It had been his duty to be sure Juno felt supported and loved during her first Season in town, even if he was too shallow to actually admit he loved his niece despite what her grandmother thought of both of them. What a fool he had been to think it would be better if he was not there to irritate the Dowager Lady Stratford and make Juno's debut a disaster. He shook his head to try to dismiss the fact his mother had hated him from the day he was born from his weary thoughts. He had always borne that burden and piling it on top of the guilt might make him forget the here and now and fall off this hard-mouthed and restive animal. He frowned at the road ahead because surely this back-of-beyond house of Yelverton's should be in sight by now? His latest hired horse was not an easy ride, but was every bit as fast as the ostler promised he would be.

Ah, there it was and a far more impressive house than expected, given Yelverton's rough manners and ruffian-like appearance this morning. As if he had any room to talk about appearances, Alaric chided himself and frowned at the streak of pale blue sky fighting the pall of cloud. Yelverton's home was nestled at the heart of a verdant valley and soon Alaric would have no more time to rail at himself for being a useless guardian. 'Aye, and do not forget you are a loser in love as well, Stratford, and Yelverton is the one you lost to,' he reminded himself out loud, thinking it was high time he slept if he was talking to himself like a lunatic. 'Even if it was not love between you and Miss Grantham, she was your best chance of finding yourself a polite, well-bred and kind-hearted viscountess,' he added under his breath. It did not help him feel any better now he had to revise Yelverton's status up a notch from the look of the substantial manor house up ahead. The road twisted and turned yet again. Was nothing in this confounded county straight or direct? Ah, there it was again and Owlet Manor was a fine and ancient gentleman's residence. Alaric already owed the man respect for the fine military career Miss Donne had outlined while Alaric ate a hot meal at her insistence before he got back in the saddle to find this place.

The worst of his fears had faded when they got that hasty message of Mrs Turner's to say Juno was safe, but the flood of emotion he felt on learning he could stop worrying about her safety had left him weak with relief. And this was no time for weakness when his niece clearly needed him to be strong. Despite his exhaustion he decided he simply had to see Juno with his own eyes and let her know he was sorry he had been such a poor guardian and protector, before he found a bed and slept for a week then thought a bit harder about his many sins of omission.

He blinked his eyes open wide again and realised he had almost nodded off in the saddle. He made himself take note of the land around the fine manor house growing ever larger on the horizon to keep himself awake. Closer in, he could see that the old house had been neglected for many a long year. The landlord in him could see that hard work and a little money had been spent on it lately. As the owner of prosperous estates he could offer Yelverton help getting this house and his land in order, if he happened to like him. As it was he had no intention of staying longer than it took him to remove Juno from Mrs Turner's care and get her back to Broadley, even if he had to beg the naggy-tempered and annoyingly unforgettable woman for the loan of her gig and a fresh horse to draw it with.

Tomorrow he would feel alive and awake enough to hire a carriage for the journey back to Stratford Park and a new life. He could worry about the details when they got there, but at least both of them would be excused his mother's cold dislike for the first time in their lives.

How could he have trusted the Dowager to put Juno's interests before her own? He had thought the obsessive love the woman had had for her eldest son would have rubbed off on George's only child, but apparently he was wrong about that as well as everything else. The Dowager Lady Stratford had told him she would never forgive Juno for being born female when they had had their last confrontation in London, before they finally washed their hands of one another and he galloped away. George's girl or not, Juno was a female, so she failed to keep the Dowager Lady Stratford's despised second son from inheriting his title and the fine estates that went with it. Of course she despised the silly chit, she told Alaric as if he was stupid not to have known it all along. And how could he have trusted Juno to his mother's care believing she must care because George was the girl's father?

'It suited you to believe in a fantasy, my lord,' he condemned himself disgustedly now.

Deep down he must have known his mother only had one chip of love in her stony heart and she had buried it with his brother. Alaric had given up trying to convince his mother he never wanted his brother's inheritance long ago, but he must have carried on dreaming impossible dreams when he passed Juno into her care after George's funeral and thought he had done the right thing. At seventeen he felt overwhelmed by the burdens that fell on him and poor little Juno was one more. But this was not about him and his excuses for behaving badly; it was about putting things right for Juno if he still could. He deserved to be so tired every bone in his body ached. He should feel the loss of an ideal wife in Miss Grantham. He had been a fool to leave her free to find and love a better man than careless, self-absorbed Alaric Defford. He truly hated himself as he dug his heels into his horse's flanks and urged the sullen animal on as fast as he would go.

He shot a disapproving look at rusted, open main gates to the venerable manor house's front door and rode on past. Grass was growing across the once-gravelled drive and there were so many weeds between the stone flags nearer the house that the flags were barely visible. He shook his head at such wanton neglect. He hoped Yelverton was ashamed of himself for not getting the path to his front door cleared straight away. How was the man's sister to receive polite visitors if they had to come in through the farmyard? 'Place is a shambles,' he muttered as he rode into the stable yard.

'Sir?' a slightly unsteady-looking farmhand asked warily, as if he thought he should have heard an order if his ears were up to it.

'Are you castaway?' Alaric demanded as he dismounted and staggered until the earth settled under his feet.

'If I am, that's two of us,' the man muttered, then stared back at Alaric with pretend innocence.

'Does your master know you despise his kind?' Alaric asked with a steady look to let the rogue know he was not deceived by forelock tugging.

'He's bin a soldier, though, ain't he?' the man said as if that excused Yelverton's sins as one of the ruling elite.

Alaric decided he had heard quite enough about Saint Darius and his heroic past for today. 'Respect for his army service does not seem to have stopped you drinking in the middle of the day when you were supposed to be hard at work for him, though, does it?' he replied to let the fellow know he was not fooled by his act and taking advantage during a crisis was reprehensible.

'No, sir, but Mrs Turner ripped up at us so there's no need to join in. Said she was going to open the taps on the cider barrels until they was empty if we didn't get back to work, so she did,' the man said with a hint of male appreciation for a fine and spirited woman in his bleary eyes Alaric did not like one bit.

'Serve you all right if she did it anyway,' Alaric informed the man coolly. 'And kindly see that my horse is tended while I speak to the lady.'

The man gave a mocking salute that hit his ear instead of his forehead and Alaric decided Mrs Turner's wrath must have been mighty indeed to work its way past all that alcohol. He supposed he should be grateful she had managed to put the fear of God into her brother's workmen, since this one took the horse's bridle and led it towards the stables without another word. At least the nag would be inside and might get watered and maybe even fed to put it in a better temper for the return journey.

Alaric stopped frowning after the rebellious farm-hand and frowned at the back of Owlet Manor in-stead. At least the narrow garden separating the house from the farmyards and the road was neat and newly planted with herbs and even one or two cottage-garden flowers to brighten it up. There was an old orchard to the side of the place that looked as if it had received some attention as well and a row of raspberry canes still glowed with the occa-sional red fruit the birds had not gobbled up. Mrs Turner's concerns were obviously more about food than decoration. Understandable if her brother did not have funds for more than the basics despite his grand house. Miss Donne had told him the manor and estate had fallen into the man's lap when he came home from the war.

Alaric eyed the narrow and mellowed Tudor brick on this side of the house and wondered how he would have felt if his grand heritage came with no money attached and years of neglect to make up for. Lucky that most Deffords had been careful landlords, then, and they never spent more than they could afford. It was no credit to him that he was a rich man and a lord, he decided as he noted the bricks needed pointing and the ancient oak porch was listing to one side like the farmhand who had done his best not to welcome Alaric to his master's new home. Ah well, none of it was any of his business, he decided and stepped through the porch to rap on the door.

'Yes, whatever is it this time?' Mrs Turner opened the door and demanded impatiently before she took the trouble to see who was out here.

Alaric supposed she had an excuse with all those fools half-drunk and maybe a little bit dangerous and her brother occupied elsewhere. 'Good afternoon,' he said with a silly echo of the awe and wonder that shot through him the first time he laid eyes on her troubling him again. He had hoped she would be less lovely and desirable than he recalled, but if anything he had undershot the mark.

'Oh, it is you,' she said as if he was the last person she wanted to see on her brother's doorstep even with a pack of half-cut rogues to be impatient with. 'I am sorry. Good day to you, Lord Stratford,' she said, sounding a lot more polite, but still not enthusiastic about their second doorstep of the day.

'I have come to see my niece,' he told her. She stood in the doorway as if trying to hide even the kitchen from his view and he was tempted to lift her aside and march in again, but could not bring himself to be so rude twice in a day.

'She is very tired,' she said and would not meet his eyes.

'I dare say, but I need to see for myself Juno is safe and well,' he insisted.

'You do not trust my word, Lord Stratford?'

'I do not know you, ma'am, and you seem to be determined to prevent me seeing my ward.'

'It is not that,' she said uneasily.

'What *is* it, then?' he barked, nearly at the end of his tether. He would invade her brother's house to make sure Juno was whole and safe if he had to.

'I am sorry, my lord,' she said as if she really meant it, 'but Miss Defford does not wish to see you.'

He put out a shaking hand to steady himself against the door jamb and wished he could lean on this noble old house, let exhaustion wash over him so he could sleep standing up and forget about those hurtful words. If he slept long enough, maybe this nightmare would end and he would wake to a world of sanity and order. 'What do you expect me to do, then?' he asked lamely at last.

'Go back to Broadley and wait until you have both had a proper night's sleep and are feeling less exhausted and more rational,' Mrs Turner said as if she thought he could meekly ride back to that wretched little town without seeing for himself Juno was safe at last.

'I cannot leave here without knowing she is unharmed,' he allowed himself to plead.

Mrs Turner looked uneasy about keeping him standing out here like a beggar hoping for scraps. 'No, of course you cannot,' she murmured her agreement. 'Juno, you must show yourself and reassure your uncle you are safe and well,' she spoke up to his lurking niece and Alaric supposed he must be glad Juno did not bolt for the nearest attic to hide in when she realised he was coming. 'We cannot let His Lordship think we are holding you to ransom or whatever nonsensical ideas he will think up if you refuse to come out. No need to say a word if you would rather not, but you must prove to him you are well and in one piece, even if you are footsore and rather oddly dressed.'

He thought he heard a soft whisper of a laugh in the cool shadows beyond the kitchen and gazed hungrily past Mrs Turner's slender form, hoping for a glimpse of his niece. 'Just let me see you are unharmed, Jojo, and I promise you I will go away again until you are feeling better,' he said quietly and willed her to step forward. He loved his niece far more than he had ever been able to let her know, but he was the adult and he should have told her all through her lonely childhood if he wanted her to believe him now.

'You used to call me that when Papa was alive,' she said so softly he had to strain his ears for the words and he longed for her to come properly inside the room so he could catch a glimpse of her for the first time in far too long.

'And how he would rip up at me for letting his little girl be so miserable in London that you felt you had to come so far to find Miss Grantham.'

'You will not make me go back to live with Grandmama, will you?' she said and finally found the courage to peer around the doorpost at him.

All he could see was two anxious blue eyes looking warily at him and her pale face looking thinner and even more worried than last time he had set eyes on her. Then he had been bidding her goodbye at his London home before he travelled on to Paris. 'No, even if I wanted to I could not since the Dowager has left the country and will live overseas from now on. I will not make you go anywhere you do not want to go ever again, Jojo,' he promised recklessly and with a wobble in his voice he wished Mrs Turner was not here to pick up on.

'I want to stay here,' Juno managed to say almost out loud.

Alaric's heart sank as he realised it could be too late to put his relationship with his niece right. Maybe he had defended himself against loving anyone for so long it had become a habit. But how could he have refused it to a child who had lost her father so young she could barely remember him? It seemed feeble and self-pitying to admit he had felt so shaken and alone when he lost his brother that he had built a wall around himself. Perhaps George had been lonely as his parents' only surviving child, but whatever the reason, he had taken to his baby brother and refused to hear their mother's orders to let the brat go to the devil and come away. Even as a boy he had taken care Alaric was happy and well looked after when he had inherited their father's title as a mere lad himself. George had always done his best to shield Alaric from the Dowager's cold dislike and it had hit him like an Arctic blast when George was killed and Alaric had to step into his brother's shoes. Within the new Viscount Stratford's barricades he must have looked self-sufficient and composed instead of bereft and terrified. Men of power were certainly fooled and they began to use him for not quite official tasks like the one in Paris to help the Duke of Wellington through an awkward situation in any way he could. Little did they know there was a coward lurking behind all that lordly composure and now Juno had paid the price.

'Then so you shall, if I can make arrangements for your board and lodging and any other expenses. And if Mrs Turner does not mind having such a demanding young lady about the place when she has a great deal to do?'

I will miss you like the devil, but that will serve me right, he did not add. It would not be fair, after all he had not done for his niece up to now, to put any pressure on her to try and get her to love him back. Serve him right if he never did after walling her out along with the rest of the world ever since her father died.

'You really do not mind if I stay, then?' Juno said and she was so eager to hear his reply she actually crept past the doorway and stood just inside the room like a feral kitten ready to bolt for cover if he made the slightest move towards her. 'I promise not to get under your feet, Mrs Turner,' she added earnestly. 'I know you are very busy, but I would love to help you clean and sort through all the curious old things you have found. Miss Grantham made it sound such an adventure I feel as if I know you and the house already.'

'I wonder if she knows how hard that work can

be. It is rough and ready living here, Juno. I have a great deal to do before this old place even feels like a proper gentleman's residence once again. If you really want to stay with us for a while and rough it and His Lordship is content for my brother and me to have you here until you have recovered from your long journey, then I am sure we would be very happy to have you stay here until you feel you are ready to face the world again.'

Mrs Turner was clearly waiting to hear whether he was resigned to his niece's wishes, if not exactly delighted by them. He could see the knowledge that Miss Grantham would shortly be part of this household in her eyes as she met his with something like an apology because his niece seemed to prefer her company to his.

'His Lordship must be content if that is what you really want, Juno,' he said wearily. 'I hope you will write to me now and again,' he allowed himself to beg before he could make himself go away and leave her with strangers.

'Yes,' she said and seemed to hesitate, as if she wanted to say more, but was afraid he might try to change her mind if she risked it.

'Good,' he said hoarsely and fought back some unmanly feeling tears as he shook his head and managed to meet Mrs Turner's gaze with a plea in his. 'Look after her for me, please?' he asked and he did trust her to do that, stranger as she was and not a particularly polite or respectful one either.

'I will,' she promised.

'Very well, then. I wish you good day, Mrs Turner, Juno,' he said gruffly and bowed, then turned on his heel before he lowered himself to beg her to trust him instead. Time to get on with the rest of his life without most of the things he thought he had when he left England on that disastrous errand to France, where it turned out nobody wanted him very much either.

Chapter Five

A tense silence settled over the usually comfortable kitchen where Marianne often sat with Darius of an evening rather than make him change back into a gentleman after his labours on the farms all day. She listened to the noise of Lord Stratford's finely made boots on the cobbles fade from hearing and wondered what Juno was thinking as she decided they sounded very lonely. She doubted Lord Stratford would want her pity, but he had it for the slap his timid niece had just landed on him without lifting a finger.

'I could not go with him, Mrs Turner, really I could not.' There was a look very like guilt on the girl's face when Marianne turned to look at her surprise guest's face.

'Well, you are not doing so, are you?' she said coolly. In her opinion forgiving someone who sincerely rued a mistake was part of being grown up and Juno was using her youth and shyness as an excuse not to do so. She supposed she should not judge the girl harshly; Juno had obviously been through a few horrible months at the mercy of an unsympathetic grandmother and the indifferent *ton*. She smiled at the girl to take the sting out of her question and thanked her lucky stars she was not rich or noble enough to be looked down on and ignored by the cream of polite society herself.

'No, but thank you for agreeing to take me in.'

'It can only be for a while, Juno. You belong with your family and I think Lord Stratford will pay much more attention to your wants and needs from now on. You have put him through a dreadful ordeal by disappearing as if you had been stolen away by the fairies and I suspect he has learnt his lesson well and will take much better care of you in future.'

'Maybe, but I still do not want to be a useless lady who sews seat covers, paints dreadful watercolours and plays the harp badly until some lord is ready to marry me for the sake of my dowry and an heir.'

Juno sounded downright sulky now and looked like an overwrought child sadly in need of her bed. Marianne sighed and supposed the girl was not so very far from the schoolroom. She certainly did not seem anywhere near mature enough to face the scarily adult dilemma she had been forced into by her grandmother. Under her crippling shyness Marianne thought the girl was angry because her uncle had not been there when she needed him most. She was certainly being unfeeling about Lord Stratford's exhausting ride and obvious weariness when he got here, but maybe he deserved it. Marianne still felt guilty about sending him back to Broadley without his niece, though. At least Lord Stratford cared enough about the girl to ride so hard he looked almost asleep on his feet now the relief of finding out Juno was safe had removed the worst of his worries about her.

'We can put the knotty problem of your future aside for now and think about what comes next instead. I would be very glad of your help with my endless pile of mending and I promise to stitch any seat covers that are in need of repair so you do not have to do it.'

Juno grimaced at the thought of sitting quietly and sewing after all the drama of the last few days, but if she thought it would be a nice little holiday from real life to stay here she might as well find out straight away nobody was allowed to sit idly by when there was so much to do. It would do Juno no harm at all to perform a few boring tasks. Marianne planned to talk about even more boring things while they worked, since she doubted Juno would agree to go up to bed and sleep off the worst of her adventures in the middle of the day. If she was good enough at her tedious tales, she might even allow herself to nod off and catch up on some much-needed sleep.

Suddenly there was a cacophony of barking and outraged neighs through the open door, followed by an ominous thud, then the sound of men shouting and arguing at the tops of their voices. Alarm spurred her into action before her mind caught up and Marianne's heart thudded with dread as she ran outside with her skirts lifted high to free her legs for action. She hardly knew the man, but fear for Lord Stratford rang around her head in a near panic. Of course she would feel like this about any human being who could have been gravely injured in what sounded like a crashing fall. Juno was right behind her now and Marianne hoped she would not shy away from whatever trouble was ahead of them and faint or get in the way.

The yard was full of men shouting and milling about and the farm dogs were still barking and that dratted horse was stamping about, looking wild-eyed and dangerous. There was Lord Stratford in the midst of it all. He was lying too still with the horse dancing and snorting with its deadly iron-shod hooves far too close to the man's prone body as it looked wild enough to lash out with intent to kill.

'Joe Nicklin, you catch that damned horse right now, before it kills the poor man,' Marianne shouted over the hullabaloo at the most sober of the men who had gathered to gawp at the chaos and argue about the fallen man at the centre of it. Thankfully Joe listened to her and made a lunge at the animal's bridle, then wrestled the beast back and away so at least it was no longer within kicking reach of Lord Stratford's dark head. Seeing Joe spring into action, the rest of the men seemed to snap out of their panicked stupor and ran to help Joe force the foam-flecked and still-protesting horse away from its fallen rider. 'We will talk about who did what, when and why once I am quite certain His Lordship will survive,' she added with a quelling glare at anyone still standing about gawping.

'Right you are, missus,' Joe's brother Seth said with an ingratiating smile. He was trying too hard to placate her and her suspicion he had something to do with this disaster hardened to a certainty. Seth was a troubled soul who had come back from the war restless and edgy and inclined to lose his temper without much cause, but he was also a superb horseman. She suspected Darius had taken him on because he recognised the faraway look in the man's eyes when he spoke of war and her brother had a soft heart under his self-contained manner. But never mind them now, Lord Stratford needed all her attention until he was his arrogant self again and she refused to believe in an alternative.

'Ride for the doctor as fast as you can go and insist he comes back with you, Seth. Tell him it could be a matter of life and death and say who is injured and if you do it well enough maybe whatever mischief you have been about today need go no further,' she ordered brusquely and at least he had the shame or wit enough to run off to the stables and not stand about arguing.

'And you can get that bad-tempered brute out of the way, Joe,' she snapped as the nag still fought the man's powerful grip. 'Put him in a stall and make it as dark as you can get it, then leave him to do his worst. We can worry about him later.'

Now Marianne's eyes were fixed on Lord Stratford's prone body as she tried to see if any of his limbs were bent under him at a worrying angle. Somehow the sight of him so vulnerable and unde- fended made her blink back a tear. She ordered her- self not to be such a widgeon and get on with finding out what was wrong with him and whether it could be put right. Her heart was in her mouth as she walked past the men dragging the still-resisting horse away to kneel at his side.

Juno sank onto her knees at her uncle's side even before Marianne got there. 'Do not even think about moving him. We must find out how bad his injuries are before we risk making bad worse,' Marianne or- dered when the girl reached out to touch him, then snatched her hand back as if it had been bitten at the thought of doing him more harm.

'Is he going to die, Mrs Turner? It will be my fault if he does. He would not even be here to be thrown from that brute if not for me.'

'Pray do not start spouting such morbid nonsense when I need your help. You are the only truly sober person here so do not have hysterics.'

'What must I do, then?'

'Stay calm while I find out how badly he is in- jured,' Marianne said, and began to explore Lord Stratford's prone body as gently as she could as she fought back her own panic and this silly feeling that if he was mortally injured it would feel like a per- sonal tragedy. She hardly even knew him. Thank goodness she had a good deal of experience nursing wounded men who stood a better chance of recovery if they could stay with the column than they would in an army hospital.

She decided none of his limbs looked twisted out of shape and began gently winnowing through his crisply curling dark hair until she found a knotty lump underneath it already beginning to swell and explaining his loss of consciousness. 'He will certainly have a headache when he wakes up,' she told Juno with as much of a smile as she could manage to reassure the girl.

'He will hate that,' Juno said with a wobble in her voice to say she knew how serious head injuries could be, but if hoping for the best would help she was ready to try it. 'Uncle Alaric hates being ill.'

'Then he is in for a torrid time. I think he has sprained his wrist as well. Was the gentleman slammed against the wall, Joe?' Marianne asked the man as he ran back into the yard. At least he must have shut the bad-tempered nag away and the men looked as if this accident had sobered them up so they might be in a fit state to help her get His Lordship inside without further endangering his life.

'Seth brought his horse out. I was thatching the rick like you said I was to, Mrs Turner. I only looked over here when our Seth shouted the horse was getting ready to bolt and it must have thrown yon lord against the wall before Seth could grab it and make it stop. Bad-tempered great brute it is. I wonder the Royal George hired him out to a proper lord.'

'I expect he was in a hurry and demanded the fastest horse they had in their stables,' Marianne said and fought the oddest feeling she knew him that well while she ran exploring hands over surprisingly heavy bands of muscle on His Lordship's torso as gently as she could to find out if he had any more serious injuries they needed to worry about.

'He would do that. He does not like to wait,' Juno agreed almost fondly.

Marianne carried on with her exploration. Now she knew Lord Stratford did not have a spare ounce anywhere on his impressively muscular body and she should not be impressed by the strength and endurance of the man at a time like this. She soothed the gentlest of touches over his waist and narrow hips and even lying in a heap like this she could tell his legs were the same length. At least there was no need to worry about a serious fracture that could put his life in danger from internal bleeding. His left ankle seemed awkward, though, and she dreaded having to cut the snug-fitting riding boot off it so she could see if it was broken. Best do it before he was awake and would feel every agonising movement and she might flinch with him and risk cutting him instead. 'I need the boning shears from the scullery, Juno. Take care, they are very sharp and please do not run on the way back—I do not have time for any more patients,' she said and Juno was gone before she even finished her sentence.

Lord Stratford was lying worryingly still, but breathing evenly. He would wake up to a dreadful headache, a sore wrist and maybe a broken ankle, so perhaps it was as well if he stayed unconscious a little longer. She spared a moment to admire the stern symmetry of his features as he lay undefended. Without his challenging blue gaze to argue he was aloof and self-contained, she could see how sensitive his mouth was when he did not have it under strict control. Now the lines of exhaustion around it were relaxed he also looked as if he was born to laugh a lot more than he did.

Being lord of so much must lie heavy on his broad shoulders and the real Alaric Defford was far more fascinating than Lord Stratford, with his lordly orders and air of owning half the world and having designs on the rest. Was it all a front, then? Having heard him with Juno before this disaster she suspected it might well be and tried hard not to pity him for needing to keep one up even with his nearest and dearest.

'Well done,' she said when Juno reappeared with the sharpest scissors they had in the house, then slipped back into her place at her uncle's side. 'Be careful,' Marianne warned her as she gripped the shears herself and gritted her teeth ready for action. 'He might grip down on your hand hard if this wakes him up. He is sure to be in a great deal of pain one way and another and he will not be in a fit state to consider who or what he has hold of.'

'Worry about him, I can look after myself.'

'So you can,' Marianne said as she slipped the cold metal under his once beautiful boot and made herself cut through the supple leather.

Alaric was having a wonderful dream where he drifted between sleep and happy fulfilment in Mrs Turner's bed. Her sky blue eyes were soft and heavy lidded with sleep and sensual satisfaction his dream self felt smug about. Warmth and openness and a heady passion weighed their limbs down in this soft bed with its fine linen sheets. He could smell the summer breezes and lavender on them as well as sated desire and breathed in the fresh scent and pure essence of Mrs Turner. He wondered why he did not know her first name as they were so gloriously intimate. Mary? What had Miss Donne called her when they first met? Margaret? No, Marianne. He recalled her name with satisfaction; first, because he liked it and, second, because it suited her. And it was always as well to remember a lady's name when you bedded her to their mutual and lingering pleasure.

A good romantic name it was, too, just right for a fine woman with lovely eyes and the slender, long-limbed body he had lusted after so fiercely at first glance. There, at least he had the trick of her name now, so he would not have to call her by another man's surname when they woke up in the morning for an even more blissful loving by daylight after this night of it he could not remember even beginning with her. He was very willing to go on now they were here and very much together in the private summer night, but that lack of memory troubled him even in his dreams.

Now he came to think of it, there was a deal of noise around in what should be a peaceful and private bedchamber in the middle of the night as well. And it felt as if the sun was beating on his head, which was wrong for the night-time, and there was a breath of wind against his cheek as well which did not seem to match a slumberous bedchamber in the blessed darkness. And this mattress was devilish uncomfortable all of a sudden. His dream began to spiral away and he could feel a stone under his hip. Even in the worst inn he had ever come across he doubted they had any of those in their mattresses.

The last shards of his lovely fantasy began to shatter as pain ran in to take its place with an evil chuckle. He frowned against the loss of what felt like earthly paradise and screwed up his eyes to protest at the light. He wished whoever was making that confounded row would be quiet so he could go back to sleep.

'He is waking up at last,' Juno said. What was she doing here? He hoped his innocent niece had not seen him slip out of Mrs Turner's bed to deal with the idiot groaning in what sounded like agony when they were all trying to sleep.

'Can you remember your name?' Mrs Turner's otherwise pleasant contralto voice demanded.

What a question to ask a man who had to deal with the idiot while he had agony coursing through him like hot knives. She grasped his good hand and squeezed it as if ordering him not to ignore her. 'Your name?' she nagged and he was far too busy with the idiot to reply to such a silly question, but he supposed he ought to oblige a lady.

'I am Alaric Defford. I wish someone would tell that fool to be quiet and let me sleep,' he murmured.

'What fool?' Marianne Turner asked as if wondering about his sanity.

'The one who keeps moaning and groaning like an idiot.'

'That is you, Uncle Alaric,' Juno said and he felt his way up through another layer of unconsciousness and immediately wished he had stayed down there.

'Is it? Then I must have been swearing as well,' he admitted and opened his eyes to look up at his niece and hope she had not been listening. Agony bit as the sunlight bored into his flinching eyeballs and made him swear all over again as a jag of pain joined up with the one at the back of his aching head and ripped through him like hot iron.

'So sorry, Jojo,' he murmured and felt her hand tighten on his. Somehow he must find a way to cut himself off from the pain and protect her from it. 'Bad uncle,' he managed to say lamely before he shut his eyes again. He wished someone would turn off the sun so the inside of his eyelids were not such a fiery red. Shade might reduce the agony to a bearable hum and maybe he could gather his senses enough to open his eyes again and find out exactly what was going on.

'No, you are the best of uncles,' Juno argued with a tremble in her voice.

Somehow he managed to force his eyelids open again and never mind the thunderclap he knew was waiting for him this time. He had to let her know he was back in the land of the living and intending to stay here.

'Lie still and be quiet,' Marianne Turner ordered him softly and he was glad to do as he was bid for once.

She had put herself between him and the sun as well. He was almost ready to worship her thoughtfulness, although he wished his dream of her as his willing and about-to-be-sated-again lover was the reality he had woken up to instead of this one. In this world Mrs Marianne Turner had disliked him on sight and did not warm to him much afterwards. She was not likely to be impressed when he moaned and groaned and swore in his sleep, so there was very little chance of that rich fantasy ever coming true.

'Gladly,' he muttered and wondered when the sledgehammer inside his head would stop beating. Then he realised he could half hear and half feel a new sort of thunder through the very ground he lay on. He seemed to be in danger of being trampled by a herd of runaway horses or panicked cattle. He vaguely remembered the ill-tempered nag he rode in on taking offence at something before dreams and that very seductive fantasy took over his head and blotted out the pain and shock of being thrown. Maybe he should get up and run, but it felt beyond him so he lay as still as he could and waited for the next calamity to strike him. 'Run!' he muttered urgently to Juno and Marianne and tried to force his eyes open and even felt for strength to put himself between them and whatever was about to run them down.

'Oh, Darius, I am so very glad to see you,' he

heard Marianne Turner call out with apparent delight as the noise of what he could now tell was a single horse's racing hooves halted sharply. Alaric finally managed to open his eyes just in time to see Darius the Paragon leap off it and run towards them like a stunt rider.

'Wonderful,' Alaric said with all the irony he had available at short notice.

'Good Gad, Nan, what has the noble idiot done to himself this time?' Yelverton exclaimed as if Alaric had fallen off his horse on purpose.

He actually felt sick with dislike because it was better than being sick with pain. He did not want to humiliate himself in front of his niece and the lovely Mrs Turner. Loathing Darius Yelverton for being whole and hearty and not in pain, as well as in love with the woman Alaric thought he wanted to marry until he came here, would have to do instead. Although his yearning for Marianne Turner in his bed even when he was knocked out whispered he had not wanted to marry Miss Grantham anywhere near as passionately as she deserved her husband to want to marry her.

'I am not sure it was his fault this time,' Marianne said.

Alaric dared open one eye against the afternoon sun to look up at her. She seemed to be staring at a hangdog-looking man just within his field of vision and he did not have the slightest inclination to get a better look at the unshaven lout so he peered up at her instead. He decided dreamily he had no great inter-

est in anyone else with her to fix his gaze on instead
and managed to forget how much his head ached for
a lovely moment.

She had a sharply determined chin to add an edge
to her oval face. It rescued her from mere prettiness
and pushed her towards a fugitive sort of beauty. So
much of her compelling attraction lay in her moods
and expression that he had to wonder how she would
go on in his exclusive circle of almost friends. No
doubt Marianne would be fascinating and full of life
and spirit if she chose to let her true nature out in
public, but quiet and avoiding the limelight if she did
not. What a conundrum of a woman she was and of
course he had met lovelier women and even managed
to bed one or two of them, but they would all fade to
insignificance next to her.

That lovely mouth of hers was too generous for
classical beauty and her nose a little too pert, but
even in a room full of accredited beauties he would
still find her compelling and the rest all but invisible. Her face had a unique charm that made her
beauty lifelong instead of a fleetingly perfect thing
made of youth and beauty and a generous hand from
Mother Nature.

He also liked the fact her honey-gold curls were
coming down again, despite all the pins she must
have skewered into it to pin the heavy weight under
that ugly cap. Why on earth did she keep trying to
turn herself into a quiz when a man would have to
be blind or daft not to see the intense blue of her intelligent gaze and the kissable softness of her lips?

'Impossible,' he murmured to argue with her cap and maybe his wits had gone begging after all.

'I will have an accounting for this later,' Yelverton was saying grimly to the silent men even Alaric could practically hear shuffling their feet and longing to get away from the man's best officer's glare.

Alaric did not have the slightest inclination to watch Yelverton instead of his sister and work out exactly what had happened. He lay here and was glad that Marianne had not transferred all her attention to her brother as she shook her head at him and shrugged to say she had no idea what he was talking about. 'Impossible what?' she asked him as everyone else was occupied with who had done what and why and it did not matter a jot as he lay still and admired the rich brown and gold and even the odd red light in her hair.

'Do you think we dare move him, Marianne?' Yelverton interrupted them and from the sound of his voice he was much closer now.

Alaric bit back a protest. He was likely to faint again if they even tried it and that would be the final humiliation, but he could hardly say so without sounding feeble.

'We must keep his head still and he is covered in bruises and has a swollen ankle to consider although luckily I do not think it is broken. We managed to cut his boot off before it swelled up too badly and I dare say a cold compress would make it feel a lot more comfortable once we can get him to bed and put one on it.'

'At last, something to look forward to,' Alaric murmured and heard her chuckle very softly.

He felt stupidly elated to share even a moment of irony with her, but dreaded losing any dignity he had left if they tried to help him up and he lost consciousness again or cast up his accounts. He wished he could snap his fingers and be out of this bright sunlight for a while before he need set out for Broadley again, though. Juno's hand tightened on his good one as if his flinch at the idea of his hurts being disturbed pained her.

'Perhaps you would like to pass out while we get you inside, Stratford,' Darius Yelverton loomed over him to say half-seriously and Alaric longed for the strength to plant him a facer.

'I think I hate you,' he muttered when the man was close enough to peer into his eyes as if checking them for dust motes.

'I know you do right now,' the man joked and grinned at Alaric as if he understood him all too well.

Chapter Six

It galled him to oblige Yelverton, but Alaric woke up hours or maybe even days later in the feather bed he had been dreaming about earlier. Except this time it felt lonely in here and there was a wary sort of silence around him. He lay still and thought about the world and his place in it and concluded it felt like night-time. He must have been out of his senses for a long time, then. He was quite happy for it to have been days if that got him closer to the end of this weakness and the pain trundling through his battered body like a bullock cart now he was awake again. He shifted against the summer-scented sheets he was fantasising about earlier and bit back a groan.

Keep still, then, man, he reasoned impatiently and tried to track down the pain.

He needed to find out if it was safe to move any of his aching body without a humiliating scream. If he stayed still, he only ached all over, but he knew real pain was lying in wait like a grinning demon carrying a pitchfork to prod him with. He tried to shift his arm, but his wrist shot a burning pain through it whenever he tried to move so it seemed sensible not to. He had to fight an urge to fidget and see if one place in this bed was better than another. Maybe he could curl into a ball and find comfort somewhere. He felt bruised from head to toe and, talking of toes, one of his feet felt just as usual, but the other throbbed if he tried to move it. So that was a wrist and a foot out of action.

He frowned and felt that horrible pounding hammer start up in his head again. A savage blow to the head must be his most dangerous hurt, then. What if he had lost his wits? What would become of Stratford Park and all the farms and cottages? So many people depended on him for a roof over their heads and bread in their bellies but, worst of all, what about Juno? If he was addled, who was going to take care of his niece until she came of age?

His mother was her only other close relative and Alaric shuddered away from the very idea of leaving Juno completely at her lack of mercy ever again. Under the provisions of the will he had made a decade ago when he came of age, Juno would inherit all the unentailed land and his private fortune when he died. Every fortune hunter in the British Isles would try to marry her by fair means or foul. At least half would not mind if it was only held in trust because he was locked up in a madhouse as they could then borrow against her expectations. The poor girl would become an object to be bought and sold rather than a sensitive being with the right to make her own choices in life. So he simply had to be well and sane. That was the only way to make sure Juno was who she wanted to be.

He made himself open his eyes, then blinked against the pain as his vision cleared and he found himself staring up at Mrs Marianne Turner's unique set of feminine features yet again. This time her face was shadow softened and he wondered if he had conjured her from his dreams and blinked again. As she was still here, at least he had not imagined her the first time.

'Are you in a great deal of pain, my lord?' she whispered as she misread his frown.

'A little, but please will you tell me if my wits are addled before I worry about anything else, Marianne,' he pleaded urgently. Her given name slipped out, but keeping guard on his tongue did not seem important with the threat of madness hanging over him. 'I beg your pardon, Mrs Turner,' he corrected himself impatiently when she frowned at him as if he was talking another language.

'As far as I can tell on less than a day's acquaintance, you are sane as you ever were,' she told him with a shrug, as if she had her doubts about his sanity at their first meeting on Miss Donne's doorstep, so that was not very sane at all.

'Good,' he murmured. 'Is it still today, then?' he asked as the rest of her words sank in. It felt as if far more time should have gone by since he first set eyes on her, but at least he had not lost days or even weeks lying here like a block.

She took a workaday sort of man's watch case out of her pocket, flicked it open and held the timepiece up to the shaded candle flame he supposed had been masked for his benefit. He silently thanked her for that, knowing even a candle's worth of light shining into his eyes would hurt like hell.

'Two o'clock in the morning,' she told him briskly, 'so it is actually tomorrow if you wish to be strictly accurate.'

'Thank you, it seems as well. While we are being precise, you might as well tell me what other injuries I have sustained.'

'Are you sure you want to know?' she asked with the wry smile he was beginning to watch out for. Teaching himself not to do that was another task he could face when he was feeling better.

'If I am of sound mind and need to remake my will because my life is in danger, I need to know about that so it can be done properly this time and my niece will be protected from fortune hunters and her property being taken over by the Crown estate,' he told her very seriously. Juno's future was much too important for him to be careless about it any longer.

'According to Dr Long, you have been very lucky although I would argue. You have to stay in a dark room for several days so we can make sure you suffer no lasting damage from that blow on the head and it is hardly good luck to be thrown against a stone wall by a bucking horse. None of the hurts you sus-

tained will be life threatening as long as you are patient and do not go galloping across the country on
another mad ride for a month or so and stay in bed
until all danger of worse consequences than a headache have passed.'

The thought of his headache jarring if he even
got on a horse made another mad dash across country seem unthinkable. He was more frustrated by
her constant 'my lording' than the idea of not being
able to get out of bed. It felt as if they should be beyond distinctions of rank by now, but he supposed
he was forced on her and her brother, so he would
just have to endure her reminders of who he was and
how poorly he fitted in here. 'What about those other
injuries you mentioned, how bad are they?'

'You must know you have sprained your wrist
by now since you tried to move it and flinched and
you have sprained and perhaps broken your ankle.'

He must have looked horrified by the possibility
of not being able to walk or ride properly for a month
or so. She gave him a wry smile and a sympathetic
shake of her head. Where were lordly aloofness and
hard-won self-control now? Lost like a highwayman's mask, he decided, and only just stopped himself shaking his head because he knew it would hurt.

'I suppose the amount of time your ankle takes to
heal will let us know whether it is broken or sprained.
And as for your head and the amount of time you
have spent sleeping since you knocked yourself out
on that wall, the ridiculous ride you put yourself
through to get here faster than a man was meant to

travel accounts for most of that, if you ask me. Dr
Long was worried the pain of being moved did not
wake you, but he did not see you at dawn on Miss
Donne's doorstep so he has no idea you were a fool
to start with, my lord. At least two days' worth of
hard riding and your refusal to be sensible even before you insisted on riding here because you did not
trust me to look after Juno meant you have had less
sleep than your body needs for several days. In my
opinion Mother Nature simply took over, Lord Stratford, and your head injury is not as severe as the doctor fears. Your long sleep only proves your body has
more sense than the rest of you.'

'He is a doctor,' Alaric said with only half his
mind on what he was saying. The rest was worrying
at the threat still hanging over him that the blow on
his head was more serious than they hoped and how
he wished she would stop calling him Lord Stratford all the time. He did not feel like a correct and
aloof viscount, lying here like a helpless infant. He
wished she really was Marianne to him and not just
a stranger so she might call him Alaric and soothe
and nag him out of affection instead of duty to an
injured stranger.

'Of a sort,' Marianne said dismissively and where
were they? Ah, yes, doctors—he had little interest
in them at the best of times. 'I met one or two like
him when I was with the army,' she went on as if she
agreed with him for once. 'They believe in malign
providence rather than a duty to heal the injured. In

my experience cleanliness and patience mend more hurts than the sawbones' gloom and purges.'

'You were with the army?' Alaric asked incredulously.

'My husband was a soldier,' she said and he thought she must be very weary herself to let him see the sadness and faraway look in her eyes, as if she was with her absent Mr Turner in spirit even if she would not be seeing him again this side of the grave.

'I am sorry for your loss,' he said sincerely, presuming on that past tense.

'So am I,' she said very quietly, then seemed to make an effort of will to snap herself out of the lonely place memory of Lieutenant or Captain Turner, or however high her late husband rose, had taken her. 'And you need more sleep in order to heal. I forgot to add you are bruised black and blue all down the side of your body that hit my brother's newly mended wall to the list of your injuries, Lord Stratford,' she told him softly but sternly, as if he might not know he was aching like the devil.

'I must have had a deal of rest already. It was no more than an hour or two after midday when I let that bad-tempered nag throw me and you say it is the middle of the night now. You are the one who is in need of sleep now, Mrs Turner. I seem to have had plenty of it to be going on with.'

'Someone has to sit with you in order to make sure you do not get out of bed and ride off into the night. Juno is too young for this much responsibility and quite worn out after all the walking and worrying she did on the way here. My brother has to be up early tomorrow to take charge of the men after yesterday's shenanigans, so I persuaded him go to bed as well.'

'You should have a chaperone,' he argued and frowned when she chuckled as if the very idea was ridiculous. 'Of course you should—you are hardly at your last prayers and neither am I.'

'You are not in any state to endanger anyone and the widow of a common soldier is not bound by the same rules as a Miss Defford, my lord,' she said and her set mouth and steady gaze dared him to be shocked by the man she had married.

Yes, he was shocked and her family must have been disappointed by the match, but she still looked like a lady to him. It must have taken great courage to defy the conventions and marry her soldier anyway. 'So you feel free to make up your own rules?' he said and there was a flicker of doubt in her eyes as if he had put his finger on something she did not want the rest of the world to know.

'I am free *not* to paint watercolours or embroider fire screens or perform good works the poor probably do not want if that is what you mean. I fear I was never a properly genteel young lady, my lord, and at least I do not even have to pretend I want to be one any more.'

He wanted to laugh out loud, but did not dare, first, because it would jar his bruises and, second, because she would be offended. She would never be quietly, boringly compliant with society's sillier edicts about what a lady could and could not do if she lived to be a hundred. Did that make her less of a lady? No, he matched her to the best examples of her kind and decided character and charm triumphed over the lack of it every time. 'Are you an improper one, then?' he joked carelessly and saw contempt in her eyes before she turned away as if looking for a better distraction than him in this pared-back bed-chamber.

'I shall never marry again and no lover could compare to my late husband, so I shall not be taking one of those either, my lord, before you ask,' she said very firmly indeed and squared her chin as if he might argue and would be wasting his breath.

He recognised a false trail when he heard one and ignored that slur on his supposed nobility. So her brother had been trying to persuade her to consider a second marriage, had he? Yes, he must have done for her to be looking at him so sternly she clearly thought he was joining a male conspiracy against her. And did she really think he wanted to be one of those lovers she was so determined not to have? If so, she was right. He did not blame Yelverton for doing what any responsible brother would rather than see his sister lonely or pestered by rakes and rogues for the rest of her life. She was dangerously unaware of her own looks and, even if most of him had no intention of offering her a carte blanche, he could have provided a comprehensive list of her form and features blindfolded and after barely as day's acquaintance. No wonder her brother was worried.

She would be happier and safer with a husband to

fight off the wolves if only she would consider the idea. Of course, if she was wed, she would not be here for him to gawp at like an overheated youth. If she had an eager lover waiting for her to come back to his bed, my Lord Stratford would have woken up alone and bewildered in a strange bed and that would never do.

'What will you do when your brother marries Miss Grantham?' he asked, using up all the tolerance an invalid could play on in one go. But at least he could talk about Miss Grantham's wedding to another man without a trace of disappointment she was not marrying him. He was not jealous of Titian-haired, quietly lovely, well-bred and accomplished Miss Grantham and Squire Yelverton. Only yesterday, he had thought he was bereft and humiliated when it became obvious those two lovers had spent the night together in every sense of the word. Now the very idea of a marriage of convenience with Juno's former governess seemed to belong to a different world, along with an Alaric Defford he did not know or understand any more. That blow on the head must have been more severe than she thought.

'For now I shall be busy getting this lovely old place back in good enough order to house their guests, then I suppose I will have to find another house in need of care and attention and apply for the post of housekeeper. My perfect employer would be a reclusive elderly lady so I did not have to avoid the gossips or be put to the trouble and mess of entertaining her non-existent friends.'

'I doubt the world will ever be incurious about you, Mrs Turner, even if it was ready to oblige your solitary and bad-tempered employer by staying away,' he warned half-seriously because the idea of her as anyone's housekeeper was absurd.

He hated the idea of her at anyone's beck and call year after year, growing careworn and depressed as day followed day in a relentless procession of sameness and duty. He shuddered to think what her life would be like if she had to work for a man instead of an elderly lady as the dog was sure to try and take advantage. His fists tightened under the covers and pain shot through his damaged wrist.

'No, you are quite wrong,' she argued earnestly. 'I would work hard and I am not important enough for anyone to take notice of, my lord.'

'All this "my lording" is sheer flummery,' he surprised them both by saying wearily. 'And worldly rank and jostling for position in high society means nothing next to family and true friends.'

She was silent, as if carefully weighing up what to say to a viscount who did not want to be one any more and they both knew he had no choice about the matter. He felt guilty and a bit stupid for letting his confusion about his life out to someone he did not even know this time yesterday. Was this a concussion after all, then, or the after-effects of his long ride and all that terrifying anxiety for Juno as Marianne claimed? Maybe he felt low because he had wasted so much time behaving as a viscount should. He re-called his horror that Juno was hiding from *him* this afternoon with a shudder and a yawning gap threatened to open inside him and let loneliness flood in. Juno did not trust him; she thought he came after her to make her wed against her will and that hurt more than any bruise or sprain or sore head.

'It seems to me we both need to review our ideas about the world, Mrs Turner,' he told her seriously. The thought of her walled up in gloomy isolation made his heart ache as well as the rest of him.

'Maybe we do, but not now,' she told him as if she was humouring him. She rose from her chair to lean over him and he meekly allowed himself to be in pain and bone-weary and in dire need of her care and compassion. Tomorrow would be soon enough to restart his whole life and she still needed to be persuaded her plans were ridiculous. That sounded enough of a challenge for now and she was right, he was very tired.

Chapter Seven

'**D**id you sleep at all last night?' Darius demanded when he came downstairs and found the back door open and his sister outside. Marianne was sitting on the low wall that separated the house from the road to the farm, gazing at the view she had become very fond of during the short time they had lived here.

'Yes,' she said and carried on watching the sky lighten and listening to the chorus of birdsong because her brother had a gift for being silent and worming more out of her than she wanted to say. Even the birds seemed to pause as if waiting to hear more and that was nonsense, but far more effective than an open demand for information. 'My patient was very well behaved and slept for most of the night. He awoke about two and seemed perfectly rational, so we should not need to ask the sawbones to come back unless Lord Stratford becomes agitated and irrational. I am quite sure His Lordship is far too strong-willed to indulge in such weakness.'

'You still do not like him, then?'

Marianne paused to think about that question before she answered, 'He is well enough, I suppose. He must be very strong to withstand the ride he put himself through on his way here searching for Juno and he certainly has a stubborn nature to go with his physical prowess. No doubt he will want to put the discomforts of Owlet Manor behind him as soon as he can endure the journey to town or his nearest mansion to recover in style, so it does not really matter what I think.'

'I take it that is a "no", then?'

'I am trying to be neutral and fair-minded, if only you will let me. Maybe we did get off to a bad start, but he is a brave and determined man, even if he is stubborn as a donkey and will be a very difficult patient as soon as he begins to feel better. And given who we are and who *he* is, I am never likely to be better acquainted with him than I am now, so it hardly matters if I like him or not,' she said defensively.

Her brother did not need to know about the odd skip and thunder in her heartbeat when she had first set eyes on the bearlike and piratical-looking man standing on Miss Donne's doorstep. Nor the odd feeling she had when he had woken up in the night that they understood one another a little bit too well. She did not even want to think about her panic and bitter regret when she had run into the yard yesterday and it had looked as if Lord Stratford was seriously injured and might even die. A cold sense of dread had shivered through her when she had seen him lying unconscious at the base of that wall, but that was her secret and her worst fears were unfounded. Darius was not getting that out of her if he stayed silent and listening for the rest of the day. 'The kettle must have boiled by now. I will go and make tea,' she said to put paid to more uncomfortable questions.

'No, stay there and let me do something for you just this once,' Darius said, then left her brooding on the waking landscape and all the changes about to reorder her life, yet again.

They were too big to consider until she felt less tired, so she just sat in the strengthening sun and let it warm and soothe her before the power of it was too much to endure bareheaded. Now it felt reviving and reassuring and she allowed herself the luxury of revelling in the peace and quiet for a few precious minutes.

'Here you are,' Darius said softly and slipped the handle of one of the kitchen mugs into her hand, then went back inside to drink his own tea, as if he knew she wanted to be quiet and not think about anything much for a few moments at the beginning of another busy day.

He probably wanted to do the same himself, but his thoughts would be of Fliss and the new life they were about to begin together in this lovely old house. If anyone deserved a peaceful life and a happy marriage, it was Darius. Fliss needed a proper home as well, so this place would be perfect for her, and Marianne only envied them because she remembered how it felt to love someone as surely and completely as they loved one another now they had finally admitted it.

If only Daniel was here to share this lovely summer morning with her; if only he had lived to find such a peaceful home with her after the war was over, even if theirs would have been far more humble than Owlet Manor. He would have come with her to help Darius sort this lovely old place and its rundown farms out first and she knew Darius missed Daniel's energy and optimism as well. It would have been such fun with Daniel here to laugh with, she thought as tears blurred her eyes.

She shook her head and refused to live in Might Have Been Land because it was such a dangerous place to be that you could forget it was not real if you were not careful. She needed to get up and do whatever came next instead of sitting about regretting a future denied her by Daniel's death. The sneaky idea that she now had to regret the one she could never have with a nobleman like Alaric, Lord Stratford, as well crept into her head and made her frown. She only met him this time yesterday; that idea was not only sneaky, it was downright impossible.

Darius surprised her by coming back outside and sitting next to her with a very serious expression, as if he had tried to leave her in peace but whatever he had to say was too urgent to put off. 'We want you to stay, Nan. Fliss and I agree we cannot live without you and, before you say no to me without even thinking about it, she asked me to tell you she has always wanted a sister and will be very hurt if you refuse to stay at Owlet Manor because she will be living here as well.'

'Oh, well, that clinches the matter,' she said with a wry smile.

'I am serious and so is she, Marianne. We need you and this was never about finding work for you until the house was its proper self again. It was built for a family and we have always mattered to one another, you and I, but we do so even more after everything we saw and did in Portugal and Spain. I want this to be your home and Viola's as well, when we can finally persuade her to stop working for that rogue Marbeck and join us.'

'Even if she did she would rather find another post than become an idle lady paying calls and fascinating all the local beaux. It is your dream for all three of us to live under the same roof again, Darius, but it is not going to come true. It is a wonderful one and shows what a good man you are under your annoying elder-brother ways, but you have a true love to share this lovely old place with now and must stop worrying about your sisters. Get on with living the life you can have with Fliss and I wish you so very happy, Darius, but sooner or later I must move on as well. Viola has her own road to travel and neither of us wants to intrude on your new lives as man and wife.'

'I will never stop trying to change Viola's mind while she is in Sir Harry Marbeck's employ,' Darius said grimly.

Marianne wondered if he was thinking of galloping to Gloucestershire and demanding their little sister pack her bags and join them at Owlet Manor straight away. 'The more you rant and rave about the man, the less she will do as you want, Darius,' she warned. 'You ought to know Viola is as obstinate as both of us put together by now.'

'Aye, you are right,' he said with a gusty sigh, 'but please don't insist on going away as well, Nan,' he added as if it would hurt him. Trust him to know using his nickname for her from her childhood would sway her as much as she was willing to be swayed.

'I will stay long enough to help you and Fliss get this fine old place in good order for the wedding, but after that I must find something else to do, Darius. You know I cannot bear to be idle and Fliss already loves this house and will soon learn to run it with the help of some good servants and all the modern refinements you two can afford now she is rich. It will be a lovely, gracious old home for you and Fliss to raise your family and the last thing you need is your sisters here to argue and interfere at every turn. You know very well we would do so as soon as the first gloss of us all being a family again had worn off because neither of us is a meek and biddable female who would tactfully fade into the background.'

'You never stand still long enough to fade into anything,' he argued.

'I cannot, Darius,' she said seriously because she knew he would not let her laugh this off and he would argue with her every step of the way if she did not make him realise she was determined to leave. 'I need to be busy. I need it as much as Fliss needs to have her own home and I think she needs it very badly. It sounds as if she could never call anywhere home for very long as a child so she must have a place of her own to love and look after without me here to interfere.'

'I think you know us both a little too well, Little Sister,' he said with a heavy sigh, as if he did not think it a very good quality.

'I know how it feels to love as strongly and truly as you two do, now you have finally admitted it and thank goodness for that.'

'Aye, we have and we do,' he said with a far-off look in his eyes as he stared down the road to Broadley where his lover was sleeping without him.

'The sooner you two are wed and left to get on with being besotted with each other in peace, the better, then,' Marianne told him with a knowing smile and he just shrugged and grinned back at her. Loving Fliss had given him his true self back after those hard years on campaign. She would have to thank her sister-in-law-to-be for that even if she didn't already like her very much indeed for her own sake as well as his.

Yelverton and his sister must have been living more or less alone here for too long to worry that anyone could hear their murmured conversations. The narrow windows that actually opened must have been left wide to stop this room becoming stifling and even through the shutters Alaric could hear most of what they said in the stillness of yet another dawn.

Listening shamelessly distracted him from his ills as he lay here like a log in the otherwise darkened room and he was not even ashamed of himself. He could not prop himself up to watch the sky lighten and doubted he could hold a book without flinching even if his battered brain could concentrate and he had enough light to read it. He needed to lie still to avoid jarring the bruise on the back of his head and making the confounded headache start up again.

So what else was there for him to do but lie here and eavesdrop? he concluded tetchily. He flinched at the thought of the pain if he rolled his head the wrong way, but thank heavens the relentlessly pounding headache of last night had abated—as long as he did nothing foolish to start it off again. In the middle of the night he had been too preoccupied with worrying about his sanity and Mrs Marianne Turner to care about the boredom of recovery from a head wound. He hated the idea of being an invalid already and he was not even a day into it yet. How long did it take to be certain the danger of concussion and further damage was over, then? And when would he be able to walk or ride out in the pure light of early morning again?

He shuddered at the very thought of doing the latter just yet. Not that he was afraid to get back on a decent horse instead of the bad-tempered nag he had ridden yesterday. His brother had taught him to get back on a horse as soon as he fell off it as a boy and he had learned not to fear them. Horses were tricky creatures, much like people really in their likes and dislikes, diverse characters and strengths and weaknesses. On the whole he preferred horses and dogs to people now he lay here and thought about it— they were generally better tempered and a lot more reliable.

Except listening to the brother and sister talking about possible futures outside his window had made him think about people he could like. They were obviously very close and seemed to understand one another better than they probably wanted to be understood. He missed his brother so badly when he looked back at the one person who had made an effort to understand a scrubby brat seven years younger than the charmed heir to their father's title and lands. George had always done his best for his annoying little brother and Yelverton and Marianne's dilemma as they faced the truth that his marriage would mean she must move on touched him as he had not let himself be touched for far too long. Maybe there was something he could do to help them both. He might not be able to follow up on his instant attraction to the lovely Mrs Turner, but the spark of an idea had come into his aching head as he listened to their conversation.

'Uncle Alaric?' Juno's voice whispered from the doorway.

'Juno?' he asked foolishly because who else could it be with Yelverton and his sister communing with the rising sun outside and no sign of any indoor servants to be seen? He rolled his head on to the bruise when he tried to look at her and bit back a pained gasp so as not to frighten her away. 'Come in here where I can see you,' he said more harshly than he meant to because of the pain thundering through his head like a steam hammer as he rolled away from that side and sighed with relief. 'It hurts to twist round and peer at you when you stand over there,' he explained and hoped she would excuse so much more than one barked order when he was in pain. He held his breath and prayed silently she would forget to be afraid of him so they could start again.

'Sorry,' she said softly and came to the foot of the bed so he could see her as clearly as he was allowed to see anything in this shadowy old room. She looked so much paler than he remembered and thin with it. His heart twisted with self-loathing as he took in all he and his mother had done to the unfortunate girl between them with the Dowager's repellent scheming and his neglect.

'Do not apologise to me, Juno,' he said. 'I have done nothing to deserve it.' He heard the anguish in his own voice and was ashamed he could not find the strength to hide it for her sake.

'No, you do deserve it, Uncle Alaric, and I am so very sorry. I have been a widgeon about my come out and so many other things since. I am supposed to be grown up. I should have argued about going to London even when Grandmama insisted it was high time I made my debut and you agreed with her because other girls do it at my age and actually enjoy it. If I had told you how much I dreaded it, I know you would not have made me go. And I should have written to you the moment Grandmama tried to bullock me into marrying that horrid old man. So you see, none of this would have happened if I was braver. You would not be hurt so badly after riding all that way to find me and when you got here I just told you to go away.'

'That was not your fault and you did steel yourself to go to London when you did not want to go and you refused to marry that fat rogue and I am proud of you even if you are not. It took great courage to run away when the Dowager tried to force your hand. I cannot even imagine how terrified you must have been when you had to set out on such a journey alone and you got all the way here with no money left as well, Jojo. All in all, I cannot think of any girl I ever met who has more courage than you.'

His imagination painted a picture of a much younger Marianne flying from her safe home at whatever vicarage she came from to find, then wed, her gallant soldier. Perhaps there was one girl who had been as brave, if not braver, than Juno when she set out to find Miss Grantham and ask for sanctuary then, but as he had not met Marianne at that age he was still telling the absolute truth. He did not want a picture in his head of how delicious and headstrong and innocently determined Miss Marianne Yelverton must have been when she set her heart on her late husband, come what may. The woman she was now plagued him badly enough without adding another layer of temptation to the mix.

'A bolder person would have got her own way without needing to run,' Juno objected, so he had to push the tempting image of a young and dreamy-eyed Marianne aside to concentrate on Juno. Had she always been so resistant to praise and how could he not know something so important about his own niece?

'I doubt it and stop finding yourself less than everyone else you know. There is no bravery in doing something you do not fear and I like you far better than the usual simpering debutante with an abacus where her heart should be,' he said and at least Juno was never going to be the sort of ruthless husband hunter he had learned to avoid since inheriting George's title and lands at seventeen. 'You are kind-hearted and clever and far nicer, as well as a lot more interesting, than those preening girls with so little to preen about. I should have done better by you than I have until now, but you must believe me, Juno, no sane person I have ever come across is as certain of themselves as you seem to think they are.'

'Not even you?'

'Especially not me and if you promise to try harder to fight your demons in the future, then I will do the same with mine,' he offered with a wry smile.

'I doubt you have ever had a shy moment in your entire life, Uncle Alaric.'

'I expect I could surprise you with one or two, but we all have our own worries and shortcomings, Jojo,' he said and he had certainly learnt a lot about his own dark places since he set out on his frantic quest to find her.

'When I saw you lying there hurt I felt...' Juno hesitated and Alaric willed her to go on. He wanted better for her, wanted her to live well in her own skin and know she always had a right to be listened to, even if he had not been very good at it in the past. 'Furious with myself,' she went on as if she had to physically push the words out of her mouth. 'You came all the way from Paris to Broadley, then out here to Owlet Manor in order to find me, although you were obviously so tired after riding all that way that you could barely stand upright when you got here. And you only came to make sure I was truly unharmed by the storm and the journey and having to walk the rest of the way here from Worcester after I was robbed. Then, when you got here, I hid away from you like a timid little child and refused to even meet your eyes across a room.'

'I was the adult and you really were a child when this all began. I should never have left you with your grandmother after your father died. I ought to have done what I wanted to at the time and found a kindly older lady to help you settle so you could live with me at Stratford Park instead of at the Dower House. Not that the Dowager has spent much time there in the last few years, but I should never have let her persuade me I was not fit to care for you and you needed her. Apparently the world would think it odd if you did not live with her and that should not have mattered one jot beside your happiness and well-being.'

'I would rather have been with you and I was very glad Grandmama spent most of her time in London,' Juno said with the ghost of a smile.

'So was I,' he confided with a wan smile back. 'I

should have realised she did not love you years ago, but I was blinded by the fact she adored your father and thought she must love you as well. I should have been old enough to stop worrying what people would think if you lived with me instead.'

'I do not think she likes either of us very much.' Juno's smile was more certain now and he managed to find a better one in return.

'No, but I really do love you, Juno, and you are going to grow very tired of me telling you so for the rest of your life to make up for being such a fool until now. I promise you I will not keep my feelings to myself from now on.'

'Things could get very complicated if you wear your heart on your sleeve all the time, Uncle Alaric.'

'Aye, you are quite right, niece. Then I had best limit myself to being open with you and anyone else I somehow manage to love or like. The rest of the world can be excused knowing exactly what I think of it.'

'Considering how little patience you have with some parts of it that would be as well.'

'True—and I think you know me a little bit too well.'

'I watch people a lot, even when I feel too shy to join in.'

'Then we must find more of them you feel happy to engage with or you will soon become a cynic.'

'No, I love Miss Grantham and already like Mrs Turner and Mr Yelverton very much. I even quite like you at times, Uncle Alaric, although obviously you do not count since you are family and obliged to like me anyway,' she teased him, this girl he had been so desperate to find on his way here it seemed to have torn open his closed heart and remade him.

His mother's cold indifference at best and hatred at worst, then George's tragically premature death in the hunting field had made him a puzzled and lonely youth. He shut that boy away and concentrated on being Lord Stratford, but it was about time he came out from behind his title and learnt to be himself—if only he knew who that was. He would have to learn to ignore his inner sceptic if he wanted to make Juno's life better and stop guarding himself against strong emotions for the rest of his life. And he was tired of being the lord who walked alone. His fine plan to wed Miss Grantham and keep his viscountess at a distance would have been a disaster, so it was as well she came here and found true love instead.

'Obviously I am very relieved about that,' he said and might have said more, but sensed Mrs Turner was nearby even before she came into the room so quietly he wondered how he had been so certain. This odd awareness of her kept his senses constantly on the alert. His heart began to race when she was within a hundred yards and he had strained his ears for every murmured word she had said to Yelverton under his window this morning, as if he could store them up like treasure against the time he must leave here and go on his lonely way.

Maybe that scheme he had been mulling over would mean not having to leave her behind when he went. It might be a bittersweet torture to be close to a woman so beguilingly unaware of her own attractions and not be able to do anything about it, but something told him he would regret it if he put his own comfort first and ignored her sad dilemma. He still hoped she would not gauge his heartbeat now because she would have the sawbones out here as fast as his horse would go.

'Ah, there you are, Juno,' she said and perhaps it was as well. He was more than delighted to be on good terms with his niece again, but he still felt as if a half-dozen horses had galloped over him yesterday. Strong emotions were exhausting, he decided. No wonder he had avoided them since his brother died.

'I meant to sit quietly by Uncle Alaric's bed until he woke up, but he was awake when I got here,' Juno said sheepishly as she faced Marianne's sceptical gaze.

'She has done me good, Mrs Turner,' Alaric defended her and it was true, or it would be tomorrow morning when he woke up feeling better *and* fairly certain his niece was not going to flee as soon as he was well enough to get up.

'I am sure your company has done your uncle more good than any tonic I have to hand, Juno, but my brother is about to come up here to help your uncle wash and shave. I doubt His Lordship will want either of us nearby while he curses his injuries and very likely my brother up hill and down dale.'

'Almost certainly him as well,' Alaric muttered grumpily, but his dislike of the man was only show by now. He had already forgiven the man for stealing his would-be fiancée. One day he might thank him for loving a young woman he admired for her learning and grace and courage, but did not love. If not for Yelverton, he would have to consider himself bound by his carefully considered offer for the admirable Miss Grantham. Something told him neither of them would have been very happy shackled together for life and they had both had a lucky escape.

Chapter Eight

After all that cursing and discomfort, her patient was so pale and exhausted Marianne insisted on leaving him to sleep despite his insistence he was not tired and had already slept for hours. He did so for several more, so at least that was half a day over without him trying to get out of bed. She had sensed his restless energy on the other side of the door before she even set eyes on him yesterday, so she knew it would only get more difficult to keep him quiet when he felt better. Watching him sleep in the shadowed room now, she was surprised to discover that she hated seeing him brought low like this. It was like a bird of prey being chained to a post or hooded when to her mind they should always fly free.

Fanciful nonsense, she told herself as she turned to go so he could sleep boredom away a little longer.

Hopefully his body had more sense than the rest of him and it would force him to rest and heal before he made any more ridiculous demands of it. Yet he had proved that he did not listen when he had pushed himself to exhaustion on his way here. It was such a fine and powerful male body as well and it seemed a crying shame to abuse it with his usual lordly bull-headedness.

'Mrs Turner?' he murmured even as she turned to leave.

'I am sorry I woke you.'

'Everybody seems to be sorry for me today, one way or the other,' he said and was that really a self-deprecating smile or just a trick of the shadows in a darkened room? If it was, then how dare he have a sense of humour to make him seem more human than he was yesterday? 'Even your brother apologised for hurting me just now, so he thinks I am as fragile as glass and was trying to be kinder than I probably deserve.'

'Do you still have the headache, my lord?'

'Not unless I roll about on the lump on the back of my head.'

'Then do you think you could endure a little light if I open the shutters slightly?' she asked to try and gauge how sensitive to light he was and if she ought to worry about him more than she already was. If there was a lingering chance of concussion it should have shown by now, but she was determined to keep him in bed for another day just in case she was wrong.

'Gladly. I would like to see even a hint of today since I seem to be sleeping so much of it away it feels like a waste of a fine summer day.'

'You *are* injured, Lord Stratford. You must take care until we are sure your head injury is less serious than the doctor feared. I knew you were going to be a difficult patient the moment you started to feel a little better,' she said with her back to him as she let in a small shaft of curious sunlight now it had moved up the sky and would not shine directly into his eyes.

She tried hard to pretend he was only a man in need of a little compassion and not in any way special as she drifted about his bedchamber, tidying little details of the room Darius had no time to worry about. If she tried hard enough, she could forget Lord Stratford possessed strength and character as well as too much money for his own good—oh, and that wretched title as well. Mother Nature had been generous with her gifts when he was born and Marianne wondered if the lady was hell-bent on mischief when she gave him energy and presence as well as an unforgettable face, even if she had withheld classically handsome features. The man was too definite for such smooth good looks, but by the time you realised that it was too late—he had already remade handsome and the rest into also-rans.

'Who, me?' he answered as if he would never dream of being awkward or lordly and she almost laughed.

She added charm, when he chose to use it, to that list of unfair ways Lord Stratford was unforgettable and frowned to make it clear that tactic would not get round her any better than a brusque series of orders. 'Yes, you. It is in your best interest to rest until your head is better and trying to charm your way down-stairs before you are ready to leave this room will not get you anywhere.'

'I shall have to confound you and endure it like a gentleman then, or is that your plan, Mrs Turner? You point out how awkward I am likely to be so I will play the perfect invalid to show you how wrong you are. Is that how you keep ugly customers like me in order?'

'I don't know, I have never had to deal with one quite as ugly as you before, Lord Stratford,' she lied smoothly, but this time he grinned at her as if he knew it was untrue. He thought he had her measure and that felt far too dangerous. The last thing she wanted was him knowing what she really thought of him. If he knew she had tried to sleep earlier, after far too many wearisome days and nights of worrying over Juno and then him, and failed because of him, he would know he had the advantage and play on it to get his own way. Even closing her eyes and try-ing to nap had been a mistake, she reminded herself.

She turned away from him again and frowned down at the short stretch of garden where the house backed on to the road to the farm and stables through the sliver of a gap in the shutters. She had thought it was prudent to allow him this so he would not get out of bed and fling them wide as soon as her back was turned. Yet as soon as she tried to relax she was haunted by silly images of him awake and aware under her searching hands, instead of unconscious and worryingly still as he was yesterday when she frantically explored his body for injuries. He had such a honed and muscular body under his once-splendid clothes as well.

She did not usually care how a man would look naked, not since she lost Daniel and thought she would never want to be intimate with a man ever again. Yet even now her fingers twitched involuntarily as if they were longing for the feel of him under them again, so she eyed them as if they had turned traitor. They still yearned to explore his firm satin skin over honed muscles and a flat belly she had been certain no aristocrat would possess, until she searched almost every inch of him for hurts she winced at finding, although she kept telling herself he was nothing to her.

'If that does not work, I shall just have to find another way to stop you doing yourself permanent damage by doing too much too soon,' she said and from the hot dare in his mesmerising blue eyes he had heard the mistake in that sentence just as she did as soon as it was out of her mouth. No, she would not be joining him in that bed to keep him there until he was well enough to get up and start ordering the world again. 'A sleeping draught, perhaps, or maybe I could get Darius to knock you out with a cudgel,' she added.

A fiery blush still stung her cheeks at the image of them in bed together with her doing all sorts of wrong and inventive things to keep him there. She cursed herself for that giveaway flush of hot colour and he could hardly miss it when there was not much else to look at in this bare bedchamber. She had only just got it clean and had had a new mattress brought in when he needed it so urgently. All the extra comforts she was planning to add hadn't seemed important. She would have another chair or two brought up so the others could sit with him and keep him amused. And she needed to consult Fliss about adding a rug and some furniture. If Lord Stratford felt more comfortable, he might be less restless and less inclined to run before he could walk on that damaged ankle. There, she had almost forgotten to be conscious of him as a man while she did her best to reduce his stay here to a domestic detail.

'I can think of better reasons to be a good patient,' he told her with a mock leer and an altogether too-disarming grin.

There was still a hot promise in his gaze so she avoided it and frowned at a fresh cobweb instead. There could never be anything between a lord and a humble widow they would not be ashamed of afterwards. 'I doubt you know how to be patient in any sense of the word, my lord,' she forced herself to say lightly.

'And I am trying so hard to be humble,' he told her half-seriously and she nearly laughed. She could not imagine a less humble man if she ran through a list of the hot-headed and entitled officers she had met from the Duke of Wellington downwards.

'It could take a lifetime,' she argued and he smiled as if he knew he was naturally arrogant and impatient, but he was less lordly and very human in private.

'I will need a lot of help, then,' he said huskily and all the images in her head earlier were hot in his piercingly blue eyes as he gazed back at her.

Even his mouth looked firm and inviting as the notion of what that help might involve sang between them. He was an invalid, for goodness' sake. And even when he was well he would still be a viscount. Before she went away again she ought to check the bandages on his wrist and ankle were tight enough, but not cutting into him, except being so close to him right now seemed a bad idea. She almost wished he would go back to being the arrogant and objectionable nobleman she met yesterday. It would be so much easier to treat him with cool and impersonal efficiency, then go back to getting the house ready for a wedding.

With any luck he would be well enough to be very gently driven to Broadley and the best inn in town very soon. He could live there in comfort until he was ready to be driven home in his own beautifully sprung carriage. And if she kept on putting his money, rank and privilege between them maybe she would stop finding him so attractive and powerfully male, even when he was lying there in Darius's nightshirt and should look less than his usual overconfident self.

She heard a stir down in the yard and thank goodness for a distraction. Now she could be taken up with whoever was out there instead of him *and* she would not have to get that close to the man without Darius here to take away the intimacy of it.

'I wonder who that can be?' she said, with a *tut-tut* to tell him she did not have time or inclination for visitors. Really, she would be glad to see anyone who would drag her away from his side and break this ridiculous spell he seemed to have cast over her at first sight. She still loved Daniel and she always would, so of course she did not want another man and she *really* did not want to want a lord like this one.

'I have no idea,' he said, 'but at least you can walk over to the window and see for yourself.'

'Hmm, well, I cannot see why anyone would be... Oh, my word,' she gasped as a team of dray horses came properly into view, then the dray itself appeared, loaded with boxes and all sorts of odd items as if half a house full of furniture and trappings were on the move, but what on earth were they doing here?

'For goodness' sake, woman, will you stop peering at whoever is out there and tell me what is going on?' His Lordship snapped from the bed in angry frustration and there he was again, Alaric the Pirate; barking orders from his sickbed. Good, he should make her temper flare and stop her having silly and overheated ideas about Alaric the man.

'If I knew that I might tell you,' she said and turned back from the window with a frown and a stern dare not to even lift his head off his pillow, let alone attempt to get out of bed and see for himself. 'There is a dray loaded with boxes and bags and furniture drawing up outside, Lord Stratford, and I have to suppose that the driver and his mate have been directed to the wrong place to deliver it since I did not order a single stick of it. I had better go downstairs and send them to wherever they are supposed to be going with it all.'

'Ah, apparently your friend Miss Donne is even more efficient than I thought.'

'What on earth can all that stuff have to do with her?'

'The lady obviously has the good sense to worry about your reputation even if you do not, Mrs Turner. If you continue to stay here without a duenna of some sort now I am in the house, your good name will be in shreds.'

'I do not have a good name for the gossips to destroy, so it does not matter what they think of me,' she said. The bitterness in her own voice shocked her. The snide remarks about ladies who wilfully married below their station she had had to pretend not to hear in Bath must have hurt her more than she realised at the time, numbed as she still thought she was by Daniel's death.

The sound of it made Lord Stratford frown, then look lordly and impatient. 'It matters to me,' he said so mildly she felt the sting of his temper more than if he had shouted at her.

A little bit of warmth and caring about her well-being was in there as well as impatience and that might have disarmed her, if she was not already furious about the silly conventions he was worrying about a lot more than she wanted him to. If such empty notions of propriety had made a friend rush here, she would far rather she stayed away. And she did not have time for any more distractions right now, or enough cleared bedrooms to receive them if they intended to stay as that wagonload of furniture and luggage made it look as if they might. 'It does not matter as much as a snap of my fingers to me,' she told him defiantly.

'You were born a lady whether you like it or not, Mrs Turner, and I do not think your brother would thank me for calling him less than a gentleman now. You are still Yelverton's sister and he has the role of lord of the manor to keep up whether you like it or not. You have to be concerned for your good name if you do not want your family suffering from your lack of one by association.'

That nagging piece of grit in her oyster made her want to blaze fury back at him and tell him he had never been more wrong in his life, but he was quite right, drat him. 'I know,' she admitted with a heavy sigh.

Her sister Viola might live in a respectable house several miles away from Chantry Old Hall with her charges and a stern maiden aunt of Sir Harry Marbeck's, but she was still in Sir Harry's employ and vulnerable to gossip about her family. For Viola's sake and for Darius and Fliss's she had to pay lip service to the conventions. Doubtless Fliss and Darius would soon add another generation of Yelvertons to the mix and the lid would be screwed down on Marianne's dreams of an independent life once and for all. So she might have to care about things she had left behind with a sigh of relief when she married Daniel, but that did not mean she must like it.

'I cannot undo the past even if I wanted to and I do not, Lord Stratford,' she told him defiantly. 'I do not regret my runaway marriage. As I was not ashamed of my husband while he was alive, I am certainly not going to be now.'

'Why should you be?' he said with a quieter challenge. 'Do you expect me to think less of your late husband because he was born in a more humble bed than you or I? He must have been a brave and honourable man for you to want to marry him in the first place and I respect such men wherever I meet them.'

He sounded offended by her assumption he would not, so she supposed she ought to stop making them. She had secretly accused him of prejudice from the moment their eyes met on that doorstep and he had mistaken her for the maid and her fury with him for that misstep felt far too personal now. She shook her head at her own stupidity, but he took it as disagreement with him and impatience flashed in his eyes as he shot a challenge back at her.

'Perhaps you ought to think harder about which of us is most inclined to rush to judgement, Mrs Turner,' he said with a hint of disgust that made her squirm.

'What you think of me is immaterial. I must go and find out what is going on down there and if you have any sense you will go back to sleep,' she told him brusquely, trying to pretend his accusation did not sting. What looked like a hired gig had arrived outside now and she saw Fliss draw the horse to a neat halt, so at least her attempt to teach her friend to drive over the last few weeks had paid off.

'Curse it, we are not done,' Lord Stratford said as she turned away from her vantage point to leave him to his solitude with what she told herself was a sigh of relief.

'We are as far as I am concerned,' she told him and at least in his current state she could walk away from an argument with him. If he was his usual self, she would probably not get halfway across the room before he stood in her way to stop her going and make her listen to his opinion of her. He might even kiss her to be certain of her attention and that was an indignity she must not even think of. So she did nothing else but wonder how it would feel to be kissed by His Lordship while she ran downstairs as if the devil was on her tail.

How fortunate that Miss Donne, Fliss and all those trappings were waiting outside to distract her from impossible fantasies. The very idea of Lord Stratford kissing her until she forgot all the differences between them and sighed for him like a dizzy schoolgirl was unthinkable. It was high time she got it right out of her head and went on with real life.

Chapter Nine

'That was well done, Defford,' Alaric muttered disgustedly as he listened to Marianne hurry away. Now he was shut up here with his wretched body aching in every bone and sinew and his head hurt like blazes. No use trying to get up and stagger after her to apologise and explain himself better. 'The lady must be feeling so much better about her hard lot in life now, you infernal idiot.'

Unfortunately for him the fantasy he had of her sleepy eyed and sated in his bed while he was drifting in and out of sleep yesterday was impossible. Mrs Turner was a lady, whether she wanted to be one or not, so he could not ask her to be his mistress. And the idea of her life being picked over and sniffed at by the Dowagers if he married her made him shudder. Only if they were deeply in love would there be any point risking all the gossip about her late husband and how on earth she had managed to hook his exact opposite the second time around. Marianne's defiance of the social conventions when she ran away to wed a so-called common soldier would outrage the high sticklers and make her the target of all sorts of wrong-headed speculation. He did not particularly want to have his sanity questioned by his peers either and he was not in love with the woman, he merely admired her beauty and her spirit and her fiery determination and her lithe and lovely figure and… Hmm, that was an awful lot of *and*s.

Never mind—admiration was not love so they were still impossible for one another and that was good. She would laugh if she knew what a sad state of longing and yearning he had got himself into when he met her sceptical blue eyes for the first time. He was very tired at the time and she was all sleepy eyed and ruffled, so of course she had looked delicious and desirable and like the embodiment of all the dreams he had refused to have as the youthful quarry of most of the husband hunters in the polite world.

As a suddenly desirable young lord instead of a younger son, at first it had taken all his energy to escape the traps laid for a single viscount in possession of all his limbs and teeth. So he had dared not dream of meeting an enchantress one night in Mayfair and falling head over heels in love lest she turn out to be a younger version of his famously beautiful mother. It was too dangerous to dream back then. Since he had acquired enough town bronze to evade the little darlings so eager to be a viscountess they would have taken him even if he had two horns and a tail, he had become too cynical to dream about anything much at all.

He could not accuse Marianne of trying to enchant him when she was obviously not at all pleased to see him that first time, but he contrarily wished she would, then he could stop thinking his way around this feral attraction and let himself just feel for once in his life. He wanted her to look at him as if she could not help tingling with sensual awareness whenever he was near.

He knew an affair was impossible and he could not ruin a woman who had risked so much for the love of a very different man even if she wanted him to. Yet he tried to define the faint scent she had left behind in this bare old room and knew if she felt anything like as itchy and tempted and frustrated about him as he did about her they would be in deep trouble. He would get over it; he knew how to lock up his emotions, but if hers were engaged he could not fight them both. Her refusal to see sense last time she had loved made her dangerous. Except the very idea of being loved so much she stopped caring who he was and did it anyway seemed magnificent and so much bigger than anything he had ever dared hope for. Just as well she did not love him, then.

He snuffled like a hound and managed to pick a few elements of Mrs Marianne Turner out of the air—hmm, there was rose water to start with and something herbal and sharper underneath it...rosemary, perhaps, or lemon balm. Or was that the scent clinging to the pillow under his head after it was

dried by fresh air and summer sun? Not a fancy prep-
aration for a lady's complexion or a faint drift of
expensive perfume anyway—he could not imagine
her spending a single penny more than necessary on
her toilette. Perhaps those faint, clean scents came
from a home-made washing ball. Yes, that seemed
a good fit. From the clean and tidy but spartan state
of this room he concluded Yelverton had naught to
spare for many of the things Alaric took for granted.
Yelverton would still lack them until he wed Miss
Grantham, so the man's sister must have worked her
fingers to the bone to provide as many as could be
had by hard work.

Alaric would be angry on her behalf if he had not
realised she was so stubborn she probably insisted
on doing everything herself here, even if Yelverton
offered to hire someone to do the rough work. She
would tell him to put the money into his land and
livestock and let her work her way through this grand
but neglected old house one room at a time. Alaric
hated the idea of her doing everything except scrub
floors and chop firewood and he would not put it past
her to do even that if her brother let her.

He reminded himself of the reality of his life and
the vast distance in station yawning between them,
even if she was not still grieving for another man.
He was interested in Marianne Turner as a potential companion for his niece in the real world where
they both had to live. Getting her to see herself as a
lady of gentle birth again was the first part of finding
Juno someone she could feel at ease with now Miss

Grantham was going to be married to Yelverton and far too busy with him and his tumbledown old house to take on any more responsibility. He could tell from that muttered conversation this morning Marianne was in a dilemma about the future and it seemed like killing two birds with one stone to offer her the post of Juno's companion to save her from being preyed on or exploited by some ruthless future employer.

His hands tightened into fists again at the very thought of some unscrupulous seducer setting eyes on the unaware but lovely Mrs Turner and deciding to get her into his bed by fair means or foul. A jag of pain shot through his injured wrist and reminded him he was lying here like a useless block and in no fit state to hit a rake preying on an honourable man's honourable widow. A widow who did not sound in the least bit receptive to a potential employer who had his own hot thoughts about her he would learn to live with. He was not important; it was his niece's happiness that mattered now. And even Juno seemed to have abandoned him for more exciting people and events. He allowed himself to feel a little aggrieved about that while getting ready to resist Mrs Turner's vibrant looks, natural charm and humour and all her other attractions for Juno's sake.

Alaric eyed the narrow shaft of sunlight slowly working its way across the room and letting him know there were much better things to do outside if only he dared get out of bed. He huffed out a sigh of self-pity and gloomily counted out the least number of days he could spend in this old-fashioned, unexciting bedchamber before he dared risk defying orders and felt even worse. 'Best go to sleep again and while away the time that way, Stratford,' he ordered himself, 'and make sure you do not dream of a sleepy-eyed siren who wants you as urgently as you want her this time.' If willpower could get him well and out of here and Juno happy with the right companion to help her face the world, he had best march it out right away.

Marianne saw the doctor out of the front door, waved a distracted farewell then sat down on one of the ancient oak benches in the grand entrance porch with a heavy sigh. There was nothing she could do to keep Lord Stratford in bed and safely out of the way now all danger of him suffering lasting damage if he stirred had been officially pronounced over and done. She hardly had time to sit and dream of an uncomplicated life without any viscounts in it when she heard the sound of His Lordship's uneven footsteps on the stone floor behind her.

She got up to eye the man with disfavour and tried to ignore the skip in her heartbeat at seeing him fully dressed and almost his arrogant self again. He was easily as handsome as the devil and could be every bit as dangerous if she let herself be beguiled by him. 'I thought you were supposed to use a stick,' she told him grumpily.

'Find me one and I will.'

'Stay there, then,' she ordered him sharply and went to raid her late great-uncle's store of them in his still-untouched study. Tempted by the mischievous image of a lord hobbling about the place with the aid of a roughly fashioned one from a country hedgerow, she snatched up a silver-mounted gentleman's walking cane Uncle Hubert must have kept for best instead, before Lord Stratford limped in here in her wake. 'Here,' she said, thrusting the cane at him as she turned round to march back into the hall and found him only a few steps behind her. 'Do you never stay where you are put?' she asked crossly. She would never see him as a rich and entitled gentleman if he kept getting so close she could almost feel him breathe.

'Not if I can help it,' he said unrepentantly, swirled his new prop with his good hand and nodded approvingly as if he was surprised about not being given a hedge stick as well. 'Now tell me what is to do here?'

'Nothing as far as you are concerned,' she told him with a frown—what was a still-injured viscount intending to do in another man's house?

'I never could abide doing that.'

'Me neither,' she said unwarily and saw him raise his eyebrows at such heartfelt agreement when they argued over most things.

'Perhaps we should stroll about the ground floor of your brother's house and take a look at what you Yelvertons laughingly call a garden. I need some exercise, you see, the doctor said so.'

'He said a little gentle walk would do your ankle no harm, not that you should stamp about the place ordering everyone about and getting in the way.'

'You do not know that I will,' he objected quite mildly and held out the elbow of his good arm for her to hold.

She placed her hand on it before her head could order the rest of her not to be so witless. 'I know you have been fretting for something to do and I heard you and Darius arguing about it while he was shaving you this morning,' she admitted.

'Did you, now—eavesdropping, Mrs Turner? How very unbecoming in a lady.'

'I told you, I am not—'

'And I believe I told you that you are very much a lady, like it or not,' he interrupted before she could make her usual disclaimer.

'And Lord Stratford's word is law?' she carped, mostly because she did not like being ridden over roughshod and a little bit because she was far too conscious of him walking at her side. She could feel his firm muscles flex under her fingertips and there was this silly sense it was right to walk at his side and argue over what should happen next and how they were to bring it about.

'With you about to disagree I very much doubt it, but on important matters it is as well to be firm from the outset.'

'And if you say I am a genteel widow I shall be one whether I like it or not?'

'Precisely, so, as your brother and Miss Grantham seem determined to marry the moment the banns have been read, where are you planning to hold the wedding breakfast?' he said as if that was her sorted out so now it was time for the next item on his list.

'You two seem to have been confiding in one another like a pair of ageing spinsters.'

'We are the only males in a houseful of females, so we men must stick together. He tells me Miss Grantham wants to have the wedding breakfast here, so where are you planning to serve food and drink and what about this dancing your brother seems to be dreading so deeply I think he envies me a sore ankle as an excuse to escape it?'

'Does he, indeed?'

'Yes, he says he has two left feet.'

'I have to admit he is right—he would never have made a staff officer since the Beau always insisted they could dance as well as they ride.'

'I dare say Miss Grantham will love him anyway.'

'I dare say.'

'So where are you intending to hold all this dissipation at such short notice?'

'The dining room and drawing room are the obvious places,' she said, not quite ready to admit the two large rooms were beyond her in the scant weeks Darius and Fliss were prepared to wait before they married.

'Hmm, difficult in three weeks, but not impossible,' he told her after they had inspected the untouched rooms.

She had done her best to ignore them ever since she and Darius arrived in Herefordshire, although

Darius would have been quite happy for her to put all her effort into them, but then he would have expected her to sit in the drawing room and receive his neighbours. She had far better things to do and no intention of being disapproved of by another set of genteel gossips after her experiences in Bath. So she concentrated on kitchens and bedchambers and the smaller parlour and morning room once used by the family.

'As it is high summer, Miss Donne has suggested using lengths of muslin or gauze to make a pretend marquee and hide the smoke stains on the ceiling,' she explained as they stood in the once-grand dining room. 'And we can put flowers in front of the damaged wainscoting. Maybe the wedding guests will not look closely if the food is lavish and a good polish will hide a multitude of sins.'

'In here, perhaps, but not in the drawing room where there is no feast or wedding toasts to distract them.'

'Maybe after all those toasts they will not care the chairs are old-fashioned and worn and the cushions and curtains moth-eaten.'

'Maybe not, but I owe your brother and Miss Grantham Juno's safety and well-being. They gave her a place to run to when she was desperate and a roof over her head when she got here. I can never thank them enough for being here for her when I was too far away to realise what was going on. Making sure their wedding is memorable for the right reasons feels like the best I can do to say thank you to them, with your help, of course. My people can help bring it about if you will supervise.'

'I know Darius will have already argued that you owe nothing.'

He stopped and frowned at the dust and neglect around them. 'This fine old place has been left to tumble down,' he said severely.

'Yes, and I know when I am being diverted from a scent, Lord Stratford,' she told him. 'And what people do you mean?'

'The servants at Stratford Park have been idle all summer so they might as well come here and make themselves useful before they forget how.'

'And why do I feel as if I am being presented with a fait accompli?'

'I have no idea,' he said. 'Perhaps we should look at the mess of weeds and brambles your brother calls a garden next,' he added and they were already on their way out of the open front door so here was another one.

'What about it?' she said with an annoyed glance at the wilderness all around them. 'And I do not think either of us would call it anything so grand.'

'If it is tamed, the wedding guests can wander round it.'

'Maybe it will be wet.'

'Oh, ye of little faith,' he teased her and somehow it was almost comfortable strolling along at his side as if she really were a lady.

It was so tempting to drift along in his power-ful wake. 'You are a very managing man,' she told him curtly.

Chapter Ten

Alaric was doing so well at reining in his baser instincts until he paid more attention to the rebellious glint in Marianne's eyes than where he was going. The tip of his cane slid on a patch of loose stones and quick as lightning she grabbed his arm, as if she thought he might break if she let him fall. He grasped her waist on an instinct he did not quite trust and told himself it was to steady them both. The novelty of being protected by a beautiful woman threatened all his resolutions not to kiss her, so he had to stop this before it got out of hand. He used his good leg to stop the slide and managed not to curse out loud in front of a lady, but however hard he tried to he could not make himself let her go.

'You must take more care,' she warned huskily.

'So must you,' he cautioned. He heard her breath stutter, then quicken. Her lips were parted and she licked them as if they suddenly felt dry and that was what really undid him. He was kissing her before his mind could scream no. It felt as if he had been starving for her mouth, her lips and her startled response as he deepened their kiss since the first moment he had laid eyes on her. And she gave herself up to their kiss as if this was what they were born for, so what had he been waiting for? *You*, an inner voice whispered.

With her lips soft yet demanding as they blotted out the world together, he felt as if they could do anything; be lovers; trust one another completely; be everything to one another. Heat and light and need shot through him and he groaned into her luxury of a mouth. He drew her closer, shaped the back of her head with shaking hands and opened his mouth on hers. And she met his tongue as he explored and teased hers—and that was the moment he took a step too far towards her and his stupid ankle slipped again.

This time he grabbed her close and shifted his balance on to his good leg to protect her from his clumsiness. He cursed himself for taking even the slightest risk with her. He should never have tried to kiss her on his first trip outside his spartan bedchamber in a week. He felt her stiffen and curve away from him even as they saved themselves from a tumble once again. Ah, yes, that was the truth of it; he should never have kissed her at all.

Breathless and flushed, she was even more delicious and desirable now she would not meet his gaze. When she tried to speak it looked as if words had deserted her. She shook her head and looked away.

They had taken a huge step into intimacy, then a hasty jump back. He wanted to tell her he was glad *and* sorry for it, so he stood tense and silent instead. What an odd tableau if anyone could see them in this wilderness, but she was more important than who knew what and when.

He was going to live a very different life from his old one and to do it he had to renounce his best fantasy of Marianne love shot and heavy-eyed in his bed. She was a lady and the widow of a man who gave his life for his country. He wanted her to feel safe at Stratford Park if she agreed to become Juno's companion and she was hardly likely to if she was afraid he would impose himself on her whenever they were alone.

'I am sorry,' he said stiffly. 'I promise you it will not happen again.'

'Good,' she managed to say at last.

Of course she agreed; why would she not? He was not a very impressive figure with a weak ankle, sore wrist and poor record as a human being. 'Please accept my sincere apology, Mrs Turner,' he asked as they stood several yards apart.

'I loved my husband, Lord Stratford,' she said, then eyed him warily as if he might be about to argue, given her fiery response to him in that fleeting, glorious moment before she recalled who she was kissing.

'I am sure you did, ma'am,' he said stiffly.

She shrugged and looked as if she still could not find the words to tell him how much less than the late Mr Turner he was. 'Don't call me ma'am,' she ordered him sharply instead.

'No, m—' he began, then hastily amended at her glare. 'Mrs Turner.'

Juno. Remember how much her happiness matters, Stratford, he reminded himself sternly.

'I am not usually so clumsy,' he added.

'You have an injured ankle.'

'I am surprised you did not kick me in the other one and make it a pair.'

'I should have resisted your kiss and you should not have kissed me in the first place—that is the beginning and end of the matter. We must try to forget it ever happened.'

'Very well, if that is what you want,' he agreed. His inner idiot was jumping up and down, wanting to know where that much forgetfulness was going to come from. It did feel as if awareness of all they could be together was branded on his very soul by that hot and deliciously passionate kiss. No, he was a cold man at heart—he must be to have ridden away from London when Juno needed him. He was sure he could will all this heat and desire stone dead if he tried hard enough and she did, too.

'I do,' she asserted and they were in complete accord for once.

That was wonderful, but it seemed like a good idea to change the subject. 'Stratford Park has been closed up for far too long,' he said and saw her puzzlement and a suspicion his wits might have been addled by that blow on his head after all.

'Indeed?' she said cautiously.

They both stared at what had once been a gravel walk covered in climbing roses as if seeing the chaos ahead of them was a lot easier than trying to explore places neither of them wanted to go. The air felt heavy with unsaid words as well as the scent of a last Bourbon rose gallantly blooming in its hard-fought-for corner. Most of the ironwork had collapsed under other roses grown wild and a mass of ivy and brambles added by Mother Nature. Luckily the wild disorder reminded him what they came out here to talk about.

'Even the servants sent to London to open up and run Stratford House for Juno's debut will have returned to Wiltshire by now,' he added, hanging on to his subject like a drowning man to lifeline.

'I hope they enjoyed their holiday.'

'If they did, it is well and truly over. Many of them are on their way here with my valet,' he confessed.

'Oh, really?' she said at last and sounded frostier than he had hoped.

He had best carry on explaining himself before she packed her bags and stormed off to stay with her parents. 'Your brother has agreed I can set them to work here instead of leaving them to argue endlessly at Stratford Park.'

'How easily led he has become since he fell in love,' she said coolly.

She was very good at making a man feel bad, wasn't she? He almost felt sorry for Turner facing his wife's wrath for some clumsy male misdemeanour.

Except the man had her passionate love and Alaric was ashamed of being so jealous of a dead man. He wanted her sharp wits and hard-earned wisdom for Juno and he would just have to lock his inner satyr in the cellar and throw away the key when they got to Stratford Park.

'Love will do that to a man,' he said blandly. She looked so horrified when she took her eyes off the undergrowth it cost him an effort not to kiss her again. 'Or so I have been told,' he added to let her know he was not speaking from experience.

'Why?'

Why what? He shot her a sideways look and she was staring at the mess in front of them again and that was a relief, was it not? 'Why do I want to help Yelverton get this wreck in some sort of order for his wedding to my niece's former governess? Or why do people fall in love with one another when life would be so much simpler if they married for sense and a settled future?'

'Why help with all this, of course,' she said as if he was a fool to even ask.

'Miss Grantham was Juno's only real friend until recently. If not for her, Juno would have had nowhere to escape my mother's heartless plans for her.'

'She could have found you, my lord.'

'All the way across the Channel and on to Paris? I very much doubt it. I must pity her lack of a real home to flee to even if you do not.'

'That I do not. You would have made one wherever you happened to be if she only had the maturity to confide in you. Indeed, I doubt you would have gone in the first place if she had admitted how terrified she was of her grandmother and the *ton*.'

And there it was again, the warmth he had lived without for so long, and he wanted it for Juno if he could not have it for himself. 'I did nothing to make her feel she had a right to confide in me.'

'Most people think a child is best in the care of a woman, so I cannot see why you insist on blaming yourself for an honest mistake.'

'You do not think women must be better with children than men, then?'

She shrugged and looked uncomfortable and he reminded himself she and Turner had not had children, so that could well be a sore spot in her life. 'Some men are every bit as caring and loving as women and some females simply do not have the heart to put the welfare of a child before their own,' she answered carefully and set him wondering if her mother was as cold and selfish as his had been. If so, someone had done a fine job raising her and her brother since they were far more open to love and life than he had ever been.

'Is that the voice of experience?' he asked because he could not help being interested in her and interest was not fascination.

'No, my mother has always wanted the best for us in her own way.'

'But her way is not your way?'

'No, our standing in the world and marrying well

was never important for me. I only wanted to be with a man I loved with all my heart.'

'I can see both sides of the coin,' he said and fully expected her to hotly declare he understood nothing about true love then, but she was silent, as if she was thinking about those sides and wondering how different her life would have been if she had been more wary.

She would be right about him, though; even as a spotty youth he had not managed to fall in love with an unsuitable girl. He had been too busy missing his brother and avoiding his mother's fury because he was still alive when George was dead to have had enough feeling left for the moody ups and downs of calf love. He supposed he had been too young and alone at seventeen to do more than survive when his world had turned upside down. Being called by his brother's title, knowing so much responsibility rested on his shoulders, had frozen the young man he should have been. Alaric Defford should have been free to do foolish things like fall in love with grocer's daughters and run about town with the fastest set that would have had him. George would have eyed his pranks with tolerant amusement and tugged him out when he was drowning in River Tick.

Then his big brother would have said he must do something useful with his life as a younger son, like join the diplomatic corps or enter politics. Except by the time he had been old enough to live that life George had been dead. As Lord Stratford, Alaric could not be the wild second son because if he had been wild and irresponsible nobody would have been able to look after his thousands of acres, several lofty mansions and the legion of staff and tenants who made it all work.

'Now I am older and perhaps a little wiser I realise a parent or guardian must worry about material things,' Marianne said and they were talking about mothers. At least hers had cared enough to argue with her choice of husband. 'At twenty years old I felt I had every right to ignore them and grab happiness with both hands. But how did we get around to my unwise marriage when we were talking about Darius and Fliss's wedding only a moment ago, Lord Stratford?'

'Would you consider becoming Juno's companion when they are safely married?' he said impulsively and found he was holding his breath for her answer.

At first she looked dumbfounded, then doubtful, as if she thought her ears were deceiving her. 'I... Well, I had no idea. I do not know why you would think it a good notion,' she said and shook her head as if that was all she could manage right now.

First he had kissed her, now he was blurting out his plans for a better future for her than staying here and feeling in the way or going back to her parents' house and enduring a life she had obviously not enjoyed. How inept could one man be? 'You would only have to keep her company and Juno likes you—that is all that really matters,' he said, but she was clearly bewildered by the idea.

'We only met a week ago, my lord, and you know nothing about me.'

'I have known Miss Grantham for several years and she likes and trusts you. Even on such a short acquaintance I can tell you are painfully honest. I just want Juno to be safe and happy and stop feeling like a misfit. My mother and I did that to her, Mrs Turner. Juno needs a better life and I hope you are willing to help her build it.'

'I cannot see how having a companion who married beneath her, then spent five years travelling on the coat-tails of an army on the march could give her enough confidence to rejoin the polite world on her own terms.'

Alaric heard the defensive note in her voice and cursed the two years of grief and gossip Darius told him his sister had endured in Bath before they had come here this spring. He hated the idea of her being picked on because she was different and that was what bullies always did. They must have chipped away at her confidence and her brave marriage until she felt she must point out her unsuitability before someone did it for her.

'It does not matter if she never wants to set foot in a ballroom again, but I do want to make her happy and the first step towards that is finding her an honest and caring companion like you, Mrs Turner.'

'There must be plenty of genteel officer's widows who would guide and help her much more surely than I can hope to,' she objected.

He suspected from the thoughtful frown into the

middle distance the notion was tempting her. She had a heart as soft as butter under her brusque manner and it was better to make this about Juno instead of her having somewhere to go after her brother's wedding. 'Can you think of one?' he risked asking her.

She opened her mouth to give him a list and hesitated. 'No,' she finally admitted with a sigh.

'Then will you think about filling some of the gaping holes my stupidity has left in Juno's life?'

'You could do that if you chose, my lord. She is very ready to love you.'

'Being a lord is not all velvet and ermine and learning to walk with your nose in the air and not fall over. I have a great many duties and I cannot be with her as much as I would like, so this role is really to be her companion and friend and I believe you are the right person for it. I think you love your brother too much to stay here and resent playing second fiddle to your sister-in-law.'

'Yes, yes—I admit you are right about that much at least. I do want him and Fliss to be left in peace to live well together and I know he is worried about me going back to Bath with our parents.'

'Then why not come back to Stratford Park with Juno and help us and your family?'

'Have you talked to Darius about this? You two seem to have been confiding in one another like a pair of bosom bows.'

'This is only between you and me until and unless you say yes. I would not push you into doing something you do not want to do by underhand methods.'

'I cannot make up my mind just like that. I need time to think, then discuss this offer of employment with my brother and sister-in-law-to-be.'

'And there I was, thinking you made up your mind about things and then told your family.'

'Then kindly give me time to do so.'

Alaric still felt like a bumbler for kissing her, then springing his wonderful idea for her future on her before she had hardly had time to catch her breath. Of course she would hesitate after that and he must let the dust settle and hope she came to the right conclusion now. Although if she was not going to be living under his roof and in his employ, perhaps... No, there was no perhaps for them. She believed in love and happy-ever-after and he most definitely did not and that was that.

Chapter Eleven

Marianne carefully avoided him for the rest of the day and one or two after that. It was not until his stone masons and carpenters began work on the chapel a couple of days later that she confronted Alaric over their mission.

'You and Yelverton were so worried about your father making the journey to the next village and back to marry him to Miss Grantham I thought they might as well be wed here instead. The chapel is only a few hundred yards away, so there is no need to worry about carriages and delays if the marriage takes place here.'

'How do you know the chapel is still consecrated?'

'Because I asked your brother and he asked the local vicar.'

'You would.'

'I did and the reverend gentleman is happy to oblige the local lord of the manor so your father can perform the ceremony.'

'Smug and managing,' she said. 'I have to admire you for it,' she added, 'although I am surprised Darius and Fliss are meekly agreeing to all your plans.'

'Apparently true love means doing almost anything for your beloved.'

'Does it indeed? I doubt it will ever do so for you, my lord.'

'So do I,' he said with a pinch of real sadness under his cynical smile. He doubted he could ever be undefended enough to love beyond reason.

'And I am far too busy supervising all the maids and handymen now flocking about the house getting in each other's way to stop here and argue with you any longer,' she informed him and marched back to her housekeeping duties.

'Avoiding me again?' Lord Stratford asked softly from behind her a week after their bewildering conversation in the garden.

Marianne was surveying the now empty and—as clean as it could be got with mops and brooms and scrubbing brushes—grand dining room. 'How *do* you manage to creep up on people like that when you still have to walk with a stick, my lord?'

'I suppose stealth comes naturally to me and if I had not, you would have left before I could get here.'

She almost smiled—no, she nearly laughed and that was worse. 'I am a very busy woman,' she told him severely instead and wished she had managed to escape him yet again. He made her feel on edge yet almost excited when he watched her with that wary

warmth in his clear blue eyes. A shiver of awareness always seemed to slip down her spine as soon
as she heard his voice in the distance and made her
tingle all over until she managed to find a task that
demanded all her attention. She had to keep on reminding herself he only wanted her for her supposed
skills as a companion and that kiss in the garden was
an impulse he regretted just as much as she did. 'Was
there something you wanted, my lord?' she asked.

'Common sense,' he told her.

'You know I cannot supply that.'

'No,' he said with a stern look. 'You have none to
spare. You are working too hard to lay claim to any
of your own, never mind giving some away.'

'There is only a fortnight to go until my brother
weds Miss Grantham now and there is so much left
to be done.'

'And you are doing far more of it than you need
to, Mrs Turner. Please stop it before you wear yourself out and ruin the day for your family.'

'My brother and Miss Grantham deserve the best
wedding they can have and I will work morning,
noon and night if that is what it takes to be sure they
have it.'

'Which is why I sent for as many of my people as
could be squeezed in here, so you would not do it all
yourself to save your brother money,' he objected and
he was right, drat him. 'My servants are well-trained
and work well together. All you need to do is set them
going and leave them to get on with their work.'

'They still need direction,' she argued stubbornly.

'Not with you to keep them going at the relentless beat you set yourself they do not.'

'There you are then, I am doing my job.'

'And wearing them out as well as yourself and I doubt your brother has ever thought of you as an employee, Marianne.'

'You cannot call me that,' she argued. She had to do something to stop it feeling so warm and intimate in this great echoing, empty room now he was in here as well.

'Why not? There is nobody else to hear.'

'I can and you know perfectly well it is not correct.'

'Yes, ma'am.'

'And I have already told you not to address me like an elderly lady.'

'Some days there is just no pleasing you, Mrs Turner,' he said with a cynical smile.

'And if you came to badger me about your extraordinary offer that I should become Juno's companion, please remember I know nothing of the polite world and please go away again.'

He stared at the newly whitewashed walls as if he found it very hard to talk about whatever it was he was planning to tell her to persuade her she was wrong. 'I must plead, then, and tell you some family history you would probably prefer not to know,' he said at last. 'My mother is a cold woman, Mrs Turner,' he admitted stiffly. 'She loved my elder brother obsessively. I thought her love for George would transfer to his only child after my brother died, but what a mistake that was.

'The Dowager Lady Stratford informed me when I confronted her with her appalling behaviour towards Juno that she had never forgiven her for not being born a boy. George's son would have inherited his title and estates instead of me and I already knew she hated me for being alive when my brother is dead, but I was too much of a fool to see the Dowager Lady Stratford does not have another jot of love in her to spare and she despises poor little Juno for not keeping me out of George's shoes when he died. So my niece grew up with the same coldness and lack of love in her life I endured as a child and you would not want her to turn out like me, now would you?'

She could hardly say he seemed to have turned out remarkably well, considering. 'My mother can be exasperating, but at least she has always loved us under all her fuss and fancies,' she told him instead and felt very lucky indeed.

'I did not tell you as a bid for sympathy on my account.'

'You still have it.'

'She has reason to dislike me,' he argued as if he actually believed it.

'I doubt it. If you are a madman or a murderer, you hide it well and nothing less could justify her turning against her own child. Even you must have been a helpless innocent once upon a time and cannot have done anything to deserve it.'

'I suspect just being born was enough to make her hate me.'

'Why?' she said.

He hesitated and seemed disinclined to say more and she badly wanted to know now—and not for Juno's sake. 'I should not discuss such matters with you.'

'Oh, for heaven's sake, I am a widow—not a shrinking spinster likely to faint at the very mention of childbirth or the marriage bed.'

'Very well, then. The Dowager told me when we were ranting at each other in London that she loathed the indignity of being with child even the first time, but at least she birthed a healthy boy and thought her travails must be over. My father did not agree and insisted on another boy as insurance before he would excuse her from her marital duties.'

'I cannot believe you even thought about making a marriage of convenience with such an example in front of you,' she said impulsively, then put a hand over her mouth when she realised where her tongue had taken her. 'I beg your pardon, my lord,' she took it away in order to say. If Fliss heard her she would have been hurt as the possible viscountess he had picked out to marry and he must be embarrassed by her clumsiness.

'Why should you? I cannot quite believe I did it myself now matters have fallen out so much more happily for Miss Grantham and your brother. It seemed a good idea at the time, but I have had my eyes opened to how bleak a marriage of convenience can be since then by my darling mama.'

'And you and Miss Grantham are better people than your parents,' she said, because now they were started on frank and free conversation.

'Thank you. I am no saint, but I would never force a reluctant wife to endure me in her bed for the sake of the succession. Not all the acres in the world and a far more lordly title could be worth the misery he caused, then and now.'

She nearly laughed at him for thinking any sane female would have to *endure* him in her bed. Her inner houri would leap at the chance to have him in hers if there was even a whisper of honour in it for either of them. 'I still cannot understand a mother loving one son and rejecting the next.'

'I was not her next child or the one after that.'

'She had other children besides you and your brother, then?'

'Apparently she miscarried several times and brought a couple nearly to term before they were born dead. In the seven years between George's birth and mine a baby girl survived long enough to be christened before she died as well. Then two years before me she had a boy who lived for a month before he followed his big sister to the family mausoleum. Then nothing until she was enceinte again at last and my father was wary enough by then to leave her be until I was safely born.'

'You would think she must have been so delighted when you were delivered safely she would love you all the more. I doubt you were weak or puny since you have grown into such a tall and powerful man.'

'Why, thank you, Mrs Turner. I am flattered you have noted my rude health and sterling character.'

'You mean you are too stubborn to give in over anything without a fight, I suppose? I would have to be a fool not to have noticed that.'

'Apparently my father was as well.'

'Oh, dear, he reneged on their agreement?' she said with a sad shake of her head for the stupidity and selfishness of both his parents.

'Yes, he refused to believe I would survive after so many of his hopes were dashed before I was born. I felt sorry for the Dowager for the first time in my life when she told me that by the time I was born she hated being with child so much she just wanted me out of her body and for the pain and intrusion and indignity to cease. Imagine how she must have felt when she was expected to go through all that again and again and he never stopped wanting more children from her. I never felt more guilty about a woman's lot in life and less eager for a viscountess of my own than I was when she told me how delighted she was when my father died on the hunting field and she was free at last.'

'None of it was your fault.'

'Maybe not, but the ridiculous laws of entail and primogeniture made it the fault of Viscount Stratford with all those inherited acres and estates and more houses than one man could ever live in to pass on only to a son.'

'You sound like a Jacobin.'

'I could not support bloody revolution after the Terror in France, but hearing the true reason for the Dowager's hatred of me and through me of Juno as well made me think I must be very sure the lady I marry is happy to be a mother and I have the sense never to be obsessed with the Defford inheritance.'

The idea of him wed to a woman who would tolerate him for the sake of a family made her want to cry for some odd reason, but she fought it back and hatred for the Dowager Lady Stratford was a good antidote for tears. She would like to tell the woman exactly what she thought of her for neglecting the fine boy this fine man grew out of.

'Being the victim of her husband's obsession with male heirs did not give her any right to treat you or your niece so badly. She was the adult and you were an innocent when she decided to hate you. The wonder is that both you and Juno are good people despite her worst efforts.'

'I am flattered you think so, but I owe whatever I am to my brother. George was a good man who refused to be spoilt by her devotion to him alone. He did his best to be my stand-in father when ours died soon after I was breeched. I owe him far more than he ever got back from me as his daughter's uncle and guardian.'

'I cannot understand such limits on a mother's affections, so why do you keep on trying to, Alaric?' she said, so disgusted with the woman she forgot to call him something formal.

'Well, I hope we are done with one another for good this time. I paid her debts on the understanding I will publicly disclaim any more and she intends to live abroad now Emperor Napoleon has been ousted from his throne. Apparently she is sick of me and England and I suppose you think me harsh and bad-tempered now and will refuse my offer of employment on principle.'

'No, I have no sympathy for your mother since she obviously has far too much for herself. She meant to sell her grandchild to an old man, so why would anyone blame you for making her live on her settlements in future? At least you can make a fresh start at Stratford Park now.'

'And I hope Juno is young enough to throw off the past and grow into a woman of character.'

'I might have known everything would lead us back to that topic and I am sure you could do better than me as her companion and watchdog.'

'And I know I could not.'

'Then give me the space I asked for and I promise I will go and have the bath I have been looking forward to all afternoon and to stop harrying your poor put-upon staff, my lord. I am too weary to argue with you just at the moment.'

'I doubt you are ever weary enough for that, Marianne,' he told her grumpily and turned round and strode off into the dusky shadows of the great hall, leaving her in possession of the field.

She was not sure she wanted it at the cost of all he had forced himself to tell her in the hope she would agree to his plan. And of course she was right not to tell him she feared her own weakness as far as he was concerned. It would be one way to get him to stop persuading her with his deepest darkest secrets how much Juno needed her. But she was not sure she could endure the humiliation of him knowing how much she longed for him in her bed of a night now he was staying under Darius's roof as an honoured guest instead of a patient forced on them by circumstance.

If she accepted Alaric's offer of employment, how could she resist the urge to throw herself at him when she was living under his roof instead and might well decide her self-respect and the family honour could go to blazes as long as she could be his mistress?

And he was such an honourable idiot he would probably ask her to marry him if they gave in to this ridiculous attraction that had sprung up between them more or less at first sight. She had not been with child even once during her five years of marriage to Daniel, so she could not let Alaric wed her if they did weaken and become lovers. However he felt about the Defford succession, she could not live with herself as year after year went by without an heir to his wealth and possessions and noble name. He was too fine a man to make her his mistress and she was too much of a lady to let him marry her, so she would do better to say no and go back to Bath.

However, the thought of never seeing him again—except in the distance, perhaps, when he escorted Juno on a trip to see Fliss and she happened to be there as well—stung her so hard she was not sure she could bear it. So was she in love with the man? Perilously close to it, she decided, but not quite there yet. Best if she did not give herself time or chance to fall the rest of the way, then. But, oh, how she would miss him when he went away thinking she was so hard-hearted that even that wrenching tale about his mother's inhuman conduct towards him as a child could not move her to make up the similar gaps in poor little Juno's life until now.

Chapter Twelve

'I can see what you have been doing with yourself all morning, Marianne,' Darius informed her from his place just inside the door of the last untouched bedchamber on the main level a week on from her last tête-à-tête with Alaric.

'Indeed, most of this dust seems to be on me instead of the furniture,' she said ruefully and turned around slowly so it would not shake back on to the clean bits. 'And what are you doing upstairs in all your dirt at this time of day?'

'The same as you, I should imagine—wishing I was clean.'

'I must get this room clean and cleared then put back together as neatly as I can before I can take a bath. Mama will carp endlessly about being given a lesser bedroom than Viola's or Miss Donne's if I do not get this room done in time and neither of us want her feeling put upon and prickly on your wedding day.'

'You do not have to do it all on your own. Fliss sent me up here, dirt or no, to tell you so because she is worried about you and so am I.'

'There is no need,' she forced herself to say calmly and stared at a spider that was daring to crawl into the light now she had stopped pulling down bed curtains and the dust-laden webs of its distant ancestors.

'You are avoiding us all and I will not let you, Marianne. I thought you liked living here, but maybe I am wrong and you intend to go back to Bath with Mama and Papa after the wedding.'

'No, I am not a martyr.'

'Then if you cannot endure our company why not accept Stratford's offer of employment he tells me he has made you and stop worrying about what to do next? I hate seeing you like this, Nan. I understand that my happiness with Fliss may be reminding you of what you and Daniel had and maybe living without him feels worse than before we fell in love, but we will not make you feel like an unwanted third if you stay.'

'No, please do not think that, Darius, never think like that. I am so very happy to see that you are as loved now as you have always deserved to be. I knew you could find joy and laughter with the right woman to laugh with you and remind you what a good man you are now and again when you forget it and brood about all the things you saw and did in the war. Darius the cynic was only cover for the soft heart you protected to survive that hard life, Big Brother, and Fliss is ideal for you.'

'You saw most of it as well, Little Sister.'

'Not the killing and the conflict,' she said, knowing what it must have cost him and Daniel to set out to wound and kill their fellow men. Love for this strong and loyal and, yes, soft-hearted, brother of hers was prodding her to accept Lord Stratford's offer of employment even if she was not sure it was the right thing to do. Could Alaric become a run-of-the-mill sort of lord to her rather than the special one he was now? Or would she fall even deeper under his spell than she had already?

She sighed and realised only by doing what he wanted and living as Juno's companion was she ever going to find out. It was a risk—either hurting herself or hurting Darius and Fliss by refusing to stay here and be the widow in the way. Her brother knew how much she had hated living in Bath. He would be even more hurt if she chose to go back there instead and suspicious of her true reason why. She certainly did not want anyone else knowing about these feral longings for a man she could not have.

'Why is it always one step forward, two back with you, then, Nan?' Darius asked as if he thought that sigh was for him instead of lordly Lord Stratford.

'No,' she insisted with a shake of the head to tell him she really meant it. 'I have come a long way since you inherited Owlet Manor. But today I need to be left in peace so I can get this one last room clean and usable. It will help me weather Mama's fussing and dramatising if I make her feel that she and Papa are important here. I robbed her of the wedding she

longed for when I ran off to find Daniel and her new
friends shunned me when I lived in Bath. I am such
an unsatisfactory daughter to her and I know she did
not defend me as fiercely as she might have done because in her heart she agrees with them, but at least
we still love one another. All three of us always knew
we were loved by our parents, however little we understand one another. Mama cannot see why I married Daniel when there are perfectly good curates
and one or two gentlemen of leisure I could have
fallen in love with if I had only tried a little harder.'

Marianne thought of Alaric's description of his
cold-hearted mother and shivered. His calm acceptance of a total lack of love between them still stung
her on his behalf. He could so easily have grown up
hating his brother for being the favourite. Marianne
sighed because it felt as if an unseen tie bound her
to the viscount and it was tugging at her heart more
strongly with every day that passed. Could she ignore
it and do as he wanted? Of course, that decision was
the real reason she was keeping the rest of the world
out with the dust of ages, but Darius did not need to
know and worry about her even more.

'If it makes you feel better to do this, then of
course you must, Nan,' he said. 'But promise me
you will stop when you get this room as perfect as
you can in such a short time. The rest can wait and I
do not care if Fliss and I wed in a church porch and
feast in a cow byre as long as we are married. Mama
can boast about my splendid wedding to Lord Neth-
erton's niece to all her friends without them knowing

the east wing is in the same sorry state Great-Uncle Hubert left it in and we have borrowed half the furniture and fittings from Miss Donne's friend Mrs Corham.'

'I want your wedding day to be wonderful so you can look back on it with a smile for the rest of your lives. If Mama is carping at me and glaring at Miss Donne all day because she feels less important than Fliss's stand-in mother, I will be miserable and on edge and Fliss will be mortified. Mama is going to be a difficult enough mother-in-law without them starting off on the wrong foot.'

'Maybe so, but the maids could do this if you let them.'

'They can help now I know exactly what needs to be done in here,' she conceded with a sigh.

'Good, perhaps it will distract them from decking out my bedchamber with every bit of finery they can find,' he said and Marianne almost laughed. The dreamy look he had been wearing so often since Miss Felicity Grantham stepped into his life one hot and sunny June day took over from brotherly concern and good riddance to it. He was thinking about his wedding night now and that was a much better idea than worrying about his sister.

'I expect Fliss will like it better with a few improvements,' she said to encourage him to see those changes with new eyes.

'I was a soldier for over a decade, sister dear. I recognise diversionary tactics when I meet them,' Darius argued nevertheless.

'Then you must know how unlikely it is I shall sit tatting while I wait for your neighbours to call,' she countered.

'I can dream,' he said lightly, but there was sadness and frustration in his eyes all the same.

He had dreamed of making a home for both his sisters, but they were too independent minded to be Squire Yelverton's dependent sisters even if he could afford to keep them. Fliss had inherited a fortune from her godmother, but Owlet Manor and its farms had been neglected for a very long time. Even thirty thousand pounds would not last forever if Darius's sisters were here to be a drain on it. Lord Stratford's offer was a godsend she would be foolish to turn down; so that was that, she would just have to polish up her willpower and try to see as little of the man as possible in future.

'Go away and dream of your bride-to-be. I am busy,' she said brusquely.

'You promised to stop trying to make this old place perfect.'

'I did not actually promise,' she said sneakily.

'Then I shall stay here until you do,' he said, leaning against the door jamb and ignoring her hard stare at his work shirt, covered in several sorts of dirt and maybe even worse from the smell.

'Oh, very well,' she conceded wearily because she knew he would stand there however long it took her to do as he wanted. 'After this room I will stop. There are things I must do before the wedding and I suppose I had best get on with them.'

'Promise?' he said implacably.

'Promise. Except if a crisis blows up you cannot expect me to sit on my hands and pretend it has naught to do with me.'

'If Fliss or Miss Donne cannot deal with it first,' he qualified and he was right, drat him. This was going to be Fliss's home and she had every right to take over the running of it.

'I agree,' she told Darius with a bland, blank smile to stop him finding out how desolate that felt.

'Very well, I will wash and change and, if I was a stern and managing sort of brother, I might suggest you do the same before you take your luncheon with Fliss and Miss Donne and me in the parlour.'

'Luckily you are only managing, then,' she muttered.

He grinned and left her to her spider and the empty old room. To her it was a pleasure to see a place like this coming alive again and now she had to give it up. In a way this was what she used to do on the march with Daniel—wrench comfort and cleanliness out of chaos. Whatever shelter she managed to commandeer after a long and weary march or a bloody and terrible battle was soon as clean and comfortable as she could make it. Then and now it felt like the least she could do for those she loved. And this time there was the added benefit of avoiding a man she did not want to love, but dreaded she might have to if she saw too much of him. It was high time she cut impulsive, romantic Marianne out of her life for good and became careful and realistic Mrs Turner, lady's companion.

'Was there anything worth saving?' Darius asked as he came back hastily washed and wearing clean clothes. He caught her standing exactly where he left her, staring at the pile of torn-down draperies and ancient bedding as if they fascinated her. That was where dreaming got you—absolutely nowhere.

'Were you hoping there was a suite of modern furniture under the piled-up wreckage of ages?'

'I doubt the word modern is one Great-Uncle Hubert would have recognised if it was painted across the house in letters ten feet high. What I *am* hoping for is hot tea and currant buns with my luncheon and you will have neither if you do not hurry up,' he said with a frown, as if he was getting ready to worry about her all over again.

'I will, then, since I know what a glutton for currant buns you are,' she replied and went to clean up and put on a better gown until he was safely busy again. Since Miss Donne's Bet had a light hand with a currant bun, it would be a pity to miss out on them altogether.

'Felicity looks so beautiful,' Miss Donne whispered tearfully as Reverend Yelverton said the last majestic words of the marriage service over the happy couple and they faced the world as Mr and Mrs Yelverton.

'And they are so happy I have no idea why I am

crying,' Marianne agreed as she watched Fliss walk down the aisle of the tiny church on Darius's arm.

'Nor do I,' the lady said as she dabbed away at her eyes with a whisper of lawn and lace and sighed happily.

'I seem to be your escort, Mrs Turner,' Lord Stratford whispered as the best man followed Darius and Fliss out with his own wife on his arm. 'I hope I will do?'

'Of course,' she said and took his offered arm and they emerged from the little church together as local children held hoops of flowers interwoven with corn over the bride and groom like a triumphal arch. The wedding party followed the bride and groom across the fields and around to the grand front of the house rather than the back door they normally used for more everyday occasions. 'It is as well it is high summer,' Marianne said as they approached the wide open front door. 'Sunlight and warmth casts such a good light on the house.'

'Indeed,' he said as if his thoughts were elsewhere.

'And Papa was so happy to marry Darius himself,' she said with an anxious glance behind them to see if her father had exhausted himself getting here.

'Marbeck has promised to stay with Reverend Yelverton until he is ready to make the return journey and as your sister is not here yet I expect all three are sitting in the shade waiting for the fuss to die down. Your father will have plenty of time to get his breath if he can walk at his own pace.'

'And Sir Harry did not mind?' The man had

brought her sister all the way here in a curricle and four as well and Marianne was not quite sure she approved, even if it was an open carriage attended by a tiger and two outriders so nobody could accuse them of impropriety. She supposed the man had exerted himself to get Viola here to see Darius and Fliss marry after some domestic crisis made it doubtful Viola could have got here in time without his help.

'Marbeck is not the yahoo some of the gossips like to believe,' Lord Stratford said as if he actually liked the raffish baronet.

'Yet I cannot help but wonder why he is trying so hard to prove his sooty reputation false today,' she said with a frown.

'Maybe he has turned over a new leaf. He has put himself out to drive your sister here and says he will drive himself back to Gloucestershire to spend a few days with his wards, so Miss Yelverton can stay and enjoy a small holiday.'

'What a considerate employer he is,' Marianne said blandly, still not sure she liked or trusted such a handsome rake with her little sister's welfare and good name.

'Whether he usually is so or not, he needs your sister a lot more than she needs him, so it is in his interests to be kind to her when he has three wards under the age of ten to cope with alone if she leaves her post. I can barely manage to look out for one eighteen-year-old with a retiring disposition myself.'

Marianne loved her sister, though, and really did not want her to suffer the sort of insinuation and slights she faced when she came back from Spain a widow. 'Maybe I am judging him on not even a whole day's acquaintance and you are right to tell me so, but I am not inclined to be fair when my sister could be gossiped about if she does not keep Sir Harry and his bad-dog reputation firmly at arm's length.'

'Hmm, I wonder,' he replied with a preoccupied frown as he turned to watch the Reverend Yelverton join the company at last, looking none the worse for his more direct walk past the farmyard while he continued to discuss some obscure piece of scholarship with his younger daughter and Sir Harry Marbeck.

Marianne tried to see them through unbiased eyes and frowned because, never mind fairness, Viola seemed different today. She had not seen Viola since she left Bath to become governess to Sir Harry's wards nearly a year ago, but her sister was more animated and less tightly in control of her thoughts and emotions than she was then. Viola even seemed to move more freely as she strolled along at her father's slow pace. And what on earth had they found to talk about so intently with wild Sir Harry Marbeck that they hardly seemed to notice the rest of the company were even present?

'Stop worrying, Marianne. Marbeck is too much the gentleman to take advantage of a lady employed to care for his wards and living under his roof.'

'It is not his roof,' Marianne replied absently. 'And she is not your sister.'

'Yet Miss Yelverton is clearly a lady of character and I expect she has her own share of stubborn Yel-

verton pride to add to it. Trust her to put him firmly
in his place if he steps over the line and Marbeck
will be so desperate for her to stay I am sure he will
not risk it. As she used to teach at Miss Thibbett's
School Miss Yelverton can pick and choose who she
works for and you can trust Harry Marbeck to know
it and treat her accordingly.'

'Is he a friend of yours?'

'An acquaintance merely, but I do not think he is
as black as he has been painted.'

'But attractive rakes like him can cloud the most
sensible lady's judgement,' Marianne objected because she did not want to be fair to the dangerously
attractive young baronet.

'Indeed?' Alaric said with a glint of devilment in
his eyes that contrarily made her want to laugh at his
almost suggestion he might have to become a rake if
she liked the idea.

Perhaps laughter was the most dangerous quality a handsome employer could offer a governess or
a young lady's companion, she mused, and decided
to concentrate on her sister's vulnerabilities rather
than her own this afternoon. 'My sister has seen far
less of the world than I have, Lord Stratford,' she
said primly.

'Maybe she has just seen different bits of it, Mrs
Turner,' he replied almost seriously.

'Maybe,' she replied. Did he think she was being
overprotective? Perhaps she was not giving her sister
enough credit for being four and twenty and a lady
of character. She shot a brooding glance at Viola,

Sir Harry and her father and decided even if Alaric was wrong and she was right she had no cause to interfere. Viola would see it as her big sister thinking she knew best and the fragile bond between them might break for good this time. 'And I have a wedding breakfast to supervise despite my mother's best efforts to create chaos, so kindly let me get on with my last duty as housekeeper here, my lord.'

'Heaven forbid you ever shirk one of those, Mrs Turner,' he said rather wearily and she refused to meet his eyes. Hard work had been her salvation these last few months and it was very useful to hide behind at times like this. She would miss it, she decided as she glanced around the polished and immaculate hall and the wide open doors into the drawing room and the dining hall, where tables groaned with bright glass and gleaming porcelain ready for the feast. And without Alaric's help and his servants' effort she could not have achieved even half of it.

Chapter Thirteen

'Have you decided to say yay or nay to me yet, Mrs Turner?' Alaric asked her several hours later, when the last of the guests were standing about feeling awkward and Fliss and Darius had departed in a flower-decked gig for Miss Donne's house in Broadley and a private wedding night.

Miss Donne and the family were to stay here and welcome the happy couple back in the morning, then they would spend the rest of the week here before they finally left the newlyweds in peace. And all Marianne could think of was that Lord Stratford would shortly be leaving for Broadley as well. After an overnight stop at the Royal George he would come back for Juno tomorrow, then they would travel on to his grand Wiltshire home and she might never see him again if she said no.

'I am willing to agree to a month's trial. If I do not suit you or you prove to be a tyrannical employer, we can reconsider at the end of it,' she said at last.

She would be a fool not to at least give it a try, would she not?

'There will be no need,' he said confidently. 'I am sure you and Juno will enjoy one another's company so much you will hardly notice my tyranny.'

'Only time will tell,' she argued and was surprised when he shook hands on their bargain and announced it to the company. Too late to go back on her word now and of course she did not want to return to Bath or stay here and play the third in Darius and Fliss's honeymoon. Alaric was cunning to make it nigh impossible for her to go back on her word and she shot him a reproachful look over her surprised mother's head even as she smiled and agreed, yes, she was very lucky and, no, she could not have told anyone sooner than this as it was Fliss and Darius's day and they deserved to be at the centre of it.

Juno was touchingly delighted with her decision and Mrs Yelverton was torn between delight her daughter was going to work for a noble family and dislike of her having to work at all.

'Is this what you truly want, Marianne?' her father asked quietly while Alaric was doing his best to reassure her mother that Mrs Turner would be valued and respected under his roof and an elderly cousin had recently come to live at Stratford Park so her good name was safe.

'Yes, Papa, you know I prefer to be occupied and Miss Defford is a bright and interesting young woman under her diffident manner. I believe I can be useful to her and my life will not be an onerous one.'

'No, but it has been so for too long. You deserve to live among good people who appreciate your fine mind and generous heart.'

Marianne blinked back tears at the quiet understanding in the blue eyes all three of his children had inherited from him. 'Thank you, Papa. I do love you and Mama dearly, but…' She let her voice tail off as she ran out of tactful words to say why she could not go home with them and endure being a chastened widow again.

'And we love you, my Marianne, but the house in Sydney Place is not big enough for us to get away from one another and I know you were not happy there.'

'I would not have been happy anywhere after Daniel was killed.'

'Maybe not, but Bath has its drawbacks as well as advantages. It is in a fine situation and we two go on very well there, but you young people need more life and freedom than a small town house can offer.'

'You were there when I needed you,' Marianne said and it was true. Never mind the less generous of her mother's new friends, she had needed to be with her parents at the darkest time in her life so far. And now she wanted the life her father spoke of and space enough to breathe. Living at Owlet Manor these last few months had taught her to value that and maybe Alaric and Juno had taught her what she had and they did not—a loving family who would always value and look after one another despite their differences.

* * *

Marianne was glad when Sir Harry Marbeck left for Gloucestershire and Viola was free to whisper, 'Congratulations', under cover of their mother's slightly drunken ramblings on the subject of undutiful daughters and their father's gentle protests they were no such thing. 'You will be much happier with them, Marianne, and Juno is such a gentle girl you should get on very well together.'

'Darius might be hurt when he finds out I do not intend to live here and Fliss was Juno's governess for several years. She might not think we are suited.'

'She is wise enough to know the girl needs to be out in the world, not tucked away at the back of beyond with two lovebirds and as they should be man and wife in peace for a while she obviously cannot stay here.'

'And when did you become so wise about love and marriage, Viola?' Marianne asked with an intent look as if to say *Don't try and turn the subject because you know I can hang on to it like a dog with a bone.*

Oh, botheration, she was interfering and she had promised herself not to. Just as well Alaric was not here to hear her and raise his dark brows in surprise.

'I watched you fall in love with Daniel and saw that same look in Fliss and Darius's eyes today, so I have been able to observe the difference between an agreeable sort of a companion and the love of one's life, Marianne. You will just have to trust me to know my own mind and take my own risks if the time ever comes for me to jump head first into love as my big brother and sister have done before me.'

'Sometimes you find yourself landing in a mess of briars if you leap without looking,' Marianne warned, not sure if she was referring to her own feelings for Alaric or those she thought Viola was developing for her careless employer.

'Maybe if you look hard enough there is a way around the briars without getting scratched,' Viola said, 'and you know I always look before I leap, Marianne. So please stop worrying about me.'

'I have to, I am your big sister.' Marianne read her sister's silent disagreement in her stubbornly firmed chin and the way her eyes went unreadable and chilly. 'I cannot pretend it is better not to rake up the past when it stands between us, Viola. I know how much I hurt you when I left the vicarage to marry Daniel. I felt guilty about leaving you behind almost every step of the way.'

'You still went.'

'I did,' she admitted starkly, 'and I would do it again in the same situation, but somehow I would find a way to take you with me.'

'And poor Daniel would have had the weight of the law and his commanding officer's fury to contend with as well as you demanding he marry you and never mind what Mama and Papa said,' Viola the woman reasoned.

It was almost as if Viola had made herself forget the lonely child who pushed Marianne out of the door and shut it on her as if she truly hated her for leaving. She could still hear Viola's sobs through the wood as she crept downstairs and out through the back door and into the night. And the sound of her little sister's desolate sorrow at being the only Yelverton left at home haunted her all the way to Daniel's latest posting.

Even when he finally agreed to marry her at the drumhead, since she had no intention of going away until they could wed without her parents' consent, it felt wrong to do it without her little sister playing bridesmaid as they always dreamed she would when they planned their ideal weddings as little girls. 'Forgive me?' she pleaded now as she had back then, her last words to her sister as she slipped out of their shared bedroom and stole away into the night.

'Of course, I am quite grown up now, Sister. Real love and a chance of such happiness are rare and should be grasped with both hands. I did just tell you I learnt to recognise true love when I see it, so forget about whatever I said back then—I was a spoilt brat who only thought about my own wants and needs. You did what you had to do, Marianne. Mama and Papa would never have let you wed a mere sergeant and I would have been very happy for you if Daniel had not taken you away and left me to worry about both of you as well as Darius living in the midst of so much violence and unrest.'

'I was not in any danger,' Marianne argued rather lamely but of course she had been once Daniel was posted to Portugal and then Spain. She shivered at the memory of the terrifying retreat to Corunna and the running battles even as the boats took the ragtag remains of Sir John Moore's army off the shore, then she recalled Daniel's fury when the army had tried to leave his wife behind. He had refused to let them and tears threatened now at the memory of him refusing to take no for an answer as he had marched her on board one of them and defied any man to make him leave his wife behind. There were other times they had been surprised by the enemy or just got lost in a storm and it had taken days of stubborn effort to find Daniel again.

'Don't lie to me,' Viola demanded sternly and suddenly Marianne could see what a formidable teacher she was with any pupils foolish enough to try to get the better of her. 'I am truly a grown-up now and I know you must have been scared and in peril time and time again in Portugal and Spain, whatever colourful comedies about your life on the march you sent back to make Mama and Papa feel better about you being there. You must treat me like an adult if we are to truly be sisters in spirit as well as fact once again, Marianne.'

'Very well, then, I will—anything to avoid more of your icy glares.'

'I have been working on them lately,' her sister admitted ruefully and Marianne's attention snapped back to the very grown-up problem of Sir Harry Marbeck and her sister's true feelings for the wretched man.

'You have?' she said cautiously.

'I have and do not allow that vivid imagination

of yours full rein because it is Sir Harry's great-aunt who has been on the receiving end of my iciest ones lately and not Sir Harry himself. If I did not stand up to the old tartar, she would have me running around at her bidding all the time instead of looking after my charges and trying to drum a few facts into their reluctant heads.'

'She sounds like a nightmare to live with.'

'No, I like her. She adds spice to the mix.'

'You really are enjoying this position, then?'

'Yes, and imagine how it would be for me as Mama's last chick if I had stayed in Bath, Marianne. Teacher or not, I was dragged off to soirées and card parties and made to play silver loo every night of the week except Sunday when I had to go and live with them before you came back.'

'So you left me to endure it and went back to live at school with a sigh of relief, then you took this post to make doubly sure you would not have to do it again, I suppose.'

'Perhaps, but you have no idea how hard I had to fight for that post at Miss Thibbett's. If not for Papa putting his foot down for once and insisting I was allowed to leave home and accept it, I would be a Bath quiz right now.'

'No, you definitely would not,' Marianne argued. 'Not with that face and blue eyes and all that lovely blonde hair. You always were the family beauty, Viola, so do not even try to tell me you did not have dozens of offers before and probably during your teaching career.'

'And it is ridiculous of you not to accept how truly lovely you are, Marianne. Even after Daniel adored you every moment you had together, and I have no doubt told you how breathtaking you are time and time again, you still refuse to see your looks are out of the common way.'

'Because they are not—I have ordinary brownish hair and trust Mama to inform me I am too thin and look older than my years the moment she arrived here.'

'I do not think Lord Stratford agrees with her,' Viola said with a sidelong glance that dared Marianne to retaliate and mention Sir Harry Marbeck.

'Lord Stratford has beautiful manners and even his worst enemy could not accuse him of being above his company.'

'Does he now?'

'Yes, and he treats all his staff with respect and consideration.'

'I am sure he does,' Viola murmured and her eyes were full of mischief and too much understanding. It felt wonderful to be teased by her sister again, but Marianne wished Viola would choose someone else to tease her about. 'Have you ever wondered if loving so deeply once would help you cope with that passionate nature of yours even better if you ever do it again?' Viola asked almost innocently.

'There is very little chance of it as far as I can see.'

'Never say never,' Viola told her in a crisp parody of their mother in Mrs Yelverton's days as the busy wife of a country vicar.

Marianne had to laugh, as her sister intended, but there was more than a pinch of sadness under it as they went arm in arm to join a half-hearted supper left over from the wedding feast. Owlet Manor was still lovely and mellow and looked like a proper gentleman's house as it basked in the evening sun, but it felt as if the glow and energy had gone out of the place for her now Alaric was no longer here.

She would be living under his roof soon so it was impossible to put the man to the back of her mind and forget she had ever met him even if she wanted to. Impossible anyway, she realised as she moved through the knot of family and friends staying the night. This should be a completely joyful occasion. Yet she had this odd sense that something crucial was missing as soon as Lord Stratford's finely sprung carriage disappeared around the first of the bends in the road.

Chapter Fourteen

As Alaric made himself climb into the carriage he told himself he had to leave Owlet Manor and the world out of time that he felt he had been living in for nigh on a month. He had meant to bring Juno with him so they would be ready to travel back to Stratford Park in the morning, but Marianne's acceptance of his offer of employment changed all that. Juno was so delighted she persuaded him to let her stay where she was for a few more days while Mrs Turner packed and said her goodbyes to her family and they had insisted they would love to have her there. Juno and the new Mrs Yelverton were close and she had a good excuse to stay, but he did not. His presence disrupted the family gathering and Mrs Yelverton Senior was on pins all the time with a real live viscount under her son's roof and her husband was embarrassed when she assumed airs to impress him.

Alaric might have dismissed her as a social climber if he had not met her children first, but now he had learnt to look beyond surface appearances and a fussy manner he rather liked the lady under the fluster and chatter. No doubt she was interfering and had been tactless with her elder daughter, but she obviously loved her children and he could see where Marianne and Darius got their energy and determination. Given the choice between his own mother and Marianne's, he knew which one he would rescue from a burning building.

He stared out of the carriage window at the darkly green trees of late summer and the fields of ripening grain they were passing at the leisurely pace country roads dictated. His life had changed so radically since he had set out from Paris to find out what was amiss with his niece, but he was not quite sure what came next. Juno would do much better now he had found her a companion instead of a heartless grandmother to keep her company, but what about Alaric Defford?

For so many years his life had been set. He had thought he would carry on being isolated from the real world by a title and possessions until he finally bit the bullet and married for the sake of an heir and even then it would be a polite sort of marriage to a well-bred and dignified lady who would not expect grand emotions from her noble husband.

Yet Stratford Park had never felt like a true home as poor rundown Owlet Manor did even before Marianne and his staff made it shine again for the wedding. But it was his family seat and he supposed it was the place he had to go to when he thought about home. Juno was familiar with it as well, even though she had been living across the park in the Dower House for most of her young life. Thank heavens Marianne had agreed to go with them when they went back—her vital presence would scout some of the ghosts from the vast house he had lived in virtually alone since George died.

Now he had solved Juno's and Marianne's lonely dilemmas in one go he should be feeling a lot better about the future. Except he ached for so much more from Mrs Marianne Turner than he had any right to expect from her. He reminded himself about his words to her this afternoon about a true gentleman not taking advantage of a lady in his employment. 'You have been too clever for your own good this time, Stratford,' he muttered at the late summer twilight outside the window.

There was Broadley on the horizon once again now and it was still too early for him to retire to the best bedchamber at the Royal George with nothing to do but curse himself for tying himself in knots over a female who was probably barely aware he existed as a mature and potent man. He wanted her so much he might have to take up fencing and rowing and horse racing in order to give himself something physical to exhaust himself on when she was living under his roof. Then he would only need to decide where life was going to take him without Viscount Stratford's protective armour against the world to keep it at bay and all might yet be well. Hmm, it might be, but just now he felt as if he had left everything that really mattered to him in life behind at Owlet Manor. Was

he cursed to always feel lonely without it for the rest
of his life?

Best not think too hard about that particular version of a wasteland and he was a patient man. He
could wait for Mrs Marianne Turner to make up her
mind about the man under his viscount disguise and
he had forgotten about boxing when he made up his
list of ways to avoid throwing himself at her in a stew
of lordly passion, had he not? He would be the fit-
test man in England as soon as his stupid ankle was
back in full working order.

Three days after the wedding Marianne waved her
parents and Viola off in Lord Stratford's comfortable
travelling coach. Fliss and Darius were busy pretending to help with the harvest and probably wandering about staring into each other's eyes and getting
in the way instead and she was escaping her pack-
ing. Her excuse was a burning need to find a book
to take with her on the journey to Stratford Park a
couple of counties away in Wiltshire. So she was in
Great-Uncle Hubert's study tidying a small part of it
because tidying was soothing and if she happened to
do some dusting while she was in here nobody could
deny the room needed it.

'Ah, so there you are.'

'Yes, here I am, Lord Stratford.'

'I thought you promised your brother to stop at-
tacking his house as if your life depended on getting
it clean from top to bottom.'

'I am not cleaning. I am looking for a book.'

'Then you would seem to have come to the right place.'

'Indeed.'

'And why are you wielding a duster?'

'You would not want me importing dust into your fine carriage or your magnificent country house, now would you, my lord?'

'Admit it, you are cleaning, Mrs Turner.'

'I am sorting,' she said and that was all she was prepared to admit.

'Why?'

'I have an orderly mind.' It felt anything but orderly just now and why did he have to stand so close to her in order to talk? Although she did have to admit she had only managed to clear a small space in the piles of books stacked all around the room when Great-Uncle Hubert had run out of bookshelves, so he had little choice but to be close to her even if his presence somehow seemed to have sucked some of the air out of this dusty old book room and she was conscious of every breath he took.

'Liar,' he accused her with so much laughter in his blue eyes she smiled back at him like an idiot.

'I am sorry,' he said at last.

'Why?'

'I am not your employer yet, but I am still supposed to be a gentleman and should not close doors behind me when there is a lady in the room.'

She felt her heartbeat thunder in her ears as the musty scent of old books and the little noises of the old house shifting on its oak bones as the sun moved around the house faded and all she could see and sense was him. 'Are you?' she murmured. 'Luckily I am not a lady.'

He stepped back as if she had bitten him. 'If anyone else said the things you say about yourself, you would loathe them,' he told her furiously.

She was glad he had to shut the door to make enough space to join her in here so nobody could hear them now. 'Best do it myself rather than wait for someone to do it for me,' she replied coolly.

'And what do you think your husband would think if he could hear you say them, Mrs Turner?'

'You have no right to bring him into it,' she told him with enough anger to hide her worry Daniel would hate the lesser version of herself she became when he died.

'Your brother seems to dread throwing you back into grief so much he does not feel he can argue when you call yourself names, but I can. I do not want to, Marianne, but you can hate me without hurting yourself. I was wrong to think I could lock my feelings away after my brother died and I cannot even start to imagine how much worse it must feel to lose the love of your life, but you can take it from me, pretending not to feel at all is not really living—it is existence and no more.'

How dare he criticise her when he had no idea how it felt to lose your true love? He had just admitted he did not and he was right. Temper hammered in her temples, but the horrible suspicion he was right was fighting it. 'You have no right to say things even my nearest relatives dare not say,' she argued.

'Darius told me the Bath tabbies made your life a misery when you were living under your parents' roof and he was still away fighting, so no wonder he does not want to upset you.'

'Even if they had welcomed me with open arms I would still just have been stumbling around in the dark after my husband was killed. I hope Darius has stopped feeling guilty because he lived when Daniel died at his side, though, and at least he has Fliss to make him see the world as it really is now,' she said and tears threatened as she remembered that terrible time in both their lives.

'While you have nobody?' Lord Stratford said so gently she had to let his words sink in and do their damage.

'Yes,' she said and a terrible sob ripped out of her like a rusty saw. 'Now look what you have done,' she told him unsteadily and clenched her fists against the fury and heartache and beat them on the air as if it might help, but of course it did not; nothing did when she let the full force of what she had lost on that terrible night at Badajoz overwhelm her.

'Come here, you stubborn woman,' Alaric said softly and pulled her into his arms so she could beat him instead, or cry if that worked better. Brave of him and she was wrong; there was comfort to be had in the world after all. Who would have thought a viscount would have a shoulder just the right height and breadth for a tall lady to weep into and feel safe as she let the storm rage at long last?

'I will damage your fine coat,' she gasped between sobs. She did not want him to let her go, but he was sure to when he felt her tears soaking into his neat but superbly cut country gentleman's clothes.

'Serve me right,' he murmured and thank goodness her stupid mob cap must have fallen off so she could feel him whisper it against her unruly hair.

And Alaric just went on holding her when she could not halt the storm of tears she had probably made worse by denying it an outlet for so long. It was such a relief to let out all the hurt and loneliness she had kept to herself in her parents' little house in Bath and even when she had come here with a brother still raw from the war. Alaric whispered the occasional word of comfort as he bent over her like a protector and she felt safe. She dare not even think the word, *lover*, but there it was in the back of her mind like a siren voice. She could almost feel her eyes going red and swollen as she tried to grab back enough self-control to remember who they were and where they were before someone came in and caught him with a weeping widow in his arms.

'I must stop this nonsense,' she murmured and tried to draw back from him.

'It is not nonsense and you have at least two years' worth of Bath gossip to get out of your system,' he told her with a wry smile when most men would hastily mumble an excuse and back away.

'They were awful and I suppose seeing Mama and

Papa again has reminded me of that time and how miserable I was there,' she told him with a grimace.

'Jealousy,' he told her as if it was so obvious it needed no more explanation.

'I am all but penniless and have lost the husband I eloped with—how can anyone be jealous of me?'

'You are a beautiful woman and that is a black mark against you for the likes of them. And you have had what they never can and never will have themselves because you dared everything for love. Can you imagine a single one of them giving up their comforts and position for a man even if they loved him to distraction?'

Marianne disregarded his flattering notion she was beautiful, but she did think hard about some of her mother's cronies and the little lives they led. She almost laughed at the very idea of a single one following in the tail of an army to be with the man they loved. 'No,' she said as all the petty limits they put on their own lives suddenly struck her as pitiful and so very unimportant she wondered she had ever let them make her feel less than they were.

'Neither can I, nor a sensible man asking them to. They would make his life a misery and I suspect they bullied and belittled you because you made their lives look so small and dull in comparison.'

Tears had made her eyes sore and the occasional sob still shook her, but he had not pulled away in disgust. Alaric's strength and humanity seemed to have melted something icy and painful inside her and she was glad. She felt as if she could breathe more freely without it, even if every breath she took drew in his warmth and the pure temptation of being alone with him in a musty old room. Reminding herself she must look terrible, she scrubbed at her eyes with her handkerchief. 'How did you know all that?' she asked him huskily.

'Perhaps I know you and all I need to do is imagine the small lives they lead and contrast them with you and there you are—jealousy and guilt. It is obvious. No wonder they disliked you, Marianne. How dare you be twice the woman they are?'

'A few were men,' she qualified with a shudder.

He frowned. 'Damn them for being spiteful when you rebuffed them, then.'

'How did you know they tried to seduce me first?'

'I have eyes and a heart and feelings, Marianne,' he told her as if he thought she might not have noticed.

'I know,' she said soothingly, but it seemed to make him even more gruff and grumpy.

She made the mistake of patting his shoulder to soothe whatever ailed him and felt the fine tension in his body. Intent on what she wanted for once she stood on tiptoe and kissed him, quick and hard, on the lips. She would have swiftly backed away if he had not taken over as if he was starving for her, then deepened it into something more intense. Their kiss in the garden had felt warm and wonderful, but this was far more passionate, much more demanding.

She felt little pulses of lightning shimmer through her wherever he touched her, but sanity might have saved them if she had not felt hesitation in his touch, as if he was afraid he might hurt her. She murmured a wordless argument and gasped at the need blazing inside her when she opened her mouth against his and forgot all about lords and soldier's widows in the glorious heat of the moment.

Passion hot and heady flamed between them. This time her tongue was bold and teased his firm mouth, then tangled with his. She ran a shaking hand over his crisp dark curls and loved the freedom of being able to touch him. She explored the nape of his neck with a touch of wonder at his latent strength under her fingertips. He was so different from Daniel she felt like a traitor for a moment as she thought about then and now, but the richness of the moment soon swallowed it up. Alaric was always himself, just as Daniel had been, and right now he was a novel pleasure under her exploring hands, then her mouth again once they took in enough air to risk driving one another out of control.

His hands were broad and strong on her back and she wriggled closer and gazed into his eyes for a luxurious moment. He stared back at her with his blue eyes blazing emotion she was desperate to read, but could not quite decipher. She wondered why his eyes were much the same colour as her own, but so very different. His pupils flared with what looked like strong, almost desperate feelings.

'Marianne,' he breathed her name so huskily it sounded like a magical spell. What they both wanted was clear enough from the grinding need inside her, but from the regret in his eyes he was not going to allow them to have it. Now his touch was meant to soothe instead of inflame. The loneliness of him drawing away from her made her want to cry, again, if she had any tears left. Except she felt them prickle her sore eyes for him this time, for the loss and lack of him even when he was still warm and strong and very much alive against her wanting body.

She shook her head. 'Alaric,' she whispered in the book-stale air of Hubert Peacey's private lair. 'You stopped,' she half accused him, although anyone might have come in and caught them entwined like lovers and that really would not do.

'I had to,' he said on a long sigh of what sounded like regret. 'Anyone could have come in and found us locked in each other's arms,' he echoed her thoughts huskily.

'I suppose that would have hurt your pride and your reputation.'

'It is not me I am worrying about,' he argued impatiently.

'Do not concern yourself about me, my lord. I will survive. I am quite good at it by now,' she said flippantly and saw fury blaze in his eyes this time.

'Survival is not good enough for you, or me. We have both survived for long enough and there has to be more than that from now on.'

'Yes, there must be to make it worthwhile,' she agreed, but it was all she could offer right now.

They avoided one another's eyes as the afternoon sun suddenly crept out from behind the clouds outside and edged curiously in around the blinds that had frayed and faded and no longer protected Great-Uncle Hubert's precious books as well as they should. That sun was already lower in the sky and soon it would be autumn and they would both be in Wiltshire at famously grand, classically splendid Stratford Park. And he would be my lord there and she would be an upper servant. Marianne the lover screamed at the rest of her to seize what she could, while she could have it. 'I am probably barren, Alaric,' she told him painfully and who asked the houri to speak?

'And I probably do not care,' he said, but how could he not?

He was a lord as well as master of large estates and all the family history dragging behind him like a ball and chain.

Ah, of course—he could not marry her, could he?

Not only was she the widow of an enlisted man and a mere vicar's daughter, but she could not give him the children he needed so badly. A mistress who was unable to breed a pack of little bastards to complicate matters when he took a wife and bred his heirs would save him so much complication.

'Well, I do,' she said. She straightened her wilting stance, telling herself not to feel the loss of those children, bastards or no. She longed for them so desperately even as she eyed him militantly and hurt herself on a shattered dream she had not even known she had until now. Now she would have to regret not carrying his child as well as her abiding sorrow that she had never borne Daniel one either. Suddenly that felt like agony and something feral uncurled inside her to defend her from any more of that.

'And you intend to use it as yet another weapon to keep me at a distance, I suppose?' he said as if *she* was hurting *him* instead of the other way around and for no good reason either.

'No, it is the plain truth, so I do not need a weapon to fight off amorous noblemen,' she snapped, her past pain and frustration at her childlessness driving her into a fury way beyond any offence he might have offered her if she gave him a chance to. 'And I would not marry you even if you wanted me to. Now if that is all I really must wish you good day, my lord. I am a very busy person and if you still want me to pack up my life once again and come with you to Stratford Park I need to hurry now, or is that scheme all over after this whatever it was we just did together?'

'Of course I want you to come with us and you agreed to become Juno's companion for at least a month, so do not use this.' He stopped and looked helpless and driven and even a little bit hurt for a moment before he stamped Lord Stratford back on his face and manner and his gaze went stony.

He even imposed rigid control on his sensitive mouth and that was what made her stop and think because his mouth was so warm, provocative, so intimate and right on hers only a few seconds ago and now she was treating him as an enemy. Brought up short by his withdrawal of all warmth from her, she realised where her stupid temper and frustrated maternal instincts had taken her and was ashamed.

She had invented most of this painful scene by deciding his motives and intentions towards her without knowing what they really were. Temper put up a wall between them and she had no idea how to tear it down again. Her fury at an improper offer he had never even begun to make had led her to break something precious. Alaric looked so hurt before he shut her out that she felt more alone than she ever had before as they stood so close and so distant in this musty old book room and listened to one another breathe.

'This altercation,' he went on stonily as if that was all it had ever been and never mind the odd kiss or two, 'of ours cannot be allowed to disappoint Juno so deeply when we have both promised to try and make her a better future.'

'I will not renege,' she said with a little bit too much dignity as well. This was her fault, she decided as she stared down at the one small pile of books she had managed to rescue from the dusty chaos all around them. Her insecurities were too ready to come to the fore and prod her into a defensive temper. Because she was so afraid she felt too much for him, she walked on briars when they were together, as if that was all she deserved.

This time she was stiff and defensive and far too sensitive to hurts he probably never meant her to feel and what a hopeless pair they were. It was probably just as well she had scuppered any chance he might be stubborn and reckless enough to ask her to marry him, whatever it was he felt for her. She wondered if either of them were quite sure what that was and bit back a regretful sigh.

'I will have to hurry up if I am to be ready to leave tomorrow,' she said as she looked down at that pile of books as if she was fascinated when she could not have said what they were or who wrote them if her life depended on it.

'I shall not inflict myself on you once you are living under my roof,' he said.

'I kissed you,' she argued stiffly.

'Whatever we did, I should not have let it happen.'

'We kissed one another because we could not help it and now we can, so that should not be a problem for us any more, should it?' Suddenly she wanted to go with him so badly the idea of staying here looked faded and blank. Was there ever a more contrary female than Marianne Turner, née Yelverton? she asked herself as she traced the tooled leather cover of one of Great-Uncle Hubert's most prized volumes and still had no idea what it said.

'Will you come to Stratford Park with us and keep your word to Juno, then?'

'Stop making everything in your life about her, Alaric,' she told him earnestly, because at least she could argue with his overdeveloped sense of guilt even if she could not take back what she had said and make this distance between them vanish. 'Juno is too young and confused to take the weight of your guilt on her shoulders. You told me to stop being ruled by the past and start living again so I will if you will.'

'Maybe I lack your courage.'

She shook her head and refused to meet his not-quite-as-chilly look. 'No, I am a coward,' she said sadly and opened the door and made herself walk away from him. She felt his gaze on her back and still made herself keep doing it. She did not want to carry the image of Alaric staring after her as she went all the way up the stairs and branched off to her room at the front of the house a floor further up in the attics because she told herself she had always liked the view and nobody else ever came up here. Except of course a picture of him before she managed to turn her back and leave did stay with her and she could not see the mellow afternoon countryside for the blur of yet more tears she blinked back furiously.

He looked so bleak and alone against the world again and it was lonely and stark up here as well, view or not. So much of her wanted to run back downstairs to tell him he could have anything he wanted of her; she would do for him what she had for Daniel and risk everything for love. Except this time she would have to cast every last caution to the four winds if she truly loved him. If she did that, she could not shackle him to a barren woman even if she insisted love was enough and would she have the courage to face the world as Viscount Stratford's mistress and not his wife?

It would be even more of a transgression than loving Daniel seemed to the wider world, but she had never regretted that one so maybe it would not be as empty and echoing as the word 'mistress' looked from outside. Yet what if he discovered love was not enough? What if he looked at her in five years or ten or even twenty and realised he had sacrificed too much for her? No, it felt like a cutting off of something precious and potentially wonderful, but maybe that petty, stupid quarrel she had forced on him was for the best.

'Forget he is anything more than your employer from now on, Marianne,' she whispered to herself once she was safely inside her bedroom with her back pressed against the door as if to keep wild and sensual Marianne out. Of course he had not come up here looking for her; Lord Stratford was too honourable to pursue a woman who had said no to him. 'And stop lying to yourself,' she told herself disgustedly. 'You did not say no, he did when he called a halt to that kiss. You would have gone on saying yes until anything else was a technicality.'

Just as well he had, then, since she could not endure being cut off from her brother and Fliss and Viola for the sake of a scandalous liaison with a man so far above her touch. She did not have a thick enough skin to be anyone's mistress, even if she could face the idea of never seeing her family again as the price for the sensual pleasure she knew she would experience in his bed. And what would Papa think when he found out his elder daughter had become a scarlet woman? He would be heartbroken and that was that, then—the last nail in the coffin of Marianne the mistress.

It did not stop her aching for Alaric the man while she got ready to pack her life up again. At least he

was in Broadley by now, not a floor down and a few
sturdy planks of oak away from her as he had been
for the last few weeks. Even that was not nearly far
enough away to let her rest peacefully tonight and
somehow she had to learn to stop being a fool about
a man she could not have.

Chapter Fifteen

After years of holding himself aloof from strong emotions, Alaric felt so many tearing away at him now it was as if he was making up for a drought. She was so vulnerable, the real Marianne under Mrs Turner's brisk efficiency, and it was too soon to risk everything they could be before he knew it was for good. What a fine pair they were; him guarding his heart after losing George and succeeding to a title and estates he never wanted and her hiding so much hurt and grief for her Daniel behind relentless hard work.

This afternoon she had trusted him enough to cry in his arms and let some of it out and that had made him feel proud and racked with guilt at the same time. He had wanted her so much even while she wept for another man against his shoulder as if her heart might break. No wonder she had responded when he kissed her so lustily; she was overwrought, all her emotions too close to the surface, and she had trusted him. Then she had distrusted him and then she went sad and distant and mysterious on him and he would never understand women as long as he lived.

'Brute,' he still accused himself as he rode back to Broadley.

He had recognised something exceptional and significant about Marianne the moment they met and now he felt a fool for not realising how much she meant to him until they quarrelled and he did not know how to cross the barriers they had each put up to keep the other at a distance again. He had known she was true and strong at first sight, despite the snap of temper in her fine eyes and her impatience with lords like him. So, yes, Marianne tugged at his senses and challenged him and made him someone better than he was before he met her. And he wanted to confront her with everything they could be to one another if they only dared, but caution whispered it was too soon. And how could he reveal his dreams and dilemmas to her now he had persuaded her to become Juno's companion? He had done it to give her a place to go when her brother married, but doing it left him tied hand and foot.

How could he tell her he felt explosive and on fire and desperate for her in every inch of his body and all his wildest fantasies when she was still grieving for her husband? Even if she was not in his employment and would not soon be living under his roof, how could he tell her that? Well, she had said they should give each other a month's trial, had she not?

Best hold her to that limit and maybe, after a month of trying his hardest to be a good and unthreatening viscount, he could finally manage to convince her he was a better man than the evidence so far suggested.

'Juno? Juno? Where are you? The carriage is coming down the drive and your uncle is here to escort us on the first leg of our journey to Wiltshire.'

Marianne realised at breakfast this morning that the girl had grown more silent as the day to leave Owlet Manor came closer and she had barely managed to eat a thing today now it was actually here. Marianne urged Fliss and Darius to say their goodbyes, then go on a visit to Miss Donne so there would not be quite so much of a break when the time came for Juno to leave. Now Seth and Joe were carrying their luggage for the journey out for the grooms to buckle or tie in place and the rest had gone ahead by carrier. Lord Stratford was waiting outside on a fine horse obviously much more suited for a gentleman to ride and waiting to escort them to his home and Juno was nowhere to be seen. Marianne heard her own voice echo up into the lofty roof timbers and beside that there were only a few murmurs as the coachman and grooms got on with preparing the luxurious carriage for the journey. She shouted Juno's name again; silence met her voice again and felt like far too much of it for comfort as her heart began to race. That terrible feeling of urgency she remembered when Juno was missing felt like ice as a fear that history was repeating itself shivered down her backbone. She ran up the stairs as fast as she could raise her skirts and sprint.

'Juno?' she shouted again as she pelted down the bedroom corridor and heard only the sound of her own feet thumping on ancient oak floorboards and the echoes of her own voice again. 'Juno?' she repeated, desperate now as she ran into the room expecting to find it empty and Juno halfway to goodness knew where. She was so convinced she was right that she nearly turned away too soon and missed the glimpse of skirts and petticoats that was all she could see of Juno from the doorway. She peered around it and saw the girl sitting on the floor in the furthest corner of the room, rocking herself backwards and forwards like a desolate child. 'Oh, Juno, why are you down there? Whatever is the matter?'

'I cannot, I just cannot,' Juno wailed incoherently and Marianne almost wished her own mother was here, or Viola. Or anyone who had experience of sobbing and incoherent girls who were not yet quite old enough to really be women would do right now. 'Tell Uncle Alaric I am sorry,' the girl said.

'You must tell him that yourself,' Marianne said and there was her lifeline. He was Juno's guardian and protector; he would know what to do and say. Or if he did not he would just have to learn fast.

'Lord Stratford!' She ran back down to the head of the stairs, calling out his name. 'Tell Lord Stratford he must come inside and you had best have the horses unharnessed and taken off to the stables, Joe. There has been a slight delay to our plans.'

Now she was feeling guilty at her panic about having to deal with Juno's distraught tears and that strange frozen look on her poor woebegone face. Alaric dashed in through the front door, then took the stairs in as few bounds as he could and she was so glad of him she almost wept herself.

'What is it?' he demanded curtly.

'I have no idea, but Juno needs you,' she told him breathlessly and was almost on his heels when he had to grab the upright of the door to stop himself in his headlong haste to get to his niece. Then he was sitting down by Juno on the floor and doing what Marianne ought to have when she found her there. He simply pulled her into his arms and rocked her like a little child as she howled into his superfine coat.

The poor man would be getting through them by the dozen if distraught females kept on weeping all over him like this, Marianne mused, feeling decidedly surplus to requirements, yet still she could not make herself go away and leave them in peace to talk about whatever Juno wanted to talk about.

Juno surprised Marianne after a few moments of unrestrained woe by sitting upright and fighting back her tears. She owed the girl an apology for expecting her to go on sobbing until she was so incoherent with misery she had to be put to bed. 'I thought I could, but I cannot,' she said rather bravely. 'Stratford Park,' she explained as a sob and a shiver hit at the same time and she buried her head in Alaric's shoulder again and seemed to find some of his strength in there. She shook her head as if she was furious with herself for reacting in this way.

'I have heard of it,' Alaric said lightly and Juno actually managed a laugh.

'The girls from London, I simply cannot go back and face them, Uncle Alaric. I tried so hard to find the nerve to, but I truly cannot do it.'

'Ah, and now we are getting to the heart of things at last. Why did you not tell me about them before I set all these ridiculous plans in motion, love?'

'I wanted you to be proud of me. I want to be brave and strong and look them in the eye and show them I am not a looby or a wantwit or even a silly little wallflower. I am, though, because I cannot do it.'

'Is that what they said? And who are they?'

At last it all came tumbling out—the full story of Juno's miserable debut Season in so-called polite society. Never had Marianne been more grateful she was too humbly born and Papa too poor for her to do more than attend a few local parties and a subscription ball at the Assembly Rooms in the nearest town when she was old enough to be considered officially out.

'I cannot understand why those girls turned against you,' Marianne said from her place on the bed where she had sunk while she heard all the vicious tricks a few haughty young women had played on Juno once they discovered they could get away with it, 'especially when some of them are your uncle's neighbours and should have known better.'

'At first they were eager for me to join in with

them, but I suppose I am too quiet and I had never been to the waltzing parties or any of the events their mamas arranged for them before they were officially out so they were at ease and I was not.'

'Idiot, I should have thought of that,' Alaric chided himself.

'No, Grandmama should. She took your money and spent it lavishly on parties and grand toilettes for herself and entertaining her friends, like that horrid man she was so insistent I had to marry. She should have done all the things for me other girls' relatives did. I will not have you blaming yourself for her self-ishness, Uncle Alaric,' she told him rather sternly and Marianne was very tempted to nod her agreement.

'Whatever I can or cannot blame myself for, we clearly cannot go to Stratford Park today, Jojo. If you will unpack one of those boxes the men have been so busy strapping safely to my travelling carriage so you may wash your face and brush your hair and meet me downstairs when you are ready, we three can decide what to do next. Come, Mrs Turner, I be-lieve Juno will come about if we leave her in peace for a few minutes to compose herself.'

Marianne followed him out like a faithful sheep-dog after her shepherd and expected to be dismissed from a position she had told herself she did not want very much anyway. Now it was fading away it seemed like a lost opportunity to be close to the man without anybody realising how badly she wanted to be close to him and that was a giveaway of her true feelings, was it not? She obviously felt far more for Viscount Stratford than she had ever wanted to feel for another man after Daniel died and this time it could not go anywhere at all. Just as well if he did dismiss her, then.

'I should have known,' she said as soon as they were out of Juno's hearing.

'Nonsense, and if we are both going to blame ourselves nothing will get done. We simply need to find another place for her to go since I do not have the heart to force her to face those little harpies. If you will help me to do so, I will be grateful and I am sure Juno will be as well.'

'You do not mind that your plans are spoilt?'

'No, I do not like Stratford Park very much myself so I will not be heartbroken if Juno does not want to live there.'

'But isn't it very grand indeed?' Marianne said, the radical idea a man might not actually like his ancestral home making him seem less lordly and more human. Sometimes she really wished he was hardhearted and arrogant so he would seem less appealing to a susceptible idiot like her.

'It is, very grand. I am not very fond of grand—I have discovered lately that I much prefer comfortable. If your brother would only sell it to me, I would far rather live here than in a vast Palladian folly like Stratford Park.'

'He will never do that, he loves it here.'

'I know, pity,' he said with a grin as if he really was relieved not to be going back to huge and famous Stratford Park.

'What do you think you might do instead?'

'If you and Juno are agreeable, we could travel until the roads become too difficult to do so freely, then we can think again. It might be good for Juno to wander about her own country and explore whatever bits of it take her fancy at the time.'

'But you are an important man of affairs and I know you have obligations to your tenants and neighbours. At least Darius only has three farms to worry himself over and all of them are within easy riding distance.'

'I envy him more and more every day,' he said lightly and Marianne almost believed him.

After a day to regroup and for Juno to recover from her tears and chagrin, they ended up taking a very leisurely journey up into Shropshire for a week or more. Then they explored Cheshire for another week or two. Derbyshire came next and by then it was agreed that Lord Stratford would soon have to leave them to their travels while he attended to some of that business he and Marianne had talked about at Owlet Manor and he also met his agent and did all the things conscientious viscounts had to do.

Marianne and Juno shared a maid now and the girl sat silent and rather glum on the seat opposite them as they rolled down yet another country road to a country town where they were to spend another countrified night. The girl could not be much older than Juno, but she ghosted about their bedchambers night and morning, laying out this and that and being so silently helpful Marianne felt inhibited by the barriers between servants and served for the first time in her life.

The maids at the vicarage where she grew up had been cheerfully loud, tossing remarks back and forth to one another as they cleaned or cooked or helped the children with their dressing and undressing until they were considered old enough to do it themselves. This sort of service was different and Marianne had to find the line superior servants seemed to want to hold between them and their noble employers and even with Miss Defford's companion. She felt subtly put in her place by the silent efficiency of the girl and even the grooms and coachman said very little as they sped through the sleepy countryside. Lord Stratford rode ahead most of the time, but he was often wrapped up in his own thoughts even when they came together at those inns along the way where they were fussed over and spoilt because of his rank and power. Perhaps he was simply enjoying the peace and quiet and the changing scene. He was obviously completely fit and healthy again after his accident, so maybe he was enjoying travelling about his homeland after several months spent among the tension and furore of a Paris struggling to come to terms with the downfall of their beloved Emperor.

Marianne sighed and shifted in her comfortable seat and heartily wished she was not such a fool. All three of them were embarking on a new life, even if this current one did feel a bit like a limbo between their old and new ones. Lord Stratford had sent in his resignation to the government, so he told Juno there would be no more duties distracting him from his family and estates from now on. Whatever he had done for them in the past, he must be a reliable and subtle diplomat if the men of power relied on his tact and discretion to smooth out some of the bumps in the Duke of Wellington's rocky road as British Ambassador to France.

Marianne knew from experience how abrasive and pernickety and downright rude the great man could be, even if he was also steadfast and subtle and brave and almost a genius when it came to the delicate balancing of troops and terrain in battle. She admired the Duke deeply and even the sight of him steady and unquestionably in charge would put heart into his army. His men had trusted him not to waste their lives on vainglory, but they did not adore him as so many Frenchmen almost seemed to worship Napoleon Bonaparte.

The carriage rounded a long bend and now she could see Lord Stratford riding in front of them again. Would this journey be less tedious if he chose to join them in the carriage rather than ride ahead in solitary state? He seemed so at home in the saddle she supposed he enjoyed the exercise and it was a little stuffy in here so who could blame him for avoiding it? However well-sprung and well-cushioned a carriage was, the novelty of travelling in such style soon wore off as mile after mile sped past and heat began to build as the sun came out. She tried not to let her gaze linger on Lord Stratford's lithe form to distract her from this jolting box on wheels. They could not even open the windows more than a crack for the pall of dust the horses were kicking up.

Alaric sat his powerful grey as if he had been born in the saddle and what was he going to do with himself now he had laid aside his self-imposed duties? The man she had begun to know under the haughty aristocrat was too restless and clever to be content with the life of a country squire for very long. She frowned at his strong back, powerfully muscled shoulders and narrow flanks and wished he was less compellingly masculine. The idea of him as an idle viscount bent on pleasure seemed laughable right now, but would he be restless and bored after a few weeks of country life and be tempted away to London for the Little Season?

She felt the hum of excitement under this odd new life she was going to be living stumble and halt at the thought of him not being with them and caught herself out in a lie. It was not entirely for Juno's sake she had agreed to this wandering journey. Of course she had nowhere she wanted to go after Darius and Fliss married and the alternative was finding work with strangers, if they would employ her, or going back to live with her parents in Bath. But there was a thread of fantasy and need under all the good reasons she had given herself to be here. She wanted him to look at her with sharp interest and seductive intent again just as he did in Great-Uncle Hubert's study that memorable day. And she did not want her own stupid insecurities to spoil it this time. Yet why would he risk such a stinging rebuke for things he had never said again? He would not, of course he would not, and he must be uncomfortable at the very thought of that frustrating encounter. So every day she told herself there would be something so fascinating and breathtaking to see out of the carriage window she would forget to watch for him like a fool and wish those hasty, bad-tempered words unsaid. And every day she was disappointed.

'We will soon be in Buxton, Mrs Turner,' Juno said as if she thought Marianne was flagging and needed encouragement.

'When will you remember to call me Marianne, Juno?' Marianne said and tore her gaze from Lord Stratford's lithe but powerful form to meet Juno's eyes.

'What if I forget and do so in public?'

'It does not matter since I hope we are friends and we can be those in public as well as in private and you really need to stop worrying about what other people will think of you all the time.'

'That is what Uncle Alaric says, but I cannot bring myself to be bold and brave and I fear I shall never be a credit to him.'

'You already are and he loves you as you are, Juno. Do you think that will change if you say a wrong word or speak out of turn by accident? If you do, then I do not think you understand him at all.'

'Perhaps not, but you obviously do,' Juno said and there was the intelligence and underlying strength of character Alaric was intent on bringing to the surface more of the time, although Marianne preferred it when Juno was not using them on her.

And this silly preoccupation with Lord Stratford had to stop. She would remember to call him that even in her head from now on; Alaric would not do for a lord and his niece's paid companion. Marianne shifted and shot a wary glance at the maid, but the girl had succumbed to the warmth of the day, the rocking of the coach and the sheer boredom of trailing around the country on the whims of the aristocracy and was fast asleep again. The girl must have slept her way through half of her native land by now.

'It does not take a great deal of insight to see love behind His Lordship's iron determination to find you when he got to Broadley so travel stained and exhausted you would barely have recognised him. A shame, perhaps, that he was shaven and tidied up by the time you saw him that day; if you had met him weary and desperate for news of you as I did when he rode in soon after the dawn you would know how deeply he longed to find you safe and well and how much he loves you.'

'And I might not have made him go away and he would not have been thrown from that horrid horse and given us all such a terrible fright.'

'We would probably not be sitting here having this conversation then, since His Lordship and I did not like one another very much at the time. I dare say he would never have realised my sterling qualities and companionable virtues for the bad blood between us back then and, if you had agreed to go back to Wiltshire with him, I would never have got to know you better either and I would miss you, Juno.'

'No, you would not, because you would never have found out how wonderful and unique I am and what excellent company I can be, but I am very glad we did stay at Owlet Manor and that you are my companion now.'

'Thank you, so am I,' Marianne said, but she was not quite sure she really meant it. If Lord Stratford had only gone away again as soon as he reclaimed his niece, maybe Marianne would have forgotten about him by now. At least then her heart would not ache whenever she thought how differently matters might have fallen out if he was born a humbler man and she was a more confident woman.

Chapter Sixteen

After Lord Stratford went off to be a dutiful lord and look after his grand house and estates and vast numbers of tenants' interests for a while it felt lonely and a little bit pointless and meandering to keep on travelling without him. Marianne sat in a coffee room of yet another comfortable inn one morning, brooding about whether it was more painful to see him every day and not be able to touch or be touched by him or not to see him at all and miss even the sight of him. Sometimes it felt as if half of her was always somewhere else, wondering how he was and what he was doing and if he missed her, too. Probably not, she concluded and sighed over her letter from Darius and Fliss and almost wished she was back at Owlet Manor with them, except Alaric would not be there either.

'You look very pensive, Marianne,' Juno interrupted her reverie and made her start guiltily.

'I was daydreaming,' she replied truthfully.

'About sad things from the look of you,' Juno said gently. 'Did you love your husband so very much?' she asked impulsively, then looked cross with herself for asking. 'I do beg your pardon. Of course you do not want to talk about him to a stranger. How clumsy of me.'

'No, it was not and you are not a stranger.'

'I know I am young and must respect your privacy as Uncle Alaric told me to, but I cannot help wondering how it feels to be in love. How do you know when you have found your special he, that he is not just another gentleman with a pleasing face and form and gentle enough manners?'

'Of course you must ask such questions or how are you to learn more about the world? Yes, I did love my husband, very deeply. I miss him so much at times it feels as if I only lost him yesterday and at others he seems so far away from me I think I must have imagined so much about him I know to be true. I dare say none of that makes any sense to you, but I pray you will never have to find out for yourself how it feels to love someone deeply and sincerely and then lose him, Juno. I hope your love affair turns out to be a lifelong one when you finally get around to falling in love with a man who deserves you.'

'But how will I know it is really love I am feeling? How did you know your husband was going to be the one you would love for life when you met him?'

'I—' Marianne broke off and met Juno's painfully honest blue gaze and for a moment she could not get past the fact her eyes were so much like her uncle's the resemblance jarred her heart with pain and nostalgia and made her think too hard about love again.

Now she was missing Lord Stratford instead of Daniel Turner and it felt disloyal. She suddenly had a mental picture of her beloved husband turning around to smile one of his loving, glowing smiles at her as he walked away with a wave towards another path she had to take without him now. This time the tears could not be held back.

She had been wrong at Owlet Manor when she cried all over Alaric—she was a watering pot. The panic and remorse in poor Juno's face at the sight of her tears made her reach for her sensible handkerchief and scrub them away. The poor girl obviously thought she had caused these tears, but they were Alaric's fault and she could not even be furious with him to stop it hurting. Under all that lordly temper and arrogance he was a good man and would probably hate the idea of causing her pain, so Juno must never find out she sometimes cried over him and not just Daniel.

She wondered as she stared out of the coffee-room window to try and fight her eyes dry if it would truly be better if she had never met the man. No, she would have missed so much. She shook her head at the thought of the hollow that she would have left in her life. He had marched into it and forced her bruised emotions back to life; it was much better to feel than simply exist from day to day, so she had to be glad of him. She sighed for the simple inevitability of her and Daniel's love for one another and supposed they were much luckier in love than Lord Stratford and Mrs Turner were fated to be. So where were they before she diverted herself with a new set of tears? Ah, yes, love. At least she could talk about her feelings for Daniel openly.

'I was not the noble heroine you seem to want to paint me as when I first met my husband, Juno. I could not believe I could really be in love with my brother's sergeant and fought my feelings for him for as long as I could fool myself it was simply not possible,' she said as honestly as she could with that forbidden *and this time I shall have to fight them for the rest of my life* caveat in her head. 'Daniel was Darius's steadfast comrade in arms and saved his life more than once and I clung to all the distinctions of rank and fortune between us for a while, as if I was a princess and he was a peasant. I wonder he did not simply shrug and march away from me with barely a second thought.'

'Obviously you did not cling to them all that hard,' Juno argued.

Marianne decided she would have to be careful not to make it sound a wildly romantic tale and tempt Juno to follow her example. There could never be two men like Daniel even if there were any more wars to fight and God send there were not. 'I had enough of my mother in me back then to do my very best to deny the fire and warmth that sparked between Daniel and me from the first moment we laid eyes on one another, Juno,' she continued as carefully as she could with the memory of that time to warm her with a smile for the man who had marched into her heart and stolen it without even trying. 'His honesty and big heart and the uniquely lovable fact of him wore my snobbery down in the end. I knew I could never even think about being happy with another man while he was alive somewhere to let me know I was wrong to even try to forget him inside a more suitable marriage for a vicar's elder daughter.'

And apparently I still possess that genius for falling in love with unsuitable men.

Marianne finally admitted the truth to herself. She was no happier about this admission of her true feelings for a man than she had been seven years ago when she finally accepted the fact Daniel would always hold her heart, never mind him being a suitable life partner or being able to keep her and any children they might have in the sort of comfort, if not much luxury, she was used to as a lady of gentle birth.

'I should never have asked you to talk about this when it obviously upsets you. Please will you ignore my nosiness, I truly did not mean to make you cry.'

Impossible to say it was the awful realisation she was actually in love with Juno's uncle that did that, not only the memory of Daniel being so gruffly silent for once when they first met and so gallantly determined not to act upon the unseemly spark of attraction between himself and Lieutenant Yelverton's sister. 'Sometimes we have to cry, Juno. It is the only right response to a situation we have no control over. I learned to hold my tears in and pretend not to be feeling anything very much while I lived with my parents in Bath after Daniel died and grief twisted in on me until I felt dead inside. Anything is better than living in a world that suddenly feels grey and hopeless and I hope I never have to go back to the wretched place again and relive the sorrow I lived with there. If you have a yearning to see the place, I would be grateful if you would dismiss me and engage another companion because I cannot endure it.'

'That I do not and even if I did I would rather have you and put off a need to visit a place that sounds far too full of dull people without enough to do. And I do hope I will be considered a disgrace to my family and far too disreputable to be allowed to join the gossips in Bath if I never marry. I would rather keep cats and a procession of scandalous lovers than end up in such a hotbed of silver loo and scandal one day because I forgot to live an exciting life.'

Marianne had to laugh at the highly unlikely scenario. 'I think perhaps you should become a playwright instead with an imagination like that,' she said.

'I really wish I had the talent for it, but was it really so awful living there?' Juno said as if she could not believe a lady so much older than she was could be bowed down by hard words and slights just as she was by those spiteful girls in London.

'Not really, I was feeling low and that colours the way you see a place, but it really was boring and full of bored people with nothing much to do but make up stories about anyone a little out of the ordinary to enliven their days.'

'I wish they would mind their own business, then.'

'So do I, but most of the time I barely heard the tutting and whispering about me. It was trying to pretend there was nothing wrong with me that made the world seem so bleak. Not being true to yourself is a curse I hope you never endure.'

'No, indeed, it sounds even worse than my miserably unsuccessful debut. So you hate Bath and I loathe London. I hope neither of us needs to set foot in them ever again, but there is not much hope of us ever being truly fashionable without one or the other of them to bring us up to scratch.'

'Perhaps we could endure it for some new clothes now and again and you could learn to endure the capital for a week or two to look suitably ravishing to enchant this beau you have been dreaming about meeting one day, I suppose? My mother has always insisted the London dressmakers are literally a cut above the rest.' Marianne thought Juno was trying to joke her out of her sadness and was touched. The girl had depth and character far beyond that of the usual debutantes and in a few years' time the polite world could be in for a shock when the Honourable Miss Defford finally came out of her shell.

'Not dressmakers, Mrs Turner, *modistes*,' Juno corrected primly. Marianne laughed at her imitation of a fine lady astonished anyone could even speak about such distinct branches of the craft in the same breath. 'And now there is Paris to outdo them all, since they say the finest modistes in the world live there and set the fashions everyone else is forever trying to catch up with,' Juno added.

'And what does Miss Defford say about Paris and all the finery she might find if only her uncle would consent to her going there?'

'That they are still only clothes and she is very happy as she is. I do not think I will care if I never see another fashion plate in my entire life.'

'Hmm,' Marianne mused. 'I expect you were always dressed in white as a debutante. With your dark hair and creamy skin you would look much better in colours and even I love the luxury and fine texture of silks and good velvet as I move, as long as I do not have to wear them all the time and be forever worrying about getting dirty.'

'I cannot imagine you sitting in state all the time in order to keep your gown from harm,' Juno said with a rueful smile.

'No, neither can I,' Marianne said and shook her head at a fantasy of being Lady Stratford, dressed in silks and satins to please her lord and make her feel more of an aristocrat. That was a fantasy that could turn into a nightmare when it rubbed up against the day-to-day reality of trying to be someone she was not, so it was just as well it would never come true.

'You never did tell me how you know when a man is the right one for you, Marianne.' Juno interrupted her reverie, thank goodness, so she owed her another try at explaining the unexplainable.

'When he makes you forget any differences of rank and fortune and expectations between you. He may be a gallant fool who thinks he ought to put you first and walk away, even if it hurts you to even think about not being there to share his life with him from that moment on, but he is your fool nevertheless. Because he lights a fire in you that refuses to go out and maybe because he is uniquely himself. In the end it is simply because you love him and if he loves you back there is no better feeling on earth. Where he walks is where you want to go, too. Where he is going is the place you need to be.

'But although we were so certain we loved one another and it was right to have risked everything for him, there were days when I wished I had never met him, Juno. Sometimes I longed for safety and certainty and home when I was with Daniel in Portugal and Spain, but I would still rather have been with him than sit safely in Lisbon waiting for him to come back, or not. There were days when I wanted to weep with fatigue and hunger and Daniel wanted to send me away so I would not suffer the privations he had to endure so we could be together, but I am so glad I am a stubborn woman and I would not go, because that way we had so much more time together than we would have done if I was a biddable sort of person who does as she is told.'

'I will be sure I feel that much for a man before I risk everything for him then, but could a person love like that more than once, do you think?' Juno added so casually Marianne eyed her with suspicion. The girl could look so innocent she made lambs seem cynical.

'Maybe,' Marianne replied tightly and hoped that was enough to let Juno know there was some ground she should not tread on.

'I fear the poor old place has not been lived in for decades, Your Lordship.'

'I can see that for myself,' Alaric replied absently.

'It was a splendid old house in my grandfather's day. He often spoke of the fine company and days of feasting and dancing here when old Miss Hungerford was young and engaged to marry a baronet.'

'What happened?' Alaric asked, still staring at the uneven shamble of roofs added piecemeal when the owners wanted more room for guests or family and what looked like a long gallery tacked on to the roof of the west wing when fashion dictated every house with any pretensions to grandeur should have one.

'He ran off with a serving wench and was never heard of again. It was the scandal of the county and the locals swear Miss Hungerford's father caught up with the rogue, ran him through in a fury then buried his body so deep in the woods nobody will ever find him.'

'And the maid?'

'I suppose she ran away,' the lawyer said as if it had never occurred to him to worry about a servant girl. 'A runaway maid would soon find work in a city and it is not far to Gloucester or Hereford or even Bristol from here. The locals claim to see Sir Edwin walk on moonless nights searching for his lover, but I do not know how they expect anyone to believe it when such darkness stops you seeing your own hand an inch in front of your face, let alone the wraith of a man who probably got clean away, then lived out his life in disguise to avoid Miss Hungerford's father's wrath. I expect the maid got old and ugly and he regretted losing all this place must have offered a man for a pretty face and a comfortable armful.'

The lawyer was clearly not a believer in the power of true love over rank and differences of fortune, even if he liked to tell an improbable tale. Alaric tried to block his ears to the man's chatter and assess the place as a possible home for himself and his family. Juno would like living anywhere that was not Stratford Park, its Dower House or Stratford House in London. And if only he could persuade her to marry him, would Marianne like this poor old place? She might relish the challenge of renewing and restoring an even more tumbledown house than her brother's equally ancient manor house was before she started. And yet... There was a forlorn air of old glories and future possibilities he felt guilty about turning his back on. If he ever managed to persuade the stubborn, challenging, extraordinary woman to let them both be happy, he would bring her here and let her make her own mind about it.

'Are there smugglers this far from the coast?' he asked as part of that story about ghosts walking rang true. Moonless nights would not betray signs the so-called Gentlemen were at work to the authorities, but they were a long way from the sea in this wild corner of Herefordshire nearly into the ancient mysteries of the Forest of Dean.

'The River Severn is tidal as far as Gloucester,' the man admitted cautiously so Alaric concluded he was right and the tale had been put about to keep the curious in bed on the darkest nights of the year.

'So an old tale of mayhem and haunting would be very useful to anyone with nefarious business in the dark,' he said, wondering if the house itself might be of use for storing cargoes since it was so forlorn and empty he doubted anyone had been employed to watch over it for a very long time. Smugglers to scout as well as spiders and vermin this time then, but if he could persuade Marianne to let them both be happy they could rid the poor old house of all its unwanted visitors and make it a perfect home for a hardworking country gentleman and his energetic lady.

'Indeed,' the lawyer said gloomily.

At least the man had fallen silent while Alaric worked through that reason for the old tale being embroidered and kept alive for such a purpose and they both brooded on the broken windows and tumbled slates of Prospect House as it sank into ruin. 'No,' Alaric said at last. 'I require a house and estate that needs hard work and dedication to get it all up to scratch and working well again, but this place has gone too far.'

It would not do to let the lawyer know he already felt angry the near-derelict old house had been allowed to get in such a state it was nearly too late to save it. He hoped to persuade Marianne to feel the same way about it as long as she would take him with it, of course. He could not live under the same roof as her one day longer and not let her and his niece and the rest of the world know he was in love with the woman. He had endured quite enough of being the honourable man and trying not to seduce his niece's companion was more than he could manage now he had spent three whole weeks riding about his native land pretending she was no more to him than any other ladylike companion for his niece might be and that he was not tortured by unsated need and yearning for her beside him in every bed he had slept in since the day he met her. She could either marry him or find another fool to drive to distraction with her stubborn temper and coolly challenging blue eyes.

He had borne weeks of it before he was wound up to such a pitch of wanting and needing her he knew he would break if he stayed with her and Juno on the road one day longer. For once it had been useful to be a lord with too many matters of business to neglect for much longer when he found an excuse to leave Juno with her and ride away. And at last that month was nearly up so she had best get ready to be thoroughly seduced by her former employer the moment he could bring that foolish contract to an end, if only she would finally admit they felt more for one another than a polite lord and Juno's companion should if they were to remain polite and companionly much longer.

'I will write to colleagues in nearby towns and see if they know of anything in the area,' the lawyer said with a last mournful look at the poor old house and a shrug as if he had done his best for it and it had been worth a try.

Luckily Alaric was looking for comfort and a house you could not lose half a regiment in without feeling crowded and this place could do very well. He was done with echoing glory and lonely staterooms; Stratford Park was far too uncomfortable and barn-like to live in day by day and he wanted far more from life than gilding and consequence and a marriage of convenience. This place was close enough to Owlet Manor to visit in a day and far enough away for them not to live in one another's pockets. And Chantry Old Hall was only twenty miles away as the crow flew, since crows could fly over water and that tidal River Severn was a significant barrier to humankind.

He suspected there was a lot more than employer and governess between Miss Yelverton and Harry Marbeck as well, but he would not lay odds on them reaching a happy ending. He sensed a troubled soul under Marbeck's determined pursuit of pleasure and deliberate provocation of the gossips, but if any female could tame him it was a Yelverton, so who knew? He was far more wrapped up in his own Yelverton female to even want to interfere and he hoped it was just a question of planning and hoping and not giving up on a very different dream than he thought he wanted before Juno went missing and his whole life seemed to collapse around him.

Chapter Seventeen

Marianne felt shaken and bewildered by the speed they had travelled since Juno received an invitation to spend a week or two with Miss Donne in Broadley and immediately wrote back accepting it and promising to be with her very shortly. The usually docile and obliging girl then insisted they travel as fast as they could go to get back to a place she had obviously been longing to be during this whole month of leisurely exploring this place and that.

So now here they were, back where they started. Marianne was not quite sure how she felt about being at Miss Donne's neat home where she had opened that lady's front door so unwarily that first memorable morning and found a travel-worn and exhausted viscount on the doorstep. Images of Alaric tense with exhaustion and worry and handsome as ten devils haunted her at the most inconvenient moments as it was. Being back in Broadley and visiting Owlet Manor without him when his presence there was imprinted on her memory as well would feel so bitter-sweet. He was hardly likely to come here when he knew Juno was safe and sound and happy with people she felt at ease with. Now he could go back to his old life and his fashionable and important friends and forget he had ever kissed a prickly woman who could not guard her tongue or her heart effectively whenever she was with him.

In a few months' time he would probably struggle to recall her name when they met to discuss Juno's next move and whether it was too soon to try and persuade his ward to try another London Season in the spring and hope for a much better outcome for her this time. Goodness, she was tired after all this travelling, though. She sighed and wondered what was wrong with her as she struggled to be glad Juno was so much happier now that her uncle obviously thought it was all right to leave her to carry on with her life without his constant presence.

Tiredness and a lack of spirits had dragged at Marianne ever since Alaric left them in Buxton. She looked back at the long days of work she had put into Owlet Manor before Darius married Fliss and sighed for the energy and single-minded verve of those first weeks and months at the dear old place, before life became complicated by love declared and fulfilled for her beloved brother and this unexpected and ridiculous love of hers for a man who probably did not want her anywhere near as much as she did him.

'Uncle Alaric!' Juno exclaimed as she stepped out

of the hired carriage ahead of Marianne and ran towards her uncle like an eager schoolgirl.

And it was true! Lord Stratford really had just
stepped out of the yard entrance to the Royal George
at Broadley and now he was striding forward to greet
his niece as if a magician conjured him up out of
Marianne's yearning thoughts and what the devil was
he doing here? Whatever it was she felt her heart race
and colour flush into her cheeks as she wondered if
she might be about to faint for the first time in her
life. The shock of seeing him so unexpectedly made
her feel light-headed and silly and then there was
this urgent need to forget the rest of the world and
run towards him and embrace him in such a very
public place as soon as Juno had finished with him.
The poor man would be horrified. Even the thought
of his face as he fended her off with a harassed expression sobered her.

But, oh, dear, he was handsome, though, wasn't
he? And strong and compelling as well and he made
the rest of the world fade to silence and never mind
the activity and noise all around them. She must be
standing here gawping at him like an open-mouthed
yokel. For a moment she dreamed of a fairy-tale
world where they were the only ones who mattered
to each other, until reality stepped back in and the
rest of the world was suddenly noisy and curious
and real again.

They were in a yard with horses and grooms and
ostlers busy all around them and even the odd curious face or two at the windows looking to see what

important personage had arrived this time in a luxurious carriage with outriders and mud-splashed and weary horses that said no expense had been spared in getting here as fast as possible. And Alaric was a lord and she was a lady's companion.

It was her own fault he had ordered himself to forget they had ever kissed one another as if they meant it, her doing. She had snapped and snarled at him so effectively he had treated her as an almost polite stranger from the moment they set out from Owlet Manor on this meandering journey to show Juno there was another world outside her schoolroom and the London ballrooms she had hated so much.

'Jojo!' he greeted the girl with a huge smile and a bear hug, then he swung her round as if she was light as a feather.

Marianne could not help but be impressed all over again by his strength, but why was he back in Broadley so soon when the *ton* must be on their way back to London to be brilliant and sophisticated and far more entertaining than they had time to be during the serious business of the spring Season and marrying off their daughters? Was he about to spirit Juno off to some elegant house party with his elegant friends and leave her here to wonder what to do next and mourn all the might-have-beens she could have had with him? She would miss the girl sorely and her new life as Juno's companion now she had come to know her so much better and value her as she deserved, but most of all she would miss him.

'Good day, my lord,' she said quietly as she stepped

down from the post-chaise in her turn and tried not
to feel breathless and elated at seeing him again. Her
heart was beating so loudly in her ears she was surprised he could not hear it from where he was standing.

'Mrs Turner,' he said warily. She wished she could
run into his arms, as sure of her welcome there as
Juno had been, but there was no chance of that and
she was seven and twenty and she did have her dignity to think about even if there had been. 'I trust
you had a good journey,' he added as if he was very
uncertain of his welcome as far as she was concerned
and that hint of nervousness made her heart threaten
to turn over with love for the annoying man right here
on the cobbles of this busy inn yard.

'Very good, I thank you. The weather was most
helpful for once,' she said stiffly instead of embarrassing him with a warmer greeting.

'Aye, the rain let up at exactly the right moment
for the roads to dry up and be easily passable. Have
you got everything you need out of the coach, Jojo?
It seems best to keep moving so you two do not
catch cold in this sharp wind, although the sun is
being kind to us today. The luggage will be brought
around to Miss Donne's house as soon as the horses
are safely stabled.'

'Indeed, and you can trust the grooms to take even
more care than usual with His Lordship's wrath to
look forward to if they drop anything,' Marianne
said.

'I can carry this bag myself,' Juno insisted.

Marianne was glad to see the stubborn set of her chin even if Lord Stratford eyed the small portmanteau as if he thought it looked too heavy for a lady to carry.

'If it means so much to have it with you, I will take it,' he insisted.

Marianne tried not to stare at the idea of a lord spoiling the effect of his expensively elegant clothes, beautifully cut greatcoat and fine beaver hat by carrying a rather feminine-looking bag in the hand that was not holding a gold-tipped cane she hoped he was now only carrying for show. She frowned as she looked back at him walking behind her and Juno as a gentleman should. She tried to see if he was still limping. If he was, then he must have overstretched his ankle too soon. She clicked her tongue in exasperation at his headlong determination to push his body to the limits, but he did seem to be moving freely, if you discounted the bag Juno could have had sent round later if she was not so eager to bring presents back from her travels for Miss Donne and even brusque and capable Bet.

'I cannot tell you how much I have missed your glower of censure, Mrs Turner,' Alaric told her with soft-voiced mockery, but did he think Juno had gone deaf in the last couple of weeks to tease her in front of his precious niece?

'Well, I have not missed yours,' she parried sharply, but what a thumping great lie that was.

She was surprised when he looked almost hurt for a brief moment before he covered it with a cynical smile. Surely she imagined that instant of vulnerability in his blue eyes before he raised his eyebrows and nodded at something in front of her to remind her she needed to look where she was going instead of gazing back at him.

She had managed to forget how clear and compelling a blue his gaze was while they were apart, she realised as she marched ahead of him with her nose in the air and she did not need to look at him to know what he was like. His eyes were the same colour as the lapis lazuli used to paint the Virgin's gown in an Italian master's painting she saw years ago in a local magnate's house and had never forgotten. There was a depth of colour and such skill and love in that painting and she could have stared at it all day if only the housekeeper who showed Reverend Yelverton and his family around her master's splendid house and wondrous possessions allowed more than a snatched five minutes in each room.

Now she wanted to gaze into Alaric's deeply blue eyes even more than she had longed to stand and stare at that reverend, breathtaking painting all those years ago. He was so alive and subtly masculine and beautiful in his own unique way. Even with that bag in his hand a part of her wanted to stand and gape at him admiringly. Shock, she decided, as she tried hard to bring the rest of the world back into focus and think about that instead. Soon they would have covered the short distance between the posting inn and Miss Donne's little town house and she would have to have her wits about her when she met that lady's shrewd gaze again.

'Oh, my dears, how lovely to see you all again,' Miss Donne greeted them on her own doorstep. At least the door was open before Alaric could knock on it this time to save Marianne the sharp memory of how she had first met those blue, blue eyes of his with all the impatience in the world looking back at her and a pinch of desperation to give away the truth under his exhaustion and bluster. 'Now come on inside and stop letting all the heat out. There is a cold wind blowing today, for all the sun is shining to welcome you back to Broadley.'

'I will leave you to settle in,' Alaric said as soon as he had handed her precious bag over to his niece and he turned to go back to the inn where he must be staying. Marianne wanted to argue and tell him of course he must stay and she had missed the sight and sound of him for far too long for him to disappear as soon as they got here, but it was not her house and certainly not her place to bid him stay or go.

'We will see you for dinner then, Lord Stratford,' Miss Donne said as if they had arranged a timetable between them that Marianne and Juno had no idea about, but might as well go along with.

Marianne decided the lady was even more formidable than she had thought she could be when she chose and had obviously chosen to discuss arrangements for their visit in general and tonight in particular before Marianne and Juno got here.

'Dinner?' Juno mused after she bade a hasty farewell to her uncle and shut the door behind him after one last hug to say both of them were delighted to be together again, even if they were not staying under the same roof.

'A meal I take at a more fashionable hour than most of my neighbours since I got used to dining late with the great and the good during my years of employment as a governess, Juno, my dear. So I suggest we have tea and some of Bet's excellent scones to stave off the hunger pangs after your journey as soon as you and Mrs Turner have taken off your outer clothing and washed your hands.'

'Marianne, not Mrs Turner,' Juno corrected and Miss Donne seemed to weigh that familiarity up and decide that, as Juno was not a schoolgirl now, it would do between a young lady and her companion, but not for her.

'You must allow an older and more old-fashioned soul like me to keep one or two formalities alive, Juno. I suspect I am several years older than Mrs Turner's mother and doubt that lady would approve of such informality between us.'

'I dare say not, but she seemed very stuffy to me and what she does not know about cannot hurt her,' Juno said and followed Marianne upstairs to the neat and sunny bedchamber she had inherited from Fliss.

Marianne hoped dinner would be more formal than usual and that Miss Donne had invited her friends to eat with such a grand gentleman. That way she would be able to fade into the background and he would hardly notice she was there among so much flutter and curiosity. So she told herself she was disappointed when she came downstairs to find only four covers set out on the dining-room table and they were obviously going to have a quiet evening together where conversation would be unavoidable. There was a feel of cosy intimacy about the room with the fire lit and several branches of fine wax candles waiting to lend a glow to highly polished furniture and immaculate tableware. So there would be no avoiding Alaric's perceptive gaze with so few people to hide behind.

She was not sure if she was glad or sorry that she had put on the silk-velvet gown Fliss and Miss Donne made for her in the summer now. The beauty of the fine stuff and the way her friends had made it drape elegantly over her slender figure meant it was a delight to wear and it was warmer and more fashionable than any of her muslin or cambric gowns. But it clung to her a little too lovingly whenever she moved. Tonight was going to be difficult enough without adding sensual awareness of her every move to the mixture, but it was too late to change her mind now.

'Ah, there you are, my dear,' Miss Donne said as she bustled in to inspect the table and twitch a few items of cutlery this way and that. 'That is much better,' she said as if a quarter of an inch here and there had made any difference. 'Flowers are the final touch we need to make it perfect, I think. Could you see to that while I help Bet with the roast duck, Mrs Turner?' she requested with a vague gesture at the two fine vases on the pier table before she went out again.

Not relishing handling the beautiful little porcelain vessels or risking making a mark on the highly polished mahogany, Marianne lifted the finely made things very carefully. She dared not trust herself with them in the busy kitchen, but made her way out of the French doors Miss Donne had put in to get to her garden without going through the rest of the house. There was a welcome feeling of peace in the twilit garden, although she was very glad of the fine cashmere shawl Darius and Fliss had presented her with when she left Owlet Manor for her present position. She carefully put the vases down on the one bare deal table in Miss Donne's neat greenhouse and found the scissors the lady used for flowers easily enough. At least it had not rained for several days now, so her most delicate evening slippers would not get wet and be ruined.

Peering around the garden and trying to recall what was where from earlier in the year, she frowned and wondered how she was going to fill even those delicately exquisite little vases with flowers in early October. Luckily there were a few late blooms on Miss Donne's precious Bourbon and China roses and a spray or two of Michaelmas daisies. Finding some fine leaves just beginning to colour for autumn and a few sprays of rich red and orange berries Marianne began to relax and even hummed a tune to herself while she snipped stems to the right length and stripped off leaves and matched this against that until she was happy with the result. Yes, that would do nicely, she decided as she stood back to admire her handiwork. Just as well that she had neither flowers nor a vase in her hand when she finally realised Lord Stratford was watching her from the deepening shadows of the autumn garden, though.

'How you made me jump,' she accused him as he came to the doorway of the glasshouse as if he might as well admit he was here now and had been so for some time until she finally noticed him.

'At least an inch by my estimation,' he told her unrepentantly. 'You were so absorbed in your creations that half the peers in the House of Lords could have been parading through the flower beds and you would not have noticed them.'

'I think I might have,' she answered him with a smile and a chuckle for the picture he had put in her head of a troop of peers dressed in velvet and ermine and wearing their coronets as if for a state occasion as they filed through Miss Donne's precious garden in solemn but puzzled lines.

'I wish you would do that more often,' he said and because he had smiled back and come a lot closer she was not quite sure what they had been talking about any more.

'Arrange flowers?'

'No, laugh and hum under your breath and forget to be grave and responsible for a while.'

'I have to be, it is my job to be serious and take care of your niece.'

'Not with Miss Donne in the house and me to take

my duty to Juno seriously for once in her life. Sometimes I see the bright, fearless and courageous girl you must have been when you met your Daniel under all that grief and responsibility you have learnt since, Mrs Turner, and I envy him like the devil.'

'He is dead,' she said bleakly and it did still feel bleak, even with this swirl of high excitement inside her making her breath come short and her heartbeat race like a mad March hare simply because Alaric was so close once again and she had missed him so very badly.

'I would never try to take him away from you because I am jealous he knew the young and reckless girl you must have been back then and I did not,' he said in a low growl of a voice that told her he was being very serious indeed. 'You are who you are because you loved him and lost him before we met and I would not change that part of you even if I could.'

'You would not?'

'No, why would I want to, I…l…' His voice tailed off as if he recalled where they were and he was obviously uncertain how she felt about him. 'I like you very well as you are,' he substituted for the word her ears had been so eager to hear and never mind all those resolutions she had made while they were apart to treat him as her lordly employer and Juno's uncle in future.

'Like?' she still said recklessly.

'Definitely,' he said with a warm and almost lazy smile as he bent his head to kiss her as if he was tired of words and not quite being able to say what he really meant.

'I like you, too,' she echoed incoherently, then nuzzled closer to his firm mouth after snatching enough breath to go on with. Ah, this was what she had been missing so dearly it felt as if she was only going through the motions every day she had had to live without him. Now she was greedy for his kisses and his nearness and his l—whatever that was.

His mouth was warm on hers and his hands felt like heaven as he explored her curves through silk velvet. Even his finely made evening gloves only made his touch seem all the more fascinating through them and the silken caress of her gown with him on the other side of it. She wriggled a little closer and pouted kisses against his mouth to ask why he would not let her right inside and do the same for her. She heard his breath speed up, felt him tremble like a finely bred racehorse under her urgent, reckless touch and hoped he was satisfied to see that sensual Marianne was alive and very present after all. He was definitely not satisfied, she realised smugly as she slid her leg between his and felt how very far he was from that state for herself.

'Not here, Marianne, and probably not now,' he told her raggedly and tried hard to step back from her and the danger they would be very impolite indeed in Miss Donne's greenhouse if they did not put a little distance between them.

'When and where, then?' she insisted on asking

wantonly as the little distance he had managed to put between them chilled her like midwinter.

'On our wedding night and in our own bed, if I have my way,' she thought she heard him murmur, but that had to be wrong.

Her mind was providing her with the words it wanted to hear out of her feverish need for him and his stubborn refusal to be less than noble about it, she told herself, as she stared up at him as if he had stuck a knife in her instead of maybe murmured something like a proposal of marriage. She shook her head to clear it of air dreams and nonsense. 'Now I am hearing things as well,' she muttered to herself as she felt him draw away and every part of her hated to let him go.

'Did I remember to dismiss you as of yesterday when you finally got here, Marianne?' he asked her huskily.

'Why? What have I done wrong?'

'Nothing yet and we did agree on a month's trial, did we not?'

'Yes, but...'

'But nothing, that month was up yesterday and never have thirty days seemed to tick by so wretchedly slow it felt as if every one of them was a month in its own right. So now you can consider yourself unemployed and free of any obligation to keep Juno company in future unless you do so out of the goodness of your heart, Mrs Turner.'

'I did not think I was doing so very badly at looking after your niece,' she said and now it was being taken from her she realised how much she had enjoyed getting to know the young woman she had spent so much time with lately and what on earth was she going to do with herself instead now she did not suit her noble employer?

'That has nothing to do with it,' he told her with a hunted look as if he was being asked to explain something very difficult indeed. 'Harry Marbeck is a gentleman,' he said at last and she could not hide a smile at his look of frustration as if even he knew he was being an idiot.

'So you told me when he brought my sister to Darius and Fliss's wedding.'

'Precisely and I believe I also told you he would not seduce a lady in his employment simply because he is one at heart, whatever the gossips say about him,' he said and at last she understood what he was trying so hard not to tell her and she had a struggle not to laugh. Or maybe even sing out loud, or jump up and down with glee because apparently he wanted to seduce her after all and she felt exactly the same way about him.

'Hence your abrupt termination of my employment, I suppose?' she said to help him out, although how on earth he thought he was going to be able to seduce her with Miss Donne as her fierce chaperone she had no idea, but her heart was still singing at the very idea.

'It has been a very long month.'

She looked a question at him and wondered about the potential for making love in a glasshouse. She glanced about at the scrubbed-out pots and tin labels and a few sleepy plants on the edge of an autumn sleep and above all so much glass to make them visible to anyone who cared to look out of an upstairs window or out of a back door and decided not; it was a highly unlikely trysting place. They would be far too obvious from the house and probably to one or two of Miss Donne's neighbours as well, if they realised what was going on down here and trooped up to their attics to peer down at a scandalous lord and a far-too-willing lady.

'And I am going to marry you,' he insisted as if primed for an argument and getting his best one in first.

'No, you are not,' she told him emphatically and backed away as if he had insulted her. 'No, no, no, you are most definitely not going to do anything of the sort, Viscount Stratford,' she added just in case he had not understood her the first time.

'No wedding, no bedding,' he drawled with knowledge of the fiery heat that was coursing through her like wildfire in his smile and probably in his eyes as well if only she could see them clearly enough in the rapidly falling dusk that made her worries about them being seen out here less relevant.

Drat the man, but he knew perfectly well what he had done to her and he probably only kissed her in the first place to remind her how he could set her senses alight with one intent look and as for an actual kiss... Well, his kisses ought to be classified as dangerous weapons. 'I am never going to marry you, my lord,' she told him with an emphatic shake of the head that would probably do terrible damage to the topknot of honey curls softened by a few cunningly escaped ringlets Bet had wound it into to go with the finery of Marianne's best velvet gown. 'You are who you are and I am who I am and I did not become pregnant during five years of marriage, so of course it would be too much of a risk to take with your vast possessions and title if you were to marry me.'

'You are a gentleman's daughter and the widow of a hero who died to preserve the liberty of his country, but I am only a man who had a title, riches and possessions landed on him at seventeen. I did nothing to deserve or win it all, it merely dropped into my lap. Juno running away made me look hard at what matters in life and she is one who does, but I soon realised you do even more, Marianne. Once I crashed at your feet like a fool and learned to see people as they really are I woke up to all the possibilities of a love match with you and felt like a complete idiot for ever thinking a marriage of convenience with the new Mrs Yelverton would be enough for either her or me. You have taught me how to love and I am daring to hope I can teach you to love me back if I keep on telling you how dearly you matter to me and how mistaken you would be to turn your back on us simply for the sake of a boy we might or might not give birth to between us and a title I do not care about.'

'I doubt you were the shallow fool you painted yourself even before Juno ran away,' she protested with the glow of all that love in his words and the light in his dear eyes she could still see in the twilight and never mind colours or daylight. She wanted to stare back and give in and accept everything they could be to one another, if only she dared believe she could be this lucky twice in one lifetime and he really would not long for a son. 'And I do wish you would stop chastising yourself for past sins only you seem to worry about now,' she added, simply to stop herself eagerly saying yes to him and all that lovely promise for the future.

'Finished?' he asked and even in the gloom she could see he had raised his eyebrows at her, as if he had worked that out for himself.

'No, it is a ridiculous idea and we should both forget you ever mentioned it.'

'I certainly will not.'

'Then you should. I can forget you said it so we can be easy again together over tonight and you will thank me for it when you come to your senses.'

'I am not a boy, Marianne,' he told her with a fearsome frown and he clasped his hands together as if he was afraid he might have to shake her for pretending he was anything less than a set and determined adult if he did not. He certainly looked set and determined on getting his own way.

'I can tell,' she admitted with a half-smile for his gruffness and the strength of the warmth and affection that bound them together as well as this constant sizzle of attraction she had cursed from the very beginning of their acquaintance. Even as she longed to be in his arms again and agreeing to anything he wanted them to be if only he would make love to her, she made herself curse it some more and told herself she could walk away from him even now.

'Stop treating me as if I am an immature fool who does not know his own mind. I love you and I intend to marry you and nobody else.'

'You love me?' she asked and gaped up at him like a fool. Even as she gasped out that almost unthinkable question warmth ran through her like quicksilver and all the cold and lonely places Daniel left her when he died suddenly felt full of light and air again. He had said he cared about her and there was that stumble over the like word, but she had not dared to hope he actually loved her. She let the wonder of it lift her up and make her feel new again and met his gaze with all she felt for him in her own dazed eyes and never mind if they could see each other clearly or not in the ever-increasing darkness. She even stepped forward, ready to walk into his arms before she remembered why she could not and would not marry him. 'But I am *barren*,' she reminded them both bleakly as if he might not have taken all the implications of that sad fact in even now.

The empty feel of that stark word reminded her how it felt not to be with child month after month, year after year. She had longed for Daniel's child because she loved him so much it would have been wonderful to make a baby between them. He would have been a fine father as well, patient and full of fun, but stern when he had to be.

And his children would be growing up without

him even now, Marianne, her sensible inner self reminded her.

They would have to live their whole lives with only vague memories of his strength and feeling secure and loved by their father and that would have been so very sad for them and for her as well. She still regretted the lack of a single one of them to say she and their father loved one another through thick and thin and that love would always live on in his children. With Alaric that lack would become monstrous because of all he had to pass on to a son and she could not endure even the thought of him coming to hate his childless marriage.

'I really and truly do not care, Marianne,' said Alaric Defford, Lord Stratford, with one of those mighty shrugs of his to say why on earth would he?

'I do, though,' she told him flatly and knew she was being unreasonable, but the memory of those miserable days when her courses returned relentlessly month after month was not easy to blot out of her mind and make her listen to reason.

'Why?'

'Because you have a title and great wealth and probably more than one fine estate to hand on to your eldest son,' she fudged because she did not want him to see the pain her childlessness had caused her during her marriage to Daniel, just as she used to guard Daniel from it at the time.

'Not good enough for me, Marianne. You must come up with a better reason to avoid me as a husband than that one. If I could be rid of my title, I would do it tomorrow. It bent me out of shape and made me look at life from the wrong side of the mirror and now it is standing between you and me. How could I even want a son of mine to be landed with something that could twist him into a man he should not be, Marianne? If there is no obscure Defford branch that fell away from the family tree many years ago to inherit my title and entailed land, then Juno's children can petition for it if they choose to. Best to let the whole vainglory die with me, but if they want it they are welcome.'

'You ought to be a father just for the joy of being one.'

'There are plenty of children out there in need of one. I thought on my way here that first time, before I had even met you, there are so many runaways without a frantic uncle on their tails desperate to see them safe and happy. We can adopt a few of them in time and offer sanctuary to more, but for now I would be content for it to be you and me and Juno until we can relax into love and be ready for our children to find us.'

'No. We are not going to be together, so how can they, my lord?' she said, almost more cross with herself for persisting in her doubts than she was with him for being high-handed.

'Now that is just plain selfish of you, Mrs Turner. Think of all the urchins who will never have you for a mother and don't you pity them for having just me instead? I will make a poor fist of things without you to put me right—just look at the mistakes I made with Juno.'

'You really mean to do this, then? Are you sure it is not a scheme you thought up to make me feel better about marrying you since I probably cannot have children?'

'Of course I do—did you ever know me to sit on my hands and only think about doing something that was crying out to be done?'

'Well, no, but I have only known you for a while.'

'It only took me a day and a half to wake up and see you were the only woman I have ever met I truly want to spend the rest of my life with.'

'So you thought up your idea for adopting orphans on the way here and made up your mind you were going to marry me when you were lying in bed battered and bruised and out of your senses? It sounds like a fairy story to me.'

'Yes. I wanted you from the moment I first set eyes on you, Marianne Turner, and at least landing on my head that day must have knocked some sense in because I know this is real and unique and true, even if you are being your usual stubborn and impatient self and are refusing to believe me.'

'And given how impatient you are…' She let her voice trail off suggestively, hoping it would suggest he got on with seducing her so she could find a way to persuade him being his mistress would be enough for her. Then maybe she could convince herself because hope was tugging away at her stubborn certainty she would not be enough for him as soon as the glow of loving passionately and even wildly wore off.

'I have been learning patience from the first moment I set eyes on you, so that fish won't bite,' he warned her with too much knowledge of what she had been planning in his mocking smile. 'I am a fully mature male, Mrs Turner, not a rampant boy to be led around by his cock.'

'As if I would and I hope you will never say such things in front of Juno.'

'Of course not and, before you ask, I will not be so forthright in front of the children either. I shall save that for you, my stubborn and unruly lady.'

'I have not said I will marry you.'

'Not yet.'

'Not at all.'

'Not yet,' he insisted with such intent in his eyes she did not need to see the colour of them, just the glint of stubborn determination and rampant need in them even in the dark. The 'yes' he seemed to want so badly trembled on her lips.

'Can you actually see any flowers in all this gloom, Mrs Turner?' Miss Donne's voice called out to remind her the rest of the world was still turning.

'You can carry one of the vases as a punishment for distracting me when I ought to have been helping,' Marianne murmured with a secret sigh of relief.

'For you, my love, anything and please do not think you have put me off with your brusque orders and severe looks because I rather like them now I know how much spice and sensuality is hidden underneath them. This is only the beginning and I will convince you I will only ever marry you. Even if I have to camp out on Miss Donne's doorstep and make you a scandal and a hissing in the town until you agree to marry me just to make me go away, I will do it.'

He would as well, she decided with a smile for the picture he had painted her and the heady hope love might truly be enough for a viscount and a widow if they believed in it enough. 'We shall see' was all she said to let him know how tempted she was to simply give in and enjoy them for the rest of her life.

For the rest of the evening they both tried to behave like polite acquaintances and eat their dinner because Miss Donne and Bet had gone to so much trouble to welcome them home. She could not have said what they ate if the fate of nations depended on it, though.

'Goodnight, sweet princess,' Alaric whispered in her ear as Miss Donne ordered Marianne to show him out while she resolved some mythical crisis in the kitchen so they could whisper at her front door once again and what a matchmaker outwardly prim and proper Miss Donne really was.

'Go away, you annoying viscount, you,' she told him as the feel of his mouth so close to her ear sent shivers of sensuous anticipation through her and made her ravenous for more. He was going to kiss it, on Miss Donne's doorstep with glimmers of light all around the square to make them visible to her neighbours. Ah, no, he was not going to kiss her. Disappointment ran a race with that fire inside her and won. 'You ought to know better,' she told them both. His low rumble of laughter sent even more shivers of frustration and need through her and she glared at him this time.

'Ah, but I know best,' he murmured and kissed her hand instead of her cheek as she had been thinking he might. Apparently hands were every bit as sensitive as the soft skin near her ear could be, if only he would linger there instead.

'Someone will see us,' she hissed and might have snatched her hand away if it was not so comfortable in his large one that her fingers seemed to have entwined with his without the rest of her giving permission.

'They will have to find out I am in love with you sooner or later, so why not now?' he said as if it was as simple as that and if only it was.

'Because nothing can come of it.'

'Do you call this nothing, Marianne?' he asked, suddenly very serious indeed as their eyes met in all that faint borrowed light from other people's lamps and lanterns. He held up their interlocked hands, brushed the index finger of his other hand over her overheated cheek that was still waiting for his kiss. His eyes held a challenge now as well as so much warmth that she could not even summon up a shiver for the whisper of winter to come behind the gentler autumn night.

'No, I call it impossible,' she said just as seriously and felt that chill after all.

'Where there is enough love there is no such thing as impossible. You should know that better than anyone, Mrs Turner,' he said with a hint of bitterness in his deep voice because she was giving him less than she had Daniel.

'And my late husband would tell you I am the most stubborn female he ever came across if he was able to. If you think my Daniel had an easy time of it with me either before or after I was his wife, you had best think again, Lord Stratford.'

'I envy him never knowing which way you might jump, not being able to expect anything but the unexpected from you, but most of all I envy him the faith and love you had in him when you set out to marry him and never mind any obstacles between you.'

'And it took me six months to admit I could not live without him and not miss what we might have been every day for the rest of our lives. I did not know then what I know now or it might have been a lot longer.'

'I will never expect you to forget him, Marianne,' he said gently, as if the news of that six months had soothed something raw inside him and made him feel better about the effort it was costing him to persuade her in his turn. 'I am jealous of him, I admit that, but I do not want to jostle him aside and demand all the love you have solely for me. You loved one another for five years, my darling. I honour him for the good life you two made together in circumstances that would have made most ladies run screaming for their mothers.'

'At least I can safely promise I will not do that,' she said and saw triumph glint back at her as she realised it had sounded like a promise for their future. 'No, that was only a perhaps. Stop trying to rush me.'

'As if I could when you must be the most stubborn and overprotective woman on earth,' he said rather sulkily. That glimpse of the boy he once was being just plain difficult because he could not get his way made her love him more instead of less.

She was in even more trouble now. So much of her longed to launch herself at him and revel in his lovemaking that a world of warmth and love and sensuality in his powerful arms felt tantalisingly close. Love meant putting your beloved's happiness first and however much he wanted her now, would he still do so as the years went past and all his roles demanded children to carry them on? And he should have a wife the world respected as his equal, not a vicar's daughter who had managed to marry beneath her before she netted herself a viscount.

'You must know I have feelings for you. I do not see how you could escape knowing it when I virtually threw myself at you earlier this evening, but I am about as unsuitable a viscountess as you could find.'

'You have obviously not looked hard enough, then. You are a respectable widow, love, not a housemaid or a courtesan. We lords and even the odd duke here and there have always married women the world thought we should not and yet the world keeps turning and the aristocracy is still in its accustomed place and love is all that matters in the end.'

'Maybe, but we can stand here arguing black is white all night long and you still will not convince me I am viscountess material, my lord. Now kindly go away and let me go to bed. You have obviously been here for days winning over my friends and laying all sorts of devious plans for my undoing, but I have had a long journey and I am weary from it and about to lose my temper.'

'Heaven forbid,' he said with such a rueful smile inviting her to laugh that she felt her heart melting another degree.

'Go away,' she demanded and turned her head away to hide the answering smile that might give her away as a lot less certain she wanted him to than she had managed to sound.

'For now,' he answered and used their entwined hands to pull her much closer and snatch an unguarded kiss from her lips almost out here in the street.

It was so brief and hot and unsatisfying that she pouted and shot him a look of reproach, but he just grinned a wildcat grin, raised his hat in a mocking salute and walked away from her with that confounded cane of his swinging triumphantly at his side to say he was rather proud of his evening's work, never mind her 'no' and 'maybes'. And he had every right to be, she conceded with the heat and sting of not enough kisses still on her sulky lips. Oh, drat the man, how the devil did he expect her to sleep a wink tonight with all this hot wanting and doubt and fascination for him and his magnificent body and uniquely handsome face and all the things about him that made her love him churning about in her head?

Chapter Eighteen

'So what do you think of the poor old place, Marianne?' For once Alaric sounded uncertain, as if a lot more depended on her answer than it ought to.

'Someone should be very ashamed at the state of it. Even my Great-Uncle Hubert kept the roof repaired and windows mended, although that was about all he did do when he was master of Owlet Manor for the last fifty years of his life.'

'I know it is in a very poor state, but roofs can be mended and windows replaced. Could you live here, do you think?'

'Is any of it habitable?' she said suspiciously, because they had only set out on a drive today and he was even more devious than she thought he was now he was presenting her with a potential home rather than a picturesque view.

'That depends on how high your standards are,' he said evasively.

Marianne could tell he had fallen in love with

the place since he had evaded her perfectly sensible question. She looked down at the derelict old house and the wild wood that had grown up around it since a gardener last came anywhere near the place. It was the perfect site for a manor house, just large enough to be a comfortable family home, if only it had a comfortable family living in it. What it could be, whispered a plea for someone to rescue it from ruin. The man was cunning, though, presenting her with a challenge like this one. With splendid views across the Severn Plain from up here and the sheltering hollow where the house was set out of the worst of the winds that would whistle up the Bristol Channel, she would need a heart of stone not to be tempted by its forlorn air of waiting for them to make things right again.

'I think we can safely say my standards are not high after some of the billets Daniel and I endured on the march, but what about you, my lord? Could you put up with the howling draughts and leaking roofs there must be in such a place while the builders repaired and redesigned the place for modern living around you, or would you visit the place occasionally until all the work was done and live in splendour at Stratford Park?'

'I would hire a house with proper windows and a roof nearby and be comfortable while I kept an eye on those builders and made sure it was all done as we wanted it. You would not have me leave them to it, would you?'

'No,' she said carefully, knowing he was expecting her to demand her say in how it would all be done and not quite ready to fall into his trap just yet. 'But why do you even want another house? Don't you have enough already?'

'I have more than I know what to do with, but this one would be yours. I know you secretly long for a home from some of the things Juno has said in her letters and my own incredible powers of observation. I want you to have one where only you can say who goes and stays and what is repaired and what replaced. I admit that I came here looking for a home where Juno could be happy if you washed your hands of both of us and walked away, but I knew as soon as I saw it that this place should be yours and somehow I would have to persuade you to let me share it with you. And if anything ever happens to me I want you to have a home that will always be yours to do with as you please.'

'Why would anything happen to you, Alaric? And how do you think I could endure living here without you? People make homes, not stones and timbers and leaky roofs.'

'My brother died when he was five and twenty, so I know I cannot promise I will live until I am ninety and die at the same moment you do, Marianne, but I have no intention of going anywhere without you if I can help it.'

'Good,' she said and her heart missed a beat as she thought about the uncertainty of life and he was right, it was all a risk, but so few things in life that were worth having came without a bundle of those.

She loved him so fiercely and truly and did not want him to think he had won her over with a house. It was important he would always know that he came before any of the riches and wonders he could shower on her and Juno and any other family they managed to make along the way. 'You have fallen in love with this poor old house, haven't you?' she said suspiciously.

And there was his shamefaced look he wore when he was trying to hide his deepest feelings and at least she recognised it now. She hid a smile when he decided they needed to take a closer look at the place to disguise his discomfort at being found out so easily. She was very glad of the warm rugs over their knees and the not-quite-so-hot brick at her feet he had provided to keep the chilly autumn air at bay as best he could.

He had surprised her by driving up to Miss Donne's house this morning in his beautifully sprung curricle and demanding her company and please to hurry before his precious pair of perfectly matched Welsh greys caught a cold. Now Alaric looped the long tail of his driving whip neatly after giving the high-stepping pair the signal to risk the first part of the drive to this forlorn old house so she could take a closer look.

'It needs someone to love it before it falls down,' he finally admitted when the ruts in the overgrown lane made it criminal to risk his horses' legs further by trying to get even closer, so he halted them again.

'It might take a lot of effort to keep on loving it at times,' she cautioned. 'Most people you ask to come and repair it will advise you to have it pulled down and build something modern and convenient in its place.'

'Would you?'

'No, but I must be as totty-headed as you are because I would rather restore it and add a few modern touches to make it easier to live in.'

'Such as?'

'I need to see more before I am able to tell you that.'

'Then we might as well go in and take a look,' he said and heaved a vast bundle of huge keys out of the boot as the tiger shook out the rugs that had been folded up in there to cover the horses. 'Walk them for me to save them from a chill, will you, Portman?' he asked the wizened little man who had not said a word in Marianne's hearing all the way here and just nodded and went to croon at his precious horses now.

'You have already bought this sad old house, have you not?' Marianne asked when Alaric offered her his free arm, since the other one was fully occupied with that ring full of ancient and heavy-looking keys.

'I thought it would make a fine place for our orphans,' he admitted with a slightly hunted look as she gave him a sceptical look, but still took his arm, because there were so many potholes in the unkempt drive it would have been foolish not to.

'Your orphans,' she corrected him nevertheless.

'Don't you like the idea of them learning to be happy here and growing up in the fresh air and sunshine?'

'Of course I do. I am not sure what the locals will think if they are unruly as some of the children who used to trail along with the army on the march.'

'There you are, you see, I shall need you to keep order.'

'I doubt it, Lord Stratford,' she told him severely, but she was warming to the scheme he seemed so set on carrying out whether she agreed to marry him or not and he knew it. 'Now stop prevaricating and let me see inside.'

'It is very bad,' Alaric admitted half an hour later and even he looked doubtful now. 'Perhaps those builders you told me about earlier are right. It could be better to pull it down and begin again.'

'I think the kitchen will have to be rebuilt before any self-respecting cook will agree to cook as much as an egg in there and you are right—and the east wing is beyond repair, but the rest seems possible. There are even more cobwebs and several tons more dust in here than there were at Owlet Manor when I got there, but most of the timbers seem sound and even where the rain has got in they can be renewed or replaced once the roof is mended.'

'And there are details it would be a shame to throw away, like the grand staircase and all this fine oak panelling. I am not sure I want to sleep in a state bed as vast as the one in the best bedchamber—I might lose you of a night.'

'You have not got me to lose yet,' she reminded him, but she was weakening and had just gone another step closer to giving in. She could feel him being a little bit smug and a lot more impatient again for her final 'yes' to Lord and Lady Stratford and their tumbledown old folly of a house.

'There is all the world yet to gain then,' he said with a pretend sigh. 'How I wish there was even one room here clean enough to seduce you in and bend you to my wicked ways with hot kisses and a great deal more,' he said with a serious question in his wary expression as he looked down at her this time.

'So do I,' she answered it quite seriously.

'And your brother has finally taken his wife on a bride journey, now all his crops are in and they have a new farm manager in place to make sure there is at least some cider left when they come home.'

'So he has,' Marianne said dreamily.

'And I have wanted to find out how far this place is from Owlet Manor ever since I first discovered it so that you will not feel cut off from your family when we live here.'

'Do not push your luck, my lord.'

'But, of course, there is the problem that without the prospect of a wedding there can be no bedding for us,' he said virtuously.

'You know how much you want me,' she said and it was not vain of her to point that fact out, it was purely practical. She was so deep in love and longing and needing him now it felt like a fever in her blood.

'I do, but I also know how much you want me, Mrs Turner.'

'Do not remind me,' she murmured and tried to

blank out the gnaw of frustrated need burning at the centre of her that was threatening to become a wild-fire blown out of control as he stared back at her with one of his own in his brilliantly blue eyes.

'I will use any means I can to persuade you into my bed and my arms and my life for good, Marianne. Otherwise we will both have to burn and we know whose fault that is. I might run mad and look what you will have done then.'

'I…' Marianne let her voice tail off because she could not think of any reason strong enough to keep this raging need at bay any longer. The burn of un-sated need deep within her and the sting of wanting and not having was sapping her rational mind and he had already turned her set-in-stone determination not to marry him into a whole flock of 'maybes' and 'yes, I will.' 'I am burning, I am so hungry for you I cannot lie about it any longer and you are right and I do love you, Alaric. But how can we make it for good when we are so very different in so many ways?'

'Because love matters and wherever and whenever it comes along it should not be ignored and pushed aside. You loved Sergeant Daniel Turner so finely and recklessly and so well, why would you make a second love with me into something less, Marianne? I honour the man for having the sense to love you so completely, but you two were supposed to be di-vided by birth and education and goodness knows how many other barriers, but you demolished them all between you. Am I so much less of a man you will not do the same for love of me?'

There was all the doubt he was a good man with a true heart in his eyes now and it was her fault. She had met the real man under the title when he was laid low by his head injury and still stinging from Juno's rejection. And now he had Marianne Yelverton-Turner to make him feel unwanted and uncertain of his many and far-too-plentiful attractions, he did not need his mother to reject and belittle him, did he? She hated herself for putting those doubts back in his clear blue gaze again and found her courage at long last.

'No, you are a wonderful man, Alaric. Strong, loving and true and your brother would be so proud of the man you are now, but how can I ever live up to your high standards if I agree to marry you?'

'If you ask me, the boot is on the other foot.'

'I do love you,' she admitted, 'and it has nothing to do with this poor forlorn old house before you get carried away by the idea I would only agree to marry you to get my hands on it. I wanted you from the instant I met your bloodshot eyes through the gap in Miss Donne's door. I knew I would have to want the instant I found out who you really were, but that did not mean you were not the unshaven pirate baron who stole my heart when I thought I did not even have one left to steal.'

'And I wanted you just as instantly, my fierce Mrs Turner, and never mind the exhaustion dragging at my heels and the driving need to find Juno and make sure she was safe. I did not know you liked unshaven pirates, by the way. I shall have to work a lot harder on some sea-dog ways.'

'Please do not. I doubt the world could cope with you rampaging around it, stealing cargoes and kidnapping lady pirates to carry off to your lair.'

'My, you do have an exotic imagination.'

'I do,' she told him with a silly, besotted smile as a good many of her fantasies offering a future of wild lovemaking could be hers if only she could reach out and grasp it and forget all her doubts that it was the right thing to do. 'What if you regret me in a few years' time, Alaric?' she asked very seriously as she pushed those tempting scenarios aside for a maybe later.

'Did you ask Turner that when you packed your bag and stole out of your father's vicarage with the dawn to find him and marry him, Marianne?'

'No.'

'Then why are you asking me to put a limit on my love for you? I will still love and need and desire you when I am in my dotage. Right now I am not quite sure which will come first, having you in my life and finally admitting we cannot live without one another or reaching my dotage before you will finally say "yes" to me.'

'I am ready to right now,' she told him, certainty that he was right exploding all her scruples at last. 'I love you so much I have to believe we can cross off all the items on my list of why we should not marry, Alaric. I will love you until my dying day.'

'Then will you marry me?' he said and got down

on both his knees, on this filthy floor inside this broken-down old house. 'I love you beyond words and promises, Marianne, but please will you help me to remake Viscount Stratford and be my love and my wife as long as we both shall live?'

'You had better do a lot of it, then,' she told him acerbically. 'I am not losing another love for life and having to spend mine without you, so you had better make up your mind to living with me for a very long time, Alaric, Lord Stratford.'

'Is that a "yes"?' he asked her, a world of hopes and dreams naked in his eyes along with a full measure of lust and a side dish of fantasy to add to the mix.

'Of course it is, you silly viscount. Now will you finally get up and kiss me properly before I faint from pure need on this very dirty floor.'

'Not yet,' he replied tensely as he got to his feet and stood a frustrating few yards away from her.

'Why not?'

'Because I am not stopping once I have started and we have already established there is nowhere in this poor old wreck of a house fit for us to make love for the first time in the very long love affair we are about to begin.'

'How fast can those horses of yours go, Alaric?' she asked with a world of hot need opening out in front of her and an urgent desire for everything she had fantasised about him coming true as soon as they could get to a clean house with a clean bed in it.

'Since I will not have you slammed about and

bruised as we tear around corners and bounce over potholes, you are not about to find out.'

'Then perhaps an inn…?' She let her voice trail off as the suggestion lit even more fires in his already hot-blue gaze. 'Your tiger would know what we were about, of course, but I really am beyond caring. I want you so much, Alaric.'

'And do you really think he is going to tell anyone? The man only speaks to horses with the occasional grunt for me if he is in a particularly good mood.'

'He does seem taciturn.'

'He is and, even if he was the best gossip in England, I do not care who knows I love you to the edge of reason and I cannot keep my hands off you for very much longer.'

'Well, that is very good news as far as I am concerned since I feel the same way about you, but fine words butter no parsnips, my lord. Action is what is needed right now.'

'I agree,' he said and they could hardly fumble the ancient great lock on the front door back into place fast enough before they joined hands and ran carefully down the wild grass at the side of the drive because they might be in love and desperate to prove it to one another, but Lord Stratford had spent enough time laid up with damaged limbs and a broken head lately.

Chapter Nineteen

They did manage to contain themselves by maintaining a tight-lipped silence all the way back to Owlet Manor, but by the time they got there they were very glad to hand the curricle and horses over to the uncommunicative little man who had been sitting up behind them for miles frowning over their heads at his precious horses.

'Hurry,' Marianne urged Alaric when he would have stopped to say something polite and gentlemanly to Fliss's new housemaids.

'Now they will gossip,' he said as they ran up the familiar stairs to the quaint old bedchamber Marianne had fallen in love with on her first day at Owlet Manor. It seemed fitting that the first place that had felt like home since she left her father's old vicarage would be the place where she first made love to her future lord and true lover.

'Let them, I do not care,' she gasped, tugging him in through the door of the room as she took a quick look around it in the fast fading light and realised Fliss had not changed a thing in here. It did still feel hers and she hoped Fliss would forgive her for this intrusion into her new domain. Marianne rather thought she would once she had explained there were no convenient shepherd's huts on their way here and this was her first time with the man she loved, so it deserved to be private as well as special from one end to the other.

'I do not expect you to love your Daniel less because you love me as well, Marianne,' Alaric managed to tell her huskily despite the frantic need she had sensed him barely holding under control for miles as he drove with almost too much care so he did not take unnecessary risks with her safety.

'Thank you,' she said sincerely and put her cold fingers against his even colder face and held them there to warm them both and because she did love him so much she wanted to touch him and warm him and show him how lovable he really was and how very, very strong and manly and kind and—

Just get on with it, Marianne; love the man before you both faint from frustration.

'But love is generous, my darling, so there is enough of it in my heart for both of you and I shall never love *you* less because I love him as well.'

'I am not sure I can give you gentle, though, and you deserve it,' he told her unsteadily.

'Do not put curbs on us, Alaric. However much you try to reason it into a corner and control it we want each other quite shamelessly.'

'That does not mean we cannot have tenderness as well as passion,' he said stubbornly and covered her hands where they still cupped his face and stared down into her eyes with his loving, lingering touch against her skin. 'Love,' he said with wonder still in his eyes.

'Yes.'

'I want you so much my eyes are crossing,' he told her and she stood on tiptoes for a closer look and nodded sagely at him to say so they were and the closer she looked the more hers were as well.

'Time to stop talking, then,' she said practically and raised her mouth for his kiss and to get him to give her the use of her hands back, so she could touch and hold and encourage him as he did the same for her. It was the lovely loving connection of it all that made her gasp and her body sing as they fell on one another with a hunger that had been too long building to be slow or carefully seductive now. Fire and fierce passion and that streak of tenderness under it all that he had promised them seemed to draw something wondrous out of them as they fell on each other and reached higher and faster than it felt they had ever been before. She fell back to earth with a sob for the loss of that ecstatic, languorous place they had just claimed as their own for the first time. It was the lovely, fiery, intimate connection of it all that thrummed through them like a force of nature as they lay together in the bed they had finally found the strength to climb into and count their racing heartbeats back to earth as breath came softer and kisses even more honeyed.

'Oh, goodness!' Viola gasped as she caught the wedding bouquet Marianne cunningly aimed at her almost by accident. Viola stared down at the posy of white camellias and dried lavender flowers and dark green and fragrant myrtle leaves. 'Typical of you two,' she said as she sniffed the herbs and stroked the velvety petals and refused to blush at the speculation in their mother's eyes.

'What? A mix of homespun and exotic?' Marianne said as she met Alaric's eyes and forgot what they were talking about at the leap of masculine interest in there for that intriguing idea. *Pirate Alaric*, she mouthed with an encouraging smile.

'No, an ideal combination for a Christmas wedding,' and Viola's voice reminded Marianne this was a doubly serious occasion with a roll of her eyes at their ridiculous preoccupation with one another.

'Or any other time of year,' Alaric told his bride of a few minutes and kissed her as if he could not help himself now they had got started on loving one another for life.

'Stop it, you two, and kindly get inside that fine carriage and let yourselves be driven up to the house so the rest of us can get warm again,' Darius told them gruffly from his place just behind the bride and groom with Fliss at his side trying not to laugh at him for playing gruff lord of the manor.

'Take no notice of him,' Fliss advised the newly

married couple. 'Having a viscount in the family seems to have gone to his head.'

'Hmm, he is not the only one, then,' Viola murmured as the sound of Mrs Yelverton condescending to Miss Donne even more than usual reached them even at the church door.

What might have spoiled a lesser day passed Marianne by on this very special one and she thought Miss Donne could cope with far sterner foes than the proud mother of the bride. With Alaric's strong hand in hers and his almost boyish delight in their simple country wedding, even her mother's love of a title seemed amusing rather than embarrassing, today anyway. So she ran out to the waiting carriage at Alaric's side and was glad when it was on its way because once they were out of it and inside it could go back for her father so that he could be got out of the cold as soon as possible and hopefully breathe more easily in the seat by the fire Fliss had saved for him.

'I love you, Husband,' Marianne said with an infatuated sigh. She had to love him even more for taking such care to get her father here by even shorter stages than last time so he would not get quite so cold and might not wheeze so badly in the damp December air.

'And I love you, Lady Stratford.'

'Let's not talk about her today, I am too happy to worry about high and mighty peeresses like her right now.'

'You are one all the same and I still love you.'

'Best not adore me too much, Alaric, I might become an idol and develop feet of clay.'

'Remind me to make a list of all your faults and read them out to you once a month then—that ought to keep you humble.'

'If you like the feel of sleeping in an empty bed each night of it, then you go right ahead and do so, my lord.'

'That I do not. It was far too empty while you were making up your mind whether to love me or not for me to risk that much loneliness ever again.'

'I had no choice but loving you when it came down to it. I could not forget you from the moment I first set eyes on you.'

'Ah, yes, pirates—I wonder if my valet has remembered to pack my cutlass.'

'The poor man would give in his notice if you asked him for one of those and you are more likely to need a hammer and chisel where we are going.'

'It will not be a very romantic place to spend our honeymoon,' Alaric said almost as if he regretted the leisurely journey to somewhere more exotic they could have had when they were about to move into the hastily refurbished Agent's House at Prospect Manor instead.

'I think it will be the perfect place for one,' Marianne said with the busyness and bustle they would stir up there making it seem the ideal way to spend the first days of their marriage. 'Far better than us flitting about from mansion to mansion as you introduce me to your friends and neighbours. I doubt they will want to know me and I am not looking forward to meeting them.'

'Stop it, love, you are as good as any of them and better than a good many.'

Seeing it really did disturb him to hear her worry what his friends would think of her, she tried to push her anxiety aside. No, it would not do. 'We cannot keep our worries quiet from one another, Alaric. We must learn to share them so they do not push us apart.'

'Very well, then, as soon as I manage to convince you I have the finest and most desirable viscountess in the land we shall take a tour of my lordly obligations and show everyone why I insisted on marrying you despite your dogged opposition to the idea. It will not help Juno realise there are good people at every level of our society if you refuse to believe it yourself.'

'I did not think of that,' Marianne said with a frown. 'I suppose I must learn to act the great lady after all, then.'

'No need to act, you are one already. I know our tenants and neighbours will breathe a sigh of relief and welcome you with open arms after so many decades of regal indifference to their needs and hopes from my mother.'

'She has a lot to answer for,' Marianne said sternly as the carriage reached the front door of Owlet Manor only moments after it set out from the church.

'Never mind her now, this is the best day of my

life so far and I am not going to spoil it by picking over old griefs and sorrows. Yours are different.'

'You mean Daniel?'

'Of course.'

'If there was a way of doing it, he would dance at our wedding today, Alaric. He truly loved me and would have hated to see me so haunted and miserable and grief-stricken as I was for so long after I got back to England and until the day I met you, if I am being strictly truthful. You are the very man he would have picked out for me because you are the best man I have ever met apart from him. I will never forget him, but that does not mean I cannot love you every bit as much as I loved him.'

Marianne felt as if this conversation was even more important than the vows they had made one another in front of God and their nearest and dearest, if that was possible. 'I love you so much, Alaric. I thought it was impossible for a woman to be lucky enough to love with all her heart twice in one lifetime, but you have proved to me how wrong I was.'

'You have all of my heart, Marianne. I never thought I could love like this at all, so just look what you have taught me,' Alaric said and they kissed under the ball of mistletoe and bright ribbons the servants must have placed there once the wedding party set out for the tiny church. Breathless and excited and looking forward to loving this man in every sense of the word once again and as soon as they could get some privacy and a bed to celebrate it in, Marianne felt the earth spin under her feet and the stars shift in their spheres. Alaric kissed her with such passion she wondered if it was possible to be driven out of your senses by love and desire and they could have been anywhere, at any time of year, for all she could feel of the lazy December wind and an overcast sky that said there might be snow in it somewhere or more probably rain what with this being England and the weather likely to change from hour to hour.

'Oh, for goodness' sake,' Darius interrupted them who knew how many minutes later as the next carriage rumbled up to the door and swept around the newly laid carriage sweep with a flourish. 'At least get inside out of the cold so we can get on with the Christmas feast you have promised us, Stratford. My sister will take to her bed with the influenza instead of the reason you want her there if you do not stop kissing one another soon and get inside.'

'Very well, Papa,' Marianne said mockingly and was astonished to see her brother blush for the first time since they were children. 'You are not, are you?' she asked him and when he only stood there on his own carriage sweep looking like a boy caught out in mischief she looked to Fliss for an answer instead.

'I told him it was to be our secret until after today, but sometimes he is such a boy I cannot rely on him to keep a still tongue in his head,' her sister-in-law scolded her large and mature husband and Marianne could see him turning to mush in front of her eyes. He was going to be such a wonderful father and if this happened to be a little girl she could just imagine him being wound around her little finger the second she was born.

'But that is such wonderful news you should not have kept it quiet for our sake.'

'No, this is your day. We had ours…um…' Fliss stopped as if remembering a bit too much of that night when she and Darius first made love up in the hills the day Juno went missing and shortly before Lord Stratford knocked at Miss Donne's door and demanded to see Fliss. 'In August,' Fliss finished bravely, although it remained to be seen if their babe might give away exactly when that day was or if he or she arrived a tactful nine months after Fliss and Darius's wedding.

'I am so pleased for you both,' Marianne said and truly meant it. She felt Alaric's anxiety for her hearing such news when they were never likely to have their own child as he wrapped a strong arm round her waist and pulled her closer. 'I have all I want right here,' she told him softly and forgot family and guests all over again. 'And there are those runaways and urchins to look forward to taking in if you truly do not mind your title going to waste one day.'

'Good riddance to it,' he said and kissed her again because it was a shame to waste a good kissing bough.

'You will wear it out,' Darius said with a push to get them inside and out of the cold at long last, then he made thorough use of it himself before pulling a blushing, laughing, flustered Fliss inside after him so they could make way for more soberly happy wedding guests who eyed the kissing bough with either suspicion or nostalgia, then sped inside unkissed rather than risk getting cold.

'Your brother is a rogue,' Alaric told Marianne between welcoming their guests and at least Mrs Yelverton was too much in awe of him to try and push her way in front of him as she had with Fliss and Darius at their wedding.

'I know, but Juno would never have come to Broadley if she was not looking for Fliss and I would never have discovered you unkempt and arrogant on the doorstep this summer. So we owe one another to Fliss, if not my brother.'

'Then he can say what he likes since I never want to imagine my life without you in it ever again,' he murmured between handshakes and smiles for these people they loved enough to invite to their very select wedding.

'Neither do I,' Marianne agreed and once again Lord and Lady Stratford proved what an unconventional pair they were by kissing one another in full view of their guests as if they could not help themselves and they really could not so they kept on doing it until the bride's brother ordered them into the dining room and made them sit on opposite sides of the groaning table in order to make them at least pay lip service to the proprieties.

'What a scandalous couple we are, love,' Alaric told her across all the pies and roast this and that and enough left over to feed everyone for miles around, just as he intended when he sent for it all.

'I love you,' she replied, 'so much that it probably is scandalous, but I don't care.'

'Nor me,' he said and after that the wedding breakfast of my Lord and Lady Stratford had to manage without them, so it was just as well most of their guests were more amused than offended by the scant attention they paid to their own nuptial feast.

'Wedding breakfast in bed, now there's a novelty,' Alaric told his wife some time later when he brought in the tray Fliss had ordered left outside their room until they were hungry, if still not feeling very sociable.

'I love experiencing new things since I met you,' Marianne told him with a siren smile and they made a very stimulating meal of it, eventually.

* * * * *

A WEDDING FOR THE SCANDALOUS HEIRESS

Chapter One

You're three and twenty, Isabella Alstone, and far too old to hide in the dark. You should stay in the ballroom and pretend to be happy, not creep out here as if you're planning to steal the silver.

Isabella was tired of being the perfect lady, though, so she stripped off her gloves and waved them in front of her overheated face, ignoring the voice of her conscience. It was hot even outside on this sultry late summer night and she wasn't going back until she was cooler, calmer and more resigned… No, not more resigned, more collected. Yet promises so logical and right when voiced to a friend seemed strange and wrong now and how could she be calm about that?

'Now, why is a lady of quality lurking in the shadows with the likes of me? Better go back to being belle of the ball instead of getting caught out here in bad company.'

The voice from the shadows startled Isabella from her reverie. The sound of his velvet-and-darkness voice told her he was right, but she was in the mood to be reckless.

'Why?' she demanded, peering into the gloom to try to see through the shadows.

His gruffly masculine voice had a pleasing hint of danger along the edge of it she shouldn't want to know more about, but she had left safe, respectable Isabella inside and it was wonderful to be a different person altogether for a few stolen moments. She could be the sort of female who'd dive into wild encounters in the dark, as if she was put on this earth to be foolish and bold with the first rake she stumbled on in the shadows. Her fantasy of being a brash and sophisticated lady who took what she wanted from life and laughed at the future, as if it wasn't heading towards her at the speed of a runaway horse, was too alluring to turn her back on just yet.

'Because I'm here,' the mysterious voice explained, as if that was all she needed to know to send her running. She stayed exactly where she was, refusing to scuttle inside like a scared rabbit, and heard him sigh, as if he couldn't believe how stupid she was not to listen and do as she was bid.

'You're no debutante, so the Bond Street Beaux must have told you how beautiful you are by now and that will make everything worse if we're caught in the moonlight together.'

He stepped forward so the light from the few hundred wax candles could illuminate his face and form and show her how right he was. With a face too much his to match any ideal of classical perfection, he wasn't the most handsome man Isabella had seen. He wasn't the tallest or broadest or most obviously powerful male she had ever met either. Of course, he *was* leanly fit and quietly muscular as well as deeply, darkly intense. *And* uniquely formed to make her shiver in her dancing slippers with an unexpected and delicious anticipation of something she'd hardly dared think about until now and usually shuddered away from when she saw that feral light in other men's eyes. Only seconds ago she'd been hot and weary and now she felt so alive there could be air and stardust under her feet instead of solid York stone. If this was how being irresponsible felt, it certainly topped being her usual sensible and reasoned self.

'I haven't the faintest idea who you are, so if you're trying to scare me, it's not working. Although you're right about one thing,' she said as lightly as she could when the world seemed to have stopped and they were the only two people left moving. 'I have been out for a long time now and know false flattery when I hear it.'

'I don't flatter, Mrs…' he shot a steely gaze at her ring finger '…apologies, Miss, and there's no need to pretend to be middle-aged,' he said with a wry smile that did hot and disturbing things to her insides. 'We'll both be old soon enough.'

'We will?' she echoed in a breathy whisper that must have given him doubts about that maturity, but she did *feel* like a giddy girl when he took her gently by the arm and urged her further into darkness and away from the pool of golden candlelight spilling out of a ballroom that now seemed almost as remote from her as the Arctic.

'Will someone come dashing out to find you any moment now, ready to usher you away?' he asked with a smile, but she felt a tension in his sleekly powerful body that made her frown briefly.

'No,' she told him like a silly debutante desperate to be ruined by a rogue. 'My family trusts me to behave,' she added with a late tilt at sophistication and a flutter in her heartbeat that suggested they shouldn't tonight.

'They don't consider the basic needs of the human heart often enough, then, or, in my case, even baser masculine ones you're better not to know about until you really are a Mrs Belle,' he replied with a cynical thread in his voice that made her frown for another sensible, bone-jarring moment before the darkness and scent from some exotic hothouse flower nearby wafted it clean away.

'So you're not to be trusted?' she heard herself ask like the fledgling idiot she'd never allowed herself to be in polite society.

Nobody was ever going to lure *her* in with showy good looks, false promises of love and passion, and heady nights like this one. She remembered her eldest sister, Miranda, falling for evil, charming Nevin Braxton at seventeen and all the horror her elopement and ruin had brought down on her family's lives too well for that. Isabella had shuddered away from rakes as if their kisses would poison her ever since. This man hadn't flattered and flirted and fawned on her, though. He seemed to see beyond her golden looks, exquisitely fashioned gown and neat figure and was speaking to the real Isabella.

And out here she could forget what was waiting for her inside the hot room only feet away. On this terrace with the scent of exotic flowers heavy in the air, only now mattered. Just enough light shone from the ballroom for her to see his eyes were ice blue and hot at the same time. Her breath stuttered when he pulled her further from the lights of the party and the glow of a waxing moon gave them a world of their own.

'You should not trust me, Belle. I'm dangerous,' he said almost seriously. 'I'm a wolf in wolf's clothing,' he added as if he believed it.

'It's not full,' she told him and sensed his bewilderment. 'The moon,' she explained with a nod towards it where it seemed almost touchable, on the horizon, 'so you can't claim the moon made you do it.'

'Do what?'

'Kiss me,' she heard herself say rashly. A sane part of her was so shocked it was as if it flopped down on to the stone bench nearby and sat there with its mouth open.

'Oh? And why would you let me do that, Belle? Perhaps you're as wild as I am,' he murmured, suddenly closer than she remembered.

She should run, dash back into the familiar noise and heat and glitter of a *ton*nish ballroom, and find the nearest respectable female to chaperon her. Instead she stayed as if her feet were rooted into the still-warm stones under their feet. She could touch and taste him if she stayed, hear the urgent saw of breath he'd been holding too long. Moonlight fell on high cheekbones and dark, dark hair springing almost to disarray despite all his efforts to tame it. The hint of a frown at his dark eyebrows told her a goodly part of him thought he ought to fight this basic, gut-deep attraction as well. But there was enough light for the sensual curve of his mouth to betray the fact urgency and passion were getting the upper hand even without her exploring touch and silent encouragement to get on and kiss her and to hell with the real world.

'I think you're right,' she whispered as she padded her fingertips against his tense jaw, feeling how it clenched and suspecting it was taking everything in him not to fall on her like the wolf he claimed to be.

But reason gave way to madness and suddenly she was in his arms. This was the kiss that would bring Isabella Penelope Alstone fully to life. The one she'd been so secretly waiting for since the day she began to be a woman. She hadn't even let herself know she wanted it until now. His mouth fitted lushly against her eager lips and he felt so familiar against her. He murmured something as if he agreed with her unspoken thoughts and she opened her mouth to say *Yes, please*, but he dipped his tongue inside first, as if he had to know more, had to know everything now she was here at last. She was melting from the outside in, or should that be the inside out? Heat beat through her in time with his hurried breaths and the dart of his gently exploring tongue, as if he knew she'd never felt passion like this before and it was a shock that echoed through them both.

Yes, *there* was the shake of novelty and wonder in his fingers as he danced them across her cheekbone and down to outline her chin as if he was learning her with every sense he had. Never before had she been tempted to burrow into a man's arms, to try to become a part of him by melding her heat with his, her mouth with his. For a minute reality threatened to pull her back and her mind told her body to flinch away, but the alluring stranger snatched all her attention back by sliding his wickedly exploring tongue over her lower lip, deepening the kiss.

She shifted even closer and copied his exploration. His cheek and jaw felt so firm under her touch and her fingers were intrigued by the contrast between her own softer features and his hawkish ones. She could feel the suggestion of his beard despite a careful shave and she spared a moment to scent the clean, sharp smell of soap and something tangy used to take the sting of the blade away when a gentleman was making himself civilised and smooth for the company of ladies.

Real life threatened to jump in again, but she told it to go away and muttered something encouraging instead. Nothing in reality could beat a meeting outside time and all the rules of polite society. Her heart beat so fast and her breath demanded air while plea-

sure and hope and a big, wide *yes* to life and this
stranger and all he could be opened up inside her.
She was shivering like a thoroughbred and rode a
tide of heat more intense and deep and demanding
than anything she'd ever felt before. There were no
words to describe how right it felt when he pulled her
closer to show her what she was doing to him. She
felt the tension of deep desire in his rigidly muscular
form. This was the carnal, primal need that carried
men and women to places they'd never intended to
go to when they started an evening not even knowing one another.

Instead of flinching back and telling him, no,
they couldn't go any further down that road when
they didn't even know one another's real names, she
pushed her curious hands under his unbuttoned evening coat and gave a pleased little grunt at the feel of
a hot, needy and intriguingly muscular male under
her exploring touch. Her fingers soothed the tight
muscles at the base of his spine, whispered inquisi-
tively downwards, desperate to know the difference
between his spare male flanks and her own sleekly
feminine curves. He gasped as if she'd stung him,
then sucked in breath as if he might need more if she
was going to carry on, so she did. She could feel his
muscles shift and soothe, then tense again as she explored the sparseness of his buttocks and the honed,
pared-down line where they met long, strong legs.
Her own legs wobbled and almost let her down as
their stance thrust his unmistakably eager manhood
emphatically against her.

This was what uncontrollable desire felt like. This was how a woman felt when she was desperate for the man she loved to take her somewhere magical. That old taboo, that stark little four-lettered word sounded like a death knell in a corner of her mind, but she was moon-mad and curious enough to ignore it for a little longer. It put a hiccup in her sigh, though, a caveat in her exploration even as she buried a gasp of awe and need against his shoulder, then stood on tiptoe so that every bit of her felt it knew every bit of him.

But they didn't, they couldn't; not with so many sharp eyes and curious minds dangerously close by. She felt him stand a little straighter, pulling back his leanly powerful shoulders so he stood more sceptically apart from her as she burrowed against the warmth and strength and certainty of him and tried to hold on to this moment for a little while longer. If she let go, she'd have to see what she'd done and what she ought to have been doing instead. Ever since she'd given in to impulse for once and stepped outside the stuffy ballroom behind them, the way her life was planned out from now on was weightless in the balance against this rebellious encounter under the stars. Let him go and that weight would tumble back and she would end up more wrong than she had ever been in her life.

As she stood in the stronghold of his arms, trying to hold the real world at bay for as long as she could, voices started to disturb the fog of her mind.

'Isabella can't be out here,' she heard Magnus

Haile's voice say in the vast, close distance between his world and the one she and the stranger and the moon inhabited.

Now just a few yards away his voice sounded pacifying with forced casualness. She stiffened and felt her fellow moon-led simpleton do the same. Magnus must be with his father for him to sound like that. The Earl of Carrowe was a despot with his family, but so sleekly charming in the polite world the stark difference between public and private man still took Isabella's breath away.

'Where is she, then? Get your engagement puffed off so I don't end up in the sponging house or have duns to breakfast. You have shilly-shallied for far too long, so you find her before her upstart brother-in-law withdraws his consent or I'll spill your secrets.'

'She's of age and so am I. We need no consent,' the Honourable Magnus Haile asserted uncomfortably, as if he was trying to remind himself that he and Isabella were two free and unencumbered adults.

Even as she stood in another man's arms and felt him go rigid before he let her go as if she'd suddenly grown horns and a tail, Isabella frowned at the flatness in Magnus's usually pleasant tenor voice. He had spent last Season courting her so half-heartedly it took her until the end of it to notice. Then he had asked his fateful question and it shocked her even now to recall she had agreed. They were *friends*, she reassured herself. They would run in harness well together and she had never met anyone who made her heart race or her inner wanton melt with greed and heady desire. Until tonight. When it was too late.

Isabella stepped cautiously away from her stranger; stiff as he was now reason had rushed back in. A sluggish breeze stirred the sticky heat and fluttered her pale gown as space opened up between them.

The Earl of Carrowe pushed his protesting second son aside and stepped away from the pool of candlelight. Still as a statue now, Isabella froze and held her breath. This familiar stranger standing so stiffly next to her felt remote and withdrawn as an iron statue. She desperately hoped the night was deep enough for the Earl not to see them standing here like guilty lovers. Who would have thought a man she never laid eyes on until tonight could show her Isabella the Undone? All in the space between the ballroom and here and now.

'You don't need consent, you need a pitchfork up your...' the Earl said in the coarse manner he saved for his family. Or at least those who depended on him for a leaky roof over their heads. Here at Haile Carr he had to hide his true self or risk the fury of his wealthy daughter-in-law and her even wealthier father.

'You'll keep a still tongue in your head about my future wife if you want me to go through with this marriage.' Magnus sounded as austere as a monk and halted his father's trail of obscenities in their tracks.

Isabella stifled a hum of sympathy as she felt the weight of real life settling back on her shoulders. It felt even more of a burden now than when she had first decided to share Magnus's responsibilities. They weren't in love, but she never wanted to be in love anyway. Love was a trap and an illusion, nothing like the fairy-tale emotion three-decker romances portrayed. Isabella had agreed to Magnus's proposal for one reason—to get him and his sisters out from under the Earl's thumb—to give her best male friend outside her family a chance to be free of the monster she had heard bully and even beat his children. She had had no idea until a visit to the Haile ladies showed her the insults and foul language of the real man under the Earl of Carrowe's urbane outer shell. The Countess had hidden Isabella's presence and even took her out down the backstairs so the Earl wouldn't know she had been there. From that moment on she was filled with a passionate desire to help the Earl's daughters and Magnus had given her a chance to do it, so she took it and him and told herself all would be well because she didn't want to be in love with her husband anyway.

Except it felt as if they had missed something vital out. Isabella had been restless and hot and uncomfortable in her own skin in the ballroom and bolted outside to get away from what she'd done with her eyes wide open. And look where that had got her; she'd taken light in the arms of a stranger and now had to live with the memory of it on her conscience while she pretended to be Magnus's glowingly happy bride-to-be.

'Renege on our deal and I'll tell the world what you did last year and who you did it with,' the Earl threatened Magnus as if he couldn't bear to be bested by another son after his heir married a rich woman and got control of his own purse strings. The atmosphere in the ballroom had felt oppressive with Viscount Haile and his wife holding court while family tensions simmered just below the surface. Or maybe she was making excuses for her own bad behaviour.

But what did Magnus do last summer? A couple of times since she arrived here Isabella had sensed something was deeply wrong with Magnus. It felt as if she knew only half of what was going on. Their engagement was supposed to be a surprise that would make this annual party even happier, but it didn't feel very joyous to Isabella. Her money and family power were pitted against the Earl's extravagant self-indulgence and his cruel grip on his family. He'd traded control of his unwed daughters for part of her fortune; Magnus would save his sisters and Isabella could start the family she longed for. But then she arrived here and the reality of marrying the man who'd been her friend since she made her debut finally hit home. To make those babies they would be intimate together and it felt like a giant factor she left out of her calculations about marrying for sense and companionship. Much as she liked Magnus she wasn't sure she wanted to couple with him. She was a country girl at heart and three and twenty; she knew enough about the mechanics of marriage to shiver at the very idea of the one she'd committed herself to while she stood so close to a man who had nearly taught her a lot more than she needed to know about how a man and a woman were together when they wanted each other so urgently they couldn't even wait for a bed.

'You need money too much to risk Isabella jilting me,' Magnus was arguing now and she felt the man at her side wince.

Not for her sake, she sensed, or for the Earl's. So he must be on Magnus's side. She could feel fury arcing across the few bare inches of late summer air between them. The shame of her own betrayal was bad enough—the wrong she'd done Magnus with this stranger. So what about him? He was furious with her, but fairness whispered he hadn't deserved to kiss another man's affianced bride as if she was free as air, then find out how wrong he was before their lips were cool from kissing. Even more guilt twisted in her belly and finally saw off the wanton Isabella who still longed for more from a lover and never mind who he was and who he wasn't.

'No, damn you, I need all that gelt to keep the duns at bay,' the Earl was saying now. 'You find the wench so we can announce the engagement before all the local clodhoppers go home.'

'I'll see if Isabella is mending a flounce or visiting the ladies' withdrawing room, because she's clearly not out here. You shouldn't judge her by your low standards. Not everyone has your genius for sin.'

'Speaking of sinners, where's your mother?'

'Maybe she's with her prospective daughter-in-law, avoiding you.'

The string of obscenities that greeted that provocation faded as father and son turned to go back inside. Isabella wasted a few moments wondering how quickly the Earl could put on the mask of genial host after his unpleasant tirade. No doubt it would be plausible as ever by the time he was back in the crowded ballroom that she now dreaded so deeply she would almost prefer to stay out here with a furious male of a very different kind than re-enter it and face the future.

'I presume you know your fiancé's mother, Miss Alstone?' he asked coldly.

She shivered despite the sticky heat that hit her again now the magic of the moonlit night had flown. 'How do you know my...?' she began, then her voice trailed off when he turned to face her.

'Who else but you would skulk on the terrace at Haile Carr, trying to avoid her fiancé in the arms of a stranger? Who else did I come here to see and maybe even steel myself to meet?'

'I don't know, but why *are* you here?'

He grasped her arms as if she was the last person he really wanted to touch and walked her towards the pool of golden light on the still-warm stones. Her gaze ran over his hawkish features and heat and excitement flashed through her once again, but there was such fury in his uncannily light blue eyes it suffocated.

'Can you see it now?' he demanded roughly, shaking her a little when she stayed silent. 'The mark of Cain you have put on me tonight,' he bit out and the rage and guilt beneath his bitter words felt formidable.

For another cowardly moment she let her gaze linger on features that seemed uniquely his. Eyes clear and pale and steely blue, yet so alive and passionate even the fury in them seemed better than the cold aloofness he was striving for. Eyebrows and wild curls so dark above his icy gaze that looked so hard now. His features were so strongly marked and masculine she couldn't sort them from a softer, more blurred version that nagged at her memory.

'The Countess, you're Lady Carrowe's...' Yet again she let her voice tail off as if she was an incoherent and bedazzled debutante. Even the thought of being so silly and unguarded made her stiffen her spine and meet his eyes as if it didn't cost such an effort. She felt sweat bead her brow. 'Youngest son,' she ended, because she knew who he was and still refused to name-call over one thing that certainly wasn't his fault.

'Say it, Miss Alstone,' he ordered with weary impatience. 'I'm my mother's publicly denounced shame since the day I had the bad taste to be born alive. I'm the cuckoo in the Earl of Carrowe's nest; Lady Carrowe's disgrace; destroyer of innocent ladies' reputations and all the names they call me if I'm stupid enough to enter a room full of your kind. And what about you, Miss Alstone? You're Magnus Haile's affianced wife and far more of a disgrace than my mother ever was in private. She married a monster and you're about to wed his very opposite; you have no excuse for luring in a lover before you even marry my big brother.'

'That's between us and none of your business,' she said coolly.

'Tell him about this and I'll tell the whole world

what you did tonight. Dare whisper a word to hurt him and I'll make sure the world finds out what we've done.'

'You can't ruin me,' she defied him and knew it was cheap to invite him to throw mud at the Earl of Carnwood's youngest sister-in-law if he dared.

'Wulf FitzDevelin may not get past generations of rank and privilege and be-damned-to-the-rest-of-you, but Dev can do it with a few flicks of his pen and a lampoon from a scurrilous friend who owes him a favour.'

'You're him; a famous writer? That Dev?' she said, incredulous he was the scourge of liars and hypocrites and fools she'd found so irresistibly funny when he wasn't directing his fury at her.

His more usual style of showing the folly and misfortune of his fellow man took his writing beyond satire. She admired his compassion and delight in ordinary and extraordinary people of great cities and small places alike. In his mind she probably qualified as liar, hypocrite and fool. That idea added a layer of sadness to her guilt she didn't want to think about right now.

'Luckily for me there's no law to stop a bastard being a writer or vice versa. And I thought I was so cynical nothing could shock me, but you proved me wrong tonight, Miss Alstone; I hope you're proud.'

'Not really,' she made herself say as if she was thinking about something more important than a trifling sin she could take to church with her on Sunday and come away with a feeling of absolution.

'Mention this aberration to my brother and I'll not only deny every word and ruin you, I'll take your family and friends down with you.'

'Don't threaten me,' she flared back at him, even as fear for those she loved and wanted to protect flared fiercely in her heart and hurt more bitterly because he was the one trying to put it there. 'Nobody will rule me or mine with fear or beatings or nasty little lies ever again,' an Isabella even she hadn't known was so furious about her childhood spat like a cornered tigress. 'Stay away from me and mine and your brother as well,' she went on in a forceful whisper for fear of being overheard. 'I'll do what I can for your half-sisters, Mr Wulf, as long as you're not glowering at me from the sidelines as if I'm the She-Wolf of France and Lucrezia Borgia rolled up together.'

'Your namesake the Queen Isabella, so-called She-Wolf of France?' he taunted her.

'A poor choice of words doesn't change facts.'

'I doubt you worry very much about them at the best of times, miss. Luckily for you I haven't the stomach to stay here and watch you promise to wed my brother as if you're worthy of even a single hair on his head.'

'You love him, don't you? All those stories about you being heartless and impervious to love and affection are more of Lord Carrowe's lies,' she said, so shaken by the fact the notorious Wulf FitzDevelin had turned out to be nothing like the man he'd been painted she forgot she was the one doing battle with him right now.

'I feel very cold and resistant to you, and if you don't hurry back inside, your undeserved reputation as a cool and lovely lady of fortune will be blasted for good. I'd be the first to dance on her grave, but Magnus wouldn't like it.'

'I certainly won't risk notoriety for the sake of someone who thinks he can threaten all I hold dear because I was stupid.'

'Stupid? A little more than that, Miss Alstone,' he said with such revulsion in his voice she decided to let him have the last word, since he liked them so much.

She gave him one last challenging look to dare him to do his worst, then turned her back. He was a mirage—a wonder that turned out nothing of the kind. Magnus and his sisters and her own loving family were real; they mattered. She used her memory of the ballroom's layout and decorations to sneak back inside unnoticed. She would get her breath back and confess to nodding off in a quiet corner from exhaustion and nerves. Yes, she could put Isabella Alstone back together and even look glowingly happy when her engagement to a good man was announced. Just a few more moments away from the stares and speculation of the cream of local society and she'd be able to playact with the best of them.

Chapter Two

Six months later Isabella wished she couldn't remember that night of rebellion as if it was only moments ago. She watched her very pregnant middle sister walk towards her like a ship in full sail and did her best to swap prickly memories for here and now.

'Are you hiding up here because you think it's the last place anyone will look, Izzie?'

'If I was, it clearly hasn't worked and, no, I'm not hiding,' she lied concisely when Kate reached her. The need to find peace felt urgent after all these weeks and months of turmoil, so here she was on the top floor of the newest part of Viscount Shuttleworth's grand and sprawling mansion, watching the spring landscape below and trying not to think.

'That's your story,' Kate said sceptically. 'I never believed them when you were the baby of the family and a sweet smile and tall tale got what you wanted nine times out of ten, and I don't believe you now.'

'Well, I'm not a baby anymore, so stop thwarting

me for the good of my soul and trust me to know my own mind.'

'You're my little sister, Izzie, and trying to pretend all's well with your world when it obviously isn't won't work. I can tell how sad and confused you are about whatever has happened between you and Magnus these last few months while I've been stuck in the country like a cow out at pasture. Don't shut me out, love; I'm on your side whether you want me there or not.'

'You wouldn't leave me alone even if I wanted you to, so it's as well I don't,' Isabella joked, then sobered when she saw genuine hurt in her sister's eyes. 'I know how lucky I am to have a lionhearted older sister like you, Kate. When we were little and Miranda eloped, then Jack died, you protected me like a lioness. You must have been so sad and lost yourself, but you somehow forced our aunt and cousin to stop beating and bullying me until I was as silent and cowed as Magnus's poor little sister Theodora. I'm sorry it cost you so much to keep me safe, but you have a family of your own to spoil and protect now, my Lady Shuttleworth, and I can take care of myself. I'm sad about the end of my betrothal to Magnus, but I expect I'll get over it soon enough.'

'I don't think you will,' Kate argued as if wistfulness and guilt were written all over Isabella's face and she really hoped they weren't. 'And you were quite right to put an end to it if you didn't love him.'

'Although you're the worst-tempered and most infuriating sister I have, Katie darling, you're loyal to a fault,' Isabella tried to joke; because she had a sore heart and conscience she didn't want Kate to know about. And she did love Magnus, just not in the way a wife should love her husband.

'You only have two sisters.'

'Exactly.'

'Hmmm, I know when I'm being led away from a subject, so trying to make me angry won't work. I'm not as gentle as Miranda is most of the time, but I can control my temper when you're not around to goad it. And you should humour me, since I'm in a *very* interesting condition,' Kate said with a rueful rub of her swollen belly.

'You'd hate it if I did.'

'True, but I might secretly be flattered you wanted to cosset me so badly you held that clever tongue of yours for once in your life.'

'You don't need flattering. You and Edmund have a lovely little daughter and a new baby on the way. No doubt all three of you will spoil him or her to the edge of reason the moment they are born and what does anyone else's opinion matter when you're the centre of their world?'

'I love them so much I pinch myself to make sure this is really happening at times, but you're my little sister, Izzie. I couldn't *not* care about you while there's breath in my body, and, come to think of it, even if I was dead, I doubt I'd be able to stop loving you.'

'Oh, Kate, I love you so much,' Isabella said, feeling shaky at the very thought of losing her beloved sister. They were all trying not to dwell on the ordeal of childbirth as Kate got closer and closer to her time, but the thought of ever having to live without her beloved sister cut through Isabella's fragile attempts to be cheerful like a grim bolt of lightning on a sunny day.

'Then tell me the truth,' Kate demanded relentlessly as if she knew she had an unfair advantage and was determined to use it.

Isabella avoided her eyes and tried not to think about the ridiculous mess her life was in. The truth? She didn't even know what it was herself, so how could she tell anyone else? 'Magnus and I found we did not suit,' she said carefully. 'So I had to break the engagement, since he couldn't.'

'And we both know a lady can change her mind if she really must, but a gentleman's word has to be his bond. It's quite absurd when you think about it, but you're too passionate to be Mr Haile's convenient wife for the next forty years because neither of you had the courage to say *no* before it was too late.'

'As I'm now considered a jilt, I doubt I'll have a chance to marry another man I respect, so we'll probably never know. I haven't met anyone else I would want to marry in five years on the marriage mart,' Isabella said with her fingers crossed under her skirts.

She'd met a man she simply wanted that night at Haile Carr, but Wulf FitzDevelin wouldn't marry her if she was the last single woman left on earth, so he didn't count. 'Half the eligible bachelors avoid me now and the rest find my fortune irresistible,' she told her sister breezily. 'I expect they think I'm desperate after whistling Magnus down the wind as if handsome and intelligent gentlemen are ten a penny.'

'You're ridiculously lovely and an heiress in your own right, Izzie. If you were desperate, you'd have clung to him like a limpet.'

'I didn't say it was logical, but at least as an old maid I'll be spared such nonsense in future.'

'You're three and twenty, love, and won't be on the shelf long,' Kate argued with a wry smile. 'There are a few other gentlemen with good eyesight and a modicum of sense in their handsome heads, so you don't need to wear the willow.'

Isabella felt tears threaten at her sister's steadfast love and loyalty, just as they had when she'd seen Kate and her husband, Edmund, stood waiting for her on the gravel carriage sweep this morning, too impatient to wait to greet their guest at the top of the wide stone steps as befitted their station as Lord and Lady Shuttleworth. Kate, Edmund and their daughter had hugged and inspected Isabella for damage, as if they were afraid she'd been broken since they saw her last. Louise Kenton, née Alstone, was the youngest sister of Miranda's husband, Kit, Seventh Earl of Carnwood. Kit and Louise and their sister Maria were distant cousins of her and Miranda and Kate and he was probably the most reluctant lord in the House when he succeeded to the family titles, but marrying Miranda seemed to have reconciled him to it and Louise simply added Kate and Isabella to her family when her brother married their big sister and she felt like another sibling now. Isabella wasn't quite sure she wanted Louise's sharp eyes on her, though she was glad Louise was here for Kate during this time. At least she knew a good deal about childbirth after bearing six children since marrying Hugh.

Isabella didn't know how Edmund convinced his wife she was too near her time to go to Derbyshire and join Kit and Miranda for the Easter festivities, but she was very glad he had. This way Kate must play hostess to as many of the family as he could assemble and what a good thing her sisters had married men who respected as well as loved them. Kit and Edmund found ingenious ways around their wives' sore spots and stubborn streaks when an invigorating argument wasn't advisable and that was the sort of marriage Isabella had tried to convince herself she could build with Magnus.

She felt like a fool about that delusion when she watched Edmund and Kate, and Hugh and Louise, together and realised she'd left something vital out. Magnus was a handsome and civilised gentleman with a clever mind, a dry sense of humour and a good heart, but he wasn't the love of her life. Although she didn't want one of those, it was probably better not to marry at all than accept less. She had spent six months at odds with herself and at the end of it found out Magnus was in love with another woman. He had offered for Isabella to silence his obnoxious father about the child he and his beloved Lady Delphine had made together and he loved *her* so much he'd been ready to sacrifice himself and Isabella for the sake of her precious reputation. So if she wasn't going to risk marrying for reason again and loving a man with all of her heart was a terrifying step she refused to take into the unknown, she would do better not to marry.

'I'm not pining for Magnus, Kate. He was the first grown-up gentleman I danced with at my come-out ball and I suppose I fooled myself into thinking we could make a good marriage out of our long friendship and mutual interests, but I was wrong. I miss him as a friend, but I won't collapse in a tearful heap whenever you say his name.'

'If you like him that much, maybe you should marry him anyway, since you always said you'd never wed for love,' Kate suggested half-seriously, as if it had been wedding nerves that made Isabella call off the wedding and the whole thing might still be salvaged. Since Kate took three years to discover she loved Edmund far too much to let him marry anyone else, Isabella forgave her sister for doubting her.

'No,' she said firmly enough to nip any well-meant schemes to throw her and Magnus back together in the bud. 'It would be a disaster.'

Never quite measuring up to a lover your spouse couldn't have would make a marriage hideous. Lucky for her it was only passion on her side and not love. Still, it was probably unfair to compare every other man she met to broodingly handsome Wulf FitzDevelin and his devilishly seductive kisses one impossible night when she took a few minutes off from being cool and careful Miss Alstone.

'You don't think you could come to love him in time, then?' Kate said with memories of her own slow-burning feelings dreamy in her dark blue eyes.

'No.'

'Then I'm glad you found out before it was too late. Edmund is my best friend, but he's also my abiding passion and it baffles me how you thought you could settle for less. A civilised and passionless marriage could never work for you, love.'

'You were hell-bent on making one yourself once upon a time,' Isabella pointed out to divert her sister from this uncomfortable topic of conversation.

'I'm not sure that's a proper way for an unmarried lady to express herself, sister dear. And, as Edmund was the man I was determined to make it with, I had perfect taste, even if my judgement was a little clouded,' Kate replied smugly. Isabella was certain Kate and Edmund still enjoyed the odd passionate, invigorating argument about it even now.

'Take a lesson from me, Izzie,' Kate persisted because she knew Izzie far better than she wanted her to, 'marriage lasts too long for any Alstone to risk it without being in love with our spouse.'

'Don't upset yourself because it didn't happen. I miss Magnus and his mother and sisters, but I'm glad we agreed to part before it was too late.'

Are you going to tell your sister what blinded you to the truth for so long, Isabella? the sneaky inner voice she wanted to ignore whispered.

I was confused, she told it firmly and it was a wonder she didn't have a permanent headache with all these contrary feelings clashing about inside.

'Gentlemen can be the most dreadful cowards about losing their freedom,' Kate said sagely as if she was an expert on the breed now she had a subtle and determined lord to try to order about for his own good.

'I don't think Magnus was waiting to say "I do" through gritted teeth because of prenuptial nerves, love,' Isabella tried to joke, then went back to staring out of the wide sash windows because it wasn't funny. 'Oh, look who's outside again, Kate. Louise did say Sophia was to stay in the schoolroom today, didn't she? The wretched girl obviously wasn't listening since she looks as if she's off to explore the lavender maze you designed by the wilderness and never mind her governess.'

'It's a lovely day and I don't blame Sophia for wanting to be outside instead of stuck in the schoolroom staring out of the windows at a blue sky and dreaming. I'm not going to lumber up to the schoolroom to betray her. You could find Louise and tell her what her youngest daughter is up to if you really want to, but she's probably doing her best not to know.'

'We were never allowed to use the weather as an excuse to avoid our books,' Isabella said halfheartedly.

'Charlotte never took her eyes off us long enough for us to escape, but I'm not sure even she could keep

Sophia in on a day like this if she was still a govern-ess instead of Ben Shaw's wife and mother of their vast tribe of children,' Kate said, peering over Isa-bella's shoulder at the half-grown girl.

'The Kentons would be a challenge even for her,' Isabella said absently. Sophia had reached the broad walk now and her scarlet cloak flew out behind her as she ran. She made a splash of vital colour against the sunlit grass and a richly periwinkle-blue sky and was nearly at her destination now. Isabella wished she was out there with her, running away from adult cares and all the gossip her cancelled wedding had brought down on her and her family. 'With parents like Louise and Hugh none of them are ever going to be pattern cards of proper behaviour.'

'They'd have to be changelings,' her sister agreed.

'Sophia and her littlest brother certainly aren't and, speaking of young Kit, I wonder where he is. Perhaps Sophia locked him in a cupboard, because I can't see him minding his primers if he can get into mischief with his big sister instead.'

'Louise could be keeping a closer eye on him as she knows what a restless little devil he is, or he could still be on his way and that's why Sophia's running to get away before he spoils her adventure.'

'You're probably right,' Isabella said and won-dered if it was too late to chase after Sophia or let little Kit lure her into mischief. 'It's a good thing their brothers are at school or I might have to go and restore order and it looks cold out there.'

'Much you'd care. Miranda is always scolding you

for ruining your complexion in the sun or the wind and you don't take much notice when you're not in town and the tabbies can't make snide remarks about her negligence.'

'Miranda will listen to their spiteful gossip and feel guilty.'

'She's never quite learnt to ignore the nay-sayers, has she? As well Kit doesn't care or we might still be wearing hair shirts because she ran off with Nevin when he was secretly wed to our vile cousin Celia. Oh, look, Izzie. Who on earth is hurrying after Sophia? I'd certainly remember if I'd met *him*, happily married or not,' Kate exclaimed and pointed at the lithe and vigorous figure striding after Sophia Kenton with a wildly gesticulating master Christopher Kenton on his shoulders.

No, it can't be him, Isabella. Wulf FitzDevelin is on the other side of the Atlantic and he wouldn't follow you to Herefordshire on a private family visit if he wasn't. He wouldn't cross the street to pick you up if you'd been knocked down by a dust cart, she told herself firmly, because her heartbeat was loud in her ears as she watched the powerful male figure hurry after Sophia and wondered if she'd really fainted and this was a nightmare.

His drab greatcoat swirled out behind him in his hurry and even from up here his crow-black locks looked wild, but there was such leashed power and energy in his loping walk, encumbered or not, that she couldn't escape the reality of him. He was here, now. She remembered the defiant set to his head and shoulders too well and couldn't fool herself her eyes were deceiving her.

How dare he? He wasn't on visiting terms with Kate and Edmund and it couldn't be because he couldn't stay away from her. He had put vast and empty miles of ocean between them after that night at Haile Carr and now he was back. A silly, moon-led part of her was dancing as if he'd come to claim her now his half-brother wasn't engaged to marry her any longer. She shook her head to deny the idiot any say and decided she must find out what he wanted before he made his contempt for her clear and Kate put two and two together.

Feeling the force of his impatient personality even from up here, she noted he was even more leanly fit and unforgettable by daylight. Large chunks of his overlong sable hair were being held captive by Master Kenton and she almost winced in sympathy, but he deserved it, didn't he? She shivered as if she was out there, in spring sunlight, close enough to see him frown as she fought to read the thoughts in that austere, almost handsome dark head of his.

'He's the Haile family ghost; Wulf FitzDevelin,' she muttered, but Kate heard and raised her eyebrows. 'I can't imagine what he's doing here, so don't ask me,' she added as coolly as she could with Kate gazing at her as if she thought differently.

'That's Lady Carrowe's Folly? Well, I never, ever did,' Kate said slowly. 'If his father was anything like him, I almost understand her fall from grace. If I wasn't married to the love of my life and Edmund wasn't such a potent lover, I might be tempted to lure a man like him into my bed and the devil take the consequences.'

'You only say that because you know it's never going to happen. Any woman who sends out lures in his direction will reap trouble and heartache. If he has a heart, he's hidden it so well nobody knows where it is.'

'Your Magnus is said to be as close to him as if he was a full brother and you think *him* a good man.'

'Magnus *is* a good man and can't see his half-brother's dark side because he loves him.'

'Whatever side you catch him on I'd wager my best bonnet debutantes' hearts beat nineteen to the dozen when they set eyes on the two of them. Their elder sisters will do more than sigh over a rogue like that and I expect he has to fight them off, if he's careless enough to venture into Carrowe House at the right time for the Countess to be at home to callers.'

'If you weren't such a country wife nowadays, you'd recall not even the most dashing of the young matrons are brave enough to visit her ladyship openly and they'd be idiots to accept a dare like him even if they did,' Isabella said with a fierce frown at the man's back as he strode away.

'Or so besotted they couldn't help themselves,' Kate suggested with another overt glance at that powerfully lean masculine figure as his long legs ate up landscaped gardens and a much sneakier sidelong look at Isabella.

The inner voice she was trying to ignore whispered Kate was right: he did improve the scenery even on such a shining spring day. Familiar little demons were whispering in her ear and how dare he wake them up when she'd tried so hard to silence them? The long, sinful nights in his bed her inner fool yearned for wouldn't be as wonderful as his leanly honed body and moody looks promised. No, of course they wouldn't; not now he despised her. No point risking her all for an itch she wanted to scratch so badly it still kept her awake at nights.

She tried to divert herself by wondering if his mother had loved his father or simply wanted him. Lady Carrowe never refuted her husband's assertion Wulf was her by-blow, but had she thought what illicit passion could cost when she lay with her lover long enough to get with child? If he was anything like Wulf, she probably couldn't see past the blind haze of wanting and so it was a good thing Wulf FitzDevelin disliked and distrusted Isabella Alstone so much, wasn't it?

'He's probably here to lecture me about his brother,' she told her sister crossly and at least he was oblivious to her fast-beating heart and weak knees as she followed his every move with hungry eyes.

'Hmmm, well, he looks to have made a firm friend of young Kit. Sophia won't be so pleased her little brother caught up with his help, or should I call it endurance?'

'Young Kit is a force of nature,' Isabella agreed absently.

'You could call it that,' Kate replied as they

watched man and boy close in on Sophia, 'but your FitzDevelin is one as well and grown-up with it.'

'He's not my FitzDevelin. I wouldn't give him a ha'penny worth of goodwill if he stooped to beg it from me and he never will.'

'Why ever not?' Kate asked so innocently Isabella bit back a groan.

'We hardly know each other and don't like what we do know,' she said flatly.

'Because he's the Countess of Carrowe's by-blow and they whisper dark scandals about him and all the lovers he's had who ought to know better?'

'He had no say in the sins his mother and father committed before he was born,' Isabella said absently as she tried not to think about all those bored society matrons rumour credited him with seducing. Kate was probably right and they lined up to be seduced and that was one more reason not to join in.

'They say the Earl made sure his wife's by-blow got an education and would have set him up in a profession if your Wulf hadn't run away. Kind of him to raise his wife's bastard, but he didn't get much thanks, did he?'

'Kind? Do you really think so?' Isabella asked absently.

She was busy watching Wulf move so fluidly he might actually be a wolf padding after his prey if he had another pair of lithe legs and a fine pelt to go with those ice-blue eyes. For a hungry moment she wished she was at his side, close enough to admire the ease of sleek muscle over elegant bones and wonder at his total focus as he ruthlessly tracked his quarry. Except he wasn't a predator and she wasn't fascinated, so it was as well she wasn't close enough to fall under his spell.

'You don't?' Kate said, sounding intrigued.

'The Earl isn't a kind man, Kate. He would have sued his wife's lover for criminal conversation and divorced her if he was.'

'She does seem very inoffensive and quiet now,' Kate said and Isabella could see her acute mind working on Lady Carrowe's unfortunate situation.

If the lady had even one more supporter among the *haut ton*, she might be less oppressed and her daughters more welcome in polite society. Isabella stared down at the empty garden where Wulf and the youngest Kentons had disappeared from view. She half-expected to see a mark in the air, a magic rune perhaps to tell unwary females danger lay ahead.

'You have given a good deal of thought to Mr FitzDevelin's shocking birth and stormy upbringing during your engagement to his brother, Izzie,' Kate said airily.

'No more than I would about anyone in such a situation,' she replied and fought not to cross her fingers against another huge lie, because not a single night had gone by since she met him when he didn't haunt her sleeping and waking.

'Of course not, but whatever you think of him he's here and can't have come all this way to see anyone but you. In your shoes I'd hear him out before Edmund and Hugh chase him away.'

'I doubt he'll go or stay unless he wants to,' Isabella muttered, but Kate was right. She didn't want her overprotective male relatives running him off before she found out what he wanted. 'Can you keep them busy long enough for me to be rid of him before they find out?'

'I'm in no fit state to stop anyone doing whatever they want, but if Hugh and Edmund think we're having a feminine coze about babies and lying-in, they won't interrupt unless the house is on fire or someone falls off the roof. We can go to my boudoir and tell my maid to be sure we're not disturbed, then you can use the garden stairs to go and find Mr FitzDevelin and I can escape the fuss Edmund will surround me with until I'm safely delivered.'

'He loves you, Kate.'

'I know and I love him, but I can't take a step without having to account for it to someone who has better things to do if they'd only get on with them.'

'Not as far as he's concerned they haven't and you'd be mortally offended if he went off to discuss crops with his tenants or horses with his cronies and left you to birth his child alone.'

'I would and quite right, too.'

'Stop being contrary and go and have a rest, then. Edmund will need to be revived with smelling salts if you don't stop behaving as if you're about to throw a trifling entertainment instead of giving birth to his second child.'

'If you promise to stop being wise about the rest of us and look at your own motives and feelings, I might.'

'There truly is a first time for everything, then,' Isabella said crossly.

'Anyone would think I was the contrary one of the three of us,' her sister said as if she really thought she wasn't. 'And stop looking like that, because Miranda and I know you're wilful as a donkey even if you fool so many with that angelic face.'

'I almost wish I'd stayed in London to be gossiped about by strangers now.'

'Really? When there must be so many more sharp eyes to watch your assignations with Mr FitzDevelin when you're in town?'

'Nonsense, I've never met him in town and this isn't an assignation.'

'You would have to know he was coming for it to be one of those, wouldn't you?' Kate said as if she was quite convinced Isabella had been waiting for him to catch up with her ever since she broke her engagement to his brother and how much more wrong-headed could one woman get?

Chapter Three

W ulf cursed himself for not being able to resist the shine of tears in a little boy's eyes when he begged for help to catch up with his big sister. He'd been excluded from so much as a boy that the little rascal couldn't have chosen a better bid for sympathy. Yet what would such a young girl think when confronted by a strange man with her brother aloft, especially one this unkempt and in need of a shave? His windswept, travel-stained appearance would probably terrify her and exhaustion was making it easier for him to frown than smile.

'How did the infernal brat persuade you to hunt me down?' this girl demanded when she saw her brother riding triumphantly on a stranger's shoulders. 'I do wish people would ignore him when he pretends to be an ill-treated waif. Every time someone believes him it only encourages him to keep doing it,' she went on and he should have known this sturdy little rogue couldn't have a shrinking violet as a sister.

'Thank you for the advice. I'll bear it in mind if

I'm not invited again,' he managed to reply with a straight face. He had ridden here too hard to get this over with. Lack of sleep and a decent meal must be making him light-headed, because there wasn't anything here to laugh about.

'We don't live here, so that won't do any good,' she told him with a resigned sigh that almost set him off again.

'I promise to learn from my mistakes, then,' Wulf said, swinging his giggling passenger down so the boy could run into a clever lavender labyrinth and gallop its paths as if he'd had enough energy to run from Herefordshire to the distant Welsh Mountains all along.

'He's a horrid brat and should be beaten at least once a day for the good of all our souls, but who the devil are you?' the girl demanded as if she'd only just taken in his windswept, bearlike appearance and realised he wasn't the sort of visitor a grand house like Cravenhill Park usually attracted by daylight.

'I'm Wulf FitzDevelin; who the devil are *you*?' he replied, wondering if the young men of the *ton* had any idea what a whirlwind was going to hit them when she was old enough to be presented at Court.

'I'm Miss Sophia Kenton, because my older sister Julia got to be Miss Kenton when our aunt married Mr Sandbatch, and Wulf's not a proper name for a gentleman.'

'I'm not a proper gentleman, but it's short for Wulfric if that helps.'

'He's my horse,' young Master Kenton shouted

breathlessly from the labyrinth and this time Wulf did laugh out loud. The sound sent a pair of crows cawing into the treetops and broke the almost uncanny peace of this place.

'I'd have thrown him off a lot sooner if I were you,' Sophia said with a frown at her little brother.

'I really don't think you would,' Wulf said, seeing reluctant affection in the girl's eyes and contrasting it with the open dislike in the eyes of his two eldest half-siblings when he'd been a scrubby brat himself.

'Probably not, but I'd be tempted,' the girl said with a wry smile.

'It *is* you, Mr FitzDevelin; I thought my eyes were deceiving me. What a very *unexpected* surprise,' Isabella Alstone's cool voice said from behind them.

Wulf felt his heart thunder; instinct should have warned him she was there. The sound made him feel as if parts of him he didn't want to think about right now could burst into flames. 'Good day, Miss Alstone,' he said flatly.

Somehow he managed to meet her dark blue eyes calmly and she obviously couldn't imagine why he was polluting the clean air of her brother-in-law's fine estate and ought to go back where he belonged. In the gutter presumably, he concluded and hoped a cynical half-smile would divert her from the ravenous hunger roaring through him like the hottest and most ill-timed lightning.

'Is my brother-in-law expecting you?' she asked

as if she had no idea how she made red-blooded males feel by being so perfectly, femininely arrogant. All he wanted right now was to kiss her and it took too much effort to recall why he'd come. She'd jilted Magnus—Gus, as he'd always been to Wulf—and he'd done so much damage between them already even the idea was madness and he should be ashamed of himself.

'I doubt Lord Shuttleworth has the least idea I'm here, but *you* should have known I'd come, Miss Alstone,' he said stiffly.

'Why would I? There's no reason for you to intrude on a private family gathering and I could hardly believe my eyes when I saw you walking up the Broad Walk with young Kit on your shoulders,' Isabella said stiffly.

Now she was faced with the real man her silly heart was racing as if she'd run all the way from the house to simper at him. She half-wished he was still on the other side of the Atlantic, building the new life he'd claimed to want when he left England. If he'd stayed away, she wouldn't have to face the fact he still stirred her as no other man ever had. She wouldn't have to feel the Isabella he woke up that night straining against the leash.

'You didn't send your brother-in-law to throw me out, though, did you?' he challenged in the husky undertone she found so ridiculously enchanting that moon-mad night.

'I don't want to embarrass my family, Mr Fitz-Develin,' she said primly.

'I presume you are part of Miss Alstone's family, Miss Sophia? Am I making you uncomfortable?'

'Yes, I am and, no, you're not. I'm far too interested in how Aunt Izzie knows you and what you've done to make her glare daggers at you. I don't think Kit has ever been embarrassed about anything in his life, so I shouldn't bother to ask him.'

'Oh, please run along, Sophia, and take young Kit with you,' Isabella interrupted before this meeting turned into an even bigger farce.

'I can't; it would be improper to leave you alone with a strange gentleman, Aunt Izzie. It's our duty to chaperon you,' Sophia said so virtuously Isabella frowned to say she was overdoing it and should do as she was bid for once.

'Maybe so, but show your little brother the way to the middle of the lavender labyrinth and at least try to mind your own business while you're doing it,' she said, in lieu of Sophia turning into a proper young lady by a minor miracle.

Sophia crossed her arms and stared back as if Isabella was the one being difficult. 'For that I should stay here and insist on listening to every word.'

'Go away, Sophia. Please?' Isabella gave up trying to reason her out of eavesdropping. 'Please?' she cajoled as she was desperate to get this over and Wulf back on the road before Edmund or Hugh knew he was here.

'Oh, very well, but you owe me half-a-dozen favours.'

'And she'll make me pay,' Isabella muttered

gloomily once Sophia demanded little Kit's attention until he found something more interesting to do.

'You don't treat her as an irritating little girl, though, do you?' he asked as if he was surprised.

'If she had any idea how difficult being grown-up is, Sophia wouldn't be in such a hurry to be one.'

'You find being a society beauty burdensome, then, Miss Alstone?'

'I do when people throw it at me like an accusation, Mr FitzDevelin.'

'I apologise,' he said impatiently.

'I doubt it, but you must have come here to speak to me, since you don't know my family and I doubt if you're a business connection of my brother-in-law. A strange man on the strange horse I assume is resting in my brother-in-law's stables as we speak won't go unnoticed long, however much you tipped the groom to look the other way. My brother-in-law will want a good reason why you came here uninvited now his family are arriving for Eastertide and my sister is in an interesting condition.'

'Before I'm grabbed by the scruff of my neck and thrown out I admit I came to plead with you.'

'*You?* Plead with *me*?' Isabella exclaimed, although he'd come a long way to play a trick if he was lying. 'I doubt you even know how.'

'Then I must learn, mustn't I?' he said impatiently. 'Magnus is a broken man,' he accused with such fury in his ice-blue eyes he must think it was her fault. 'He's shockingly thin and can't shake off the influenza I'm told he contracted at Christmas. He needs you. I can't imagine why when you kiss strange men at the drop of a hat and threw him over when you got tired of being engaged to marry him.'

'Please don't bother stretching your poor, under-used imagination any further, then, because I'm not the woman your half-brother needs.'

'You really are stony-hearted, aren't you?'

'Apparently,' she said calmly.

Letting him know his accusation hurt as if a knife had been plunged into her chest would be even more stupid than finding the air at Cravenhill Park fresher and the sunlight brighter because he was here, even while he was flinging insults at her. If she had any sense, she'd turn her back on him and walk away; prove how indifferent she was to him *and* his mis-conceptions. A foolish part of her was far too pleased he was here to do that, despite the fury in his gaze as he let it slide over her.

'What will get me past the ice between you and nobodies like me so I can reason with you?' he asked and began to pace, as if that was the only way he could stop himself shaking her.

'Nothing you can say,' she told him steadily and refused to let him know he'd hurt her. His picture of events was so wide of the mark she'd laugh if she wasn't feeling so sick.

'And I dare say you'd turn his life upside down and treat him like a fool if you did agree to wed him after all, but even that would be better than watch-ing him waste away for the lack of you in his life.'

'I shall not and certainly not to please you. Please

me by going away and avoiding me like the plague from now on, Mr FitzDevelin. Your brother and I had our own very good reasons not to go ahead with our wedding, but not one of them is any of your business.'

'Yes, it is. I got back to England a week ago to find Magnus half the man he was when I left and he's worth a hundred of either of us. I won't let you set him at naught because his devotion has become tiresome.'

'Find a fresh horse and go home, because you've had a wasted journey. Your insults won't change a thing and next time you set out on a wild goose chase you should talk to your brother about it before you begin.'

'He won't talk to me,' the wrong-headed idiot mumbled as if he didn't want to admit he'd failed.

'Neither will I,' she said quietly.

Was it right to enjoy the blaze of anger and frustration lighting his eyes to purest ice blue before he turned to pace up and down the path again to stop himself taking her back to London by force for his brother like a juicy bone someone stole?

'He obviously loves you to distraction,' Wulf Fitz-Develin threw out as he paced close enough to vent his fury without Sophia hearing. 'Heaven knows why when you treat him like a whining dog you can kick aside when you're weary of it.'

'I don't kick dogs. Your arguments are so persuasive I'm surprised you're not employed as a diplomat, Mr Wulf,' she retaliated sweetly. She was stoking an already scorching fire and it felt wickedly enjoyable as well as oddly powerful to bait him when he couldn't lay a finger on her without having to explain it to a pair of children and her furious male relatives, but she really should stop it. 'You'll scare the children and as they're Kentons it takes a lot of doing.'

He frowned even more fiercely and looked over at Sophia, who was staring at him while little Kit ran round the maze making war whoops as if he witnessed fiery adult battles of will every day of the week. He might well, given who his parents were and the fact they were notorious for enjoying a good argument. This wasn't a good argument, though, was it? Still, Wulf looked a little sheepish when he turned back to her.

'I'm sorry,' he said abruptly, as if every word cost a fortune.

'Are you? Now I've seen your true colours I'm not surprised Magnus doesn't confide in you.'

'We were close as real brothers until he got engaged to you. He's been closed as an oyster ever since and now just drinks and looks miserable as sin whenever someone mentions your name. You broke off the engagement days before you were due to marry; you've broken his heart.'

'Don't be so melodramatic; it was two months until our wedding and the invitations hadn't even been sent out.'

'Be grateful we're being watched by innocents, Miss Alstone. I'm so tempted to find out if there's red blood in your veins I doubt much else would hold me back.'

A hard and feverish sort of wanting blazed in his ice-blue eyes as if his steely will was all that stopped him kissing her witless, so she'd have to be grateful Sophia and little Kit were nearby, wouldn't she? 'I'd bite you if you tried it, Mr FitzDevelin, then we'd see what yours is like and never mind mine.'

'How very *uncivil* of you,' he snapped back sarcastically as if he hoped his words would freeze in mid-air and physically hurt her.

Isabella was hard-pressed not to wince. 'Lucky we are being watched, then, since I don't care to lower myself to your level,' she replied and she needed to feed that fury; keep him standing across the green dell glaring at her like an enemy. She was almost terrified by the wild emotions burning the frosty air yet fascinated by the idea of exploring them and never mind conventions, relatives by marriage or her thorny Alstone pride.

'You're afraid you might kiss the bastard back, again.'

'No, I could never want a man who despises me,' she lied.

'Why not, you did last time, Isabella,' he reminded her with such deadly softness she felt his words scorch as if he'd written them in Greek fire on her flinching skin.

He was quite right; that night she kissed him as if her last breath depended on it and why was she such a confounded idiot as to want him and not his half-brother? She felt the merciless heat of longing for a dark and dangerous man she'd never been able to feel for gentlemanly, handsome and much kinder Magnus Haile. Raw wanting ran through her like wildfire, but this time she'd keep it to herself.

'Go away,' she demanded in a voice rasped and on the edge of admitting something dreadful.

'And tell Magnus he's right, you're cold as an iceberg under all that golden beauty?'

A shard of pain her good friend could say such a thing about her threatened her serenity. She managed a haughty stare and told herself he'd made it up.

'I can't persuade you to drag my half-brother out of the pit of despair he's tumbled into since you jilted him? He doesn't deserve to be treated like a piece of rubbish by a woman he loves for some reason that's beyond me.'

'No, you can't and find out what he really wants next time you set out to get it for him by fair means or foul,' she replied so sweetly she heard him grind his teeth and was savagely glad.

Chapter Four

Wulf struggled with a powerful urge to shake Isabella until she was as disarrayed as he was after galloping all the way here as if the devil was on his heels. But he couldn't do that with the young Kentons looking on. Even if their softly hostile words didn't carry on the clear air, such acute children must already know something was amiss and that would send them running for their father. Tension was stiffening every muscle and sinew he had and he wanted Isabella with a burning hunger he'd never felt the like of before. It roared to life the instant he set eyes on her hesitating on the edge of the terrace at Haile Carr while he was trying to convince himself to go inside the hot and brightly lit ballroom because Magnus needed his support and never mind the Earl and his eldest half-brother's order to stay away. If only he'd fought his doubts a little harder, he might have been introduced to this golden-haired and lovely heiress as Magnus's intended bride instead of kissing her as if his heart and soul depended on it.

An image of his brother six months on, pale, bony and unshaven as he brooded over a brandy glass at the breakfast table, reminded him why he was here. But as Isabella Alstone was as cool as the frosty air around them as she stared back at him, there seemed no point repeating the speech he'd put together word by painful word as he rode here. His inner devil took over his tongue at first sight of her and hurt was still screaming for air inside him. For months this sense of betrayal had wanted to tumble out in a toxic stream of bitter words, but they weren't for Magnus, were they?

'Quiet men have unquiet souls and dark needs and it could be too late to draw back and say a polite "no, thank you" to the next one you hook as firmly as you caught my brother,' he warned. The thought of her playing with another idiot in the dark made him feel as if madness was lying in wait.

'You have no idea what your brother and I mean to each other. *You* should be wary of thinking you know him better than he does himself, Mr FitzDevelin. I would like you to leave before you cause the sort of scene I would rather not put my family through at Eastertide with my sister so near her time.'

'No doubt your brothers-in-law will enjoy crushing my pretensions if they find me, but I rode here for my brother's sake and would rather be a thousand miles away for mine. Will you mend this public rift and take up your betrothal to Magnus again?'

'No,' she said stiffly.

Was it the hint of hurt too deep for an ice princess that made his breath catch and a whisper of forbidden longing catch at his heart? No, she was his brother's dream and Wulf FitzDevelin's worst nightmare. 'You don't care a fig for my brother,' he said flatly and turned away in disgust. Yes, that was it; her regal indifference to Magnus's sufferings disgusted him. He should disregard the little part of him that was dancing a jig because she was free to enjoy all kinds of forbidden mischief with Magnus's bastard brother at last.

'Maybe I care too much,' he thought he heard her whisper and his inner devil tripped up in mid-skip and fell flat on its ugly face.

Wulf spun on his heel to glare a challenge at her and she met it, nodded at their youthful audience to remind him to be quiet. 'Why break your engagement, then?' he rumbled gruffly.

'Because it was the right thing to do,' she murmured, watching the Kenton children explore the labyrinth as if they'd been the centre of her interest all this time and the hard tension in the air between them didn't fascinate her as well.

'And you always do the right thing, do you?'

'No, but I own my mistakes when I realise I've made them, Mr FitzDevelin.'

'Was it because I kissed you at the Summer Ball?' he finally gritted out the question that had alternatively appalled and elated him since he read a notice the marriage between the Honourable Magnus Haile and Miss Isabella Alstone would not take place. The newssheet had appeared just as he returned from running away from his stark betrayal of his brother's trust.

'You do have a high opinion of yourself, Mr Fitz-Develin.'

'Was it?' he persisted.

'No, I might have managed to forget that outrage…'

'You didn't respond with outrage at the time; I wish you had.'

'So do I and stop interrupting—it's rude as well as a waste of time. Where was I? Oh, yes, I *might* have forgotten that outrage, but I chose to keep it in my memory as a reminder never to wander out of a hot ballroom and expect to find a gentleman in the dark. Your conduct that night had no influence on my decision not to marry your half-brother. Be glad of it, Mr FitzDevelin, and stop glaring at me as if I made you do it when we both know you fell on me like the lust-driven yahoo you are.'

He ought to be as furious as she was trying to make him, but when she put on that high-nosed lady manner, it lit a fire inside him she ought to be a lot more wary of. It had burnt out of control that night at Haile Carr; heat had scorched the sense out of both of them, as if being close as they could get was all that mattered in this life. Gus would have every right to despise him if he found out what they nearly did the first night they laid eyes on one another, but this wasn't about them and stealing illicit kisses in the moonlight. He had come here to plead with her to take his half-brother back and marry him,

not to remind them both how disgracefully they behaved when they forgot who they were. *So how is
that going, Wulfric?* Badly. The uncomfortable truth
was he didn't want her to wed anyone else. Fury at
the very idea of her in another man's arms thundered
up against his love for his brother and trumped it.
He made himself recall the sickening fall back to
earth that night after he'd kissed this beautiful, vital
woman as if his life depended on it, then found out
who she was. A Miss Alstone of Wychwood would
never truly want a misfit like him. Even if he had
half a kingdom to offer her, she'd turn up her nose
and say a chilly 'No, thank you'.

'Did Gus ever kiss you like that?' he heard himself ask and only just smothered a groan of disbelief.

'He never asked for more than a lady cares to give
before marriage.'

'Less than nothing, then,' he stated flatly and she
blushed and lowered her eyes. He tried to stamp on a
low sense of satisfaction he'd ruffled her ice-maiden
calm when Gus could not.

'I gave your brother his freedom, and if you want
to know more, you must ask him,' she ended with so
much ice in her voice he shivered.

'Do you think I haven't?'

'Ah, but you don't ask, do you? You demand.'

Wulf blushed and was surprised he still could.
'I'm sorry I was rude,' he said a little more loudly
so the children might hear him, if they hadn't run
off to find enough strong men to throw him out. He
flicked a glance in their direction and saw they were

still there, keeping half an eye on him as if he might do something very interesting if they turned their backs and they didn't want to miss it.

'You only ever wanted me because of how I look,' she accused so softly he could barely hear her. 'And don't twit me on being vain, because it's more of a trial than a blessing. Men have wanted me since before I left the schoolroom because of my fortune and a set of even features, but I was always more than that to Magnus—would I could say the same for you.'

'Marry him, then,' he said harshly, secretly hurt she thought him wanting and why wouldn't she when Magnus was worth a dozen of him?

She sighed and shook her head. 'Do try listening for once,' she said as if she was running out of patience. 'Magnus confided in me, and if you can't trust my word we should not wed, ask him to do the same for you.'

'You could marry me,' he heard himself say as if his voice was coming from a great distance.

'Because you kissed me once and feel guilty? No, thank you. I wouldn't marry now unless I was so deep in love I couldn't help myself, which means I shall never marry because I don't want to be in love.'

'Perhaps you won't have a choice, but you wouldn't wed a bastard even if you loved me from head to foot, would you? Miss Alstone of Wychwood and the by-blow of an erring countess? Unthinkable.'

'I would dislike you if you had a ducal coronet, vast numbers of houses and thousands of acres to your name. Being housed and fed by a vindictive man during your early years has bent you out of shape, Mr FitzDevelin. Maybe Lord Carrowe isn't the tolerant, sophisticated gentleman the polite world think him, but you're not either.'

'I hope you don't mean he raised me in his own image.'

'No, but I think you became hard and angry in order to survive his harsh regime and you shouldn't let him shape your view of the world.'

'You have no idea how it feels to be blamed for anything amiss in your family's life.'

'My sister Kate and I were left in our great-aunt and cousin's hands as small children. I doubt there's much your stepfather could teach them about humiliating those too small or poor to thumb their noses and walk away. You ran as soon as you were old enough, didn't you? I can't tell you how we would have envied you the strength and cunning to survive in the wider world when we were to blame for anything that went wrong at Wychwood before our brother-in-law inherited it.'

Wulf felt his heart lurch at the thought of tiny, defiant Isabella surviving such a harsh regime. She ought to have been doted on and valued from the moment she was born, as the outgoing and confident children on the other side of this coolly peaceful garden obviously were. He itched to drag the hags who inflicted such cruelty on two little girls to the nearest Bridewell and show them how it felt to be whipped and humiliated until tears and pleas sank into despair and your only refuge was unconsciousness. He'd sworn as a boy never to lay violent hands on a woman or child, so he'd have to trust the Earl of Carnwood to make sure those harpies never had control of a child's life again and reminded himself the Alstone sisters were nothing to do with him, then or now.

'You do understand, then,' he admitted gruffly.

'I do, but we were rescued by my eldest sister's godmama after she spent a year or two nagging my grandfather to send us to school so persistently he gave in to get some peace. Then Miranda married Kit and we had a fine governess and all the love we were starved of when Miranda left and my brother died. So Kate and I only had a few years of being wronged before our older sister and brother-in-law showered us with enough love and attention to make up for that time.'

'Those women left their mark on you,' he argued quietly and at least now he knew why she held herself a little aloof in case she met gleeful spite in a stranger's eye or saw a bully under their skin.

'Not as big as the one your stepfather left on you,' she countered.

'He doesn't rule my life; I won't let him.'

'Then if you get over this conviction you know what's best for your brother and anyone else you care about, we might get on better.'

'We might, except Magnus is still miserable and you're still here. Relations between us won't improve until you change that situation.'

'Here we go again, so it's probably as well my brother-in-law is about to interrupt us.'

'Damn it, I'm not done.'

'Well, I am and here he comes anyway. Go back to London and talk to your half-brother before you blunder into any more private homes without an invitation. If you tell Magnus half the wrong-headed nonsense you spouted at me, I'm sure he'll confide before you dash about the countryside doing more damage.'

Two purposeful males were striding ever closer and she was pushing him aside as if he was a problem she'd confronted and solved. Except Wulf felt more like an arsenal of gunpowder ready to blow with the smallest spark. He wouldn't be going away satisfied he could now forget Miss Alstone's vital beauty, acute mind and waspish tongue as if he'd never met her one hot and spellbound August night.

'Papa, Papa, we're over here,' little Kit shouted as if he and his sister must be more important than any mysterious stranger.

'Mr Fitz-something helped him catch up with me,' Sophia informed her father with an exasperated look at her brother, as if she already knew he wouldn't get the rebuke she half-wanted him to have for spoiling her adventure.

'And your mother has a great deal to say about you setting him a bad example twice in one day, so I'd keep quiet about his sins if I were you,' her father told her gently as he sat young Kit on his shoulders. 'Did you invite FitzDevelin here, Shuttleworth?' Sir Hugh Kenton asked very coolly indeed and Wulf no

longer wondered how the man kept six children almost in order. He had an urge to go and stand in a
corner until he'd learnt how to behave himself and
he was supposed to be grown-up.

'No,' Lord Shuttleworth said baldly.

Wulf felt as if his fur was being rubbed the wrong
way, but he couldn't accuse either of them of the sort
of lazy prejudice his stepfather lived by. They clearly
disliked him for his own sake and never mind the
bed he shouldn't have been born in.

'Mr FitzDevelin is on his way into Wales and has
called in to pass on a message from his mother, Edmund,' Miss Alstone said as she rashly stepped in to
protect him from making a very sudden exit with the
force of a gentleman's boot to speed him on his way.

'How unexpected of her ladyship to send you as
her envoy, FitzDevelin,' the Viscount Shuttleworth
said blandly.

'And how invisible her letter is, too,' Wulf thought
he heard Sir Hugh mutter as if he'd been looking
forward to throwing the unwanted guest out for his
whatever he and Lord Shuttleworth were to one another. Brother-in-law; cousin-by-marriage? Whatever complex relation his lordship was to Sir Hugh
Kenton, the Alstone clan moved as one formidable
whole when threatened. How Wulf wished his own
family were so uncomplicated.

'I suppose your horse has had a short rest, Mr
FitzDevelin, so you can be on your way to Brecon
again,' Isabella said as if a mythical journey would
save him from her relatives' protective wrath.

Tempted to argue he had nowhere else to go just for the hell of it, Wulf obliged with a silent bow because he didn't feel like lying outright to these two aristocrats.

'A shame we can't put you up for the night, Fitz-Develin, but I must be inhospitable,' Lord Shuttleworth said as if he was only mildly amused by playing host to such an unwelcome visitor for however short a time it took to get rid of him.

Wulf read the warning underneath his bland comment and decided to go quietly. No point arguing when he'd wasted a long ride hoping he could put the world right for his half-brother. For once in his life he'd tried to be unselfish, noble even, and Miss Alstone was so obstinate he wondered why he'd bothered. He'd fought all the way here to blot out the snide, self-mocking voice that whispered he was a fool in time to the pounding of hooves as he ate at the miles between him and Isabella Alstone. It argued he was desperate to see her again and never mind his brother. And now he was here why had he ever thought anything he had to say could make a difference when Magnus couldn't change her mind?

'You'd best hurry. I'm told it could rain so hard tonight the roads will be impassable,' Sir Hugh warned and even his son stopped telling his father about his day so far as if he'd caught something implacable in his quiet voice.

'Then I'd best get on my way before I'm marooned,' Wulf agreed blandly, although they all knew he'd be heading back to London and it didn't look like rain.

'Thank you for delivering the Countess's message and do give her my best wishes when you see her next, Mr FitzDevelin,' Miss Alstone chimed in to speed him on his way.

What else could he do but bow as gracefully as he could, then smile a quick farewell at Miss Sophia Kenton and the little rogue sitting on his father's shoulders? Miss Alstone was already discussing the weather with Kenton while Lord Shuttleworth waited impatiently to see Wulf off the property.

'My wife is very near her time, FitzDevelin,' his lordship told him as they strolled away. 'Come here again and I'll have you roped on your horse and left to wander wherever he takes you. And stay away from my sister-in-law.'

'I came on my brother's behalf, my lord,' Wulf made himself argue. He wanted to thump someone to make himself feel better as well, but it would do neither of them any good to alarm the very pregnant Viscountess.

'I trust my sister-in-law to know her own mind and so should you. She and Mr Haile will only have parted after a lot of heartache and I hate to see her troubled.'

'You are in her confidence, then?' Wulf heard himself say urgently, as if he was her rebuffed suitor and not Magnus.

'No, but she hates to break a promise and you can tell your brother so when you get back to London. He obviously doesn't know her as well as he thinks if he thought sending you to plead his case would get her to change her mind.'

'He doesn't know I've come.'

'Then you'll be the butt of his displeasure as well, won't you?'

'Probably,' Wulf said with the sort of defensive young man's shrug he thought he'd grown out of.

'I suppose you cared enough to come here on a pointless quest bullheaded,' his lordship said as if he was trying to find excuses for the sort of boyish mischief Wulf never had the chance to commit.

'My brother is eating his heart out. He's taken to the bottle and refuses to shave for days on end and not even our younger sisters can get a smile out of him. If you had a half-brother you loved, wouldn't *you* do anything to see him happy when he's hurting so badly?'

'Yes, which is why you're walking to my stables to collect your horse and not being carried there by my grooms to be put on it and driven off fast as the nag will go.'

'I'd best be grateful for small mercies, then,' Wulf said with a rueful grin and decided he'd like this man under other circumstances.

'Don't try too hard until you're away without arousing my wife's suspicion you're here on a mission of your own,' Lord Shuttleworth said as if he knew Wulf's reasons for coming here were only half-unselfish and that was impossible, wasn't it?

'Consider me warned off, my lord.'

'A shame, but I won't have my wife or her sister

upset if there's anything I can do to prevent it and that's a fault I've long shared with Sir Hugh and the current Earl of Carnwood.'

'I'm not your equal, my lord, but there's no need to point it out with every second word. Trust my stepfather to be sure my irregular birth is engraved on my heart, much as Mary Tudor claimed Calais was on hers.'

'It's not a matter of quality or inequality, but common sense. Tangling with you or your brother now will drag my sister-in-law's good name through more mud and I can't have that.'

'Nobody will know I was here if you don't tell them and I didn't give your stableman a name.'

'Which was why he sought me out and, as a reward, I'll be granting him a cottage of his own this Eastertide so he can wed his sweetheart. So some good came of your impromptu visit.'

'I shall preen myself even as I ride away with my tail metaphorically between my legs, my lord,' Wulf said and was surprised by a bark of genuine laughter from his reluctant host.

'Smug or not, that will be a challenge.'

'I'm used to it,' Wulf said ruefully and wasn't that the truth?

'I suppose you must be and as a rule I care more about a man's head and heart than the way he came into the world, but I know my sister-in-law has been hurt and I care more about her than your sensitivities, so I'm prepared to be inhospitable in your case.'

'I came here on my half-brother's business,' Wulf

said as his temper began to tug at its tethers. Magnus was ill and Isabella Alstone was clearly in perfect health and coolly composed, so why was she the one who needed protecting?

'And you think me rude to harp on it, but I don't think you're sure how you feel about my wife's little sister, are you, FitzDevelin?' he added unexpectedly.

Wulf almost cursed aloud again and gave even more away to this frighteningly acute and deceptively mild-mannered man. 'What can I say? You threatened me with indignity if I breathe even a bad word about her and now you want to know how I feel. I feel my brother is sad and ill after the abrupt ending of their betrothal, but things may not be as simple as I thought when I rode here to plead his case.'

'Against your own interests as well,' the man said cynically, as if he knew Wulf's inner devils lusted for Isabella and never mind fraternal love. 'I'm in love with an Alstone sister myself, FitzDevelin. Did you really think I wouldn't recognise the dazed look in a man's eye when he gazes at one of them as if he hasn't a hope in hell of ever laying hands on her but can't help himself longing all the same? I longed unrewarded for three very long years and know everything there is to know about longing and not having, but still doing it.'

Wulf frowned moodily at the neat stable yard they were nearing so rapidly, aware he'd better guard his tongue even more carefully. 'I'm not in love. I have no personal interest beyond my brother's welfare and sanity,' he bit out, feeling as if the lie might snap back and bite him.

'Then you're wilfully blind or a fool. I'm not your enemy, but I will be if you harm my wife's little sister.'

'If my half-brother marries your sister-in-law, I'll go abroad and none of your kind will miss me.'

'Hmmm, Lord Carrowe makes no effort to provide for your younger sisters, so they'd miss you and Magnus Haile seems to like you,' Lord Shuttleworth argued.

This clever man clearly had all sorts of wrongheaded ideas about the passion Wulf had for Lady Shuttleworth's younger sister. Passion was all it was. He'd get over it.

'Magnus and my mother will find the girls a good husband each and I expect they'll be abetted by your sister-in-law even if she doesn't marry him.'

'They're your family, FitzDevelin, not Miss Alstone's.'

'Have you tried telling her that?'

'No, I've no fancy to get my nose snapped off and you're right, she won't let a broken engagement stop her matchmaking,' Lord Shuttleworth admitted.

'My sisters' welfare comes first and they'll do better when I'm gone,' Wulf said.

'You're set on leaving England again, then?'

'Yes,' Wulf said gruffly.

'Then I must wonder why you came back.'

'So must I.'

'Although the Earl can't stave off his creditors

much longer,' this lord warned as if Wulf ought to weigh that in the balance when planning his future.

As if the problem of how his mother and sisters would survive hadn't haunted him all the way across the Atlantic and back. It was the idea of his mother and sisters being destitute that dragged him back to England, wasn't it? He'd been desperate not to see his brother marry Isabella. This fiery need for her, from the instant he had laid eyes on her, sent him across the Atlantic in the teeth of winter storms, but it was wrong to have been elated for even a minute when he came back to find the wedding had been cancelled. He rode here dogged by guilt and pity for Magnus's low state of mind mixed with irritation he hadn't come here to plead for himself.

'Lord Carrowe has the legal right to dictate his wife and unwed daughters' lives. He doesn't thank me for interfering,' he said carefully.

'You might need help if he's in the Fleet for debt,' Lord Shuttleworth replied, taking a visiting card out of his pocket and scribbling on it with a fine silver pencil before he handed it over. 'Ben Shaw is a lord's love child but has a powerful enough reach to make your stepfather wary of tangling with him.'

'Thank you, although I've no idea why you'd help me.'

'My wife and her sister were neglected and abused by those supposed to care for them as children and I'd hate to see your sisters left vulnerable, even if they are grown-up and too old to be bullied and coerced.'

Wulf frowned his disagreement because his youngest half-sisters were so terrified of their father they might walk off a cliff if he told them to. The twins were eighteen and Aline seven years older and more stubborn and defiant than her little sisters, but Shuttleworth was quite right and he had to put their needs before his own. Any scheme to leave the country with his mother and three unwed sister would need a lot of fine tuning, and if Ben Shaw, whom he'd already met causally, could help, he'd lower his pride and ask for it if the time came.

'I will put them first,' he promised curtly as they walked into the stable yard and he thought that he and the Viscount might have been friends in different circumstances.

Chapter Five

'Another fool's comin' gallopin' up the drive 'ell for leather, your lordship,' a different groom from the one who had first greeted Wulf told his master gloomily as they waited for Wulf's horse to be saddled. 'Seems like a day for them, don't it, m'lord?'

'Indeed,' Lord Shuttleworth responded with a frown that made Wulf glad he was playing first intruder today and not second. 'I'll see who it is and what he wants while you bring that nag out for this gentleman, Alworth.' His lordship invited Wulf to precede him out with an impatient gesture.

'Hell and the devil, that's Gus,' Wulf was shocked into exclaiming when he saw a hard-ridden horse tearing towards them with his weary rider looking as if he was barely hanging on to the reins. 'What is he doing riding here as if his life depends on it when he's supposed to be convalescing?'

'The same thing as you, I expect,' Shuttleworth replied shortly.

Had Miss Alstone's family secretly opposed what

seemed a perfectly good match to the rest of the world? Wulf felt contrary emotions churn inside him as he waited for Gus to gallop across Lord Shuttleworth's park and tell them why he was in such a hurry.

'Wulf, thank God I was right although you're a damned fool,' Magnus gasped out when he was close enough to be heard.

He hadn't bothered with the shave he had needed even when he set out and looked more the wild man than Wulf and quite unlike his usual dapper and gentlemanly self. He wondered fleetingly if Miss Alstone would like Gus better thin as a rake, romantically unkempt, wild-eyed and even looking a little bit dangerous. Wulf's heart plunged, then hammered to a marching beat at the thought of having to watch them blissfully reunited.

'I'm leaving,' he said coolly. 'No doubt you'll have a warmer welcome.'

He turned to reclaim his horse and ride away. He could leave Magnus to it now he'd pushed him into doing what he should have weeks ago: beg Isabella Alstone to take him back. Wulf turned away to hide his feelings and Gus scrambled off his horse with such haste Wulf turned to stare at him openmouthed. Gus seemed more interested in Wulf than finding the woman he had ridden here so hard to see.

'Damn it, Wulf, don't you turn your back on me as well,' his brother gasped out as if he was the social outcast of the two of them. He swayed so alarmingly Lord Shuttleworth started forward to stop him falling to the ground as if he was having a seizure. Deeply shocked by his brother's wild state, Wulf got there first and felt the lesser shock of Gus's newly bony body under his supporting grip. No woman was worth this much agony, he silently chided his brother, certainly not one who could coolly dismiss his sufferings as if they had nothing to do with her.

'Brace up, Gus,' he ordered as if impatient instead of sad and furious at the effort it cost him to get out the words struggling on his tongue.

'He's been murdered, Wulf—dead as mutton,' his brother managed before he went limp and Wulf was left to wonder for a terrible moment if his brother was mad.

'Who's dead, Gus?' he asked urgently as he fought to stay upright under their joint weight. 'And why would you think he's been murdered?'

'Saw him with my own eyes, Wulf. My father. Stiff as a doornail and covered in his own gore, but at least he won't trouble us any more.'

For a terrible moment relief sang in Wulf's heart, but he smothered it and shivered when he remembered their startled audience. 'My brother is not in his right mind,' he informed the Viscount, not sure a temporary derangement of spirits could cover the fact Gus had given a magistrate good reason to suspect him of patricide.

'The gentleman is exhausted,' Lord Shuttleworth said brusquely. 'Alworth, get both these nags stabled, then find a hurdle to carry him into the house to be cared for. We need to get him out of the cold and stop this faint turning to an ague.'

'Aye, m'lord,' the groom said with one last glance at this latest strange gentleman who seemed only half-alive after his long ride.

Wulf was battling shock and terror at his brother's hastily gasped-out words. Magnus must have been struggling with such terror ever since he set out in Wulf's tracks. No doubt he'd had to deal with the magistrates and get the corpse out of the house before he set the Runners on the killer's scent. And then he'd set out to fetch Wulf back when he was far too weak from his illness to withstand another shock. He'd always thought Gus the sensible one, a steady hand who would keep the rest of his family functioning despite their father's worst efforts.

If the Earl of Carrowe had been murdered, Wulf must get to Carrowe House as fast as he could and whisk his mother and sisters out of there. Torn between his concern for Gus's welfare and the urgency of getting back to London as fast as he could, he watched Miss Alstone arrive breathless in the stable yard with a familiar thump in his heart even now, when he should have nobler things on his mind than longing for a fine lady in a state of mild disarray. She looked as if she'd been running since she saw Gus dash over the horizon like the hero out of a ballad. She came to a hasty stop to stare down at his unconscious brother as if she couldn't quite believe her eyes. Not sure if she was delighted or horrified, Wulf used the excuse of brotherly concern not to watch love warm her shocked blue gaze as she examined Gus's pale face for signs of life and at last his brother blinked and opened his eyes.

'Why have you come dashing all this way in such a headlong fashion?' she said as if Gus was in a fit state to reply. She seemed to realise he was drifting in and out of consciousness when she shot Wulf an impatient glare instead. 'What's the matter with him? What have you done?' she said and the accusation made his gorge rise.

How could she think he'd harm his brother when Gus had dared the Earl's wrath to protect him as a boy and he loved him for it? How could she think him so little? 'Nothing,' he said coldly. 'You should look closer to home for a cause, since I'm told he hasn't been the same since you jilted him.'

'Be quiet. I won't listen to you two trading insults at a time like this.'

Shuttleworth's rebuke jolted Wulf and the man was right, he mustn't lose his temper, however much her accusation hurt. He had to keep a cool head and get his brother home as fast as a coach and horses could carry them, since Gus was obviously in no state to ride. Scandal was about to descend on the Haile family yet again and there was nothing he could do to keep it quiet if Gus's grim tale was true, but Shuttleworth and his family shouldn't be involved.

'You're right, my lord, and I'll be very grateful if you could let us borrow a carriage as far as the next coaching inn.'

'Wait until our local physician arrives, man. The moment he says your brother is fit to travel I promise to set you on your way as fast as can be.'

'As nobody knows who we are here, you can call us Smith or Butcher or Baker if it makes life easier,' Wulf offered distractedly and gazed down at his brother's haggard face. If the Earl had really been murdered, the Viscount wouldn't want the notoriety of having one of the Haile family as his guest and Wulf almost wished Gus would faint properly so he could forget the blind terror on his face when he gasped out his reason for coming.

'Or Candlestick-Maker?' Miss Alstone offered sarcastically. Her scorn pulled him back into every day, which was where he needed to be if he was going to get his family out of this latest calamity unscathed, so he ought to thank her.

'A bit long-winded, don't you think?' he argued against the uproar as three grooms and a footman arrived at the same time as Sir Hugh and his two available offspring.

'Forgive me?' she asked rather sheepishly, as if she thought her accusations were appalling as well, but he should absolve her, since she'd asked nicely.

'I'll try,' he said, making it clear he was preoccupied. Magnus helped by jolting out of his trance at the noise and staring about him in a panic. Lord Shuttleworth was right; if this was Gus's reaction to people who ran to help him, then a party of Bow Street Runners and a constable or two galloping in his wake could send him into a decline. Wulf shuddered for his brother's life and his sanity and decided who he chose to marry didn't seem very important now. 'Quietly, Gus,' he cautioned as the rescue party eyed his brother warily as if horror might be contagious. 'My brother exhausted himself tracking me down as our mother has been taken ill,' he explained as if that was the top and bottom of their woes.

And it wasn't an outright lie; the Countess's usual method of coping with problems was to be too delicate to face them. A murder in the house would require at least a nervous collapse and how her husband would have raged at her for it. At least the Dowager Countess of Carrowe could have hysterics whenever she chose from now on and Wulf doubted he or Magnus had the heart to deny her such a small solace for her hard life under the Earl's thumb. The word *Dowager* echoed dully in Wulf's head as he supervised the lifting of his brother on to the hurdle and soothed Magnus when he protested at being carried about like an invalid.

The Earl is no more, long live the Earl, Wulf mused numbly as he watched his brother's pallid face while the little procession slowly made its way to the house. Gresley would inherit little more than his father's title and Wulf already knew there was no point expecting very much from the new Earl. Gresley had never taken much interest in his younger brother and sisters and Wulf couldn't see that changing. Gresley would inherit Haile Carr officially and his wife had long ago decided she preferred it to London and the snobbish reminders the high sticklers knew how to make that she wasn't a born lady even if she was a countess now.

Indifferent to the new Earl at the best of times, Wulf turned his attention to the half-brother he did love. If Magnus had discovered the Earl's dead body, it might explain his half-crazed state when he got here. After he ran away from Carrowe House as a lad himself, he'd seen things that would shock a trooper, but Gus was far more sensitive and sheltered than Wulf had been and the Earl *was* his father. Add the stress and heartache of his parting from Miss Alstone and his illness earlier this year and it seemed little wonder Gus had buckled under the burden of it all.

'Carry him to the green bedchamber in the old wing,' Lord Shuttleworth ordered as they got Gus up the steps and inside the mansion. 'I don't want my wife to get wind of this yet,' he added. 'Even without your brother's current state of health this is an awkward situation for my wife and sister-in-law,' the Viscount murmured.

'His news has put everything else out of my head,' he admitted as Miss Alstone's exasperated snort of impatience seemed almost to argue that propriety and the gossips be damned. However, he couldn't quite believe in her anxiety for a man she'd brushed aside like a buzzing fly when she broke their betrothal and talked of so coldly not half an hour ago. He wished she'd go away and stop distracting him.

'Brandy,' Lord Shuttleworth ordered briskly when the little procession reached a clean if rather old-fashioned bedchamber. 'The rest of you can go.' His lordship added a few words of thanks for the grooms who had carried Magnus upstairs and now stepped back obediently.

'You two as well,' Sir Hugh Kenton told his off-spring with a severe enough look to make them do as they were bid. 'And no listening at doors,' he added as they turned away.

'He might, but I wouldn't,' Miss Sophia said with an accusing look at her little brother and a saintly ex-pression Wulf didn't believe for a moment.

'If either of you even try it, I'll tell your mother what you were up to this afternoon,' their father threatened. From their slumped shoulders they re-ally would go this time and Wulf was glad they hadn't heard Magnus's startling opening statement and didn't realise what a fine, grisly story they were missing.

'My brother will be best out of these clothes; it looks as if he slept in them before he set out to track me down,' Wulf said, hoping to get Isabella out of the room as well.

'Yes, that's a good idea and here's the brandy you ordered, Shuttleworth. One exhausted man against three of us—I think we can cope, don't you?' Sir Hugh said with a cool look at the female too stub-born to have left the room.

'You're trying to get rid of me, aren't you?' Isa-bella challenged him and Wulf realised he'd under-estimated her yet again.

'Yes, is it working?' Shuttleworth asked blandly.

'Considering I'm a single lady, I don't see how it can't. You two think you're sharp as needles, though, don't you?'

'We are,' Sir Hugh said modestly.

Wulf pretended he was too busy pressing a brandy glass to his brother's lips to hear the by-play and shrugged aside a ridiculous urge to beg her to stay.

'It's very annoying of you and I expect a full account of whatever goes on in this room later, so if you don't want me to put Kate on your tail, you'd best give it to me as soon as you can,' she threatened, then left the room with her nose in the air, snapping the door closed behind her to make her feelings plain.

'She won't tell Kate,' Shuttleworth reassured himself out loud.

'Especially if we fob her off with some plausible tale,' Sir Hugh agreed.

Wulf thought they looked uneasy about the chances of her complying with anything she didn't want to comply with. 'Never mind Miss Alstone; where's the sawbones?' he demanded and hoped a lady wouldn't lower herself to listen at doors.

Isabella wouldn't dream of doing anything as unladylike as putting her ear to the keyhole when she was far too likely to get caught. She racked her brains for a better way to find out what was being said in a closed room. If they thought hiding Magnus in the older part of the house would stop Kate finding out he was here, they didn't know her sister as well as they thought and Isabella *had* to know why Mag-

Elizabeth Beacon 83

nus had galloped after his half-brother so hard he'd endangered his health even further. Her pulse thundered at the very thought someone might have told Magnus what she and his brother did at Haile Carr that night. No, that wasn't possible—nobody knew about that but her and Wulf and he loved Magnus. He'd never hurt him even if he despised her. Not even, her uneasy conscience whispered, if he had truly set sail for America to avoid her and his own sense of treachery to his half-brother.

She had to know what all this was about. If someone had seen and whispered about her and Wulf's disgraceful encounter in the shadows at Haile Carr, she must decide now if she could deny her sins in public or dare to admit it and be pointed out as Wicked Miss Alstone for the rest of her days.

Inspiration suddenly hit as to how she could get answers to her questions. The poor state of the floors and ceilings in the older parts of the house had been a theme running through Kate's letters these last few months. Hopefully the carpenters had been put off thumping and hammering for a few weeks while the family assembled. Maybe their unfinished works could let her listen to what was being said by a pack of men who thought they knew best.

Creeping up the elaborately carved staircase that indicated this had once been a more important part of the house was a lot easier than she expected. The drop cloths and drugget put down to protect finely carved and polished oak against work boots and the dust and dirt nobody could keep at bay on a worksite muffled the slight noises of creaking treads and settling timbers as she moved as if walking on egg-shells. She must be even more wary once she was above the room they'd taken Magnus to. If news got about of his hasty visit, the gossips would poke and pry for a reason, so she should know what had brought him here and she had to admit to herself she was more than curious to know what had happened between Magnus and his half-brother.

She grabbed the hem of her gown so she could tie it round her waist and keep her skirts out of the dust. At least ladies' waists were lower and skirts wider now; the idea of trying to do this in a narrow column of cambric or muslin made her shudder for the con-tortions it would cost her. Mentally apologising to her maid for the state she was about to get her petticoats in, she glanced out of the nearest window to orient herself to the room below. She crept past three dusty and half-repaired attic rooms before halting at the doorway of the one where she could see the fountain court from the same angle she'd glimpsed from Mag-nus's room. Yes, that was about right. Three sets of acute masculine ears would be directly underneath her, maybe even four if Magnus was less faint than he had been at first. Her maid would have more to scold about than dusty petticoats and Isabella sighed for her stockings as she removed her soft-soled shoes and stepped on to oak boards she was delighted to see in place over only half the floor. She held her breath as she measured every step like an acrobat. Maybe she should become a government spy, she decided when she got to the edge of the floorboards without more than a creak so slight it sounded like an old house settling. The gap was too wide to jump without giving herself away. If she wanted to hear more than the murmur she could pick out now, she would have to creep across bare joists and hope the laths were poorer or more worm-holed so she could hear through them. She quailed at the idea of stepping on a splinter or a nail and overbalancing and falling into the room below, or even being left suspended halfway with her legs sticking through. Listening hard to be certain they hadn't heard her as she crept closer to the gap, she bent over it in the hope of catching what the men were saying. Ah, here was a piece of luck. The plaster was exposed below and she could see a crack and a few slivers of daylight through it. She edged along a beam that looked sound enough to get her closer. Her stockings were ruined already and she'd scraped her knees, but at least she could hear words now instead of just manly rumbles and grumbles.

'Do you think your little demons have really gone this time, Kenton?' she heard Edmund ask.

'Aye, they soon get bored and it's still a lovely day and their mother isn't looking for them yet.'

'Good, then we'd best get on before anyone else tries to find out your secrets, Haile,' Edmund said almost as if he was joking.

Isabella nodded emphatically at thin air. *Yes, do get on with it. This position is uncomfortable in so many different ways.*

'The Earl—he's stone-dead and he was murdered,' she heard Magnus say and suddenly it didn't matter she was perched up here like a chicken. Murder, no, surely that was impossible. Murder happened in newssheets and sensational ballads, not to people she knew.

Chapter Six

No, it's a fever raging through him; Magnus is delirious. Even the Earl of Carrowe doesn't deserve to die like that.

Isabella shook her head in disbelief and all her blood seemed to rush to her head as Magnus's words echoed in her ears like the crack of doom. Murder? Her ears were deceiving her or Magnus was raving. He was so torn and tortured by the awful situation he was caught up in that his mind had been turned. Yes, that was it; he must be suffering from brain fever. She was praying the doctor would come and save his sanity before it was too late when his next muttered sentence disillusioned her.

'I found my father done to death, Wulf. He was murdered, foully murdered,' Magnus was saying and Wulf muttered something soothing she didn't catch because she was too busy lingering on the gruff rumble of his voice like a besotted debutante while poor Magnus was in the grip of horror. 'Foully murdered,' he echoed his own words as if he couldn't stop now he'd got to Wulf and told him his terrible news.

'So you said,' his brother said coolly. 'Tell us where and how the Earl died, Gus, before the sawbones gets here and pours laudanum down your throat. We'll not get even this much sense out of you for hours after that.'

She heard Magnus chuckle and could even imagine him smiling weakly, so perhaps Wulf understood him after all. She was suddenly glad they were as close as they were. They, too, had shared a harsh childhood and deserved something more than bitter memories out of it. For some reason the old lord had only seemed to care about his two eldest children. After half a year of trying to avoid her future father-in-law, she'd concluded he blamed his younger children for the disaster his marriage turned into. Isabella shuddered at the thought of being imprisoned in such a marriage herself and wondered how Lady Carrowe stopped herself from murdering him long ago. No! She mustn't even think such things. Tempted to rock back and forth on her beam to comfort herself, she shook her head at the very idea Lady Carrowe had put a knife into her husband. If she was going to do that, she would have done it when Wulf was born and the man denounced him.

'He must have come back home that night after his usual debauch and we didn't even know it,' Magnus was saying. 'We found him in the morning and by that time he was long gone, Wulf. He was sitting in the Small Drawing Room with his eyes wide open and staring at us as if he'd met the devil. Remember how it was called the Red Room before Mama had it painted white to try to make it seem less gloomy? Heaven knows it's red again now,' Magnus reported with a dash of hysteria in his deep voice again, as if he was remembering the sight of his murdered father and might truly run mad if they weren't careful how they teased this terrible story out of him.

Shivering like a greyhound in a thunderstorm now, Isabella felt her heart stutter at the terrible ring of truth in his words. Now *she* couldn't shake off the awful image of the Earl staring into the pit of hell while his lifeblood drained out of him.

'I have to suppose he was stabbed, then, since there was so much blood,' his brother was saying as if they were discussing the weather.

Isabella shook her head; how could Wulf be so calm about a soul being snuffed out so horribly? Even if it was the Earl's. Surely he had a spark of pity in him for a life ended so violently? He'd be a lesser man if he didn't and she didn't want him to be somehow. He might be the most contrary, abrasive and downright annoying man she'd ever met and she was almost sure she didn't like him, but she didn't want him to be smaller than she'd thought when he stepped out of the shadows on that dratted terrace at Haile Carr.

'Maybe he was, but we couldn't see a knife,' Magnus was saying more steadily now, so she must listen instead of thinking uncomfortable thoughts she could dwell on later. She would have tried to soothe and calm him, but Wulf obviously knew truths this brutal couldn't be wrapped in clean linen. She supposed she ought to respect him for knowing better.

'From what little I could see before Mama had hysterics and I had to carry her to her bedchamber, he could have been stabbed as well, Wulf,' Magnus said, 'but he had certainly been hit on the head. That plaster bust of Ovid he used to throw his hat on when he came home drunk was lying broken and bloody by his chair. The side of his head was beaten in and he was covered in his own gore.'

'You're certain it was him?'

'Even I'm not fool enough to ride here on a maybe, Wulf, and before you ask me, yes, I made sure he was dead and didn't leave Mama and the girls alone in that house with his corpse. The sight of him lying in his chair like butcher's meat will haunt me to my dying day, so heaven knows what it'll do to poor Theodora, who found him first and ran to get me. I have to get back to them instead of cosseting myself like a Bath breakdown, they need me.'

'Lie back down, you idiot, you're exhausted. I'll look after them until you're rested and fit to help— you're too ill to be any use to them now, Gus. We're both going to need our full strength to deal with what comes next. I've wished him dead in the past but never thought I'd see this day.'

'Don't say that, Wulf,' Magnus said a little more strongly. 'Someone might hear and think you had a hand in his murder. And think how happy he'd be to drag you down with him, even if he had to die to do it.'

'You're right,' Wulf admitted and Isabella could imagine him frowning. 'Don't expect me to pretend I'm sorry he's gone, though,' he added gruffly.

'That's too much to ask, but we'll all be suspects now. You'd best keep a still tongue if you don't want it to be more than an unproven suspicion we wanted him to die sooner rather than later.'

'Everyone knows I hated him, Gus. Shuttleworth and Kenton aren't the sort of men to grasp the first straw of suspicion that drifts their way,' Wulf argued and Isabella silently nodded her agreement.

'FitzDevelin's right, Haile—you're going to need all the friends you can get, so you'd best not offend us,' Edmund said, sounding as calm and steady as if these two unlikely visitors had called in to pass the time of day.

'We need to leave as soon as we can so you keep you and yours safe from this grim business,' Wulf added.

'I can't lie about like this when we're needed at home,' Isabella heard Magnus fretting and was glad he wasn't absorbed in his own miserable situation for the moment, even if it was for such a terrible reason.

'If we can borrow a carriage to get to London all the sooner, I'll be grateful to you, Lord Shuttleworth. I shall send it back as soon as we can hire a decent vehicle and hopefully your family will hardly notice the horses have gone before they're back again.'

'You don't know our families like we do if you

think that, FitzDevelin, but you're welcome to borrow my travelling carriage and a fast team the moment your brother is declared fit to travel. In the meantime, we three should prepare ourselves for a hard ride.'

Edmund sounded doubtful about it even as he spoke. As well he might with Kate in such an advanced state of pregnancy, Isabella thought, wishing she was down there and allowed a say in their plans. She had been Magnus's fiancée for half a year and knew the Countess of Carrowe and her younger daughters as well as any outsider. So she, too, must return to town only hours after she had arrived in the country. Edmund had to stay here with Kate, but there was nothing much Isabella could do to help her sister once Kate was in labour. A single lady wouldn't be allowed into the room to hold her sister's hand while she laboured with doctors, midwives and an experienced mother of six on hand.

'Can't stay here, must go back,' she heard Magnus mutter distractedly.

'You're in no fit state to go anywhere,' Sir Hugh Kenton argued briskly. 'And there's no question of you leaving your wife when she's about to give birth either, Shuttleworth. I'm the best person to go back to town with FitzDevelin and your job will be to keep Haile here and his identity a secret until he's fit to travel. I have experience of such dark matters and at least I can help FitzDevelin and the Countess untangle their affairs, so stop playing the dutiful lord, Edmund, and remember Kate needs you here.'

Isabella recalled how scandal had dogged Hugh for years after he had been suspected of murdering his first wife. The Navy decided to dispense with his services so he became a merchant captain for Isabella's brother-in-law Kit. He was still in Kit's service when he met Louise in some wild and scandalous manner they refused to discuss even now. As a result of his past, there was very little Hugh didn't know about false witnesses and the sort of vicious rumours that could blacken an innocent man's name. Of course he was the right person to help the Hailes, but so was she. Lady Carrowe was living in a broken-down, barely habitable mansion her husband had been plundering for years to fund his extravagant lifestyle. Then there were her younger daughters; their slender hopes of a decent marriage could be snuffed out by this latest scandal if it wasn't handled very carefully. Isabella might as well make herself useful to the Haile girls and their mother and she was sure she could stay out of the way of Magnus and Wulf if she tried hard enough.

'It's true; I shouldn't leave my wife,' Edmund admitted at last, 'but you'll need help to get your family out of this mess without a great deal of scandal and danger, FitzDevelin. Don't turn Kenton's offer down because you're too stiff-necked to accept help.'

'I know a good deal about danger and my mother and sisters are used to scandal; they have me to thank for that,' Wulf replied with bitter irony.

It was true, though, wasn't it? He'd lived where he

wasn't wanted until he was old enough to run away and at an age when he should have been dreaming of wild adventures rather than facing them daily as he fought to survive on the streets. He was a strong man and the Haile family needed one now more than ever; no wonder his brother had ridden here so frantically to fetch Wulf back. Feeling uncomfortably disloyal, she reminded herself Magnus had been through his own private hell and a long illness these last few months, so it was little wonder he was felled by this heavy blow on top of all the others.

'I suspect you're the least of their worries right now, FitzDevelin. Time to stop harping on the past and get on with the present now your stepfather is dead and his killer is at large,' Hugh warned.

Isabella shivered, listening even harder for anything she could catch through feet of dusty air and a crumbling ceiling.

'And your mother and sisters need you,' Hugh continued.

'I promised to do everything I could to get you back to London by tomorrow morning, Wulf,' Magnus said restlessly, as it was his fault they weren't on the road already.

'I can ride all night if I have to,' Wulf said dismissively. Isabella could imagine him doing it as well, despite the punishing ride he must have had to get here already, driven to confront her with her sins and bully her to take Magnus back and marry him. At least no self-respecting highwayman would hold up such an angry man for fear of being mown down as if as unimportant as a fly on a horse's ear, primed pistols or no.

'Start now,' his brother urged breathlessly, 'I'll follow when I can, but you'll be far more use than I am right now, Wulf.'

Silence descended while the men tried not to agree out loud and Isabella plotted her own hasty departure from Cravenhill Park and the rural peace and quiet she'd come here to find. If she stayed, news of Magnus's presence would leak out and the local gossips would seize on it as a sign of reconciliation in the teeth of the biggest scandal to hit the Hailes for centuries. She needed to get to London before the polite world had a chance to write off the Haile ladies for good this time.

'Give me half an hour and we'll set out together, FitzDevelin,' Hugh said so firmly she knew Wulf might as well accept his company as eat his dust all the way back to town, since Hugh could afford the best horses and he couldn't.

'My thanks, then, Sir Hugh. I hope you'll return here once I've got my mother and sisters out of that dusty old mausoleum and away from the gossips.'

'No, don't make them hide away as if they're guilty of something, you great manly idiot,' Isabella actually muttered under her voice before shaking her head at her own stupidity. It was high time she crept away and got on with frustrating all their well-meant masculine plans. She wriggled precariously around on her beam to face the door again, then shuffled along until she got to dusty floorboards and could take to hands and knees while the men were busy arguing about who was going where and what they were doing when they got there. They didn't seem suspicious of the sounds of an old building restless on ancient foundations and she knew enough to insist on returning to London now, whatever arguments Edmund thought up to stop her.

Isabella glanced down at her dusty person and undid her knotted skirts. At least they would cover grimy petticoats and her once-white pantalettes, but neither would ever be the same again. Even if her underpinnings were boiled for hours to get them white again, the lace was damaged. The last few minutes would have been much trickier if she had to twist about on a beam with nothing to keep her knees from the splinters. Dirty feet and torn stockings were bad enough, she decided as she shuffled her shoes back on at the far end of the interconnected rooms. Now all she wanted was to get back to her room unseen and wash off the dust of ages before making her rapid departure.

Had Hugh and Wulf gone yet or were they still waiting for the doctor? She stole along makeshift corridors added long after this part of the house was built, musing how folk managed to live huggermugger in such times. The very idea of one room opening off another struck her as absurdly intimate, but maybe everyday life *was* more intimate in a rich man's house back then. Wulf FitzDevelin's latest intrusion into her life seemed to have made her think about things she usually accepted as everyday parts of life she didn't even need to wonder about. Perhaps she needed his abrasive scorn of fine ladies to make her question how her life ran along so smoothly she rarely questioned the rights and wrongs of it.

Somehow she found her way through the warren of rooms back to the main house without having to go back the way she'd come and risk them knowing she had heard most of what they had said. Now all she need do was explain her hasty departure to Kate and Louise, persuade her maid to pack everything she'd only just finished unpacking and retrace the journey they'd only just completed.

During the three frustrating days it had taken Isabella to journey from Herefordshire to London at a respectable pace, so nobody could accuse her of unladylike haste, she had far too much time to think. So much for her resolution to change the way she lived when they had to crawl along because she didn't want to draw attention to her return to the capital by doing it at the same breakneck speed Hugh and Wulf would be galloping at. At last, though, she was staring out of mud-spattered carriage windows at the busy streets and closely packed houses and sighing with relief that they were back in London when she had been so pleased to quit it less than a week ago.

Magnus would have to stay at Cravenhill until he was well enough for the long journey home, so it should be obvious why she left her brother-in-law's house for the time being. Louise and Kate would have sent out the right letters to the right people by now, explaining how poor Mr Haile was laid up at Cravenhill after foolishly riding all the way there at breakneck speed to beg for Sir Hugh's help in his family's hour of need. The poor man had some sort of brain fever earlier this year so how could they turn him away at the risk of his health being permanently broken? Although his timing was unfortunate to say the least and poor Isabella had been forced to leave Cravenhill for London in order to stay with dear Charlotte Shaw, her former governess, until Mr Haile was well enough to leave. Nobody could blame the Countess of Carrowe for being too bowed down with her own troubles and sorrows to drive all the way to Herefordshire to attend to Mr Haile herself, but really it was *most* inconvenient.

There would still be murmurs about why Magnus Haile was in Herefordshire when he should have been at Carrowe House. He would probably be portrayed as the devoted, broken-hearted suitor seeking comfort at the darkest time in his life; she would be the hard-hearted female who hotfooted it to London rather than give in and marry him after all. Enduring a few whispers and the odd sneer was nothing next to the horrors haunting Magnus's mother and sisters at this very moment, though. They had to live with the sort of wild speculation and storytelling that could cost an innocent life if the wrong person was found guilty of the Earl's murder. Her own lot in life suddenly seemed very easy in comparison.

'Drive straight round to Hanover Square, Samson,' Isabella ordered briskly. 'Carnwood House will be closed up, so there's no point in stopping there.'

'Very well, Miss Alstone,' Kate's well-trained coachman replied impassively.

Glad her personal maid, Heloise, was new and not given to arguing about anything that didn't concern fashion or her mistress being perfectly turned out whenever she left her bedchamber, Isabella sat back on the comfortable cushions and hoped Charlotte was home.

'Izzie, what on earth...?' Charlotte shifted the baby in her arms to kiss her former pupil, then raised her eyebrows at the small mountain of luggage piling up in her spacious hallway under Heloise's stern supervision. 'You'd best come into my sitting room and tell me all about it,' she said softly. 'Have everything conveyed to the Blue Bedchamber if you please, Harris,' she said to the butler before leading Isabella into the cosy parlour she favoured, because it was next to her husband's office and he frequently dashed in to join her for half an hour or so.

'What are you doing back in London less than a week after you left?'

'Magnus came to Cravenhill in great haste, then had to stay to be nursed through a recurrence of that illness he had earlier in the year.'

'Is it catching?'

'No, not after all these weeks. Edmund is a kind Christian gentleman, but he would have sent Magnus somewhere else to be cared for if there was the slightest risk of infection for Kate and the children.

Oh, don't look at me like that; the babe hasn't been born yet. Or at least it hadn't been when I left. By now it may have come into the world, since Kate was the size of a small cottage.'

Charlotte raised her eyebrows again and looked unconvinced by Isabella's misplaced humour, as well as her telling of half the story. The horrid tale of the Earl of Carrowe's murder must be flying about London faster than a family of hungry kites by now, so it was little wonder Charlotte refused to be diverted.

'Oh, very well, Magnus suffered what the doctor called a "nervous collapse". It's not my fault he's been under so much strain of late, so don't you start blaming me as well. And don't expect me to tell you what *did* cause it either.'

'As well as whom?' Charlotte demanded. Trust her to latch on to the one part of her sentence Isabella wished she hadn't let slip.

'The rest of the world,' she explained so airily it ought to divert attention from her flushed cheeks. 'Who should mind their own business for once.'

'I doubt even the gossips care about your part in the Haile family's woes now.'

'They would have done if I hadn't left Cravenhill the day Magnus arrived unfit to ride another yard, let alone go a mile to the village inn. I didn't dare wait for Kate's baby to be born before I left, but why must the gossips tattle and fabricate stories and put me and the Haile family to so much trouble, Charlotte?'

'Mainly because you were born with such spectacularly good looks it's impossible to avoid it, but that's the burden you bear, poor love.'

'Don't mock me, Charlotte. It feels heavier than usual right now.'

'Because gentlemen can't see the real Isabella for your looks and fortune?'

'Maybe,' Isabella said cautiously.

If Charlotte ever guessed there was one man in particular who thought the social gulf between them so wide it was unbridgeable, she'd dig until she found out who he was. Charlotte was the only grandchild of a duke and she had wed a nobleman's by-blow. No argument about Wulf's unsuitability or the scandal he was born into would cut ice with Mrs Ben Shaw.

'Love can creep into even the most carefully guarded heart when you least expect it,' Charlotte warned with all that personal experience waiting to back her argument up.

'Not into mine it won't and Miss Margaret seems to have exhausted herself with her protests about her teeth coming through,' she said as the baby in Charlotte's arms let out a wail.

'I'll try putting her in her cradle so we can have a cup of tea and eat one of Cook's best sugar buns in peace.'

Charlotte rose very carefully and eased the child gently into her cradle. A little stir of protest and she sang softly until the little girl settled back to sleep with an angelic sigh of content.

'At last,' Charlotte breathed as she lowered herself to a chair. She looked so weary Isabella mur-

mured she was going to order that tea herself instead
of ringing for it and left them to sleep off their disturbed night side by side.

Isabella sat in her own private sitting room attached to the large guest bedchamber in the corner
of the Shaws' house that was furthest away from the
nursery wing and wondered how Wulf FitzDevelin
was faring under very different circumstances. The
murder of a peer of the realm couldn't quietly fade
from public memory after a day or two of shocked
gossip and a few soothing murmurs from the authorities. She hoped Hugh had managed to set the right
hounds on the right trails to find the killer, because
until he was tracked down and punished, the Hailes
would be eyed with suspicion wherever they went.
Isabella puzzled over the challenge of visiting the
ladies of the family. It would have to be done in secret, however much she wanted to march in through
the front door and make it clear she didn't care about
the newssheets or the gossips. If she was an independent lady without close family and many friends
and well-wishers, she could do just that, but given
that she had two sisters and a clutch of very good
friends whose reputations and wellbeing were bound
up with her own she had to be discreet and careful
about her own reputation.

If Magnus's supposed love, the woman who was
too timid to admit to him even when his father hadn't
been murdered, really loved him, she would come to
town and stay at his mother and sisters' side even if

she couldn't bring herself to support him as openly as Isabella thought she should. Lady Delphine's family estate marched with that of Haile Carr and the lady knew the family very well. Isabella frowned and couldn't recall much about her own past meetings with Lady Delphine Drace. She knew Lady Drace was widowed last year and her pompous husband had been the sort of political baronet she always avoided as carefully as she could herself. The man would prose on for ever about his own views and beliefs, then condescend to all women as if they were incapable of rational thought and put on this earth to listen to the wisdom of pompous idiots like him. The Lady Delphine she remembered had anxious blue eyes set in a thin face and hands that seemed restless and almost outside of the lady's control. Who would think a woman like that could inspire such passion in Magnus he hadn't cared very much if he lived or died once she'd turned her back on him after he'd fathered her supposedly posthumous child?

Isabella was tempted to write and order the woman to live up to her obligations for once in her life. The Hailes needed a friend and Lady Drace was the logical person to be there for them, but she clearly wasn't coming. News of the murder must have reached Norfolk and the Drace Dower House by now and she hadn't driven up to town to show her support or even written a sturdy message of support for her old friends. Lady Delphine was clearly a broken reed, so Miss Alstone would step into the shoes of supporter and friend. Yes, now she was here and it wasn't quite time for the Season yet, she would be able to find lots of good excuses to slip away on errands for her sisters or fittings for a new gown or an endless search for exactly the right bonnet to match her new pelisse. If she also happened to visit the creaking old Carrowe mansion while she was out, that would be by the by, as long as she didn't allow herself to be seen by the hordes of spectators still haunting the scene of the crime like expectant carrion crows.

Chapter Seven

After another pointless and frustrating morning with the lawyers and magistrates, Wulf strode back to Carrowe House to fend off the curious. This morning he'd needed all Sir Hugh Kenton's clear-sighted logic to help him cut through the jargon and ritual as they went over the whys and how and perhaps of his stepfather's murder yet again. Until now he'd thought he understood his native language well enough, but he hadn't encountered a room full of legal minds hell-bent on contradicting one another as incomprehensibly as possible. Sir Hugh could cut through their nonsense and get to the nub of the matter as Wulf couldn't quite bring himself to, with the lives and reputations of his closest family weighing so heavily on his mind. He frowned at the thought of all the contrary forces tugging him in different directions right now and was doubly glad he'd listened to Lord Shuttleworth and accepted help when it was offered by a man who understood his situation all too well.

Wulf wanted to know who broke into ruinous old Carrowe House that night to murder the Earl and he didn't want suspicion falling on his family. Trying to weigh their lives and wellbeing against the mystery of who hated the old man enough to kill him was enough to give King Solomon in all his wisdom a headache and Wulf didn't feel very wise at all right now. Cutting down the list of suspects would mean his family could become more and more prominent on it. His mother and sisters had been there that night, as had Magnus, even if he had been out for a goodly part of it. If they knew where he'd been, he might be left off the inventory of suspects. Wulf was only missing from it himself because he was more than halfway to Cravenhill Park when the Earl was killed. There were too many reliable witnesses to his journey and nobody had been able to show how Wulf Fitz-Develin could kill his stepfather and be in Herefordshire so quickly unless he'd mastered the dark art of being in two places at once. If not for his guilt-driven obsession with begging Isabella to take his brother back and marry him, he would have been in London that night and would likely be in Newgate awaiting trial for his life at this very moment.

Whoever killed the old man when Wulf wasn't there to take the blame couldn't have been thinking very hard. Or perhaps they loved him enough to make sure no sane magistrate could accuse him of the murder. That simply wasn't possible and implied careful planning, which didn't seem very likely given the impulsive, excessive violence of the crime.

The coroner stated that the Earl had been stabbed *and* bludgeoned to death. It was apparently impossible to work out which wound had actually killed him, but both needed enough force to almost excuse Lady Carrowe and her equally slight, petite daughters from the list of suspects. But extreme passion could lend superhuman strength, one of the magistrates had pointed out unhelpfully.

Wulf tried to block that caveat from his mind as he went in through the strong, ancient oak back door of shabby and tumbledown Carrowe House. He walked past the kitchens without even noticing the soot and decay or the empty and echoing sound of his own footsteps as he strode past deserted rooms that had once bustled with life and hectic activity. It seemed better to consider the everyday annoyance of his eldest half-brother, Gresley—now Fifth Earl of Carrowe—than let his thoughts linger on the uncomfortable notion someone he loved could be a murderer. Early this morning he'd received Gresley's reply to his express telling him the Earl had been murdered and it was time for his successor to take up his responsibility as head of the family. Apparently the new Earl of Carrowe was too busy to come to town and the new Lady Carrowe too overcome by nerves and grief for him to leave her even if he wasn't. Wulf must sort it all out and keep the curious at bay, meet the old Earl's creditors and do whatever necessary to keep their mother happy until Magnus was well enough to take over. Since Gresley hardly trusted Wulf to put on his own shoes without detailed instructions, that was almost as bad as declaring he didn't give a damn what had happened to his father or the family he was born into. The old Earl had always favoured his eldest son and now Gresley wasn't even willing to come and fetch his body home. That was what undertakers were for apparently; something else to add to Wulf's list of things to do. At least Gresley would have to foot their bill, Wulf thought, the new Earl's callousness proving him a lot more like his father than he'd want to admit.

Wulf was tempted to whisk his sisters and mother off to stay at his own house on the wildest heath he could find near London and leave Carrowe House to the rats and the duns and the curious. Gresley would have no choice but to come and sort the poor old place out then, but it would look bad if they all ran away before the new Earl came to take up his responsibilities. Wulf paused at the bottom of the stairs and felt a sly glimmer of satisfaction at the neglect so obvious all around him now the Earl wasn't here to brazen out the shabbiness of his London home as if this was how he liked it. Not much of an inheritance for his successor, was it? Gilding was flaking off any fine plasterwork still clinging to the damp marred walls and cracked ceilings. The odd paintings the old man hadn't sold were so tattered or darkened by smoke and age not even the most optimistic collector was prepared to waste a few shillings to find out if a masterpiece lay under the gloom. Wulf couldn't even remember what colour the curtains, cushions and carpets were in their youth because it was so long ago they should be in a museum, if they took the moth-eaten debris of past glories.

Why wasn't Gresley here sizing up the value of anything that had escaped his father's careless eye and consigning the rest to the bonfire, though? Gresley could pretend he doted on his plump little wife all he liked, but Wulf knew money was his true passion. The new Countess of Carrowe's grandfather had owned the richest plantation in Jamaica and a fleet of slave ships and now she held the purse strings at Haile Carr. If not for her fortune, Gresley would never have married her, so it didn't ring true to stay away because she was feeling squeamish about her father-in-law's murder, not when something might still be salvaged from the wreck of his father's once-splendid assets. Perhaps the new Earl of Carrowe had the old ruin earmarked for a grand square and a few rows of neat town houses to bring him in a healthy income. Some enterprising architect could have ridden up to Haile Carr and be laying out his grandiose ideas to Gresley at this very moment.

Wulf shook his head, managing to relax the grim set of his mouth and unclench his teeth. After being bullied, then ignored by his eldest half-brother as soon as he got too big to terrorise, Wulf always looked twice at Gresley's motives. Maybe Gresley would be different now he was a true lord instead of a courtesy one. The sense of right and wrong Wulf had clung to even while being beaten for something he didn't do in this very house as a boy forbade him to pass the blame for the Earl's death on to Gresley simply because he wanted him to have it. Gresley's natural cowardice explained his absence every bit as well as guilt might do, but if any of his kin must be guilty of murder, he'd prefer it to be Gresley. Better if it was a passing maniac or some habitual criminal with a grudge and a capital sentence hanging over him already, but if Wulf had to sacrifice a family member, Gresley would do nicely.

'Ah, I'm so glad I have caught you at last, Mr FitzDevelin,' Isabella Alstone's dulcet tones greeted him brusquely from the shadows as if he ought to have been expecting her and he was deplorably late.

He groaned and why wouldn't he? She was the last person he wanted tangled up in this dark business. He had half-hoped she'd stay at Cravenhill Park to mop Gus's brow, or join her other sister in Derbyshire and stay out of his way.

'Are you now?' he replied concisely.

'Yes. We need to talk about your mother and your sisters,' she told him with such determination he might have groaned again if it wouldn't give too much away.

'What have you done; locked them in a convenient attic?'

Even in the gloom of a hall where the windows probably hadn't been washed for a decade he saw her lips tighten. She seemed to be making an almost physical effort to hang on to her temper and he felt ashamed of himself for taunting her so absurdly when everything about his family was serious right now.

'If you're going to be difficult, at least do it where they can't hear you,' she said as if addressing a fractious child.

He could see the aunt of a variety of hopeful nieces and nephews in her patient expression and badly wanted to kiss her so they could both forget to be practical for a few blissful moments. 'The estate office is as neglected as the rest of this dust heap, but at least we won't be disturbed in there,' he said, waving her into the cobweb-decorated room behind what had once been the state rooms. If she was scared of spiders, she should have stayed away from Carrowe House.

'How busy and full of life this place must have been once upon a time,' she said after a cool look around dusty deed boxes and chaotic piles of faded and mouse-chewed paper scattered here, there and everywhere after several decades of lordly impatience when the Earl decided not to pay a secretary.

'It's quite busy with it now,' he said as a giveaway scuttle in the corner of the room said some of those mice were still here.

She didn't even flinch. 'My maid will have hysterics if I take this home with me,' she told him calmly as she plucked a spider off her richly blue pelisse sleeve and put it on a tottering heap of official-looking parchment rolls.

'You have strong nerves, Miss Alstone.'

'Maybe, but I also have an aversion to being dismissed as a flighty female sure to bolt at the first sign of something I might not like the look or feel of, Mr FitzDevelin,' she told him with a very straight look.

'So I can't terrify you with our furtive wildlife. Foolish and ungallant of me to try, I suppose, but I've always been very protective of my mother and little sisters.'

'Good, it's about time someone was.'

'If you want us to have a civilised conversation, don't throw accusations of neglect at Magnus. He's not here to defend himself.'

'I didn't mean him. You know we badly wanted to get them away from here,' she said and he could see the truth in her deepest of blue eyes as she refused to be swerved from her chosen subject.

'You and your family?'

'No, me and Magnus. That's why we…'

Her tongue had clearly taken her further than she'd meant to go. He knew a truth she hadn't meant to let slip out when he heard it and, from her quick grimace and the frown knitting her brows, so did she.

'That's why you agreed to marry Magnus?' he said incredulously. 'You thought rescuing them was so important you were ready to wed my brother to do it?'

'No, of course not. Magnus is a handsome and kindly gentleman with a keen sense of humour and he'd been a good friend since I made my come out. I had more reasons than I can count to say yes when he asked me to marry him.'

'And they all dropped away barely a month before the wedding? They don't sound like the sort of reasons I could ever risk marrying for.'

'Two months and you're not the marrying kind,' she told him sternly.

'Neither are you if you needed all those reasons to say yes to my brother.'

'No, I really don't think I am,' she said rather sadly and stared at a dusty cobweb for a long moment before she seemed to recall who she was talking to. She shook her head impatiently and looked as if she wanted to be done with him and this shabby old wreck of a house now their conversation wasn't going to plan.

'But you wanted to be?' he guessed.

'I did; it was a mistake.'

He'd been right the first time he set eyes on her, then; she really did have a generous and yearning heart under all that cool poise and perfection. She *was* gallant and impulsive and protective and would make some lucky child a wonderful mother one day. How wrong-headed of Magnus to think friendship and common interests were enough to build a good marriage on with a woman like her. He'd had their mother's example of what happened when a passionate, loving woman married the wrong man in front of him all these years, yet Magnus still asked Isabella Alstone to marry him without loving her? Now Wulf was angry with his brother instead of himself or this unattainable woman he'd longed for all the way across a vast ocean and back again. What the devil was Gus thinking of to tangle such an exceptional female up in a mess like this one, then turn himself into a shadow of his former self when she saw sense and refused to marry him? No, he suddenly knew it wasn't her behind all the changes in his brother. There wasn't that sort of intensity between them, so there must be something deeper and darker behind Magnus's unhappiness than his broken engagement. At last he could see a malaise deeper than his brother's physical ills behind Gus's actions when he looked back over the last year or so and he wondered why he hadn't seen it at the time. Of course, he'd spent six months of struggling with a malaise of his own, so could a woman be at the root of Magnus's melancholy and irrational actions as well?

'A mistake you don't intend to repeat?' he asked now, feeling guilty at the sudden thought that although he couldn't have her in his bed, he didn't want her in anyone else's.

'Indeed not.'

When he rode to Cravenhill Park as if his life depended on persuading her to marry his brother, he'd almost hated her for the jealousy roaring through him at the thought of the union going ahead. He'd looked up to and loved Magnus all this life, but last year he left England so he wouldn't be able to do everything in his power to seduce Gus's bride-to-be away from him. Then Gus let her slip through his fingers as if she wasn't the most magnificent female either of them had ever laid eyes on anyway, and if the idiot *didn't* love her to distraction, he must be in love with someone else. Wulf couldn't think of any other reason why a sane and vigorous man wouldn't fall in love with her and Gus had certainly been one of those until whoever got her claws into him fixed them so deep she managed to blind Gus to Isabella's extraordinary beauty.

'How were you planning on helping my sisters?' he prompted to get them away from the nerve-jangling topic of her being anywhere near a marriage bed with another man.

'We made it a condition of the marriage settlements that they would live with us once we were married—' she began.

'The Earl must have been delighted,' he interrupted, because they were on that thorny subject of marriage again, and if he wasn't careful, he'd lose control and kiss her again to keep her quiet.

'He was so overjoyed at the idea of getting his hands on part of my dowry he would have put them on a boat to China if I had asked him to.'

'I'm amazed your brother-in-law was prepared to let him have access to even a penny of your fortune.'

'He didn't want to, but money didn't feel important when your sisters were so firmly under the thumb of a brute and a bully. Anyway, I'm three and twenty and Kit can't order me to do as I'm bid any more.'

'Can anyone?'

'Once upon a time they could, but never again.'

Another reason why she had agreed to wed Magnus, Wulf realised with a bite of something like pity in his heart for the bewildered little girl she must

have been once upon a time. She trusted his brother
not to dominate her or terrify their children, because
Magnus was too terrified as a child himself to inflict
it on anyone else. What would it take to get her to
trust any man with all of herself when she had such
gaps and grief still stark in her memory? More than
him, he admitted, frowning down at the moth-eaten
scrap of carpet under their feet as if he hated it.

'We have been in here alone long enough even
if nobody else knows we're here. I can call on you
in Hanover Square to discuss this at a more suitable time, if we really must,' he said in the hope
they could forget continuing this conversation if he
avoided her long enough. The less he had to do with
her, the better, for both their sakes.

'An outsider won't know I'm not walking home
from Bond Street or idling in the Park with my maid
at this very moment. If you come to Ben and Charlotte's house, one of them will have to be present for
the sake of propriety and I prefer to do this without
a listener.'

'You trust me to behave like a gentleman, then?'

'Yes, I suppose I do,' she replied, looking surprised, and it felt like another burden on his already-
braced shoulders instead of a compliment.

'Very well, let's get it over with before someone
accuses us of having an assignation among the ruins,'
he tried to joke, although the idea of secretly meeting her anywhere made his heart thunder and his
loins tighten so shamefully he was glad it was almost twilight in here.

'At times I almost like you, Wulf FitzDevelin.'

'Don't, Isabella Alstone. I'm not a good man. Say your piece and go, before the rogue in me overcomes my bare half-share of gentleman.'

'I suspect you underestimate yourself. Anyway, that's by the by; my eldest sister and her husband wish you to know they will be very happy if your sisters agree to stay at Carnwood House. Obviously Mrs Shaw cannot uproot her whole family and stay there to chaperon us all until my sister gets back from Derbyshire, but Lady Carrowe can lend us countenance and my former engagement to your brother would be reason enough for us to share a home until you find a suitable alternative.'

'I doubt the gossips would agree with you and I've offered to have my mother and half-sisters live with me until her house is ready for them if they can't bring themselves to stay here after what happened. According to her, that would be running away and she's done too much of that already.'

'She does seem quite resolute now his lordship is no longer here to belittle her at every step,' Isabella told him, then frowned as if she'd said too much.

'Don't expect me to pretend he was anything more than a bully and a hypocrite, Isabella,' he argued impatiently.

'I won't, then, but don't call me Isabella.'

'Very well, then, Miss Alstone,' he said with a stiff bow.

'My sins reflect on my sisters,' she explained earnestly, as if she was afraid she'd hurt his feelings. If only that was all that was hurting right now, he'd be a mighty relieved man. 'After her early experience with the gossips, Miranda is oversensitive to their spite,' she went on as if she'd decided to confide in him and he really wished she wouldn't. 'I try hard not to give them any ammunition to snipe at her with and we came in here to discuss your sisters and not mine, didn't we?' she said as if he was the one who kept changing the subject.

'My mother insists she will stay here until I persuade the tenants of her late father's house in Hampstead to move out and my sisters won't go without her. Develin House could fit into this barrack twenty times over, but it's only half a century old and maybe they will find some peace at last when they live a little further from town.'

'Is that the sum of your ambition for them?'

'For now, yes. Money and rank matter less when you don't have them.'

'You don't aspire for them to be happy?'

'A society marriage won't guarantee that,' he said and forgot the barb in the tail of that clumsy comment until she coloured up, then paled as if he'd slapped her. 'Society has never opened its arms to my younger sisters and now they're penniless. If they tried to go about in polite society at the moment, they'd be fawned on for any morsel of gossip they might let drop if they are pushed hard enough,' he went on earnestly, because he really hadn't meant to take a tilt at her failed engagement to Magnus. 'I don't want that sort of attention on them, Miss Alstone, not when they've had to endure the after-effects of the Countess of Carrowe's Scandal all their lives. Maybe that's why Aline grew up impatient of sly questions and false friends and Dorrie is so protective of Theo she's more likely to land a prospective beau a facer because he's ignored her twin than simper at him as a good little debutante should. My sisters grew up with a father who despised them for being born female and a mother they love dearly but whose name was blasted by my existence before they were even born. Maybe half a year of publicly mourning the old devil whilst knowing he can never beat or intimidate them ever again will make them more like the usual run of society ladies. They might even be comfortable enough with strangers to attend one of your sisters' parties by the time the Little Season comes around again, if they happen to be invited.'

'They will be. Meantime they need friends even if they decide not to marry,' she said sagely and he sensed fellow feeling in her words and almost laughed out loud, although it really wasn't all that funny.

'And lovers if they do,' he added to tease her, since she was being absurd. She could marry who she wanted, and when the Season began, suitors would swarm around Miss Alstone like bees to honey now she was free.

'Indeed,' she said too brightly. 'Every young lady needs a choice of them.'

'Indeed,' he agreed blankly and bowed as if he was a gentleman, then held the door open for her to precede him. 'I'm glad we have had this talk, but we should postpone any more of them until my family are settled elsewhere and you are suitably chaperoned,' he said, the mental picture of her surrounded by eager beaux competing for a dance or even a smile having choked the life out of his sense of humour.

'Anywhere would be better than this,' she said with a severe look around the dusty and water-damaged marble hall.

'Do you really think so?' he replied, surprised when there were far worse places in his experience. Apparently he thought more of her than the usual sort of fine lady, so now he was in trouble twice over—he wanted to kiss her whenever they were in the same room, but he also admired her strong character, clever mind *and* her superb figure and shining beauty. He didn't want to feel anything for her at all, but somehow he couldn't help it.

'No, of course I know there are houses more decrepit than this not even a stone's throw away from Mayfair. It was a figure of speech and I should have thought more carefully before I trotted it out,' she said with a wry grimace even more dangerous than her usual heart-shaking smile.

'Now I'm ashamed of myself for picking you up on it, but please have a care if you ever visit the Rookeries to look more closely at the poor, Miss Alstone. The places spawn crime in every form you can and can't imagine and you'd be a rich prize. Last time I was forced to rescue a lady from the stews, it didn't end well for either of us.'

'What happened?'

'She mistook me for a gallant knight dashing to the rescue. Her father wasn't quite so enchanted with me, though; he caught me smuggling her back into his house in a state of grateful fluster and disarray and jumped to all the wrong conclusions.'

'What did he do?'

'He made his footmen hold me while he liberally applied his horsewhip to my disreputable person to teach me to keep my filthy hands off my betters. Apparently he couldn't meet me as a gentleman, since I'm not one.' Wulf could feel the bitterness of the day he found out he was younger and more idealistic than he'd realised even after his rough upbringing. The burn of that past indignity threatened his guard, so he forced it into outer darkness and paid attention to getting them through the present unscathed.

'What happened when she told him the truth?'

He shrugged, not sure that the heedless and spoilt young girl ever had. 'He couldn't apologise to a bastard even if he wanted to,' he said as casually as he could, which probably meant not indifferently enough with her blue eyes focused on him as if she wanted to read his very soul. *Heaven forbid, Wulf*, his inner cynic whispered in his ear and for once he agreed with the rogue.

'And that was the start of your dark and wolfish reputation?'

'I doubt it and don't pity me, because I lustily enjoyed making his kind squirm in a very different way for some time afterwards, but being a dangerous lover to bored and duty-done *ton*nish ladies palls after a while even for the likes of me, Miss Alstone.'

'Stop it. I don't deal in clichés, FitzDevelin, and you're trying too hard.'

'I'm trying very hard, but not about that,' he muttered under his breath and why did she have to pick that particular word? He was rigid with wanting her and the effort not to fall on her like the hungriest wolf was costing him more than she'd ever know.

'I promise not to run about the squalid areas of the largest and probably richest city in the world and need rescuing,' she went on blithely. 'Even if I did, I would never let someone else take the consequences of my folly after they put themselves out in all sorts of ways I know you're refusing to talk about. The selfish and silly girl who did that is the one who needed horsewhipping if you ask me.'

She waited expectantly for him to tell her more of the silly little story that had set him on the path to becoming the wolfish bastard the *ton* still liked to see him as, when it saw him at all. He was too busy struggling with overheated desire and this strange sensation in the pit of his stomach that might be even more dangerous to his composure if he let himself examine it closely. What could he say? Nothing civilised, so he kept quiet and that seemed to make her even more determined to defend him from her own kind and even against his own scathing opinion of a much younger Wulf FitzDevelin who still had a few dreams worth shattering.

'And I know how squalid and desperate the

poorest areas are already by the way, because Lady Pemberley is my eldest sister's godmother,' she innocently went on with her counterargument. Wulf had to be glad she had no idea how dark and wolf-ish his thoughts were right now and tried not to let it show in his gaze. 'I expect you know as well as I do she works among the destitute and desperate whenever she can and you may be sure she takes very good care to keep me safe when we go to the slums together. So at least you will never be called upon to save me from the consequences of my own naivety. Trust Lady Pemberley for that, even if you consider me a fool simply because I was born in a rich man's bed.'

'I doubt you're a fool of any sort,' he said and why did she look as if that admission made her angrier than anything he'd managed to say to her so far?

'Then no doubt you think me a spoilt and over-privileged fine lady who likes to boast of her compassion by visiting nice, clean little children in foundling hospitals and talks about them the whole time as if they can't hear her. I almost wish you still saw me as a heartless jilt, Mr FitzDevelin,' she told him with her nose so far in the air he was surprised she didn't fall over.

'So do I,' he murmured dourly and knew she heard him, because she sniffed so loudly she sneezed from inhaling so much dust as she marched ahead of him like an offended empress.

Chapter Eight

Wulf ran up the last few stairs of the once-grand staircase at Carrowe House a week after his surprise encounter with Miss Alstone at the bottom of them and strode impatiently along the dusty corridor leading to the Dowager Countess's suite. He'd just heard that Develin House would be empty much sooner than he'd dared to hope. If he could persuade his mother to change her mind and leave this decrepit old mausoleum, she wouldn't have to endure a set of rooms so long emptied of comfort and valuables. Here worn old rugs nobody else wanted had replaced the exquisite Aubusson rugs he dimly remembered from his early childhood and the once-fine silk hangings had rotted to gossamer. He frowned at the notion they'd struggle to buy necessities for Develin House between them. He wanted his mother to have the best of everything after enduring this dusty poverty for so long, but all he could come up with was the everyday and most of that would be second-hand.

Impatient with himself for wanting what she didn't covet for herself, he knew deep down he'd learnt what really mattered as a runaway and they all had far more than that now. Food in your belly, enough heat to stave off the chill of night and clothes to cover your nakedness could be enough if you were free. Live through today and take tomorrow when it came. He would love to get his mother and sisters out of here if he could persuade them it wasn't running away from the chill and dust and unease of Carrowe House if they moved to his mother's old home to live just a few miles away in Hampstead. If only Gresley would come, Wulf could put it about that they were leaving the place free for its new owner. But Gresley was still refusing to do his duty as the new Earl of Carrowe. Once their mother and the girls were safely at Develin House, at least he could stop worrying about them living in a rambling old ruin. Wulf and his manservant, Jem Caudle, had secured an inner core of rooms here to cut the ladies off from the rest of the house at night so Wulf could sleep now and again, but even nailed-up doors and windows and the stoutest bolts wouldn't keep out a maniac if the Earl's attacker came back. No, best get them out of here and they'd worry about new this and that once he earned enough money to buy it, or they managed to squeeze the jointure their mother was entitled to under her marriage settlement as well as the portions Magnus and the girls were due from Gresley and his nip-farthing wife. In the end Gresley would pay to keep them out of the poorhouse and avoid being lampooned by Wulf's friends.

Feeling his fingers tighten into fists again at the thought of having to ask his eldest half-brother for anything, Wulf reminded himself to save his fury for those who deserved it. His mother and sisters knew too much about angry men already, so he distracted himself by wondering if there was anything about this old ruin they would miss. Wulf decided he might miss the sheer space of it and all the history that now sat so sadly on it. Except there was space enough around his house on the Heath even for him and history was everywhere he looked in London and much of it as rotten and dilapidated as this vast old house.

He knocked on the door kept closed to keep some warmth in and called out, 'It's only me', to reassure his mother before he went in. The Dowager Lady Carrowe wasn't yet sixty and today she looked younger, despite her pallor. Her hair was still dark enough to show what a dusky-haired beauty she had been in her youth. He took a moment to admire the purity of her bone structure and fine blue-grey eyes even as he worried about the thinness that accentuated them so starkly. They might share colouring to an almost uncanny degree, but her eyes were softer and more trusting than his had ever been, despite all she'd endured at the Earl's hands.

'Oh, here you are at last, my darling, how wonderful. We've been having the most delightful coze,' she said as she hurried towards him with an instinctive grace not even the late Earl of Carrowe had managed to knock out of her.

She kissed his cheek, something she never dared do when the Earl was here to object and perhaps it was as well Gresley wasn't here to glare and fume at her for daring to kiss her bastard son either. Gresley grumbled like a bad-tempered bulldog if their mother showed the least sign of loving anyone more than him, but if he truly cared, he'd be here right now, wouldn't he?

'Hail, Wulf,' Lady Aline Haile joked and she wouldn't have done that without a defiant glare at the door when her father was alive either.

'All hail, Aline Haile,' he obliged her by fetching out their old way of defying her father behind his back and dusting it off, but his gaze had fastened on someone else. 'Good day to you, Miss Alstone,' he managed steadily enough even though his voice wanted to stutter at the vital beauty of her in this shabby setting.

'Isabella isn't here to pry,' Lady Dorothea Haile told him earnestly.

Her twin sister, Theodora, shook her head in agreement, but she still didn't speak. Wulf cursed the old Earl under his breath for that silence. The old viper had blamed her for something he caused by shouting at her until she was too terrified to get a single word out of her mouth and Theo had not spoken since. Even her family had all but forgotten she once had a voice.

'As if she would,' Aline said scornfully. 'Isabella

is our friend, Wulf, so there's no need to glower at her like a suspicious mastiff.'

'I'm sure you're right,' he said, smoothing out his frown as best he could, though it wasn't there because he thought she was here to dig out their secrets and spread them about.

Today Isabella was neat and quietly elegant, but he was struggling with a picture of her breathless and a little tousled by the wind off the distant Welsh Mountains when she rushed outside to intercept him at Cravenhill Park. Raw need to feel her lips invite and yield under his was a weakness threatening to tie knots in his tongue and his innards and it was even more impossible than usual for him to be so wound up in wanting her like this.

As he'd spent another morning with the trappings of violent death, he tried to convince himself the frustration and misery of it all must be sapping his will to resist her bright allure. He let himself imagine how it would feel to come home to her for a moment—as if every sin ever committed against him was wiped out, he concluded.

Forget it, Wulf, you've no place in her world and a sick brother, three sisters and a mother to support.

That was the slap he needed to restore him to sanity and he almost reeled under the weight of it.

'Thank you for having such touching faith in my goodwill, Mr FitzDevelin,' she said stiffly as if he wasn't a very welcome surprise to her either.

Thank goodness; if she'd smiled that sunlight-and-roses smile she kept for her true friends, he might have forgotten who was looking on and kissed her anyway. He felt the stir and shout of her proximity in his sex and insisted it behave like a gentleman for once before he fell at her feet and begged. 'How d'you do after your long journey back to London, ma'am?' he asked stiffly, because they were not supposed to have met since he galloped to Herefordshire on a fool's errand.

'Very well, I thank you, sir,' she replied and he heard a faint trace of mockery in her voice, as if she knew he had to be stiff as a tin solider in order not to embarrass them all. If she knew, then why the devil wasn't she more wary of rousing his inner beast?

'I trust the roads were not too churned up after the rain?' he asked clumsily and marvelled at his own lack of easy small talk when it mattered most.

'I had a smooth journey, Mr FitzDevelin; it was very nearly the most tedious trip into the country and back that I've ever had,' she said and now he knew she was mocking his hasty ride there, the witchy minx.

'Then I have to thank you for bearing my mother and sisters company so often since your return.'

'It's always a pleasure to see *them*,' she replied, as if the Earl's murder wasn't the sensation he knew it was. Laying sneaky emphasis on the last word was even more provocation and thank heavens his mother and sisters didn't appear to have noticed.

Now she was eyeing her gloves and the elegant bonnet lying on an unsteady pier table nearby and Wulf supposed his arrival must have stopped her feeling joy in his favourite females' company and was doubly sorry he'd come back too early to miss her latest visit.

'Would the rest of the world thought it one as well,' Aline said with such bitterness in her voice Wulf wanted to comfort her for the hard lot life had handed her when she was born a girl to her father's bitter disappointment.

From the outset the *haut ton* had looked down their collective noses at her—maybe because she had no portion and had inherited her father's Roman nose, or perhaps because so much mud had stuck to her mother some of it rubbed off on her daughters. He had no idea how their minds worked. The fact was Aline was so busy defending their mother and little sisters from sneers and snubs nobody seemed to notice there was a clever, vibrant woman behind her haughty frown.

'I don't want them coming here to gawp, then going away to gossip about us as if they know more than the angels,' Dorrie said bitterly.

Wulf hugged her close and kissed her in a parody of a fulsome big brother until she giggled at last and ordered him to stop. 'Don't let them win, love,' he said as earnestly as he dared with Isabella listening. 'You've held your dignity so far and it would be a shame to lose it now.'

'I'm not sure I care what the wider world thinks of us any more, Wulf,' Dorrie said wearily.

'Then Theo and I will care for you, won't we, adorable Theodora?' he asked her twin with another old joke as he drew Theo close as well, made her part of the circle of love his mother and sisters always made even at the worst times. Theo didn't speak, but at least she seemed to forget to be scared for a few precious moments.

'Of course you must care, Dorothea,' Lady Carrowe told her daughter with uncharacteristic briskness.

Was this the real Gwenllian Develin, the woman who grew out of the lovely, light-hearted girl the old Earl had courted with single-minded determination, then treated so ill she became a meek ghost of her former self? Wulf wondered why the old windbag hadn't troubled a lesser female with his mean desires and jealous rages.

'We have to mourn your father because his life was ripped violently away and nobody deserves to be murdered,' his mother said. 'After a suitable time has passed, we will be able to find you good husbands to make you happy.'

'I don't want to rely on a man for that, Mama,' Aline argued quietly. Wulf wondered if she was being brave about her limited prospects or truly meant it.

'No, indeed, there is such a slim chance of finding true love among so many unlikely candidates,' Miss Alstone said with a wry grimace that made Theo laugh shyly into his shoulder as if she had to hide her mirth so nobody could take it away.

'A chance both your sisters took,' Wulf argued while he hugged his youngest sister even closer to show her she could laugh as much as she liked now her father wasn't here to call her a grinning idiot.

'Maybe they are braver than I am, Mr FitzDevelin,' Miss Alstone said lightly.

Nothing would ever make his mother's bastard an acceptable suitor for Lady Carnwood's little sister, but he was secretly delighted she wasn't planning on entering another betrothal just yet. Tickets to cross the Atlantic were expensive and he wasn't sure the Continent would ever be far enough away if she married someone else when he still longed for her as if she was uniquely branded on his senses.

'True love comes with bravery added, my dear, but it's still an act of faith,' his mother said with a reminiscent sigh. There was silence while they considered what love had cost her and Wulf silently repeated an old promise not to risk it himself.

'I'm sorry Magnus and I couldn't make that leap, Lady Carrowe,' Isabella said as if she couldn't keep the words in even with Wulf listening.

He caught another glimpse of the striving and burningly honest soul she usually kept hidden and cursed under his breath. She looked as if she'd wanted to love his brother so badly he could almost feel her yearning to be a wife and mother and jealousy stabbed him because she would never let herself love the likes of him.

'It's not something you feel to order, Isabella,' his mother replied with a look of concern. 'Love is a gift, not a duty to be squared up to. If you loved Magnus as more than a friend, I might be angry with

you for refusing to see your betrothal through, but
that depth of feeling was never there between you.
To tell the truth I was relieved when you ended it,
for both your sakes.'

The sadness in her voice when she spoke of true
love touched Wulf even if he was the product of a
love church and state said she had no right to feel.
He saw the tears swim in Isabella's glorious blue
eyes before she blinked as if she had no right to feel
it either. Lust was tempered by tenderness for a dangerous moment, but his next sister down saved him
with a denial of her own.

'Well, I'm not going to fall in love with anyone,
ever,' Aline said firmly.

Wulf smiled across Theo's head to say, *Well done,
little sister, neither am I.*

'If you don't, it's my fault,' his mother said sadly.
Wulf wished himself a hundred miles away so he
didn't have to be here as the inescapable truth of
how much the Dowager Lady Carrowe had risked
for love.

'Nonsense, Mama, it's nothing to do with you.
We shall set up a ladies-only republic in Hampstead
and make a pledge to one another never to fall in
love or marry,' Dorrie joked with a frantic cheerful-
ness that ate into Wulf's heart like acid. She came
across the room to hug Aline and Theo joined in as
Wulf stepped back, glad the bond between his sisters was so strong nobody could break it, not even
the late Lord Carrowe. 'You will need a passport to
visit us, Wulf,' Dorrie went on, 'and even Magnus

won't be allowed inside our borders without a written invitation.'

'I'm not sure if I should be insulted at the differences you make between us, Lady Dorothea,' he said in a lame attempt to go along with her.

'You should, I suspect,' Isabella whispered as she stepped past him to catch up her errant bonnet as if it was alive and on the verge of scampering away.

'Now, my dear, if you really are determined to leave us so soon, you cannot be left to wander around this mausoleum getting lost until Crumble chances upon you. I doubt he has time to escort you out and we really must finish sewing our mourning weeds,' his mother intervened before Wulf could bow and go away and brood somewhere quiet and devoid of feminine company. 'Wulf will escort you,' she went on blithely, 'and I do hope your maid won't give notice after being forced to endure our ramshackle servants' hall yet again.'

Wulf frowned and waited for Isabella to point out his mother had contradicted herself shamelessly. Apparently Miss Alstone was a frequent visitor to Carrowe House but couldn't be trusted to find her way downstairs and call for her maid to accompany her home on her own. Unlikely, he decided and wondered what game his mother was trying to play by throwing them together like this.

'If Heloise was going to resign, I'm sure she'd have done it the day I chose to return to London the very moment she finished unpacking all my luggage so she then had to pack it all up again,' Isabella joked as if she had done it on a whim.

Wulf tried to feel impatient instead of at odds with himself and a little bit glum as he waited for the Haile ladies to bid an affectionate farewell to Miss Alstone and promise to spend a day in Hanover Square. He was glad his mother and sisters had such a good friend. He just wished she wasn't Miss Isabella Alstone.

Chapter Nine

'**Y**our mother has more courage and character than people credit,' Isabella said carefully as they made their way downstairs. Wulf was doing his stern best to escort her out in silence, as if she was his least-welcome duty in a day packed full of them, and she didn't feel like obliging him today.

'She has need of it,' he said as if he had been given a strict ration of words for the day and didn't intend to waste many on her.

He had felt the shadow the late Lord Carrowe cast over his family more than anyone, so she tried to be fair. 'I do know the late Earl wasn't a good man,' she persisted because even though this stiff and guarded conversation felt wrong it was better than stony silence. 'So there's no need to tiptoe around the truth with me.'

He looked deeply uncomfortable. 'Did he try to force himself on you? He wasn't above coercing women who didn't respond to his so-called charm and he had a vile reputation according to the kind of women the *ton* would never lower itself to listen to.'

'No,' she said coolly, refusing to be kept quiet because they both knew he shouldn't mention such women to a lady. She didn't see why she should be deaf, dumb and stupid about the harshest realities of life any longer and he wouldn't put her off that easily. 'I'm wary of ageing rakes and dark corners and it was my fortune he lusted after.'

'You think you're wary?' he asked incredulously. She felt her cheeks flush as she recalled one night when she truly threw all caution to the four winds, but that was different. 'And I know the Earl always tried to act the enlightened gentleman in polite company, so why would you even think you needed to be cautious?'

'Lord Carrowe was so harsh with your mother and sisters I'm amazed he managed to deceive so many people that he was anything other than a brute,' she said carefully.

'It wasn't like him to let the brute out when he could be overheard,' Wulf murmured as if the old man was still alive and might dash out and yell at him if he was criticised here in his own home.

She looked for signs of a small boy who lived here in constant fear of the Earl's fury in the sternly self-contained man in front of her and almost laughed out loud at her own naivety. He'd tower over the man now and all the terror would be on the other side, since the late Earl of Carrowe had been a coward as well as a bully. 'He was so hard with them I knew he was a charlatan even before...' In the nick of time she stopped herself. She had to persuade Magnus to tell his brother the truth before it fell off her tongue by accident. His family knew how to keep secrets, for goodness' sake, so why not confide in them before more damage was done?

'Even before...you found out the old jackal had a hold over Magnus that the great bumbling idiot refuses to discuss even now?' Wulf continued for her and Isabella decided her best defence was silence. 'If you could persuade him to confide in me, I'd be grateful,' he said stiffly, stopping on the stairs while they were alone in order to get as close to pleading for her help as such a proud man would ever get.

And he knew all the best places to whisper secrets here, didn't he? Such caution wrenched at her heart for the beaten and bewildered child he'd been in this house all those years ago. Still, Magnus's secrets had been so important to him they got him within a hair's breadth of marriage to the wrong woman and he had to tell his brother himself, in his own time.

'You know your brother better than anyone else does, Mr FitzDevelin, and I dare say he would have told you if you were here to tell.'

'I had to go away,' he said gruffly.

'I'm sure you did. Telling your family you weren't coming back probably wasn't wise, though, especially as you lied.'

She didn't want to remember the aching hollow at the pit of her stomach his absence had left her struggling with. When he wasn't looming over her like a sternly puzzled Roman general, she might find time to recall how desolate it felt to think she would never meet Wulf's wary winter-sky eyes again or see his firm mouth set in a sceptical line when he silently accused her of being a pampered society beauty who played with men's hearts for sport. Shock hit like a slap, then raced in her blood at the thought of never being alone with him again like this, but they were having a workaday conversation on the stairs, in a tumbledown house, with several conniving and possibly matchmaking females nearby, and that was all it was to him. She had to remember that fact and learn to live with it.

'I meant to make a new life when I left,' he said stiffly. 'I had offers to write for periodicals and newssheets and perhaps a book about my adventures. I was weary of being the Bastard Wolf and wanted to be free of him as well as my parents' sins and Lord Carrowe's malice. At least in a new world I could be my own man.'

He was already his own man, Isabella decided and wondered why he didn't know it. He still refused to meet her eyes and seemed to have no idea she secretly longed for him to admit he went because she was going to marry his brother and he couldn't endure being in the same country when she became Mrs Magnus Haile. Wulf FitzDevelin was far too guarded to do anything of the kind, though, even if it was true and she had no proof of that. Maybe a new country could give a countess's natural son a much freer and more hopeful life than hidebound and dynastic old England. She wasn't used to feeling this uncertain since she grew up and took command of her own life. It felt acutely uncomfortable and a little bit lonely.

'I soon realised I'd made a mistake; my mother and sisters need me,' he went on with a manly, defensive shrug.

'They do,' she agreed and this wasn't the time or place to want to kiss the gruff idiot again. 'Can you endure the gossip now you're back?'

'I was a fool to listen to it in the first place, and now my mother's house in Hampstead is empty, life will be much easier for her and my sisters if I can persuade them to live there with Magnus. Any help you can give me on that front would be appreciated. It may not offer the sort of gentleman-about-town appeal he's used to and Magnus has suffered a reverse of fortune as well as love.'

'It was never about money for him and we were not in love. What about you, Mr FitzDevelin?'

'I'm not in love either,' he said facetiously.

She already knew that. 'That's not what I meant and you know it. What will you do when your family are living together in Hampstead?'

'I will go my own way, Miss Alstone.'

'I know you love them too much to do that; I'm not quite the spoilt fool you think me,' she said coolly.

'You have no idea what I think of you,' he argued softly.

'Then tell me,' she demanded recklessly.

'I think you're a lovely young woman who has

been indulged by a family who love you. You are stubborn and hot-headed and a little bit too convinced you know what's best for those you love. You have far more intense passions and ambitions than most ladies of quality and will blossom into a great lady when you wed the right husband and I wish you both well.'

'How kind,' she said hollowly. 'But I don't expect to marry.'

'Then I have to conclude you love Magnus after all and can't endure marrying anyone else,' he said so flatly she wondered if he found the notion painful.

'No,' she said patiently, wondering how many times she had to say so before he believed her. 'We were good friends, and if that is all you have to say, I really must be about my business, Mr FitzDevelin. I know you're busy and have little time in your life for standing about talking to outsiders like me at the best of times.'

'My mother and sisters don't consider you one of those, Miss Alstone,' he said as if he had reservations, 'but you're right; we can't stay here all day and someone has to tidy up the mess the Earl left behind.'

'And perhaps it *is* stupid of me to think I can do anything to help your mama and sisters through it,' she conceded reluctantly. 'I suppose you'd like me to stop interfering and go away?'

She might manage to stay in Hanover Square and twiddle her thumbs until Kit and Miranda arrived in town if she tried hard enough. Except she didn't exactly trip over dozens of well-wishers when she came here to keep the Haile ladies company by furtive routes and back alleys, and if she didn't come, who else would? But Wulf still seemed to seriously consider saying, *Yes, please stay away*, before he shook his head belatedly as if his sisters' and mother's needs came before his own.

'My mother and sisters need you and I can stay out of the way.'

'And you don't need anyone, least of all me?' she said, ignoring the forbidden ground under her feet.

Silence as thick and tense as the one they were suspended in while they stood in the darkness and hoped the Earl wouldn't spot them in the shadows that night at Haile Carr fell around them like a shroud. She shivered at the tension she could sense in his rigidly still body and what a devilish time she'd chosen to be shy of his ice-blue gaze because she was too afraid to imagine he was fighting a need to reach for her when she wanted to feel his hands on her so urgently she was shaking. She grasped her own behind her back to stop herself from reaching up to smooth his frown away. If she was alone in this need, she had to accept it and walk away. It was a foolish dream. When he'd left England for a new life without even saying goodbye to her, she had all but sleepwalked into marrying Magnus because she didn't want to wake up and face the truth about all three of them, but she was awake now. Barely possible chances made her heart race as he stared down at her as if he'd never seen the likes of her before, and if she could be unique for him, nothing else would matter.

'I was born on the wrong side of the blanket, Miss Alstone,' he said bleakly and made her ache for that innocent babe even while she wanted to stamp her foot at him for thinking she'd care.

'None of us have a say in when and where that happens,' she managed to say in a rather rusty voice he could interpret how he liked, but if she wasn't careful, she'd cry for what might have been and that would be a disaster for both of them.

'True, but you were born in your father's bed. Best if you let me speculate who mine was alone,' he said and refused to even meet her eyes this time. She had to hope it was because he thought they would give too much away. Hope was the last thing left in Pandora's box when all the cares of the world escaped it after all, and since she'd spent half a year trying to crush it, she knew it was almost indestructible.

'You don't know who he was, then?' she asked cautiously.

'My mother won't say and apparently the man she loved died before I was born, so he isn't here for me to suspect. Since she was wed to a man who only ever loved himself, I can't blame her for finding consolation and affection elsewhere, but our marriage laws are cruel, aren't they, Miss Alstone?'

Isabella felt as if every muscle she had was stiff at the thought she might have been irrevocably tied to his brother in a week or two and never a shred of real love to bind them for life between them. It felt as if she'd stood on the edge of a chasm and stepped back just in time. Because? Because marrying your best friend when he loved another woman was a mistake and Wulf was right, the law was cruel.

'At least when I ran away, her husband couldn't use me to try to break her any more,' Wulf said hoarsely, as if talking about that time made it feel too real again.

'You went for her sake?' Her heart stumbled at the thought of him doing so when he was far too young to be so brutally alone.

He was so male and self-sufficient now it was nearly impossible to picture him as a helpless boy a grown man had ranted at and beat whenever he felt like it. Isabella wondered if Lady Carrowe had thought her lover worth the price their son paid and almost ran back to ask. No, that was the ultimate impertinent question and she wasn't prepared to strip her own heart bare to find a good enough reason for asking it quite yet.

'It doesn't matter now,' he said with would-be cynicism, as if he'd consigned his feelings to a dark cupboard many years ago and wanted them to stop there. 'And don't convince yourself the gossips are wrong about me, Miss Alstone, because I truly hated the Earl and I'm a bastard in more ways than one.'

'You clearly have a talent for melodrama, sir. Perhaps you'll grow out of it now the chief cause has gone.'

He hesitated in mid-glower and laughed instead. The surprisingly joyous sound of his deep chuckle seemed to lighten the shadows of even this poor old house and his genuine smile made her knees wobble.

'I have lived on my wits since I was a boy, so maybe you should excuse me.'

'And perhaps that's why you haven't found out what you're truly capable of yet.'

'Have you read something I wrote, then, Isabella?' he asked softly. 'And does that make you less indifferent to me than you pretend or just curious?

She blushed. 'Yes, and the latter,' she admitted as casually as she could with his eyes watchful and almost amused on her as if he knew differently.

'What did you think?' he asked, not quite managing to be indifferent.

'That you take a reader to places they might never see and show them what really happens there. You write vividly and passionately about matters that ought to worry your readers a lot more than they do, but you still hold something of yourself back. Perhaps it would cost you too much to test your talent to the limit. The Earl did so little to deserve your attention in life that you'd do better to live up to your own standards than defy his.'

His ice-blue eyes were intent and even a little defiant now and she wanted to shiver with something beyond coldness as she met them as steadfastly as she could. He nodded as if acknowledging she was right. 'I'm glad he wasn't my father and even more so that he didn't bother to pretend he might be.'

'And I like your mother's maiden name better than his. In your shoes I'd be proud to own it and never mind the rest.'

'Maybe you would, but Wulf is easier on the

tongue and you have a fine name when you're not being ma'am,' he said with his tongue firmly in his cheek.

'I do believe you just called me a little madam.'

'No, how could I be so crass, Belle?' he parried and the teasing glint in his eyes when he named her that way warmed them so much she heard herself sigh like a besotted schoolroom miss.

'My brother used to call me that,' she said with a catch in her voice she thought she'd managed to train out of it.

'I'll settle for Isabella, then, if we're ever this strictly alone again,' he told her as if trying to tip-toe around a grief that was part of her and she was touched he cared enough to try.

'No, don't; I like it. My brother Jack would have liked you. You're honest and trustworthy, unlike the snake his school sent to escort him home when he grew ill. Jack would have refused to share a carriage with Nevin Braxton if he'd been well enough to push him out of it.'

'That's the name of the viper who pretended to wed your eldest sister when he was already secretly married to your cousin, isn't it?' he asked gently.

She was glad he didn't pretend not to know about the scandals in her own family closet. 'Yes, and a worm of the first order he was, too. We Alstones aren't really calm and civilised folk at all, Wulf. That devil's spawn did everything he could to ruin my sister's life when she was only seventeen and I find that unforgivable.'

'Clearly,' he agreed, meeting her eyes full on and how wonderful it felt to be understood. Apparently he agreed she had every right to hate the couple who did their best to make the Alstone sisters' lives a misery when they were too young and unprotected to fight back.

Heady warmth fizzed through her like a slow-burning firework. He understood her and hadn't backed away as if she was unnatural and wicked to hate those two so much even today, when she was old enough to at least try to forgive and forget the terrible chaos Nevin Braxton and Cousin Celia wrought on her young life. Instead of condemnation in his eyes, there was warmth and fellow feeling and something a lot more exhilarating. Isabella's heart raced with excitement and something even headier she wasn't quite ready to put a name to even in her own head yet.

She did know no other man made her feel as if the world had faded away and they were the only people left in it. She had longed to feel like this again since the moment she left the terrace at Haile Carr, feeling as if a crucial part of her had had to be lopped off so she could do it without breaking down and refusing to take another step away from him and what might have been. Now she could stare into his supposedly icy-blue eyes again and stop pretending she didn't want to be scorched by his heat so close she could feel him breathe. She was free to be foolish this time and reckless enough not to want to be wise.

'You don't think me hard and unnatural because I can't forgive them, then?'

'I think they don't matter, they don't deserve to. I also think every inch of you is beautiful and never mind how nature made you. Your temper and thorny pride and all those other reasons you're about to come out with to put me off are all part of you, Belle Isabella,' he said so softly she had to stretch up to hear.

'And I think you should hurry up and kiss me, Wulf,' she said even more softly and licked her lips very deliberately. Wasn't she brazen?

His hands on her as he urged her even closer were urgent and far more than mere touch. It felt like a merging of him and her, a familiar presence in her heart that she knew as well as she did her own. She struggled to find words or a way to tell him how he made her feel and couldn't. He was here and reaching for whatever this was at last and that had to be enough. He mouthed her name against her lips; his tongue licked the edges of it as if he had to know the fullness of them from the outside in and she felt a long sigh run through her body like overheated magic. He was gentle against the half-open question of it as she gasped and breathed him in, desperate for Wulf-warmed air. Then his mouth was teasing against her lips so she would part them further and she couldn't say anything at all.

Here he is again. A familiar, strange and longed-for rush of heady wanting shot through her as he groaned something silently urgent against her mouth.

Her fingers trembled as she reached up to feel every bit of him they could get to in the shortest time possible. *Ah, here*; smooth, firm skin over a wilful jaw; the tension of raw passion on his high cheekbones; the feel of long, unfairly luxuriant lashes against the sensitive pads of her fingers as he closed his eyes to the outside world and plundered her mouth as if he could never saturate himself in enough of her, would always come back for more, so he could sip and demand and beg for another taste, more kisses, more Isabella, more of anything she was willing to give, utterly unable to hold back from him.

So she pulled his head further down, further into her, fully engaged her mouth against his in a demand they echo the roaring need for more, for everything, for all of him. She wriggled against his arms in an attempt to get him to give the last bit of himself he didn't want her to know about, locked together by passion and the most urgent wanting she could ever imagine feeling if they both lived for ever. She coveted him so wildly now it drove her on with hot need, sharp, goading and demanding. Was it too much to want a man like this? It could be, perhaps it should be. She could feel her pride prickling warily in the far distance, knew the edge of danger in being so close to this uniquely wonderful man in every way. And why couldn't he ignore it as well and be the same sort of wanting, needing idiot she was?

She keened something inarticulate and needy against his mouth as he still seemed to hold back. She was so close to the edge she wanted to jump straight off and be damned to any tomorrows. Even his breath was short and deep now, almost a groan as his body leapt against hers, despite his gallant attempt not to let her know it. He did want her desperately, though; his sex needed her even if his mind didn't want to let it. She savoured the fact, sipped it from his opened mouth as he stifled a moan of frustration against her lips. How wanton a lady's hands could be as she wilfully tried to undo his manly scruples. A little whisper of sanity said he was right, this wasn't the place or time for such a naughty exploration. She tipped her head back so he could work his hot mouth down her throat and she could tangle his crow-dark curls with her fingers and feel the shape of him, learn the secrets of his muscle-corded neck, finely made ears and the sensitive line of his jaw while he drove her to the edge of madness by licking the pulse at the base of her neck, as if he was in awe of the frantic beating of her heart under his ravenous mouth and wanted to explore and incite it even more.

His hands shifted to keep her at his mercy when she wriggled her frustration. She wanted his hands to be busy undoing her. She longed to be utterly open with him as she'd never wanted to be with another man in her entire life. She couldn't even begin to imagine wanting any other man except this one so hugely. Shock trembled on the edges of this sweet, relentless, driven need inside her.

Here she was, swamped in raw, relentless need and a curiosity it felt impossible to fight was pushing her ever closer to the edge of that chasm. An opening up inside her that felt more than physical wanted to invite him in: *Take all I have and give me every way of being between a man and a woman; show me everything.* She must have whispered something almost as untamed as that in his ear while she was round there to make him groan, then try to stifle it against her skin before he gave them away, spellbound together in this vast, deserted stairwell. He trailed kisses back along the pathway he'd burnt down her throat and up to sip at her mouth as if he couldn't quite bring himself to part from her, but he was still going to. She silently cursed his formidable self-control, hated his ability to detach himself from what their senses and their bodies wanted so much all her scruples were flown. His will was stronger than hers. His experience so far ahead he knew where they might get up to if they dared and had decided, no, they would not dare. It had felt so precious and unique for her to long to be his lover like this and now he was drawing away? Distancing himself, she accused silently. She met his eyes with a challenge and dared him to risk her anyway.

'We can't,' he whispered raggedly and at least that meant he was less cool than he wanted to be while he was busy shutting down the real Wulf FitzDevelin as if she'd imagined him. 'Not here—not like this,' he added as he met her eyes again and let her see more than he probably wanted her to.

'Why not?' she whispered as if it was halfway between a threat and a promise. Was he protecting himself from the myth no lady could love the Count-

ess of Carrowe's bastard? Or maybe he didn't want to
love her more than he didn't want to love any other
woman. If she wasn't hurting so much at the idea he
was backing away from her more than any other female, she might wonder if she was insane to want to
take the last tumble into love with such a stubborn,
complex and utterly infuriating man.

'You're not getting away that easily,' she threatened half-jokingly, seeing the promise of true intimacy if only he'd believe in it in his wary eyes.
Warmth threatened the cool of his ice-blue irises as
he looked down at her and almost smiled. She knew
if he ever let himself love her, he'd do it more fully
and deeply than any other man could. If only she
was the woman he could love and trust, he would
make her feel extraordinary for the rest of their lives,
she thought wistfully. 'I'm not letting you get away
with running to avoid me this time, FitzDevelin,' she
threatened softly. 'I'll chase after you if you go anywhere near a port, and if you get aboard one ship,
I'll simply board the next one.'

He ignored her attempts to joke and managed to
put enough distance between them to watch her reluctantly make herself as neat and smoothed down
as she ought to be after calling on his mother. She
deliberately didn't mention the fact his own dark hair
looked as if he'd been out in a gale after her amorous
attention. Was that because she half-wanted them to
be found out? Maybe—perhaps she secretly wanted
his mother and sisters to know he meant more to her
than a polite almost-gentleman who could escort her

downstairs as coolly and calmly as if she really was only a nodding acquaintance.

'You should let me go,' he said bleakly, eyes back to the arctic wastes he used to set the world at a distance, as if she was a brief madness he'd recklessly allowed himself and now regretted.

'Never tell an Alstone what to do, Mr Wulf. We tend to do the opposite simply to prove we can,' she half-warned and half-threatened.

'If you refuse to be careful for your own sake, then do it for my mother's and learn from her example,' he said soberly. 'She thought she could take an impossible lover and look where that got her.'

'You, it got her you. I think your parents loved to very good effect, even if you don't,' she said brazenly.

At last he smiled reluctantly, as if her refusal to be brushed off had to amuse him because it flew so wildly in the face of common sense. 'I believe I've just been deeply flattered, Belle.'

'So do I, Wulf, although you've done little enough to deserve it.'

He quirked an eyebrow at her to challenge that denial and stood back to survey her as if she was a novelty he couldn't quite believe he was seeing. 'Be careful where you light wildfires, Miss Alstone,' he warned soberly. 'They smoulder for days before they set whole forests ablaze, hot enough to terrify the damned back into hell.'

'There you are again; melodramatic to a fault. I was right about you, Mr FitzDevelin.'

'Wulf,' he corrected sharply, as if it mattered that she thought of him as he truly was and it felt like a small victory. 'And I'm still illegitimate and have three sisters, a mother and an elder brother to set up before I can afford a wife.'

'I don't need supporting.'

'And that's supposed to make me feel better?'

The offended pride in his deep voice was evident, but he had no idea how determined she was when she really wanted something, or how dirtily an Alstone could fight when they wanted to win badly enough. Perhaps he should take a closer look at her ruthless piratical ancestors if he thought she was about to go away and give up on him simply because he thought she ought to.

'No, it's supposed to make you realise most of your scruples about offering for me are irrelevant.'

'They will be real enough if we're caught here like this and whispers start doing the rounds about us. Can you even imagine how many of your relatives and friends will line up to challenge me if they find out what we were doing just now? Oh, no, that's right,' he said as he stood further away to look back at her, 'I forgot; I'm not worthy of a sword or a pistol, am I? So will it be an ambush in the dark and a good whipping or two in order to teach me not to tilt at windmills?'

'Not on my account. I'm quite capable of standing up for what I want and I'm not sure I like being called a windmill.'

'Don't make a joke of it, Isabella,' he said rather

painfully. 'I know you're an independent woman of means who thinks she knows her own mind, but I won't let you be ostracised and mocked for the sake of a by-blow other ladies used to toy with in secret. You might think you could dare to be a pariah and a laughing stock with such a lover, but I won't let you risk it,' he said grimly and she could see from the stubborn set of his mouth he believed it.

'Do you really think I care what the scandalmongers think of me?'

'You might not, but I do.'

Chapter Ten

'Is that you, Miss Isabella?' Heloise asked uncertainly from the dusty hallway below. 'Are you all right?'

Isabella felt her heartbeat start to race at a gallop and told herself of course her personal maid hadn't heard anything they had said or done up here. When they found time to speak, they spoke softly and Wulf would have known if anyone was listening because his ears seemed to be uniquely honed for trouble whenever he was in this poor old house. There was no need for her to jump guiltily as if they'd been caught plotting a scandal between upstairs and down, but if he wasn't prepared to own up to what they were, she would have to be guilty about it as well.

'I'm not quite sure,' she murmured.

'If you don't know, nobody else will,' Wulf mocked softly, then bowed stiffly and ghosted back up his half of the stairs as if he'd never come this far down them to swap secrets and kisses with her.

'Perhaps I imagined him,' Isabella whispered wistfully to herself, then spoke up to reassure her maid all was well and now the sun had come out it wouldn't be such a hardship to walk back to Hanover Square after all, would it?

Heloise sniffed so loudly Isabella heard her even up here and smiled ruefully at her own reflection in a dusty and badly speckled mirror on the half-landing. She felt so flat and alone now Wulf had withdrawn his vital presence, but she still looked as if someone had lit a good chandelier's worth of candles inside her. So she took a moment to remind herself he hadn't even whispered a word of love to salt all that drivel about gossip and duty for her. Apparently even if he did love her he wouldn't marry her and risk a lifetime of being more important than the polite world to her, so she really had no reason to look kissed and sleepily on fire as well as more alive than she'd felt in six long months while he was away.

'I suppose we can let ourselves out through the front door, since the latest flood of callers seem to have given up and gone away,' she said to her maid as she finally reached ground level and hoped Heloise wouldn't notice her latest employer was nowhere near as calm and carefree as she sounded behind a hastily donned bonnet.

'I'll look outside before you walk out there, then, Miss Alstone,' Heloise said doubtfully, peering through the dusty glass of a Judas opening from another age. 'I knew it was a reckless notion. A lady has just arrived and from the look of the horses she's come a fair way.'

'What sort of lady?' Isabella asked warily, picturing one of the formidable matrons who had tried so hard to bluff their way through these doors the last few days after staying away for twenty-seven years after the Countess of Carrowe was publicly disgraced by her own husband. Cursing Wulf for leaving her to deal with his family's visitors as if they were nothing to do with him, she wished she had stolen out of the back door as usual now and not decided to pin her colours to the front door of Carrowe House whether Wulf wanted them there or not.

'She looks a few years older than you, Miss Isabella, and a quietly dressed, decent sort of lady.'

'Not the kind who would come here solely to collect gossip about her ladyship and the Miss Hailes and spread it abroad?'

'She's gone to a lot of trouble if that's all she's here for.'

'Then we might as well open the door and see what she wants, since we are on our way out and Lady Carrowe's staff are otherwise engaged.'

'Aye, both of them,' Heloise murmured and stepped back so Isabella was the one to let whoever was out there into another lady's house as if she had a right to.

'Oh, hello,' Isabella greeted the lady on the doorstep as if she'd had no idea she was there when she opened the door.

'Hello; do you know if Lady Carrowe is at home?'

the stranger asked as if she'd travelled too far and too fast to bother swapping polite formalities with a stranger.

Feeling dismissed and chilled by the cool and wary look the newcomer was sending her from a pair of wide blue eyes gentlemen probably found irresistibly vulnerable, Isabella shrugged. 'That depends quite a lot on who you are,' she said and stood in the way so this stranger couldn't simply march inside uninvited.

'Obviously she was at home to you and I've never set eyes on you before, so she is sure to welcome me,' the woman said with an arrogance Isabella suspected was mostly for show, but it felt quite real when you were on the wrong side of it.

'So you say,' she challenged back. She had a strong suspicion who this was and, if she was right, she'd decided not to like Lady Delphine Drace the moment Magnus confessed the real reason why he proposed marriage to her on his father's orders and the appalling dilemma this woman had left him in. Isabella might have put an end to the engagement with a secret sigh of relief, but this woman had hurt a friend and could have helped trap her and Magnus in a chilly marriage where both of them secretly longed for lovers they couldn't have.

'Delphine! Oh, it's so good to see you again at long last. But why on earth are you standing on the doorstep arguing with Miss Alstone? Mama and the girls will be so pleased to see you and Wulf's here as well,' Aline said, beginning at the top of the stairs

and chattering all the way down as if she couldn't get
here fast enough to hug the wretched woman. Isabella stepped out of Lady Delphine's path and wondered if she should get ready to break Aline's fall, but
she'd underestimated the energy behind her friend's
normally contained manner. Aline managed not to
crash into the newel post before she launched herself
at the newcomer to hug her as if she thought everything would be all right now the wretched woman
was here at long last.

'Lady Delphine; what the deuce?' Wulf's deep
voice called as he strode hastily down from his vantage point at the top of the stairs and whatever room
he'd retreated to so he could pretend he had no idea
why Miss Alstone was still here. Then he grabbed
the newcomer and hugged her in turn and Isabella
wasn't jealous in the least. No, not at all. He wouldn't
hug the woman like that if he knew what she'd done
to his brother, though.

'Thank heavens you're here at long last,' he said
easily to the woman and Isabella's fists tightened so
much she had to relax them before her nails ate holes
in her soft leather gloves. 'Mama and the girls have
missed you sorely,' he added and jealousy twisted
viciously in Isabella's gut until she had to get away
or shout something hot and furious at the woman
for being at the heart of this family after what she'd
done.

'Come, Heloise,' she murmured and hustled her
maid away in order to avoid being formally introduced to the reason why there had been so many

bumps in her own road lately. Lady Delphine Drace was the very last female she wanted to meet when she was still trying to deal with the consequences of the silly woman's actions, or lack of them.

'Magnus, oh, my darling. It's lovely to see you again, but you shouldn't have made the journey back here until you were feeling a lot better than you look right now,' Lady Carrowe scolded Wulf's brother later the same day.

She stood back to view her second son at arm's length and Wulf knew she was trying her hardest not to cry. Gus probably did as well. There was barely a sign of the once light-hearted and sociable Honourable Mr Haile in his brother's thin face and shadowed eyes, but Gus's smile made a brave attempt at resurrecting him.

'Now, do make your mind up, Mama,' he said. 'Either you want me here or you don't and how could I stay at Cravenhill Park cosseting myself like an ageing spinster when I knew you needed me here?'

'I've been stuck here longing to come to you and spoil you shamelessly, but I knew the gossips would trouble you all the more if I persuaded Wulf and the girls we should travel to Herefordshire to look after you. Maybe I should have because Lady Shuttleworth ought not to have let you travel when you look as if a strong wind might blow you over.'

Gus shot Wulf a reproachful look as if he should not have even told their mother about his collapse, but what else would excuse his absence when his father had been horribly murdered? 'Perhaps I'll ape my little brother a little late in the day and run away from home,' Magnus said lightly and made their mother laugh.

Wulf thought even this sad old house couldn't quite kill the sound of his mother's spirit reviving after years of forced penance, but Gus deliberately refused to meet his eyes to agree he could see the change in her as well. Wulf felt impatient with his brother's old habit of being visibly put out when his life wasn't going as easily as he thought it should. *You'd have thought he'd have got over it after the turmoil and upset he's been through lately, wouldn't you?* Wulf told an invisible listener in his head who looked very much like Isabella. He was in even more trouble than he'd thought if he was holding inner debates with her instead of himself.

'I might come with you,' Lady Carrowe told Gus with a smile.

'I did offer my house if you want to do that; it's a bit small, but we could manage if the girls don't mind sharing a room,' Wulf said.

'No, my love. I'm not bringing trouble down on you in your place of sanctuary. If we came to you, we would be sure to be accused of hiding away and I won't have that. I'm done with that, but if we went to Haile Carr with our goods and chattels, your brother would be obliged to let me live in the Dower House, if only because it would look bad if he didn't,' their mother went on, trying to make the best of things.

'Now he and Constance have the Big House they can't claim they need it themselves.'

Wulf had often wondered why his mother seemed to like Gresley almost as little as he did himself. Apparently she didn't feel duty-bound to hide her feelings towards her eldest son now his father was dead and he was a hundred miles away and hadn't come as soon as he heard the old Earl was murdered. Wulf puzzled over the old enigma of a doting mother who loved all her children except one and couldn't solve it this time either. Even Lady Mary Junget, the Dowager Countess's first child and eldest daughter, received a rapturous welcome when she came up to town. Lady Carrowe would sit with her fractious elder daughter for hours, patiently soothing her into a more hopeful state of mind and doing her best to get her to realise she was lucky to have a faithful, if rather dull, husband and a tribe of healthy children. Yet for her firstborn son their mother would give a wary nod of greeting and the blank, almost defensive smile she usually kept for her husband.

'I do hope we won't have to go there to beg for shelter,' she added, confirming Wulf's idea it would be a great sacrifice to ask for the home she had every right to as mother of a current earl and widow of the last one.

'We won't beg for anything, Mama,' Magnus said, looking a lot more like his cool and self-confident old self as his expression said the idea of having to plead for what was theirs by right revolted him.

Wulf thought he might have to swallow his pride

if Gresley proved too mean to give up his mother's jointure, Magnus's own patrimony and the girl's small fortunes without a fight. 'If Gresley holds off claiming this place a few more days, you can all go to Hampstead and not have to,' he said soothingly because Gus had been ill and would find out the harsh realities of his new life soon enough. 'As it was once your home and your father left it to you for life, living there as soon as Gresley deigns to come to town and take possession of this wreck won't be interpreted as running away from your obligations as Dowager Lady Carrowe.'

'I forget I'm one of those now. I shall have to practise a disapproving frown in the mirror,' she said and Wulf thought those self-appointed guardians of the rules of polite society would have more of a battle than they thought if they tried to put her back in the corner her husband ordered her into when Wulf was born.

'Please don't, but will you agree to move out of this ruinous old barrack for the girls and Magnus's sake if you won't do it for your own, Mama? We can soon have Develin House replastered and repainted and you and the girls can fuss over Gus as much as you please and use his health as an excuse to seek clear air and open spaces for the poor old breakdown to recuperate in.'

'Thank you for that, dear brother,' Magnus said with a long-suffering sigh Wulf thought largely put on.

He had to discover what was troubling his brother

and he believed Isabella now—it wasn't her refusal to wed him that had brought Gus so low he couldn't throw off the lethargy that fever he'd had after Christmas left him struggling against.

'Develin House has always felt like home to me and this *is* Gresley's house now. I suppose he can do what he likes with it if we don't need it and Hampstead isn't that far away,' his mother said as if her resolution to stay here and defy the gossips was weakening now she could see Gus needed to get away from this vast and smoky city to recover his strength.

'Well, I won't be sad to go,' Aline said brightly. 'This poor old house has needed knocking down and starting again for the last fifty years.'

'Probably more, my love,' her mother said with a rueful glance at cracked plaster, rotted panelling and the faded runners and crumbling brocade curtains in what had once been a Restoration Lady Carrowe's luxurious parlour. 'Yes, let's go to Hampstead,' she finally agreed and Wulf felt his burdens lighten a little as he calculated how much easier it would be to keep them safe from stray maniacs in a much smaller, more modern house.

Magnus was home and Aline and their last housemaid had done the best they could with the food available to at least make a gesture at killing the fatted calf. Wulf felt he must stay with them all tonight although he'd prefer to be at home alone, with maybe a bottle and a warm fire to sit and brood by.

Then he'd be free to think about Isabella instead of worrying about his brother and what sort of life he could have when he recovered. Wulf refused to entertain the notion stubborn, funny and compassionate Magnus Haile would give up on life as if it didn't matter. Yet if he went home, something told him Gus would be the one sitting up with a brandy bottle and that wasn't a way out he was prepared to allow either. Stay he must, then, and he'd better try to take part in this muted family reunion instead of sitting here brooding about a woman he couldn't have.

Except his mind would keep wandering back to this afternoon and his latest attempt to pretend he wasn't in thrall to Isabella.

And be honest with yourself, at least, Wulf. You've longed for her like a love-sick puppy ever since that night at Haile Carr. One passionate and stealthy kiss could be written off as an accident, twice is a habit. You have a burning need for a lady you can't have and isn't it lucky no one knows about it except her?

He couldn't snuff out the thought of Isabella warm and real in his arms a few hours ago. Even while he ate dutifully, listened to his family and occasionally joined in their banter, he couldn't stop wondering what she was doing and feeling right now. Here the Earl of Carrowe had been missing from his wife and daughters' lives for so long his death hadn't touched them as deeply as the murder of a better father would have done. Thinking about the man lying horribly and pitiably dead a few rooms away one dreadful morning a few weeks ago was enough to put Wulf off his cheese pie and whatever greens were cheapest at the market when it was closing. Isabella was a much more inviting subject and thinking about her seemed inevitable, so he might as well indulge himself and forget the old devil for an evening.

The Isabella underneath that glamorous protective shell of hers was frighteningly alluring as well as so complex he wondered if she'd stop surprising him even if they had a lifetime to explore each other. The resolute version of her he first met in the ramshackle estate office down the hall was even more unforgettable than the glamorous and lovely society lady who coolly ordered him to go away at Cravenhill Park a few weeks ago. His inner fool might whisper that the real Isabella saw past his scandalous birth and lack of fortune, but all he had was a modest account at Coutts and his pen. The account and his career both suffered from him crossing the Atlantic twice to try to forget a woman he couldn't have. And that reminded him he should be working on the account of his travels he'd promised to have with a printer as soon as possible to earn some of it back again.

Even if Isabella would have him as the most disreputable husband she could choose to infuriate her family with, he refused to be a kept man. Living off his wealthy wife wasn't for him. Not knowing quite how to be a man while he wasted his life trying to keep up with her and all her social obligations sounded like a nightmare to a man who had learnt to rely on himself very young. Maybe he should make her a formal proposal so one of her brothers-in-law could shoot him for daring to ask and he wouldn't have to worry about impossible things any more.

Idiot, he told himself as he tried to retune his ears to the conversation and face reality. Even when the Earl had beat him to the edge of sanity or locked him in the dark until he was so terrified and hungry that he'd agree to do anything he was told to, the escape of self-destruction had never occurred to him. Hatred had driven him to succeed, to spite a brute in the skin of a civilised man. No, he wouldn't let it be *because* of the old Earl he'd made anything of himself but *despite* him. And perhaps it was time to do it for a better reason. A picture of the best reason there was hit him like a brick in the face and finally shocked him back to the present, because he wanted Isabella in his life so badly, but he still couldn't have her.

He was distracted from his thoughts by Delphine Drace entering the room after her long rest from the journey. The tense silence when Magnus stood up and stared at her as if he'd received a mortal blow wrenched Wulf's attention away from Isabella and made him question another lot of assumptions.

Delphine was staring back at his brother and Wulf had to wonder at the tension between them. Delphine must have thought she was safe from seeing Magnus when rumour said he was ill and over a hundred miles away from Carrowe House. Wulf wondered fiercely what she'd done to hurt his beloved brother so badly that Magnus would flinch at the sight of her.

'Magnus, I thought you were fixed at Lord Shuttle-worth's country seat until you were better,' she said at last and it sounded like an accusation.

'I was,' Gus said, looking as if he found it hard to string more than two words together in her presence without cursing.

'Yet here you are,' she added hollowly.

As a boy Wulf had been jealous of the bond between Gus and the girl he was so close to when they were in the country, where Wulf wasn't often permitted to go. After Wulf ran away from home, Lady Delphine Bowers had been Gus's playmate and partner in crime more than ever. Wulf used to wonder sulkily if his brother had missed him at all. Then they all grew up; Gus went to Oxford and Lady Delphine was tidied up, polished and turned into a young lady to make her debut in polite society. Then she met Sir Edgar Drace and Wulf hadn't given her much thought until she turned up on the doorstep earlier today. He'd felt pleased she was being a faithful enough friend of his family to turn up even this late in the day and thought no more of it.

'I couldn't stay away from my home and family at a time like this, Lady Drace,' Magnus was replying stiffly. 'As soon as I was well enough I insisted on coming back. Lord Shuttleworth was kind enough to send his coachman and two grooms to make sure I didn't topple out of his travelling coach halfway here.'

'You were very ill, then?' she asked.

Wulf recognised something yearning and bitter in

her eyes when she stared at his half-brother, because he felt that ache when he watched Isabella when he thought nobody was looking. What was keeping them apart? Magnus was legitimate and the woman he yearned for a widow. He recalled Isabella's hints that he needed to talk to Gus about the reason why their marriage didn't take place and cursed under his breath. If Delphine and Gus were in love, then why the hell had Gus asked Isabella to marry him? And who else was knotted up in the mess they'd made?

His brother had a lot of questions to answer and it was high time Wulf asked them and refused to let Gus slide out of telling him the truth.

Chapter Eleven

'Are you quite sure you wish to dine with us to-night, Isabella?'

'Of course, Charlotte; you keep such interesting company I'd be a fool to stay away when I will have to endure so much of the other sort once the new social Season is in full swing and all the debutantes are busy giggling in corners.'

'Do stop being so old and sophisticated, my love, but you must know how endlessly Ben and his friends like to argue over their pet projects by now,' Charlotte said with a shrug that almost convinced Isabella she was worried her guests would rattle on about steam engines and lathes and celestial bodies and Isabella would be bored.

'Lucky I'm not the empty-headed society female some people think me. I find the talk around your table on such nights fascinating and I don't *think* I've ever sat about fanning myself and trying to grab the limelight at any of your entertainments so far. I could always stay in my room if you'd rather not risk me putting on a public display of fashionable boredom.'

'That's not what I mean and you know it. Even if you were bored to the edge of mania, your company manners are far too good for you to let it show. I was the one who had to drill them into you and Kate after your wicked aunt left you to raise yourselves like a pair of wild ponies abandoned on a mountainside.'

'Then if you can trust my manners, why don't you trust me to be as richly entertained by your clever friends as I usually am?'

Charlotte frowned at her own feet as if to avoid Isabella's gaze, so her friend was seriously worried but didn't want to admit it. Silence stretched uneasily between them for once. 'It's not you I don't trust,' she said uneasily at last.

'Then who *don't* you have so much faith in?'

'Whom,' Charlotte corrected half-heartedly and looked wistfully at her baby daughter's cradle, as if she wished the little mite would wake up furious just this once.

'Whom don't you trust, then?' Isabella asked with exaggerated patience.

'It's not that I don't trust him exactly.'

'Am I supposed to know whom you mean?' Isabella said shortly.

'I know *you*, Isabella. There's a capacity for deep feeling in you I don't think even you know about and it's a pity you engaged yourself to marry Magnus Haile without loving him with every fibre of your being, but I'm so glad you saw sense and refused to wed him.'

Charlotte met Isabella's eyes so steadfastly she suspected her friend had been trying not to say what she thought since she first read about her engagement in the *Morning Post*. And hadn't she found endless reasons not to call on Charlotte and Ben before she left for Haile Carr so she couldn't tell them about her engagement? As she thought back, that said so much about her secret doubts she was surprised she hadn't questioned it at the time. Maybe Wulf was the shock she had needed to make her wonder if the life Miss Isabella Alstone had built was as flawless as she'd managed to convince herself it would be once she married a good man.

'And what's that got to do with the price of fish?' she asked brusquely. 'Or a dinner you and Ben arranged for a few friends before I came to stay?'

'You don't know all our friends,' Charlotte said glumly and shifted in her comfortably padded chair as if she might have sat on a pin.

'Is one of them a murderer or a thief, then?' Isabella heard herself joke lamely and how could she even say that in jest after the Earl's terrible death? Charlotte had caught her off guard with that jibe about thinking she could control her feelings when she knew how impossible that was now.

'No, criminals are such bad *ton*.'

Isabella chuckled at her friend's imitation of one of the *grandes dames* expressing their views as if they were all that mattered, but she knew a red herring when she smelt it. 'So, no criminals—who don't you want me to meet at your dinner table tonight, Charlotte dear?'

'It might be better for both of you if you don't meet right now.'

'I'm even more intrigued about whom you think I'm going to be rude to.'

'Not rude precisely,' Charlotte said carefully.

'What, then?'

'Intrigued and pretending not to be.' Charlotte's words came out in a rush, as if she'd been trying to hold them back, but truthfulness wouldn't allow it.

'You will have to be plainer to convince me it's a good idea to stay away when you have rashly invited me to live here until Miranda and Kit are back.'

'If you must have it, Wulf FitzDevelin accepted our invitation to dine before his recent family drama unfolded. We can't tell him not to come because you're staying with us, Isabella. He's too sensitive about his illegitimate birth as it is and we've been trying to set this meeting of minds up since he got back from America.'

'Ah, I see,' Isabella said carefully and wished she wasn't blushing. 'You think I can't be civil after what happened, or didn't happen, between me and his brother?'

'I'm sure you'll be crushingly polite as only you know how.'

Isabella felt herself flush again under her former governess's steady gaze and almost admitted she sometimes used an excess of good manners to defend herself against the more curious and malicious among the *haut ton*.

'I have met Mr FitzDevelin more than once at Carrowe House since I came back to London in such a hurry, Charlotte, and I won't hide the fact I visit the Hailes behind society's back from you. You know I can't turn mine on people I grew very fond of when we all thought they would be my family by marriage. Mr FitzDevelin and I even manage to be polite to one another most of the time, despite my lack of common civility.'

'Now I've offended you.'

'No, but I admit to being a little hurt you think I'd snub him in public.'

'Under all that polish you're still the same ruthlessly outspoken little madam I first met, aren't you?' Charlotte said with a grimace. For a moment she seemed ready to abandon the subject and leave things be, but that was too much to hope for. 'No, it won't do, Isabella. I can't let you pretend I'm mistaken and ought to keep my worries to myself. You're attracted to the wrong brother, aren't you?'

'What on earth have I done to deserve that outrageous slur, Charlotte?' Isabella tried not to let her voice squeak as she fought to control her shock that her best friend had worked out her darkest secret. 'I jilted his eligible, handsome and amusing elder brother whom he loves. Mr FitzDevelin wouldn't want me if I was sent to him wrapped in silver gilt and tied up with pure gold ribbons.'

'Attraction and mutual need don't follow rules,

Isabella. If they did, I'd be a governess or school-marm and Ben would be who knows what by now.'

'This isn't love and yours was.'

'Ben was born a bastard and felt it in every inch of his giant, gallant, daft frame, but I'll never regret marrying him. I love him as I could never love another man if I had to live without him for a millennium.'

'I know that, but why are you telling me?'

'Because it's wonderful to love such a prickly bear of a man and find out he loves you back.'

'Oh, no, don't tell me you're matchmaking now. A minute or so ago you were trying to keep us from meeting at your dinner table tonight and what I feel for Mr FitzDevelin isn't love, or anything close to it. Don't get carried away and start building castles in Spain.'

'How do you know?'

'How do I know what?'

'That he doesn't love you?'

'Because I've seen far too much of love matches, thanks to you and my sisters, to mistake this for love,' Isabella said and crossed her fingers under her skirts. It might *not* be love, and even if it was, it wouldn't lead to a happy ending.

'I suppose you're old enough to know your own mind.'

'I do; I'm not in love with Mr FitzDevelin.'

'I don't think you'd dare admit it if he was the man from all those wild dreams you never admitted having, but you can't reason away love and I suspect at least half of you doesn't want to.'

That was too close to the bone. Isabella wondered what she needed to say or do to persuade her friend to let the notion she and Wulf were more than nodding acquaintances go. 'Mr FitzDevelin doesn't even like me.'

'Then since you're so definite about not loving him, I'll try to treat you as fellow guests attending the same simple meal. It could be a struggle, since you usually leave the room or close the conversation if his name is mentioned, but I'll try.'

'There's nothing simple about your dinners,' Isabella said lightly, 'but if you and Ben can't get your odd ideas about Mr FitzDevelin out of your stubborn heads, I might as well have my supper in the nursery or go to Carnwood House.'

'With the knocker off the door and most of the staff in Derbyshire with Kit and Miranda? I'll cancel the whole affair before you spend a glum evening with a maid of all work, the bootboy and a taciturn footman for company.'

'I'll stay, then, but rid yourself of the notion I like Mr FitzDevelin more than any other nodding acquaintance. Kit would laugh himself hoarse if the poor man galloped to Wychwood in order to demand my hand in marriage and so would I.'

'Would you now? I wonder,' Charlotte said as if she had her own ideas about how funny it might be.

'Yes, Mr FitzDevelin would be horrified to hear you talk so.'

'Would he? Poor Dev,' her friend said softly.

'If ever I've met a man capable of looking after himself, it's Mr FitzDevelin.'

'Wouldn't that make him your perfect man? He might elbow past that fine control you pride yourself on before you knew he was doing it.'

'Oh, be quiet, Charlotte. Waste your breath on one of your children or save it for Ben, but please write me off as a hopeless case and leave me be.' Isabella stuck her nose in the air and went upstairs to pick out her most modestly stunning gown in the hope of making Wulf suffer for being the cause of the last half-hour of relentless interrogation, even if he didn't know it was his fault.

Chapter Twelve

She should have been prepared for the shock of Wulf FitzDevelin looking handsome as the devil in a dark evening coat and immaculate linen after her conversation with Charlotte earlier. Isabella shot a sidelong glance at the man when she thought nobody else would notice. Tonight he seemed quite happy to ignore the clever conversation and free flow of ideas around the table for the fine eyes of the lady seated next to him. Part of her hoped he was throwing up a smokescreen to mask his interest in her instead of the eagerly wicked Mrs Fonthill. This could be his clumsy way of protecting her from the curiosity of her friends.

Charlotte had placed them opposite one another at the dinner table and Isabella dearly wished she didn't have to watch him flirt with someone else every time she looked up from her dinner. The bit of her that wasn't reasonable hoped Wulf knew her every move as acutely as she knew his. That Isabella was bitingly jealous every time she caught him smiling at the overblown creature, or openly admiring her cunningly displayed bosom. If he was acting, he was so good it looked as if he wouldn't notice if Miss Alstone took to dancing stark naked among the entrées in an attempt to wrench his attention away from the woman at his side. She glared down at her plate because her eyes were oddly misty for some reason she didn't want to think about. Perhaps she'd caught a cold from the children. At least that would give her an excuse to retire early from this delicious but somehow rather awful dinner and that seemed a very alluring idea right now.

It was the thought of all those experienced and eager women he once confessed he'd made love to that had made her faith in him threaten to melt away. She tried to tell herself Wulf was only pretending to run true to form for her sake, but the image of one or two of the ladies she knew considered their duty to their husbands done and a young and handsome lover their just reward for bearing all those sons played over and over in her mind and made the whole evening hideous before it had hardly begun.

Wulf was so fascinated by his dining companion he didn't seem to notice Isabella sneaking side-long glances at him when she wasn't trying hard to be polite to the gentlemen on either side of her. She couldn't enjoy the company of all these clever, enterprising and interesting people because Wulf was behaving like a moon-led idiot with an overblown female who ought to know better. She felt insulted he'd been the same with her in secret and suddenly began to doubt his sincerity during their shadowy encounters. She ought to dismiss him from her thoughts as if he was no more than a stupid fly buzzing around another woman as if he'd never heard of Miss Isabella Alstone. Yet the other men in the room faded to watercolour next to him. She had to clench her nails into her palm until it hurt in order not to leap out of her chair and rant at him for ignoring her after their latest snatched kiss in the gloom.

For an awful moment she also wanted to stab a pin in the woman he was so engrossed with. She longed to be the cool and aloof Miss Alstone she was before she met him. No good; that version of her packed her bags and left six months ago—on the night she met Wulf FitzDevelin. The night Isabella was shocked, intrigued and sensually excited by every last handsome, bitter, faithless inch of him between one breath and the next. How could she be intrigued by a man who was blatantly flirting with another woman while she watched from the sidelines, even if it was a pretence? She shouldn't hate the woman he was ogling, but sympathise with her. Mrs Fonthill was falling for the same sensual promises in his ice-blue eyes Isabella had.

Blaming the object of his flattery instead of the man who fixed his eyes on her as if *she* was the one female in the world he wanted only yesterday was wrong. Wulf didn't belong to her because of a few stupid kisses they should never have snatched. So of course she wasn't jealous or vindictive; she was disgusted by the lures a married woman could cast with her husband sitting nearby. By now the rich curves of the woman's generous breasts was holding Wulf's attention like iron to a magnet and reasonable Isabella was giving up. He did nothing to discourage Mrs Fonthill's possessive little touches and blatantly seductive glances under her skilfully darkened lashes. Little doubt these two would have a more satisfying end to their evening than he'd ever allowed her, but if the lady deserved censure because she was married, what about him?

He deserved her contempt, she decided. When he woke up next to a tawdry and overripe bedmate tomorrow morning, he'd get his just deserts. Isabella imagined the lady's sleek brows and lashes without the lampblack she used to darken them. It could end up smeared across Mrs Fonthill's suspiciously blushing cheeks if she didn't wash it all off before she lured him into her bed. Next Isabella considered the lady's elaborately looped and bejewelled hair and decided her luxurious locks could be padded out with false curls as well. She let them fall down on the smeared and ruffled pillows to shock Wulf in the morning, too, and it would serve him right for not seeing past the very obvious lures of a woman who wouldn't admit to being a day over thirty in a court of law.

She was quite enjoying her vengeful fantasy now and was almost charming to her immediate neighbour for a few minutes as satisfying images of Wulf reaping the price of his sins ran through her head like a bad play. How dare he use another woman to deny the attraction that sang between them even as they said a stiffly polite good evening to each other?

Stop right there, Isabella, she silently corrected herself. *This is the lesson you badly needed to learn and never mind the one he'll get in the morning. These are his true colours.*

Except she didn't want them to be; she didn't want him to lie in another woman's arms tonight and soar to whatever heights lovers achieved in the witchy darkness.

'No, he *can't* be the lover I long for and can't have. I won't let him be,' she whispered under her breath, horrified when Ben picked up her tension if not her words and followed the direction of her eyes. He had the cheek to grin as if he thought it was a fine joke she was watching Wulf with hungry eyes while he flirted with another woman.

Feeling out of sorts with herself and almost everyone else, she remembered Charlotte's warning: Mrs Fonthill was bored by talk of arts and natural science and the inventions her husband doted on. Apparently the lady had a generous dowry and it was her money that had set the Fonthill Works on its feet and kept his innovations going until the markets realised they had need of them. Now he was successful in his own right, the lady had lost interest. In fairness she *had* thrown herself at Wulf and maybe the gallant great fool was too kind under all that hawkish male beauty and aloofness to humiliate a lonely and frustrated woman in public. If it wasn't Wulf's sleeve the woman was clutching, Isabella might pity her for being married to a man who cared more about steam-powered engines than his rich wife.

She shuddered at the thought of how Magnus might have come to view her after a few decades of marriage. He was far too much of a gentleman to treat a lady he wed for money so shabbily. Isabella shuddered at the thought of the life they would have had together if she hadn't found the courage to call off their wedding. At least Wulf was born of love and not duty—he endured a rough and bitter upbringing because of it, but he never had to doubt his heart and instincts as his half-sisters and brothers did because of the man who fathered them.

Now she was thinking about his brother to try to blot Wulf out of her mind and that wasn't working out very well, was it? She clung to it in the hope she could do better. Magnus's life had been pulled out of shape by being the Earl of Carrowe's second son, a spare in case his elder brother failed the succession. Magnus was sent to Eton and Oxford and thrown on the *ton* with too small an income to be fully part of it, but no space for a bigger dream. It was a wonder he had grown up so good-humoured and blasé about his role, she mused while the ladies quit the dining room at Charlotte's signal.

With any luck, she might manage to forget this silly fascination with Wulf's every move and glance if she thought about his half-brother long enough. Mrs Fonthill had peeled herself away from Wulf with open reluctance and at the last possible moment as the ladies followed Charlotte to the drawing room.

Isabella willed her fingers not to clench into claws and made a murmured excuse about checking on the children. If she stayed, she'd lose her temper and say what she thought of Mrs Fonthill flaunting her lush bosom to attract a man's attention. To truly deserve a Wulf FitzDevelin in her bed she'd need more than a full figure and a lusty imagination.

The children were asleep for once and the night nursery disappointingly calm. Since Isabella couldn't face watching Wulf flirt with another woman any longer, she decided to stay away. Charlotte could twit her in the morning if she liked after she'd sworn she could be indifferent to Wulf for a whole evening, but she couldn't do it now. Isabella rang for Heloise and told her she had a headache and would try to sleep it away. Her maid would convey a message to Charlotte before she decided there must be a crisis in the nursery and came up to find out what it was and never mind her guests.

Ever since she found out Wulf would be here to-night Isabella had been secretly elated. This would be their first out-in-the-open, social meeting. As a very real headache throbbed in her temples she blinked back tears for the lonely feel of an evening when the man she longed for spent all his time with someone else. Knowing she had lied to Heloise and couldn't sleep if she tried, she waited a few moments to make sure her maid had gone away, then wrapped herself in her warmest shawl against the spring chill and went out to pace the spacious garden alone. At least out there she could breathe fresh air and have room to be properly alone. She longed for cool clear air off the Pennines and the freedom of the hills above Wychwood that she had tramped so often as a girl. Perhaps if she could get back there, she wouldn't hurt so much. She tried to tell herself it was only her pride that hurt, but she knew it was a lie.

She paced past the French windows towards the airy family garden Charlotte and Ben had made. Pausing for a moment, she yielded to temptation and looked back into the drawing room. Instead of bending over Mrs Fonthill as if he couldn't take his eyes off her, Wulf was staring out of the windows, as if he knew she was out here by instinct, but that was impossible, wasn't it? Far easier for her to see him than for him to look out with the light from the candles that were making the darkness deeper than ever behind her. She eased back a little and held her breath until he looked away and turned to answer someone's question, or perhaps slant his latest *inamorata* an easy smile. Isabella wandered deeper into the wide gardens that were the main reason Charlotte and Ben took this house, allowing their growing family as much freedom as town children ever had.

It was far too early in the year for the roses to be in flower yet, but the pale glimmer of a late primrose or the tall and glossy pale pink tulips the gardener had carefully placed wherever the boys didn't run were lighter marks in the darkness. The moon didn't look anywhere near as big or bright here in sooty London. She compared it to that night last summer at Haile Carr and found it wanting in so many ways—no heat, no heady and exotic perfume and, worst of all, no Wulf. No comparison at all, then. Drat the man. Without him this was night-time in a pleasant enough garden where she could find a little peace after a noisy and disappointing evening, but essentially it was as blank and lonely as all the other nights since.

She shivered; time to live with what was instead of yearning for everything Wulf wouldn't allow himself to be. So she wandered a little further into the walks and even smiled briefly when she spotted a new den the children had built in the wilder bit here at the back of the gardens. She moved on despite a childish urge to crawl inside and cry for a bit, then curl up safely until morning. There was a neat bench almost tempting her to be still in the faint moonlight, but she didn't sit. If she wanted to be still, she would be inside, tucked up in bed while the most determined guests lingered over the fading sparkle of ideas and a last glass of brandy. This far from the front of the house and the mews, she had no idea if most of the carriages had already rattled home with their sleepy occupants drunk on ideas or Ben's fine cognac. She didn't care anyway, she assured herself and wondered if Mrs Fonthill was brazen enough to take her newest lover up in hers and leave her husband here to be called for later.

'Fool,' she muttered and paced restlessly along narrow paths and back on herself because it was a largish garden for London, but not by Wychwood's vast proportions or Edmund's rolling acres. Either would do now, except she had a whole London Season to get through before she could get to real, wide countryside and truly fresh air. She heard a faint click and a hint of movement off to her right and stopped in her tracks to consider if she ought to run or shout for help first. Neither, instinct told her as a tall and very masculine shadow loomed out of the back of the garden, but what the devil was he doing here?

'How dare you?' she whispered not quite loudly enough to be heard by anyone close enough to find them, as if they'd had an assignation planned all along.

'I'm hardly going to lose a fine reputation or a good name if I'm caught, so why not?' he murmured.

'No, and wouldn't it be a shame if you had to cultivate one of those?' she sniped back, but he was too busy frowning down at her as if he had every right to be here quizzing her to rise to her goad.

'I hurt you,' he told her huskily, and did he think she didn't know?

'I doubt it,' she snapped and wished she could think of the perfect response to his abrupt words now instead of having it occur to her long after he'd gone.

'Charlotte Shaw was watching us so closely I thought a light flirtation with another woman would stop her speculating about me and you.'

'Why?'

'Because Ben Shaw would kill me if he thought I had designs on you, if he didn't send for your brothers-in-law to do it for him.'

'What a faint-heart you are, Mr Wulf.'

'No, I'm a realist,' he said grimly and looked so certain and stern about it in the faint moonlight it might take gunpowder to shake his stubborn belief he had no right to be involved with a lady of birth and fortune.

'You're an idiot,' she told him severely. 'And if that's all you came to tell me, you can go away again.'

'I haven't finished.'

'Well, I have and I have a headache.'

'So I understand, but you looked so lonely out here, Isabella,' he said as if that explained why he came back to keep her company.

'You must have eyes like a wolf as well as their bad reputation, then. How did you get in here so easily?'

'I was taught to pick locks by a very fine craftsman,' he said modestly.

'And you think that's a good thing for a gentleman to know?'

'I think it's the sort of thing wolves like me are expected to know and there's no harm in being predictable when it gets me where I want to go.'

'There's no story in here, Wulf; nor a Mrs Fonthill to make it worthwhile for the Wulf FitzDevelin to creep about in the shadows. If you think Ben's safe is easy to crack, you should have brought your friend and half the contents of the Woolwich Arsenal with you because you're wrong.'

'I'm not a thief,' he told her as if she'd tweaked his pride.

'You obviously consort with one.'

'He's reformed, I hope,' he said impatiently and there was just enough moonlight to see him frown as if he wasn't quite sure about that and it worried him.

She didn't want to find that admirable, so she turned away from the sight of him, the shadowed, lurking-in-darkness and barely visible man he seemed to think was all she deserved. 'You should go now before someone sees you.'

'Who could?'

'Whom,' she corrected him snippily and was almost ashamed of herself until she recalled Mrs Fonthill's low-cut gown and hungry eyes.

'You should open a school,' he teased softly and how she wanted to be gently teased into a better humour and perhaps more, but she was so tired of peering through the night or the dust heavy shade of Carrowe House at him like this that she wasn't going to be as easily distracted this time.

'I should go inside and refuse to speak to you until you're prepared to own up to me in public,' she told him bleakly and felt him wince.

'Put the shoe on the other foot, Miss Alstone. You can't want a bastard like me attracting attention to you in public when you were betrothed to my half-brother until very recently. If I was considered pitch before that and the murder, I'm a whole lake of it now.'

'I make it a rule only to kiss men who admit to knowing me whenever and wherever we meet.'

Maybe she had been cursed to fall in love with

the wrong brother and none of the neat endings she had mapped out at the start led to the right place. There—that was the snap of reality she needed to meet his accusing look with cool reserve even if he probably couldn't see it. She *couldn't* love him. And what right did he have to question her when he'd spent the entire evening wooing a potential mistress?

Isabella swept down the nearest path to the house in a swirl of expensive silk and finest lawn petticoats, Wulf trailing slowly behind her. Yes, this was the gown she chose with both her sisters last autumn, wasn't it? When she was trying so hard to believe this man was nothing to her and it didn't matter if he *had* left England never to return. Sensing she wasn't quite her usual self after a scandalous meeting under the stars she couldn't tell them about, Kate and Miranda had carried her off to their favourite silk merchant to pick something fine and frivolous and hoped it would help whatever was troubling her when she was engaged to marry a fine and handsome gentleman and ought to be dancing on air. So it wasn't so much a quietly fashionable gown as a hug from her beloved sisters, a reminder she was loved. A contrast to Mrs Fonthill's blatantly low-cut gown and brutally corseted waist and there was that nasty little clutch of jealousy in her belly again. It made her feel sick and uneasy and he shouldn't have come after her, she decided crossly and glared back at him again.

'They would be gentlemen, then, wouldn't they?' he said cynically and she wanted to slap him, except there was a hint of jealousy in his voice that made her silly heart race although she'd forbidden it to.

'Not if they tried to kiss me in the dark to find out if I would kiss them back. And who are you, Wulf, if you're *not* a gentleman?' she said relentlessly.

'A man who doesn't know who his father is,' he said as if that was all he'd ever be and this time hot tears prickled at her eyes. She told herself it was her fury at his intransigence that put them there.

'A man who doesn't know who he is for the lack of one?' she said and turned to face him. He was so heartbreakingly handsome and so determined to be the big, bad wolf, yet he'd got in here past Ben's careful defences, and all the reckless risks he'd have run if he was caught, because he thought he'd hurt her. 'That's not enough to sum you up now, Wulfric FitzDevelin—you've made yourself and never mind who your father was.'

'Aye, I've made myself into a fool,' he said as if he was joking.

He'd stepped closer still as if he had to convince her by proximity alone he was unsuitable to even be seen with Miss Alstone by the clear light of day. Instead he was pure, or perhaps impure, temptation and more so than ever when he was being so ridiculously modest.

Her fingers shook with the effort of not reaching for him as she tried to smooth an imaginary crease from the skirt of her gown. 'You've made me into one as well and more than once,' she admitted huskily and what sort of an idiot was she to remind them of that when she ought to be raging at him for his sins, but the root of his dalliance with Mrs Fonthill was in his stupid blindness about himself as a man she wanted and had let herself fall in love with somewhere along the line. How could she go on being furious with him when his stubborn conviction he was too much of a rogue to deserve her was part of the reason she loved him in the first place?

'Oh, the deuce; why did you have to bring that up now?' he muttered crossly.

'You have so many questions and not enough answers,' she replied lightly and would have walked away if he hadn't hooked his arm round her waist as if it belonged there.

She tried to imagine she hadn't longed to be in his arms, but couldn't dig up the right sort of petty little insults it would take to make him let her go. She'd wanted him mercilessly since he walked into Charlotte's drawing room looking so darkly dangerous and determined to ignore her. She did her best to stiffen in his arms and think of winter to cool her ardour. 'Take your hands off me, you lecher,' she whispered not quite fiercely enough, 'and that's a polite term for Mrs Fonthill's lover, by the way. I'm sure you know more impolite ones than I do. Choose one and wear it, Mr FitzDevelin, because you earned it tonight.'

'I'm such a dirty dog and you want me, so I might as well add to my sins.'

Isabella hardly heard her own gasp when he pulled her even closer and kissed her fiercely before she could think of a protest. Well, no, that was a lie. She *thought* of several, but he wasn't going to leave her any breath to speak anyway, so she drew his head down so she could kiss him back. It was such lusty pleasure to be in his arms and she shouldn't even know such delights existed until she was a respectably married woman. Except she did. It was like being adrift in the most exotic and lovely country she could ever imagine visiting and coming home all at the same time. Her heart was beating so fast and light now she wondered if it was thundering in his ears as loudly as it was in hers. His mouth was ravenous on hers as if he'd been starving for her and at least there was no hint of Fonthill's perfume or another woman's easy hunger on his lips. Wulf FitzDevelin wanted Isabella Alstone. She wriggled triumphantly and heard him groan at the feel of her restless body moving against his before he slid an even more passionate kiss across her willing mouth and stilled her with pure heat.

'Isabella,' he half-protested and half-praised her when he finally managed to lift his head and murmur her name.

'Wulf,' she muttered back and he kissed her again as if he had to imprint the taste and scent and touch of her on his memory. Sadness pinched at her even as the urgent heat of him spoke of long hot nights and lazy summer days of loving without boundaries and she knew it was a lie. Only he could take her there and he was far too much of a gentleman to risk it, the great fool. It was a joyous sort of pain, this outrageous need of him that gnawed at her in a way she couldn't find words to tell herself about, let alone him. She felt the jet buttons of his waistcoat bite into the soft skin of her torso through gossamer layers of silk, boned satin and lace, and stretched sensually against him to let him know she wanted it all gone. She wanted him naked; just him and her. With nothing between them but salty skin and lovers' whispers of praise and encouragement.

'I want you so much; I want it all,' she murmured with lips that felt numb. Their mouths were made for loving and not talking right now.

'No, Belle, we can't,' he muttered low and gruff as the injured wolf he looked like when he raised his head as if every fraction of an inch he made himself put between them hurt in some vital way.

'Not here and not now, I know that; but tell me where and when and I'll come to you.' She offered all of herself, rashly, completely and with such exhilarating feelings inside that all the lies they'd told each other since they met that first night melted away. 'I will,' she argued with a frantic nod as his eyes told her he'd already made up his mind not to let her.

He shook his head as if he couldn't quite believe his ears weren't making up lies about her. 'No, you won't,' he said firmly, getting his inner warrior on to the parade ground with unseemly haste. 'Stop it, Isabella. You can't ruin yourself with a bastard like me, however willing you are.'

'Willing?' she said as if it was poison on her tongue, which it felt like as she watched him be all the things she loved him for but almost hated right now. He could say what he liked about being a bastard; it was his damned honour and his pride standing between them—like twin statues of virtue and nobility she wanted to smash to tiny pieces and dance on. 'You think I'm only *willing*?' she demanded. She was desperate for them to love one another right now, not passively willing to let him have his wicked way with her as if she was some milksop out of a bad play.

'Yes, in every way there is,' he said as grittily as if he'd been turned to stone despite the warm wonder of his body so firm and masculine against hers.

He couldn't quite draw completely away from her to leave her achingly lonely in the shadows again, though, could he? He wasn't going to let them be lovers and what else could they be out here in the little hours and the darkness if he meant to be noble? So he was distancing himself from her as if he was about to board another ship bound for New York, but this was different. Now she knew Wulf longed for her as acutely as she did for him. Although she would be being loved to the last degree of heat-soaked pleasure right now if they were equals in that, wouldn't she?

'Is that all you think I am?' she asked in a voice that sounded as if all the blood and life in her was soaking into the cold stone pavers under her feet while he stepped round her with a polite *excuse me*.

'Yes,' he said stiffly, as if he really wanted to be a thousand miles away now, 'that's all.'

'Liar,' she hissed at him. He flinched; his eyes

closed to deny it and he shook his head as if he desperately wanted to mean it. 'You want me every bit as much as I want you,' she went on fiercely. 'You want me, Wulf; denying it won't make it go away. You've done that for more than half a year now and it hasn't worked, has it?'

'Do you want me to admit I need you as urgently as my father did my mother?' he said harshly, as if who he was explained everything. Why were they back with that tired excuse?

'Or as much as she wanted him,' she challenged. 'Knowing her, as I have come to since I engaged myself to marry the wrong brother, I can see your mother must have loved your father more than life itself to take such a risk with you,' she ended more gently. He didn't think anyone could love him so much; she could swear it until she was blue in the face and he'd never believe her. 'She loves you so very dearly, Wulf,' she said softly, feeling her whole future swung on making him see he was lovable and worth the risk she would take if she let herself love him for life. Something told her she had already made that giant step without leaving herself a way back. 'Since she loved your father passionately enough to break her marriage vows, she must have loved him nearly as dearly as she does their son.'

'Then why didn't she fight for us? Why not leave the Earl and proclaim me and my father boldly from the rooftops? She's a Develin, for heaven's sake, she could have thumbed her nose at the world and her father would have sighed and tut-tutted for a while, then shrugged and taken us in and made the best of a bad lot.'

'What would have happened to your elder brothers and sister? However much she loved you and your father, she couldn't walk away knowing what Lord Carrowe would do to them when she wasn't there to protect them from his fury.'

'So she chose to live not even half a life for their sake, with no power or influence to alter what I was made to do? Don't you think they would have been better off without her, given the Earl's never-ending need to punish her for daring to take a lover, and I can't believe she ever loved *him*.'

'Neither can I, but she's not the sort of woman to marry solely for advantage, so she must have felt something for him,' Isabella argued and wondered why she was defending Lady Carrowe when she'd never found the courage to do it herself.

'If she ever did, it was long gone by the time I arrived. She must have hated him for keeping me under her nose to beat every time he thought she was tempted to stray again. I wish she'd told him so every time he did it rather than close down and grit her teeth as if she deserved whatever filth he threw at her.'

He said it as if only by hating her husband could his mother be halfway right not to have rescued him. Isabella frowned and thought harder about the lady's reactions to a man she had come to hate too much herself to see things clearly until now. 'I think she pitied him,' she said slowly as the truth dawned.

'How could she pity such a hyena, Isabella?'

'For being one, I suppose.'

'She's a saint, then, but I'm not and never will be.'

'No,' she agreed and couldn't stop herself from giving his tense face a loving pat to console him for everything he'd endured, 'but somehow I still like you quite immoderately.'

'Don't,' he argued gruffly, putting his hands about her waist as if he was about to push her away before she got past more of his defences. 'Don't forgive me for anything I've done, Isabella. It's hard enough to walk away from you as it is.'

'Then don't do it, Wulf. Accept me as I am, as we are, equals before God.'

'You're Miss Alstone and I'm Lady Carrowe's bastard and once upon a time I would have gone home with that lonely rich woman while her husband was busy with his steam-powered engines. I would have scooped up her frustration and loneliness and enjoyed her body until I went on my way, whistling with the dawn.'

'And even that horrible image won't convince me you're as rackety as you think. You cling to a method of measuring the world out in grudging parcels, Mr FitzDevelin. Luckily I don't think so little of myself or the rest of the world, so why must you?'

'Because that man made me this way,' he said as if she'd driven the truth out of him and ought to be ashamed of herself. 'I'm a nameless fool with nothing but my pen between me and the devil. I have my mother, three half-sisters and Magnus to keep and can't afford the luxury of a Miss Alstone in my bed. Your noble brothers-in-law would kill me and quite right, too; then where would my family be?'

Now he'd said it he stood and glared at her with such furious longing in his eyes she wished she could laugh and dismiss his scruples as petty and unimportant. All she had could be his as well, if that was the only thing keeping them apart. Wealth and grand houses would feel less than nothing without him. She wanted to rage and stamp her feet and demand he put her and the life they could have together before this stubborn folly, but she knew him too well by now to batter her poor heart against his stony pride again tonight. Tomorrow or the next day maybe, but tonight he'd worn her down and her head was aching again.

'I might be worth it,' she joked rather lamely, the hardness of tears threatening at the back of her throat as she acknowledged a harsh truth and felt infinitely weary at long last. If he didn't love her enough to grasp what they could be together, there wasn't much point in humiliating herself again.

'I'll never risk making a bastard with you, Isabella.'

'Then marry me instead,' she offered rashly, feeling the rightness of it slide into her mind as if it had always been waiting to be recognised as the glowing piece of good sense it truly was. 'Your family would be safe and with Kit and the rest of my family behind us you wouldn't need to worry about them again.'

'I would be a kept man. A tame fool dressed up to impress your friends. Dragged to fashionable parties and soirées to be pointed out as a rich woman's folly. No, thank you, Miss Alstone; I'd rather be laughed at as an example of my mother's idiocy than mocked as my wife's.'

So this was how it felt when the tears you were struggling with faded away because your sorrow was too big to cry away. No wonder Edmund left London for three years when Kate turned his love down again and again as if it was of no importance. Suddenly she longed for her brother-in-law's wise counsel, wanted the comfort of Kate's loyal and loving arms around her and for both of them to tell her they loved her, even if Wulfric FitzDevelin couldn't, or wouldn't. He'd never admit he felt more than simple lust for her even if he longed for her every hour of life God allotted him. He'd got it so firmly lodged in his silly head he could only do her harm there was no point in him even considering loving her.

'Good evening to you, then, sir. I can't make small talk with you here in the middle of the night any longer, so I suggest you truly scurry off home and forget you ever saw me out here.'

'How can I do that when I've hurt you again?'

'Have you, Mr FitzDevelin? Ah well, such things will happen to reckless ladies of fortune who take risks with the likes of you. I wish you goodnight,' she said lightly and dodged past him and marched back to the house as if she really did.

Chapter Thirteen

'How can you wish me anything of the sort, Belle?'
Wulf murmured. 'How can you be that kind and how
do you think I'll ever sleep softly again without you
in my bed?'

He thrust a distracted hand through his hair and
briefly thought he must look as if he'd been out in a
gale with sooty locks all awry and neckcloth disarrayed by her exploring hands. He touched the mess
she'd made of careful grooming and his body turned
against him as he ran over places she'd been, as if
some of her must linger there to be savoured and treasured. He'd said no and made her walk away when
she felt as if she could be his whole world; everything
that would make his life feel so rich and generous it
would never matter who was born in what bed when
they were together. Except it did. He would always
feel ashamed of being dependent on his wife and
hadn't he once taken a long hard look at his mother's
marriage and sworn never to make such ball-and-
chain promises himself? Marriage had trapped the

last Earl and Countess of Carrowe in a lifelong cycle of jealousy, frustration and contempt on one side and fear and a weary sort of pity for a man who turned out so much less than he could have been on the other.

Wulf was less than Isabella Alstone. Less hopeful, less joyous and a lot less of a gentleman than she deserved him to be. Even without his own shortcomings his lack of a real name would drag her down if she shared it with him. Imagining how their children would be teased for his own lack of a father, he shuddered at the memory of pinches, name-calling and spite when he was included in some childhood party he'd done his best to forget for Magnus's sake. They had never talked about his brother's clutch of schoolboy friends who met up to create havoc together in the holidays again after that hellish day. Poor Gus felt guilty for not turning his back on his friends and being recklessly loyal to his half-brother ever since and that was what torn loyalties and being a bastard really meant. Isabella had no idea how it felt or how she would feel if he was stupid enough to expose her to it, so he wasn't going to let her find out, especially if he loved her. He wasn't quite ready to admit that disaster just yet, but he was afraid he might if he looked harder.

An argumentative inner voice whispered he could refuse to take a penny of her fortune, spend the odd holiday on one of her grand estates at his own expense and go on working hard at his chosen profession to prove the gossips wrong when they said he married her for money. And were they all blind?

What fool would marry Isabella Alstone for her money? She was everything a man could fantasise about in a woman and a lot more he'd never dared to dream about before he met her. To own the everyday privilege of making love to her exclusively for the rest of their natural lives was something a man might sell his very soul for, if he had one. The Countess of Carrowe's natural son could only bring her conflict and unhappiness; her world would reject and revile them as a pair of fools who'd regret what they did when the novelty of playing against the rules wore off.

So where was he with his catalogue of reasons why not? If only he lived another life, then he could pride himself on being an independent man and just about manage to ignore the differences in birth and fortune between them. In this one he would have to take from her and he'd rather risk the sheer terror of his family having nothing much to live on if Gresley refused to honour his commitments. The so-called polite world would mock Isabella if she married him when she could have wed Magnus and taken Wulf as a lover once she was done with securing the Haile succession. Not that they had much left to succeed to; the old Earl had spent everything he could and Gresley was the only one with a penny to his name.

The very thought of Isabella in Magnus's bed made his fists clench so hard his knuckles went white even now. He'd had to put the width of the Atlantic between him and this terrible image of her and Gus wed and busily securing that succession together.

He'd been tortured there and back by the idea he'd got far too close to something exceptional with his brother's wife-to-be that night at Haile Carr. Now he felt a blinding, unreasoning rage threaten to suck him under at the very thought of any other man laying a finger on Isabella with more than the most innocent reverence in his mind and he loved his brother. He was a mess, he decided, and cursed viciously under his breath.

Even that finger would probably be too much for him. The burn and thunder of blind fury running through him at the very thought made him clench his fists and he had to remind himself where he was and that he wasn't supposed to be here. His inner fool wanted Isabella to be a coolly reserved and faintly amused great lady with every man she ever came across for the rest of her life except him. He wanted her so desperately and in every way there was that it hurt. Temptation roared at him to forget scruples and burgle every bedchamber in that innocently sleeping house yonder until he found hers. Then he'd stop and adore every last inch of her until Ben came and pounded him into a pulp. They'd snatch satisfaction for however brief a time they were allowed before some busybody realised nobody could get through Miss Isabella's locked door to find the intruder. They could love gloriously at least once. Given his size and temper, Ben would roar and rage at the sight of any man taking advantage of Isabella, even if she'd asked him to do it, and Wulf would not be able to defend himself or his actions, because he still wouldn't marry her.

Yet the need to feel her under him, around him, with him as they made love soared so wildly he smashed his fist into the nearest tree trunk. He tried to bless the agony he'd inflicted on himself as it jagged through him like hot metal so sickness bloomed in his belly instead of lust. Once he'd stopped being sick and sorry for himself, he had to get out of here as stealthily as he got in and then forget why he came. Isabella had looked so alone and lonely in the darkness out here when he'd glanced up from flirting with another woman to show the world Wulf FitzDevelin was on the prowl again, snapping up bored wives their husbands were foolish enough to leave untended. He was as bad as ever, so no need to speculate about the odd wolfish glance he cast at the unattainable Miss Alstone he couldn't quite suppress. Now all he had to do was walk a few miles across dark and dangerous London to try to sleep in his own home, since he couldn't endure Carrowe House tonight and pretend nothing was amiss. Maybe he could honour his overdue appointment with the brandy bottle to take away the taste of using one disappointed woman to hide his interest in another.

'Wulf, Wulf! Don't just lie there; wake up,' Magnus demanded, but what right did he have to interfere?

Wulf had to grope his way up from a very peculiar dream and felt a hard jag of pain in his misused right hand when Magnus shook his shoulder. He cursed and kept his eyes closed as he tried to come to terms with life in a newly tarnished world he was going to have to get used to. He didn't want to emerge from his coward's cocoon of drunken sleep and even inside his chilly stupor it didn't feel much like morning. Gus wouldn't be shaking him as if he ought to be wide awake if it wasn't time to face the world, though, so it must be, mustn't it?

He groaned, remembered Isabella marching away from him last night and refusing to shed a single tear although he'd seen the shine of them in her eyes. Perhaps he preferred the nightmare he'd just emerged from of Mrs Fonthill pursuing him around the Shaws' drawing room like Diana the Huntress with hounds in full cry as her husband obliviously built some sort of shiny machine and laughed very loudly. Odd, but at least the memory of it distracted him. If he'd ever felt the need to chase animals about the countryside on horseback, he'd give it up here and now. 'Dratted woman,' he murmured and felt his brother's attention waver from whatever he'd woken him up to talk about.

'Never mind her, whoever she is. You need to read this or, given the state you're in, perhaps I'll read it to you as you're probably seeing double.'

'You woke me up to *read* to me?' Wulf asked and opened bleary eyes to stare at Gus, too shocked he'd run mad to be furious with him.

'You'll understand when you hear, or perhaps you'd like to wake up to find half of London on the doorstep and you with no idea why they're here?'

'Half of London don't know I've got one, let alone where it is,' Wulf argued grumpily, but he yawned and tried to find enough attention for whatever Gus thought he should know.

'They will find it now,' his brother said grimly.

'Why? What have I done?'

'Not you; him.'

'Oh, *him*,' Wulf replied hollowly, knowing Gus must mean the Earl, since that was the 'him' who had blighted both their childhoods. 'You'd have thought we'd be safe now he's on the other side of the grave. Still, at least he's no kin of mine.'

'I shouldn't be so sure,' he thought he heard his brother mutter under his breath, but his ears were too drunk and sleep-shot to listen properly.

'What does he want?' Wulf said grumpily as he heard the first stirrings of the dawn chorus begin outside his bedroom window and knew he'd only just slept and any moment all that brandy would sour his head and stomach. 'I'm awake as I'll ever be at this hour.'

'You'd best get up and dress first,' Magnus warned, eyeing the wild spectacle Wulf knew he presented.

'Come on, Gus, tell me what he said or did and get it over with,' he said and felt a suspicious shiver ice its way down his spine, as if the old snake had managed to slither into his room somehow, but that was impossible now.

'Just read it, Wulf,' his brother said wearily and he might as well.

* * *

Charlotte had the *Morning Post* in her hands and was staring at the wall opposite as if it had suddenly become fascinating.

'What is it, Charlotte? Not bad news about someone close to us, I hope,' Isabella asked.

'No, nothing like that. I thought it was an advertisement slipped inside when they delivered the papers when I first saw it, but it's worse than that.'

'Then what is it,' Isabella demanded.

This morning her head hurt and her eyes ached and she was surprised her friends hadn't noticed how out of sorts she was when she made herself join them at the breakfast table as if nothing much had happened last night. She ached when she thought about that interlude in the garden, yet hugged it to her like a miser. Wulf parcelled out their time together in such meagre little portions she might have to make a few minutes last a lifetime if she couldn't convince him what an idiot he was being.

'It's described as a special notice,' Charlotte said. 'I suppose they didn't know what else to call it, since the man is already dead.'

'Do tell us who you're talking about, my love, before Isabella throws her breakfast at you,'' Ben said.

'You don't want to know what it says, then?'

'If you would like to tell me, then I promise to listen,' he told his wife with a grin he knew perfectly well was infuriating.

'Harrumph,' Isabella coughed as politely as she could. 'The special notice?' she said airily when they both looked at her as if arguing was far more interesting than anything the outside world could offer them.

'Oh, yes, you would be interested, wouldn't you?'

'I don't know, since you haven't told me what it says yet,' Isabella replied with what she considered exemplary patience.

'It begins with a list of the late Earl of Carrowe's names and titles.'

'Lord Carrowe?' Isabella gasped.

'I shall not read them out. He should have had his mind on higher things when he wrote this and not listed all the reasons he could find to feel self-important. Oh, my! Oh, my goodness. This is quite dreadful and horribly unseemly. The printers should have refused to put it into print and I should have read all the way through before I teased you.'

Isabella began to dread what the late Earl of Carrowe's last twist of the knife would turn out to be. 'Go on,' she said hoarsely.

'He goes on: "I, the most noble Earl of Carrowe et cetera, aver and attest that my wife, Gwenllian Augusta Develin-Haile, Countess of Carrowe, has borne me three legitimate sons during her lifetime, despite her treasonous infidelity with another man between the birth of my second and third sons. Sealed proof of Wulfric Develin-Haile's true birth as my son, as well as a record of the death of his mother's lover a twelvemonth before his advent, is lodged with my lawyer and the relevant authorities at the House of Lords, lest it should prove necessary to assert his rightful place among my heirs and their successors.

My wife is a weak, sinful and easily led woman, but Wulfric Develin-Haile is truly and legally my son. I commend my soul to God as a wronged and much injured husband. No doubt He will judge my wife both before and after she follows me to the grave and at least there she must lie beside me for all eternity and truly repent her sins of adultery and betrayal.'''

Isabella sat silent and horrified as the echo of Charlotte's recital of those cold and unrepentant words died and the world changed around her. At last she shook her head, because she couldn't find the right words to say how furious and sad and stunned she was on Wulf's behalf. The old Earl's self-serving wickedness was now public knowledge and she hated to think how the Haile family felt this morning, but what about Wulf? He was an innocent victim of his father's cruelty. When Lord Carrowe set out to punish and vilify his wife all those years ago, he did it by rejecting and abusing his own son and her heart bled for the bewildered little boy he once was. For the first time in her life she felt as if that cliché was true as she rubbed a hand over it to make the ache seem smaller. The selfish, brutal and wilfully cruel waste of it was breathtaking.

'Oh, how could he do such a monstrous thing?' she whispered numbly.

'Poor Lady Carrowe, this will hit her so hard. I can hardly bear to think how she must be feeling this morning,' Charlotte said after a shocked silence.

'And poor Dev,' Ben added.

'Around every breakfast table in every house *this*

is delivered to of a morning people will read this wickedness,' Isabella said, pointing at the printed sheet she so badly wanted to burn, except to do any good it would have to be the original, wouldn't it? And it was far too late. 'They will read it to anyone willing to listen in their turn and his life and all his father's shameless spite will be a sensation over the teacups for the world to wonder at for their amusement.'

'He will hate the Earl even more now,' Charlotte said.

'How can he not? That evil old man was a stone-hearted basilisk and I pity Wulf's eldest brother for having to wear the title in turn,' Isabella said in a flinty voice and met Charlotte's eyes even knowing there was bitter fury in her own and she was giving far too much away. All she wanted was to be with Wulf, to make him realise it didn't matter; none of it made a ha'penny worth of difference. He could have anyone he liked as his father, even the one he was cursed with at birth, and she would still love him and he still couldn't stop her doing it.

'Don't expect me to argue with you, my love, but I think you need to sit down and take a sip of your coffee,' Charlotte said as if she was afraid Isabella might break if she didn't. 'There's no point being ill for the sake of a man who used his own son as a weapon to beat his wife with.'

'Aye, breathe in, Isabella,' Ben ordered sharply.

At least the urgency in his deep voice broke through the watery unreality she had almost got lost in and Isabella gasped as if he'd slapped her. Air rushed into her lungs and she swayed as the reality of this cheerful, intimate family room reformed. She was back from the edge of fainting for the first time in her life and the world she'd come back to was a different place.

'I'll be perfectly fine in a moment,' she said and took a few sips of coffee to prove it.

'Good, you gave us quite a shock by reacting as if the old viper has taken a potshot at you instead of his wife and son. I'm sorry not to have seen how serious it was when I first lit upon it,' Charlotte said with a bewildered flick of the hand at the sheet of newsprint lying on the floor where she'd dropped it when she started to her feet to catch Isabella if she really lost her senses.

'As well I was with you when I heard this instead of getting it from a chance-met acquaintance eager to spread the latest delicious morsel of scandal.'

'Since you reacted as if he took a shot at you instead of his son I have to agree,' Ben said.

'My feelings are my problem,' Isabella challenged his giant stature and fierce protectiveness. 'The last thing I want is you standing over Wulf glowering at him or dashing off to make Kit to do it instead. I know my own mind, so until Wulf Fitz-whoever-he-is-now makes up his mind how he feels about me and the world, I expect you to respect my judgement and leave him be.'

'You do like a challenge, don't you?' Charlotte put in mildly enough and Wulf was right, her friend did seem to have strong suspicions about their feelings for one another, whatever he actually felt.

'The tittle-tattlers will be nigh breathless with self-importance when they hurry out to spread this folly abroad,' Ben warned. She could see he wasn't happy about her choices, but he'd sat back in his chair to brood about them, so she supposed he must have listened.

'Never mind about them; the Countess and her daughters are my friends and I want to help if I can,' Isabella said.

'Best get them somewhere quiet where nobody knows who they are and make certain it remains that way,' Ben replied.

'No, they must stay where they are and pretend they knew all along. That way it might seem like a wearisome matter they all got tired of long ago. They need to shrug it off as if they're surprised the world took Lord Carrowe's word against his wife in the first place and it's always been obvious he was lying,' Charlotte argued.

'So there's nothing we can do?' Isabella asked, feeling useless.

'We could invite the girls to stay with us for a few days, Izzie, but I don't know if they will agree to come. They seem devoted to their brother and will probably want to stay at Carrowe House to show the world they were never ashamed of him in the first place, so why would they run away now?'

'I'm sure it would help him to know his sisters have at least the offer of a safe place to get away if they choose to,' Ben said gently.

It didn't feel like enough and even the thought

of Wulf's shock, bitterness and betrayal when he read his father's chilling statement made Isabella clench her fists. She desperately wanted to be there for him, not his sisters. She cared about them, but she would be able to offer Wulf comfort when nobody else could. The man who sired him had only owned up to him because he thought the precious Haile succession might be in danger one day. There was no love in it; not even a single word of remorse or acknowledgement the old Earl was a sinner and a monster in life and intended to carry on being one after death with this hurtful, self-justifying piece of bluster. And of course it was true. Her heart sank even further than when he left her standing like an idiot on the terrace at Haile Carr, feeling as if she'd been struck by a natural wonder and the world would never look the same again. The feeling she had about him the instant their eyes met had sat uneasily on an Alstone sister who swore never to want a man as urgently as she wanted Wulf FitzDevelin. She didn't take the time to look deeper into his dark looks and the silver-blue eyes he inherited from his mother sharpened and edited by wary cynicism so they were uniquely his back then.

He was the man she tried so hard to wish she'd never met—bastard Wulf who defied her to think him less than his brothers because he was born in the wrong bed. A man who stood proud and challenging after that moment of true shock when Magnus spoke and he realised exactly who he'd kissed under the hot August stars; a man who dared her to suddenly find him unworthy of her heat and desire because he was her fiancé's half-brother. That last part of it blinded her with shame, but she should have looked harder, should have known there was nothing simple about him or his family. He carried his mother's stamp so distinctively his father must have seen it at his birth and realised he could take revenge on his wife in the cruellest way possible. That wicked old man knew his lies wouldn't be challenged by a Haile nose or their dark brown eyes. Even now she was finding excuses for her refusal to see past an accident of birth by arguing the Countess should have fought for her son. Nature gave her husband the perfect cover for his ill intent, but she could have challenged him. And how could the bitter, jealous monster the late Earl had become disown his own son simply to punish Lady Carrowe for daring to love a better man? Knowing Wulf's mother, her lover would have been a better man; she wouldn't have loved him if he wasn't.

Isabella tried hard to see past her hatred of the old Earl. Maybe there was the faint shadow of a better man under his misplaced pride and selfishness once upon a time. At least that would account for the Countess marrying him in the first place. Their children had so much talent and character it would be a freak of nature if every scrap came from their mother. Most did, of course, but the man who wrote this terrible admission of what he'd done to his son also sired at least five good and clever people. She couldn't claim to know the new Earl, or Lady Carrowe's elder daughter—they were older than the Hailes she knew and rather aloof. Yet all the Hailes she did know had a deep integrity and humanity that made their father's folly seem even worse. Perhaps they showed the world what their father might have been before he wasted his promise so terribly it was all gone by the time he denounced his third son as a bastard.

'If the Earl had proof his wife's lover was dead a year before his son came into the world, she could have used it to defend herself and her baby against his wicked lies,' she said at last.

Ben nodded his agreement; 'Common justice argues she was wrong not to, but who knows what he did to keep her quiet?'

'It's not about justice, it's about control,' Charlotte said with a shudder and Isabella remembered her friend knew all about that from the wrong side. 'The great and noble can say what they like,' Charlotte went on, 'because the world listens to those with a title. The rest of us endure their arrogance and pretend it doesn't hurt us.'

'But it still does. I'd never ignore or slight you, my Amazon Queen, whoever told me I ought to,' Ben said and met his tall and vital wife's eyes with love and passion and a fierce protectiveness in his own.

'Sometimes you two make me realise how lucky I am in my family,' Isabella said because there wasn't much point pretending she wasn't here.

'Then sometimes we should be quiet. We're more than fortunate in the one we've made together, as well as in the love of Ben's natural father, his step-mama and his two little half-brothers.'

'It was a shame my first half-brother didn't turn out so well, but Charlotte is right, Izzie, we are blessed.'

'And at least none of us had to own up to a father like Lord Carrowe,' Isabella said and almost managed to make it a joke. Yet the bite of that self-serving announcement still hurt her on Wulf's behalf. She had to blink back tears of fury and the sort of pity he'd hate.

Wulf was the man she loved, if only he loved her back. There was a slender chance he might have let himself to begin with, but now he'd think he was cursed tenfold. At war with himself for being his father's son, he'd step back from any woman who might want him as the third son of an earl now. Wulf was so much his own man she mentally raged at him before he could even say it. As if his birth made the slightest difference to her. She loved him and would go on doing so when he didn't offer for her now he was legitimate and a suitably noble match for the late Earl of Carnwood's youngest granddaughter. He was a stubborn idiot who thought he knew what was best for her and somehow that made her love him even more, so she was clearly a hopeless case.

'I must find Heloise,' she said numbly, 'My new gowns are ready to be fitted, so I might as well go to the dressmakers' while they're quiet. The polite world will soon flock to London and the seamstresses will be so busy they might rush the alterations.' It was the best excuse she could come up with on the spur of the moment, but luckily Charlotte didn't have time to sit about waiting for seamstresses to hem a gown or alter a sleeve and she didn't suggest coming along.

'Are you sure you're well enough to stand still for hours while they tweak your new gowns until they're perfect, Izzie?' she said.

'I might as well be busy and at least Heloise will be happy in the temples of fashion.'

'To make up for all the hours she's spent sitting waiting for you at Carrowe House of late?' Charlotte said as if warning Isabella even the most discreet lady's maid might not keep those hours to herself much longer.

Chapter Fourteen

Sending Heloise to the workrooms of the most exclusive Bond Street dressmaker with a minute map of measurements and a list of required alterations wasn't devious, it was necessary, Isabella told herself. She ghosted down the side roads and alleys that would get her and the taciturn footman Miranda and Kit had left in London round to the back of Carrowe House without being seen. Yet again there would be clusters of interested idlers outside the front, watching liveried footmen hammer on the vast doors with calling cards while their masters and mistresses watched from carriages and expected the Hailes to naively let them in.

She knew this visit was ill-timed and probably wrong, but she still needed to see Wulf. The late Earl's appalling announcement cut to the very foundations of who he was and she cared about the man Wulf made himself and never mind the Earl's nasty little games. He could call himself what he liked, he was Wulf and that was all that mattered to her. He wouldn't want to hear her say so right now and might not believe a word she said, but that didn't mean she didn't have to say it.

'Ah, I thought Jem or his mother must be back earlier than expected,' Magnus told her when he cracked open the kitchen door, then reluctantly held it wide enough for Isabella and her stern protector to slip in before he closed and barred it against invaders again. 'They went out marketing for us, since the girls can't show their faces for fear of being mobbed by the curious.'

Isabella knew Jem was the name of Wulf's manservant, or friend or whatever the lad and his mother were. She suspected they could have met when Wulf was a wild boy alone on the streets, since he treated them more like family than servants. Even hardened by the Earl's mistreatment Wulf must have been an innocent in that underworld. She was glad he'd found at least two friends, although Jem must have been little more than a baby back then. Isabella thought it unlikely an eager tabby or sneaky recorder of other people's misery would get a word out of them about Wulf or his family or indeed anything much at all.

'Gregory is large and strong and very close-mouthed, aren't you, Gregory?' Isabella said and her companion nodded to prove it. 'He will hold this door against all comers for as long as you need him to, but you'd best give him a good description of both the Caudles, Mr Haile, or he won't let them in either.'

'I suppose I would be better employed elsewhere,' Magnus said as if even today he didn't have the strength to argue and she obviously wasn't going to leave. He knew her well enough not to accuse her of idle curiosity and she desperately hoped Wulf agreed with him.

'Then I shall accompany you upstairs,' she said and waited as patiently as she could while Magnus gave Gregory a detailed account of Jem and his mother. They left Gregory glaring at the closed door with the suspicious determination of a medieval retainer relishing the prospect of seeing off an invading army.

'He doesn't get out much,' she said when they were out of earshot, 'and I had to see Wulf.

'He's not feeling sociable,' he warned and led her through the labyrinth of kitchens and storerooms and up to once-grand reception rooms.

'I expect you're right, but I still need to see him.'

'It's been a heavy blow; he's not quite himself.'

'That's not his fault, though, is it? You have to tell him what your father did last summer, Magnus. He won't feel he can trust anyone if he has to find out from someone else.'

'He's got enough to cope with right now.'

'Honestly, you Hailes are stubborn as mules. I should have known you were full brothers the moment I met him.'

'We're like the old Earl?' he said, looking revolted.

'No, you're both good men and very like each other under the skin.'

'Wulf is definitely a good man, but I'm not so

sure about me,' he said with something like his old rueful and charming smile.

'Weren't you supposed to make sure nobody got in to gawp at us, Gus?'

The fury in Wulf's voice said he was already in a fine temper after reading his father's iniquitous notice and now he was jealous as well. 'Wulf,' she greeted him flatly.

'Miss Alstone, how delightfully unexpected,' he replied with mocking politeness and an exaggeratedly elegant bow.

'I suspect you are castaway, Mr FitzDevelin, so I shall come back when you're sober enough to know a hawk from a handsaw.'

'I'm not sure it's polite to call my brother a handsaw and please don't trouble yourself. Mr FitzDevelin will not be at home. He never was at home here and he certainly isn't now.'

'Oh, for goodness sake, stop feeling sorry for yourself,' she said impatiently.

'If I waited for you to do it, I'd die of old age,' he grumbled half-heartedly.

'You don't need any help with that,' she argued and maybe he needed a nice refreshing argument to make him drag his head out of the nearest brandy bottle.

'I'm drunk,' he informed her grumpily.

'And that excuses you from being anything else, does it? When did they write that into the rules for gentlemen, Mr Haile?'

'Don't ask Magnus how I should be; he doesn't know how I feel.'

'I wasn't asking him.'

'Oh, the devil. I'm him, aren't I?'

'The devil? Not quite yet…' Isabella hesitated to call him that by his true name again and compromised on '…sir.'

'Give me a few more hours and another bottle and I'll be halfway to hell, so I'll be sure to give him your regards,' Wulf said and Isabella almost wished she'd left him to escape into a bottle for a few more hours.

'You are Mr Haile, though, Wulf,' Magnus pointed out helpfully.

'Thank you, I've just found out that mad old fool was my father after all and you're expecting me to be happy about it?'

'He was my father all my life, why should you get off so lightly?'

'Oh, Gus,' Wulf said and lurched a little as he strode down the remaining stairs to hug his brother so fiercely Magnus nearly toppled over in his weakened state. 'How the hell have you lived with knowing it all this time? He's put the devils that ran him into me as well now with that cursed announcement of his.'

'You live with it by not letting him do it, Little Brother Wulf. By trying everything you can think of to make yourself a better man,' Magnus said steadily.

There was the truly kind, honourable and determined man Magnus was before life and love and his father tried so hard to break him. 'Your brother is right,' Isabella intervened when Wulf opened his mouth to argue.

'And if you think he's so wonderful, why didn't you marry him?' he growled and glared at them both.

'Mind your own business,' she told him loftily.

'You are my business,' he said fiercely, 'and he's my brother.'

'He's got a point, Isabella. Best not to repeat ourselves, but we could always try again,' Magnus said so lightly she wondered if he knew he was tugging a tiger by the tail. 'We could elope.'

For a moment Isabella was horrified by the idea he might be serious. 'I think you're forgetting the last six months and the fact we both have interests elsewhere,' she said carefully, because this probably wasn't the right moment for the confession she'd urged on Magnus earlier.

'Ah, yes, they're quite difficult to ignore, aren't they?' Magnus said sadly and she almost wished she'd held her tongue.

'What interests?' Wulf barked.

'You really are a very stupid man,' she told him haughtily, so frustrated he didn't realise what he was to her she almost wished she hadn't come.

'Not stupid enough to be interesting because I'm the third son of a lord,' he sneered.

'Oh, I don't know; you're not very interesting in your own right at the moment, are you?' she said with a contemptuous glance at his wildly disordered sable hair and unshaven chin.

'No, but I was the bastard I thought I was last night and today I'm only one in spirit,' he said.

'I'm sure you're too hard on yourself.'

'Oh, go away,' he told her as if her company was suddenly too much to endure. Yet she caught sight of his reluctant half-smile when he turned away from her with a gesture of pretend revulsion. 'If I wanted my ears assaulted by the opinions of strangers, I could open the front door and hear them in droves.'

'I'm not a stranger.'

'By the opinions of a lady I happen to have met before and who refuses to mind her own business and leave me be when I beg her to, then,' he corrected himself with exaggerated patience and almost a grin of complicity, but she wasn't ready to be complicit or meekly go away as he bid.

'A lady who won't let you ignore and slight her because you're not who you thought you were and I won't be making any more furtive assignations with you so you can pretend I'm virtually a stranger when you happen to meet me in company, Mr Wulf Whoever-you-want-to-call-yourself-now. And if you ever kiss me again, you can do it in daylight with half the world looking on or not bother because I'm done with hiding in dark corners with you, whatever name you settle on,' she told him brusquely and turned on her heel to leave because this seemed like a good place to start.

It would give him something to think about other than his obnoxious father and she *was* tired of hiding in corners. If he felt anything real for her, he could follow her into the light and prove it to both of them. She couldn't stop herself looking back when she reached the door to the kitchens, where Gregory was stoically waiting for her. Wulf's eyes were blank with shock after her reference to their trysts in front of Magnus, so at least her ultimatum had given his thoughts a new turn.

She finally noticed Lady Carrowe and her younger daughters looking on with eager attention when she wrenched her gaze from him long enough to see them on the last half-landing. She'd been so engrossed in how Wulf felt about her she hadn't even noticed them creep downstairs. At least she didn't need to explain the situation to his family next time they met and she refused to let him pretend he hardly knew her. She nodded to say she meant every word and didn't care if they knew about those kisses because she refused to be ashamed. Even so she hoped they weren't too shocked and knew she considered them true friends whatever happened from now on.

'I wish you all a good morning,' she said and swept out because there were times when there really wasn't anything else to say and this felt like one of them.

Chapter Fifteen

'Well, that's certainly told you, Wulf,' Magnus said with the once-familiar careless grin he ought to be pleased to see back on his brother's face, Wulf realised rather numbly.

'Don't you think you should go after her?' Aline put in as she seemed to snap out of the trance she'd gone into after hearing Isabella's impossible invitation to kiss her in front of them all or leave her alone in future.

'And do what?' he said wearily.

'Well, kiss her again, I suppose.'

'I thought you didn't approve of such mawkish nonsense.'

'I don't, but I suppose you two must enjoy it, since it sounds as if you've been doing it quite a lot,' Aline said with a puzzled shake of the head as if she couldn't quite imagine how anyone could, but each to their own.

'She had no business telling anyone,' Wulf managed with a defensive frown and wished everyone

would go away until he'd got over the self-inflicted
pain beating in his head like a war drum now she
was gone and he was in no fit state to run after her.
He'd probably be arrested for bothering a lady in his
present state and he still wasn't sure he was as ready
to throw caution to the winds as she thought he ought
to be. After all, his caution was for her, wasn't it?
He might be the Honourable Wulfric Haile now, but
he felt like a shabby sort of a gentleman and he still
couldn't offer her much more than himself. What
sort of prize was he for a beautiful, clever lady of
character like Isabella?

'It sounds as if Isabella had every right to drag
whatever you've been up to out into the light, my
son,' his mother told him severely and Wulf groaned
and put a hand to his aching forehead and rubbed
as if that might make it all go away—as if anything could now Isabella had made that reckless,
ruthless and ridiculously brave ultimatum in front
of them all.

'Fresh air is what you need most right now, Little
Brother,' Magnus told him sagely. 'Well, that and a
shave. Oh, and probably a bath as well because you
might as well begin clean and tidy. After all that I
know just the place where you can hire a fast horse
and you'll get as much fresh air as you can handle
on the road to chase away that headache,' he added
helpfully and grinned despite Wulf's best frown to
tell him what he thought of his misplaced humour.

Dorrie exchanged a puzzled look with her twin.
Theo mouthed something at her and she gasped, then

nodded as if she was fool not to have got the mean-
ing of Magnus's ridiculous insinuation straight away.
'Oh, yes, Derbyshire; of course,' she said wisely and
as if that clinched things. He wasn't going to gallop all the way to Wychwood on a wild goose chase
when the Earl of Carnwood was likely to set the dogs
on him when he got there, third son of an earl or not.

'I'm going home,' Wulf said dourly, then stamped
out the back way because he didn't care what his
family or Isabella said about the value of openness,
he wasn't risking the front one in this state. He might
hit somebody if they got in his way and that would
never do, now would it? 'And there's plenty of fresh
air to be had at my house on the Heath, thank you
very much, loving family of mine,' he muttered
under his breath as he slipped through back alleys
in Isabella's wake. 'Women!' he confided in a startled groom from the next-door mews, then stamped
off into bustling, busy London to walk off some of
his temper and most of his headache and try very
hard not to think about anything at all.

'Gres! Well, I never. We thought you'd quite forgotten the way to London,' his next brother-in-line
greeted the new Earl of Carrowe not very enthusi-
astically as soon as he'd managed to shoulder his
way past the crowd of still-hopeful onlookers outside
Carrowe House a few days after his father's startling
announcement from beyond the grave that Wulf was
his get after all.

'I tried to, Magnus; believe me, I tried,' Gresley

said wearily as soon as he was safe inside the house and out of earshot of those interested spectators.

'I wager he's actually telling the truth, for once,' Wulf muttered from where he stood in the shadiest corner of the hall, watching the family reunion with a cynical eye.

In a way it was his fault his family were still being besieged by the curious, so it felt like his duty to pretend to work here instead of at home today and take his turn at keeping the curious at bay. It wasn't as if he'd got much done since the latest set of bombshells blew his life apart, so no matter if Gresley's arrival shot any chance of concentrating on the article he was supposed to be writing out of the water.

His mother shook her head reproachfully as she picked up on his cynical comment. She had been doing that a lot since Isabella made her startling statement, then marched out of the house to leave him to deal with his family's feelings as well as his own. With a last look to say *If you can't be pleasant, be quiet*, Lady Carrowe stepped forward to receive her eldest son's dutiful kiss on the cheek. 'You should have sent word you were coming, my dear, so we could put on a better welcome,' she rebuked and hugged Gresley before stepping back to survey his travel-worn appearance with a frown.

'This house would have to be knocked down and rebuilt before there's much of a one to be had here,' he responded gloomily.

Most of his family had had to endure all this dust and decay day in and day out, so why couldn't

Gresley hear how crass that comment sounded? He lacked the imagination to put himself in someone else's shoes, Wulf decided and perhaps that was the real reason he seemed most like his father out of all of them. How odd to be one of seven instead of one of one and Wulf wasn't sure how he was going to like being Gresley and Mary's little brother.

'It is a wreck, isn't it? And quite beyond repair, even if you actually wanted to repair it,' Aline said almost triumphantly, gazing around the dusty and worn marble hall with affection. 'Thank goodness the state of it usually keeps the *ton* at bay without us even having to try very hard to fend them off and it would have been good to have some help with that, by the way.'

'I was busy,' Gresley blustered.

'You said that when we begged you to come here to deal with the coroner and magistrates and lawyers,' Aline challenged impatiently.

Wulf stayed silent so he wouldn't rage uselessly at his eldest brother because Gresley was so like his father it was almost uncanny. Later, when Gresley was rested and fed after his journey, they would have to discuss Wulf's dealings with the magistrates and constables, but there wasn't a great deal to tell. Even Sir Hugh Kenton hadn't been able to find a clue to who the murderer was or how he got into this leaky old house and out again without being seen by a living soul. Carrowe House, with only two elderly servants and so many rotten old rooms even the family had forgotten about, was the ideal place to slip into, murder a man who expected his family to respect his privacy at all times, then slip out again without being noticed. How anyone wasn't noticed wandering about this great city covered in blood was beyond Wulf, but there was no trail of it to give them a direction to look in. Had the man been devilishly lucky or simply devilish? Best not add the supernatural to the list of things to worry about when there was quite enough on it to keep him awake at nights already. Wulf thought there must have been more than one person with the Earl when he died—one to murder him in what looked very like hot blood and the other cool enough to make sure they didn't leave a trail for anyone to follow. Sir Hugh had told him to keep that idea to himself because the less the villains knew about their ideas for catching them the better.

Wulf was glad he'd persuaded the Caudles to move in and paid a couple of heavies to watch the place from the outside every night. He resolved to hammer shut another set of doors and windows to keep his mother and sisters doubly safe for however much longer they insisted on staying here. He had already made an inner core of rooms as secure as possible without rebuilding the place from the ground up. It was locking the stable door after the horse bolted, he admitted to himself, but the very thought of whoever killed the Earl coming back kept him awake at nights even when this endless longing for Isabella in his bed didn't. The villain could have murdered them all or done other unthinkable things without anyone outside the house hearing a thing. His own wild ride to Herefordshire on a wasted errand left only Gus between their mother and sisters and a murderer. Wulf shuddered at the idea of his brother confronting a desperate man when he was in such a weakened state after his illness. He was furious with himself for being more than a hundred miles away when they needed him most, so how could Gresley leave them to face the world without him when their father was murdered here? He was supposed to be the head of the family, for goodness' sake.

'Fell off my horse,' Gresley finally admitted sheepishly, as if owning up to that was worse than patricide. 'Sprained my ankle and looked like the loser in a prize fight for a fortnight.'

'You didn't want to come here and help Mama cope with our father's death and all that followed because you looked a little the worse for wear?'

'No, Magnus, I didn't. I didn't want to now, but Connie insisted. Well, at least she and her father and the grandees from the Home Office did. Connie says I can't ignore what amounts to a royal order to come here and sort things out and I had to admit she was right to get any peace at all.'

'A royal order?' Lady Carrowe asked in a hollow voice.

'Yes, apparently the fuss caused by that nonsensical letter the Earl left behind him was the final straw for the King. He can't intervene openly for fear of stirring up even more public outrage against him. The Earl was one of his friends and the least said about that the soonest mended, so the King's cronies sent a messenger to tell me that while they are ready to write Papa's murder off as an unlucky encounter with a burglar, they can't close their eyes to his tangled private affairs any longer and insist on knowing the truth of his untimely ending. They sent for some bloodhound the Crown employs to deal with matters they want sorted out discreetly, then quietly lost as only the Home Office can lose things. First they've got to find him, however, as they carelessly sent him abroad on another matter. In the meantime I have to take an interest in this old wreck of a house and say bland and soothing things to calm everyone's nerves.'

'Oh, dear. Well, never mind, we'll soon be off to Hampstead and you can hardly be expected to stay here on your own,' Lady Carrowe said soothingly.

Wulf marvelled how skewed things were when his mother thought that would make Gresley feel better. Since he was looking resentful and defensive and troubled all at the same time, someone had clearly put the fear of God into him. Wulf secretly admired the forcefulness of whoever made Gresley face reality, and if this hunter they set such store by was half as good at his job, the murderer had better watch his step.

'The King is worried his reputation might suffer because Father was a friend of his? As if he could be more unpopular if he'd set out to make his people hate him,' Aline said scornfully.

Wulf nodded, although he shouldn't encourage her to be so outspoken. Aline might yet find a man brave or reckless enough to marry her, but she'd have to mind her tongue if her hero wasn't to run away screaming.

'It took royal intervention to get you here?' Magnus prompted, very likely to stop Gresley scolding Aline and set off a furious argument.

'Revolution,' Gresley added sagely. 'The King is afraid of the mob.'

'I can't see why our private disasters would stir them up,' Wulf said as he stepped out of the shadows as his true self for the first time.

'It's not private, though, is it? The old fool made a sensation of us all with that notice on top of everything else.' Gresley refused to meet his eyes, but the fact he'd replied was an admission Wulf had a right to take part in this conversation and he'd always tried to ignore his very existence until today.

'Frederick wasn't to know he would die violently,' their mother defended her late husband halfheartedly.

'Then he should have done,' Wulf muttered darkly. He saw his eldest brother's lips twitch as if he wanted to agree, but apparently that was going too far.

'Lucky you were too far off to be accused of his murder,' Gresley grumbled instead. 'If anyone had reason to do the old dog to death, it's you.' That was probably the only apology Wulf would ever get from his elder brother for years of pretending he didn't exist.

'None of my children are capable of murder,' Lady Carrowe said firmly.

Wulf wondered why Gresley flinched when their mother was asserting his innocence as well.

'Someone is,' Gresley said heavily.

Wulf almost wished the men of power had left well alone, but the longer the Earl's death was a mystery the more gossip and suspicion would do the rounds. Someone had the sin of murder on their head, but he still wasn't quite sure he really wanted to know who it was.

'I'd better sleep here, I suppose,' Gresley said as if to change the subject. 'It's more comfortable at White's, but Connie says it will look bad if I don't put up here. At least when the formalities are over and the will is read, I can go back to Yorkshire and you'll all be happier in Hampstead away from this.'

'It is your house now, so you must do as you please,' their mother told him.

'Let's all get our hammers out, then,' Gresley joked and Wulf chuckled, then noticed Gresley was staring at their mother as if he longed for more than she could give him. How had he missed that need for so long?

'Not until the upholsterers are quite finished with Develin House, if you please, boys,' she said.

'No, that would be unseemly,' Gresley said and he was his usual stiff and insensitive self again, so maybe Wulf had imagined it. 'When you are ready to move out, then, Mama,' he added and went off to hurry his valet and grooms.

Again Wulf had an odd feeling of kinship with his eldest brother he'd love to crush to powder and wondered if he'd ever get a firm hold on who he really was. He wasn't who he thought, but how could he be an earl's third son when the old man had denied him at birth? Add the burning regret and hunger and sheer bloody-minded stubbornness roiling away inside him since he'd refused to chase after Isabella and accept her terms and it was little wonder he hadn't slept properly for days. If only she would break through the wall he'd built round his privacy and demand he marry her again, he could give in and pretend he wasn't too much of a coward to admit he couldn't live without her. Well, he could live, the last half-year proved that, but it wouldn't really be living, would it? Existing was the best he could look forward to.

Meeting Isabella opened him up to a whole world of feelings he hadn't wanted to know about, but had he got so used to living in the shadows he couldn't see the sun? It hurt to feel, so he hadn't let himself. Until he met her and her breathtaking beauty and energy and sheer love of life demolished the walls he'd built round his inner Wulf as a boy. What he was going to do about all these untidy, unsafe emotions he wasn't sure right now, but her ultimatum meant he couldn't go on trying to pretend he didn't have them much longer. But if he couldn't bring himself to beg her to marry him when he was Wulf Fitz-Develin, how could he now he was the legitimate son of a lord? A lord he cursed every time he closed his eyes, then woke to the memory of who he really was stark in his mind.

It felt as if something loathsome lived inside him and he didn't think he was going to be anywhere near as good at overcoming their dark heritage as Magnus had proved himself to be. Wulf couldn't get his mother to talk about it either, apart from a sad shake of the head and an assertion she had always known exactly who he was. She gave birth to him, so of course she knew that, but why hadn't she challenged the Earl? Wulf FitzDevelin was an illusion, the only certainty he'd had as a child was that his parents must have loved each other for his mother to risk so much making him. Even that certainty had gone and he felt like a chair with a leg missing and bound for the bonfire. If he loved a woman as unique as Isabella Alstone, wouldn't an unsuitable, unsavoury character like him do better to stay away from her and not risk letting her down? To marry him she would have to take so many reckless risks it seemed impossible to ask her for them when he looked at how little he had to offer in return.

'Now Gresley is finally here, will you at least tell *me* why you let the Earl disown me at birth before he wheedles it out of you?' he murmured to his mother when the others had returned to the least cavernous reception room available and were waiting to see what Gresley would do next.

'He was closer to his father than the rest of you, so he might know Frederick's reasons for what he did better than I do, but I will tell you some of mine,' she said as if choosing her words so they couldn't trip her up later. She gestured towards the old estate office he had inflicted on Isabella after she returned from the country. More secrets to hide; more lies to tell—she was quite right about him, wasn't she?

'Anything that would help me make sense of who I really am would do,' he said rather desperately and hoped he could concentrate on what might be a very important conversation for him in spite of the memories of Isabella here, so vividly beautiful and alive against the shabby hopelessness of this used-up room. He was beyond being angry with his mother anyway. She'd paid such a heavy price for not arguing against her husband's lies. Wulf always thought he was the outward proof love was more important than anything else in his mother's life, even him. As a boy, that made the bond between them seem more special than the one between her and the others and now he felt as if he didn't know her at all.

'Your father did it to control me, and as having him as their father did his other sons so much harm, I thought at least one of you could be your own man if he stuck to his lie and disowned you.'

At first it sounded like a flimsy excuse for being so spineless, but Gresley and Magnus really had been pushed into a mould the Earl thought would make perfect Haile men of them. Magnus's determination not to be the arrogant and thankless man his father wanted saved him from being made in the Earl's image. Would *he* have had the strength of mind and heart to do as Gus did? Or would he have been even more wild and defiant to prove he was his own man and maybe even downright dangerous, considering the bad blood in his veins? Standing here thinking about how hard he'd tried not to love Isabella in this very room, he wondered if his mother wasn't almost right to have stopped him being the Dishonourable Wulfric Haile at birth.

'I had to be my own boy first,' he reminded her all the same. 'The world didn't even wait for me to turn my back before it sneered at Lady Carrowe's Shame.'

'I was wrong to stay silent then and later when he beat and bullied you to show me I couldn't stop him treating you exactly as he chose. He had already told his silly story by then and I doubt anyone would have believed me if I'd argued with him when you were old enough to be hurt by his lies and it was already too late.'

'So your lover was a fantasy of his as well?'

'No, he was very real. I loved him so deeply and desperately, but I had children and already knew what a devil your father could be. I couldn't leave them in his hands to run away with the man I longed to be with so deeply it almost broke me.'

She watched him with a challenge in the cool blue eyes he was the only one of her children to inherit, as if she thought he'd say she was wrong to look at another man when she was married to the Earl of Carrowe as well as all the other things she might have been wrong about after her lover accepted his marching orders.

'You mean you didn't…?'

'Yes, that's exactly what I mean. I wished I had when your father denounced me and called you a bastard anyway. I could have offered you a truly noble parent if I'd only taken my true love as my lover, Wulf. I regret not being able to do that for you, although I expect the Earl would have tried to throw another man's son on the parish. I would have stopped him, of course, but he would still have tried and thought he could get away with it.'

'He was mad enough to have killed us both and said it was your fault.'

'Oh, my love, don't condemn yourself to a life-time of waiting to go insane. Your father wasn't mad. He was appallingly spoilt from the day he was born as his parents' only child and heir. They were very much to blame for making him weak and querulous and quite unable to control his temper, but he was as sane as the next lord. No, that's a bad example; he was a lot more sane than one or two of them.'

'True,' he agreed, realising Isabella had been right, his mother really was the strong one of the pair, despite the Earl's physical strength and self-righteous anger and all the bluster that went with it.

'I wouldn't turn real love away if I had my life to live again,' she told him. 'Living without it cost us both too much.'

Chapter Sixteen

'Why did Isabella jilt you, Gus?' Wulf asked his brother as casually as he could manage when they were strolling in unfashionable Green Park to try to build Magnus's strength back up a little at a time.

'Why would I tell you that?' his brother said after such a long time Wulf was wondering if he'd heard.

'I need to know,' he replied, fighting the instinct to say it didn't matter.

'Why?'

'Is that all you're going to say?'

'Until you give me a better reason, yes.'

'She told me to ask you,' Wulf admitted gruffly.

'Really? You did a lot of lurking in corners before she called a halt, didn't you?'

'I don't think there's a law against it,' Wulf said defensively.

'You remind me of yourself as a sulky boy, Little Brother,' Magnus said and leaned against a tree with some of the careless ease and confidence he used to exude.

'You remind me of yourself as a not-much-older insufferable know-it-all.'

Wulf *had* to know why his brother's betrothal ended abruptly. Secretly he had rejoiced to hear it was all over between Magnus and Isabella, of course, but he realised he would have had to sail away and not come back again if the wedding had gone ahead. Funny, his heart had never told his head how much it didn't want the wedding to happen while he had sat in a cramped cabin week after endless week willing the ship to return to England faster than wind and sail could get it there.

'Ah, but I'm not the one with the burning desire to root through my brother's private affairs,' Magnus said with some of the old steel back under his cool society manners.

Wulf would normally have rejoiced that his brother was acting more himself, but right now he needed answers more than confirmation his brother's spirits were beginning to revive. 'I haven't got any for you to find,' he replied gruffly.

'Isabella has my sympathy; I never realised you were a slow top.'

'You were in the way. How could I barge past you and pounce on her like the wolf the Earl named me for?' There, now he'd admitted he wanted Isabella and Gus smiled as if that was exactly what he'd been waiting to hear.

'I didn't even know you'd met Isabella until you galloped off to Cravenhill Park to confront her on my behalf, you blundering great idiot.'

'We met on the night of your betrothal ball.'

'You were there after all, then? Despite saying you weren't going all the way to Haile Carr to be thrown out.' Magnus raised his eyebrows in that infuriating fashionable habit he had before he fell to earth.

'You're my brother,' Wulf said tersely.

'I looked for you, Wulf, and made a point of telling Gres and the Earl if they tried to humiliate you I'd call off the wedding. I needed your support more than you'll ever know and you stayed away and before I knew it you'd left for the New World. I felt more alone standing on that quayside watching you sail away than I've ever felt in my life.'

'I'm sorry, Gus. I let you down as well.'

'As well as who?'

'Whom, Big Brother, whom.'

'Do you want to live to get much older, Wulf?'

'Tell me why you asked the most beautiful female I have ever laid eyes on to marry you when you don't appear to love her and she doesn't love you.'

'Ah, now that sounds like a very personal interest indeed. Why does she want you to know?'

Wulf paced the just-about-green grass because he couldn't stand still. He hadn't managed to say it to Isabella yet, so how could he admit it to Gus? 'You're right, it's very personal,' he said tersely.

'How personal?'

'Too much—I have nothing to offer her. My name stinks even more since the Earl made things worse by making a show out of hating Mama so much he disowned his own son to punish her for looking at another man. No wonder the King wants to forget he ever had a friend whose marriage was an even bigger mess than his own turned out to be.'

'I don't think that's possible, but Isabella won't care about what the world thinks if she loves you.'

'How do you know?'

'Because I know her better than you do from the sound of things. I also know you'd like to hit me, despite the fact I'm not up to brawling with you right now.'

'Ah well, we always knew I wasn't a gentleman.'

'No, you believed what our father told you; the rest of us knew he was wrong,' Magnus said and turned away to pace in his turn. 'I don't want you to despise me,' he admitted at last.

'You let me out of cupboards the Earl locked me in when we were boys and fed me when he forbade it. You even took his blows when you could and taught me to ride and drive up and down the local mews and got me to swim in the Serpentine because he wouldn't take me to the country with the rest of you because I liked it and that would never do. If we live to be a hundred and quarrel like fishwives for the rest of our days, I couldn't turn my back on you, Gus.'

'I felt guilty because when the Earl took his anger out on you he didn't have so much of it left for me.'

'Gresley probably felt guilty about that as well, but he didn't help me. You could always tell me what I want to know now and we'll call it even.'

'Clever, but I suppose I owe it to Isabella to tell

you the truth, even if I do lose your esteem,' Magnus said as if truly he believed he could.

Wulf would turn a blind eye even if his brother confessed to murdering the Earl, but Isabella was right, he needed to know the secret haunting his brother. 'Just tell me and we'll deal with it,' he urged.

'We can't, nobody can,' Magnus said with a sigh that sounded as if it came from his boots. 'But you still need to know, so I suppose I should tell you. It really began when Sir Edgar Drace died.'

'I *knew* Lady Delphine was at the bottom of it somehow,' Wulf said, remembering that night at Carrowe House when tension felt so tight between Magnus and Lady Delphine he almost expected to hear something snap.

'Don't interrupt if you want to hear more. I'd rather not tell this tale at all, so it's up to you.'

'Consider me silent as the grave.'

'Don't, you have no idea how often I wished Drace in one.'

'He wasn't much of an asset to the human race,' Wulf said. 'I had to report his fury at the poor for the sin of being poor too often to mistake him for one of those.'

'Ah, but it wasn't for the sake of suffering humanity I wanted him dead, Wulf. Drace made Delphi give up riding and she must not dance or drive or do any of the things I know she loved to do before he married her. He wouldn't even allow her to visit Mama and the girls when he took her to stay with her parents for a few days. I hardly saw her, but when

I called one day, she was wearing long sleeves and even they couldn't quite cover up the bruises. When I challenged her about them, she told me the law allows a man to chastise his wife as long as he doesn't kill her. He was a Member of Parliament and the magistrates might have looked the other way even if he killed her in a rage, so I did what she wanted and stayed away, but I hated him for being such a bully.'

'As well you weren't anywhere near when he broke his neck, then.'

'I rode all night to find her as soon as I heard he was dead,' Magnus admitted, 'and I didn't even stop to wonder why until I got there. She was so thin I could nearly count her bones through her skin, Wulf. She was nothing like the harum-scarum Delphi I used to run wild with all summer and missed when I was back at school. The plain truth is I love her, Wulf. All those years the real reason I hated Drace was because he got to her before I could.'

'He and the Earl will be company for one another in hell,' Wulf said and couldn't find a single spark of outrage in his heart for his brother's guilty secret so far.

'Don't make light of it. I should have found a way to make him stop beating and humiliating Delphi. I should have stopped the Earl doing the same to you as well, so don't ever call me a good man again,' Magnus said bitterly.

Wulf could see him shaking with the effort of sharing his dark truth and even for Isabella's sake he couldn't put his brother through more pain. 'Never mind, Gus, Isabella and I will find a way past it,' he said.

'You both deserve the truth.'

'I doubt I do.'

'Then you need to hear my story, so you don't hurt her like Delphi hurt me.'

Wulf was shocked by the idea he could turn bright and vibrant Miss Alstone into a pale shadow of herself. The thought horrified him.

'What on earth did Lady Delphine do to you, then?'

'She took me as her lover for every stolen moment we could snatch together in a summerhouse on a neighbouring estate unlived in for years, accepted my rampant adoration and all the pent-up love I'd only just admitted to myself, and enjoyed it as if that was what she was born for. She embraced her own sensuality and threw herself into being adored and I thought I'd found heaven on earth for six whole glorious weeks of bliss. I stayed at an inn a few miles away, but my horse could have found his way there blindfolded by the end of them.'

'What happened?'

'She told me it was over. It had been a pleasure to find out what the sins of the flesh really felt like and she thanked me politely, as if I'd given her a pretty fan or a lace handkerchief. And, oh, no, of course she didn't love me and never had. I was a convenient lover when she needed to feel warm and wicked after all those years of cold and propriety with Drace. Now I'd taught her all I knew she had her eye on her next lover who, by the way, had far more money and power than I'd ever have.'

'Bitch,' Wulf gritted out and meant it.

'No,' Magnus argued. 'Count, Wulf. Count backwards and use your brains.'

Wulf shook his head to clear it and saw what Magnus meant. 'Her *daughter*?'

'She's mine,' Magnus agreed as if more words would undo him.

'Delphine's passed her off as Drace's and I doubt that's much of a favour in the long-term,' Wulf said with the snicker of his own supposedly illegitimate birth in the back of his mind.

'She's the image of me, poor little mite. Nobody could look at her and me side by side and mistake her for Drace's get. That's why Delphine brought her child to London when she came to visit us, then made her maid stay nearby with the baby instead of openly bringing my daughter to Carrowe House, where we Hailes couldn't fail to recognise one of our own.'

'So why haven't you married her and claimed the baby as yours anyway?'

'Delphi won't say yes. Delphi's woman sent me a letter begging me to visit her mistress a couple of months after Delphi gave me my marching orders. I delayed because I knew it would hurt to see her decked out in the spoils of her next love affair. By then she was visibly with child and had to admit it was mine because there was no chance the baby was Drace's, never much chance he was capable of siring one at all actually.'

'A boy would have taken his title and estates, though.'

'She promised to admit the child wasn't her husband's if she birthed a boy because she couldn't live with the imposture if her child took so much from the true heir. Thanks to her parents' insistence their private fortune was settled on her and any children when she married that apology for a gentleman, she didn't need his money, but my little girl saved her the trouble of confessing what she sees as her sins.'

'You've seen the child?'

'Yes, and loved her the moment I laid eyes on her, Wulf. I can't claim her because her mother won't let me. I've tried everything to convince Delphi to marry me, but she refuses to even consider it.'

'She's a fool, Gus,' Wulf told him.

'No, I'm the fool. If only I'd stayed away for a few months after Drace's death, she would have had to marry me when I got her with child as there would be no question of it being his in law. Delphi's rejection was bad enough, then Father found out and she still wouldn't marry me. That would be to admit what we did when her husband's body was hardly cold in his grave and she couldn't brave the censure of the polite world for being so wicked and actually enjoying herself for once in her life. She thinks she can pretend we didn't do anything of the kind, that her daughter will grow to look more like her as she gets older. According to Delphi, a baby's brown eyes can turn green or blue and her hair will pale into something less like mine. She will grow up a baronet's posthumous daughter unless we put doubts in people's heads by marrying each other.'

'She's an idiot and doesn't deserve you.'

'Drace had to beat and abuse her to make himself want a woman enough to even try to get her with child, Wulf. Then I threw myself at her like a greedy boy before she had hardly even taken in the fact her prison door was open. The longer it goes on the worse the puzzle and any scandal gets when we're found out. I suppose I'm not much of a catch anyway.'

'You would make yourself one if she said yes,' Wulf told his brother. 'You might have been raised a gentleman, but you'd work for love if only she would let you.'

'Well, she won't, not even when the Earl decided to blackmail me with our lovely little secret. If I didn't marry a fortune and hand it to him, he said he would tell the world Lady Drace's daughter is my bastard.'

'So you offered for Isabella?' Wulf whispered as if saying it out loud might break them both.

'I should have let him do his worst.'

'He would have done it. He would have ruined the woman you love out of pique if you didn't do as he bid you.'

'Yes,' Magnus admitted bleakly. 'So I let Isabella be the ransom.'

'Did she know?'

'Not then. When I asked her to marry me, you can imagine how relieved I was when she said no. Then she came back to me with a scheme to pay the old devil part of her dowry on condition Aline, Dorrie and Theo lived with us. I hadn't told her about Delphi and our affair, of course, but Isabella saw through the old man's surface charm and insisted he assign guardianship of Dorrie and Theo to me before he'd get a penny of her dowry. Isabella insisted she didn't want to be in love and a rational marriage would suit her very well. I suppose she could see how unhappy the girls were at Carrowe House under the Earl's thumb, too, and we were such good friends, Wulf. And once I'd offered for her, how could I withdraw? So we agreed to wed and I believe that must be where you came in.'

'You nearly married her.'

'I expect we would have come to our senses sooner or later.'

'Don't lie, you would have wed Isabella because you couldn't marry Lady Delphine and no woman deserves that.'

'Isabella least of all?'

Wulf glared at the tree Magnus was leaning against as if he needed it to hold him up. 'I love her,' he confessed at last.

'Shouldn't you be telling her instead of me?'

'Yes,' Wulf grumbled. 'How did she find out about Lady Delphine?'

'Another letter.'

'Lady Delphine's maid seems to be on your side.'

'Not noticeably.'

'Then why interfere?'

'Because of the child and maybe she wants her mistress to be happy and cared for despite herself as well. Perhaps I never deserved to be happy after what it did, but you deserve Isabella.'

'I don't, but living without her is worse than offering for her so she can turn me down.'

'You'll always regret not taking a chance, but how are you planning to make this grudging proposal?'

'You're not the only Haile who can offer an elopement to a lady.'

'However you offer for her be sure you make her happy, Wulf. I might have to kill you if you don't. If Carnwood or Shuttleworth or your friend Kenton don't get there first, of course.'

'She has to say yes first,' Wulf said gloomily.

Chapter Seventeen

A whole weary week had passed since she humiliated herself in front of Wulf and most of his family at Carrowe House. Isabella counted off the days and decided her reckless throw of the dice had been a failure and she didn't know what else to do. Maybe she was going to have to drag herself through the new social Season without him after all. Even the idea of pretending she couldn't imagine anything more delightful than hot rooms, sharp-eyed critics and too much warm lemonade made her feel slightly sick, so the reality was bound to be even worse.

'I hope you really are planning to have your new gowns fitted this time, Isabella,' Charlotte said with a frown when she saw Isabella's outdoor clothes and her best bonnet waiting to be set on her perfectly arranged locks.

'Heloise won't let me escape twice.'

'Good, you're going to need every one of them for the new Season now you're unattached again,' Charlotte said cheerfully and carried her still-teething baby daughter back into the sitting room as if there was no more to be said.

'I'll be glad to go home, too,' Isabella muttered at the closed door and only just managed not to stick her tongue out. 'Come, Heloise, if you had kept a still tongue in your head, I wouldn't have to do this, so don't try to creep upstairs as if you never even heard the word *mantua-maker* and don't dote upon every aspect of fashion.'

'Your gloves, Miss Alstone,' Heloise said and held them out reproachfully.

'Thank you,' Isabella said, slipping them on and trying not to remember a hot night at Haile Carr when she'd used her evening gloves to fan her hot cheeks. She turned briskly for the door.

'Your bonnet, Miss Alstone.' Heloise caught her up with a look of deep shock that any lady would go out without one.

'Confound my bonnet,' she said and jammed it on as she ran down the steps.

'Never damn a bonnet like that one, Miss Alstone; it's probably sacrilege,' Wulf said as she reached the bottom and realised he was waiting there for her. He took off his silk hat and bowed gracefully, then offered her his arm as if they had trivial social encounters of this sort every day.

'What are you doing here?'

'Well, that's not very polite. You should send your mistress off to learn better manners somewhere very refined indeed, Heloise,' he told her maid and the wretched woman tittered and got ready to follow them as if she thought the whole event run-of-the-mill as well.

'Never mind my manners, you are not the type of man to wear clothes like that or stroll about Mayfair as if you have all the time in the world and not a lot to do with it.'

'I do today. I am busy walking the beautiful Miss Alstone to an engagement, or at least I would be if you could start moving instead of standing there glaring at me as if I've just said something outrageous.'

'But why?'

'Why not?' he countered as if it was quite normal for him to come here looking like that, offer her his arm and expect her to meekly go with him. He looked even more dark and dangerous than usual in the elegant day attire of a gentleman he wore with his own unique flair. And now she was supposed to stroll along by his side as if the very sight of him in full daylight didn't make her knees wobble?

'You did say no more hiding in dark corners,' he pointed out helpfully, and what else could she do but take his arm with that demand in her mind to say this was her fault?

'True, but I can't believe you listened.'

'Neither can I,' he said with a rueful smile that made it even more difficult to stroll along at his side as if they were polite acquaintances. 'I haven't been very good at it so far, have I?'

This was her own fault. She had asked for him to admit he wanted her company in full daylight as well as the intimate darkness they usually met in, but the best thing about the dark was that it *was* intimate. They could feel each other move with slavish fascination and nobody could hear or see them and whisper about them behind their backs. Out here, strolling along the broad streets and squares of fashionable Mayfair, it felt far too exposed and public. She was even more conscious of his lithe body as they walked side by side because she couldn't reach out and touch him. It would cause a scandal if she did any of the things she longed to do right now. So of course she only wanted to do them all the more.

'No, but I'm so glad you decided to this time,' she said and smiled because he had listened to her for once and come out of the darkness.

If she had to endure not doing any of the things they had been doing in the shadows since the night they met, it was worth it to walk at his side and show the world she knew and appreciated the youngest Haile brother no matter his parentage. Knew him and was so proud to walk side by side with him on a beautiful spring morning she didn't want to say goodbye when they reached the dressmakers'. They couldn't linger and stare into each other's eyes here, though, because this was how things were when you were out in the open, under the critical gaze of the fashionable ladies and gentlemen strolling up and down the most fashionable of streets. He bowed in farewell and raised one eyebrow at her as if he knew about all that heat and breathlessness and wanting she was trembling on the edge of.

'Mrs Shaw believes we might happen to meet in the park at the fashionable hour tomorrow. Apparently her new barouche has plenty of room for a chance-met acquaintance if I get there quickly enough to oust all the other ones who will be queuing up to claim a ride around the park with the beautiful Miss Alstone,' he said so calmly she had to wonder if she was the only one burning up with need.

'Shouldn't we make our own assignations?'

'We aren't very good at arranging them in the open, though, are we?'

'No,' she had to admit and this was the new reality she had wanted, so she supposed she had best get used to it.

Driving in the park together, walking to museums and art galleries, sharing Charlotte's box at the theatre with half a dozen others, and even a small and exclusive evening party for a few hundred of the hostess's closest friends where Wulf made what he called his 'debut in polite society' was very well, but Isabella enjoyed the day they spent at Develin House with his family, inspecting works done and planning what would fit where, so much more. Isabella had changed so much since this time last year she hardly recognised herself as the same woman when she looked back. The old Isabella was prepared to settle for less than her sisters had. She didn't believe in love, so for her love would never exist because she had reasoned it away. Marriage to a good friend for the sake of a family and rescuing his sisters from a dire situation seemed so sensible why turn Magnus down when he asked her to marry him? This Isabella who lived in the now cringed at the idea of her then self blithely ignoring all the passion and need inside her and for what? For the sake of building a safe little box to put her life in, then forget how small she had to make herself in order to fit inside it.

At least today they had been allowed to drive back from Hampstead in Ben Shaw's pared-down racing curricle alone but for the tiger—the groom dressed in striped livery—as long as they stayed in sight of the others following them in Charlotte's barouche. The diminutive tiger was so busy clinging on and watching Wulf's driving with an eagle eye to listen to them, so it was almost like being alone. All these proper social meetings had left Isabella feeling desperate for half an hour's unregulated conversation with the Honourable Wulfric Haile.

'You do know I don't need all the trappings of fashionable life to be happy, don't you, Wulf?' she asked and watched the hazy, smoky city grow ever closer in the evening sunlight as she tried to pretend his answer wasn't vitally important.

'You don't need to meet your family and friends and talk and shop and maybe even gossip a little now and again?' he asked as if he wasn't quite so sure about that.

'I do need *them*, but not half the peerage and a few hundred of their hangers-on along with them. When I said I wanted to meet you in the light of day,

I didn't mean you should change into someone else to make it happen.'

'I'm not; I'm finding out who I am and who I'm not. You said you needed us to know each other by daylight and I'm Wulf Haile as well as Dev and Fitz-Develin now, so we need to find out who he is between us. The me I am at heart sometimes ends up shut in a room for days until I get a chapter or a book or even a page just how I want it and I doubt I'm very easy to live with.'

'You think finding out about the man you really are behind all the dash and devilment will frighten me off, don't you? You should know that I am quite capable of amusing myself, then. Don't lump me with the spoilt little socialites who need constant attention and flattery if they're not going to turn into a Mrs Fonthill or another of your bored lady friends the moment a husband finds something serious to do with himself. Perhaps I'm more like you than you think as well, because I'm only just getting to know myself as well and I owe a lot of that to you, Wulf.'

'I thought you were pretty much perfect as you were the night we met,' he said as if he meant it and she had to be flattered even if it wasn't true.

'No, I was lonely and uncertain of what I wanted that night and even a touch terrified by what I'd done in agreeing to wed Magnus. I thought I could never be in love because I didn't *want* to be; it wasn't to be trusted and I thought good sense, a few mutual interests and plenty of friendship and respect made a better basis for marriage than some fleeting passion that would melt away as soon as desire faded. I was so wrong, Wulf, about that and so many other things. I have never been perfect and never will be, but I'm not prepared to accept second-best ever again or be second-best for someone else.'

'How could you be?'

'Ask your brother,' she said with a wry smile.

'I already have and you were right, I did need to know his sad story.'

'And now you do know it, what's next?' she asked as they reached the city and her heart sank at the idea of parting from him again until their next frustrating encounter in front of too many people.

'Will you marry me, Isabella?' he asked, an anxious glance betraying how much her answer mattered to him.

'Why?'

'Well, not because of my lack of fortune, noxious reputation and dubious charm obviously. So it would have to be because I love you. I can't promise you much, but I can promise you'll never be second-best for me, Belle.'

'You love me?'

'I wouldn't have dressed up like a dandy or made my debut in polite society if I didn't.'

'You don't sound very happy about it.'

'I would be if I wasn't waiting for an answer and even more desperate for you than ever in so many different ways.'

'Of course I will, you idiot. I thought you were never going to ask.'

'And I can't believe you said yes,' he said on a huge sigh of relief and a look of pure joy that made her love him even more. 'Don't make me wait long, Belle. I think I might burst into flames out of sheer frustrated desire if you don't marry me very soon.'

'Your brother promised me an elopement, but I suppose one Haile brother will do as well as another,' she joked and joy was so real in her heart now. Then there was that wicked ache deeper down and it felt utterly wonderful to be alive and by his side, even if they did have to wait a few more days for much more.

'This is one thing I intend to do a hundred times better than Magnus and I've got off to a fine start by loving you with every fibre of my being. I'm so glad he's an idiot.'

'No, he's a good friend, but that's all. I used to wonder why I wasn't in love with him now and again during the years after I met him during my first Season. He's a fine and handsome man and I truly hope he'll find love again and this time with a woman who has enough courage to love him back whatever anyone has to say about them being together, but he's not you, Wulf. That's why I could never quite persuade myself to fall in love with him. It's why I misbehaved so scandalously with you in the dark that first night at Haile Carr. You're you and he's simply my friend Magnus.'

'Well, that's a relief, then. We won't have to emigrate after all.'

'Do you really want to live in a new country?'

'Only the one you're in, love; if you want to explore one, I do as well.'

'Not just now I don't; we have far too much to do here to go skipping across the Atlantic Ocean and back because you feel like a change again. Maybe when your sisters are happy and your mother is quite settled and your brother is himself again we could think about an adventure or two.' Isabella considered that list and couldn't leave off the biggest reason they had to stay because they had to begin as they went on and be honest with one another from now on. 'And then there's your father's murderer to be tracked down and punished before someone else gets the blame.'

'Are you sure you want to share in our notoriety, Isabella?' he asked as if she might throw his love aside even now because she lacked the courage to recognise it for the huge gift it was.

'I want your closeness and our love and laughter, all the shared jokes and sharp corners and loyalty, Wulf, and the Earl truly doesn't matter any more. His murder is important because your family will only be free of him when it's solved, but his petty jealousy and self-indulgence and meanness are dead and done with and I love you and want to share everything that makes you as you are for the rest of our lives.'

'Good, then if you still want to elope, I can be free next Tuesday.'

'I need a gown,' she said in a panic all of a sudden because it was only five days away and she couldn't marry him with the trousseau she had made when she was going to marry his brother.

'I'm not sure I agree with that statement,' he said wolfishly and she laughed joyously and, as they were back at Ben and Charlotte's now, he threw the reins to the tiger and lifted her down from the precarious vehicle as if she was little more than a featherweight.

'I'm certainly not marrying you naked, you wolf,' she murmured as he slid her down his rigidly eager body and made sure she knew he wanted her so urgently the days ahead already felt like an eternity.

'You can wed me in a suit of armour if you want to, just make sure you do.'

'I will,' she promised and kissed him boldly on the mouth in front of Ben's grooms and anyone else who happened to be looking because this was the man she loved and the world would just have to get used to it.

Chapter Eighteen

Wulf neatly turned Ben's curricle into a lane that looked as if it didn't go anywhere very much. Isabella wondered if the wheels would ever be the same again and how they would get up and down this road in the winter. Right now the prospect of being marooned here with her new husband seemed very appealing, so she supposed they were right about there being a silver lining to every cloud.

'A fine catch I am, bringing you home in another man's carriage,' Wulf said as if he was still worrying about the differences in their respective fortunes and how she would feel about being isolated by mud and perhaps even snow up here come winter. She thought she'd managed to convince him money didn't matter to her as long as they were together, but she would manage it in the end now they had proved to one another that love could overcome far bigger odds than they had set it so far.

'You're my fish and I'm proud of you,' she joked but wondered fleetingly if Ben's gleaming paintwork could survive wide hedges and a narrow lane unscathed much longer, despite Wulf's skill with such a dashing equipage. The lane began to climb more steeply and the tiger Ben insisted on sending along looked as if he had doubts about maintaining his dignity if he fell off the back of his master's fine carriage.

A short way up and the road improved and widened a little to welcome visitors brave enough to get this far. Isabella was a countrywoman at heart, so it certainly didn't frighten her to be this far away from other people. She wondered how Wulf's devoted manservant and his mother would rub along with Heloise, though, and was surprised the woman agreed to stay now Isabella Haile was determined to be as unfashionable as possible most of the time.

'Oh, now I see why you love this place so much,' Isabella exclaimed with a gasp at the wide expanse of open heath and woodland spread out in front of them like one of the most beautiful landscape paintings she could ever imagine seeing. 'You feel you could set out to explore the whole world from up here and why wouldn't you love it?' she murmured.

'Welcome to my home, then, ours now, until you find us one that suits you better,' Wulf said and helped Isabella down before leading her towards the back of the substantial cottage, leaving the tiger and Jem Caudle, the manservant, to deal with the horses and luggage. 'Once upon a time I came here to get away from people, but since I met you, any time we spent apart felt lonely. For more than half a year now I've longed to have you here where nobody much even knows there is a house at all and we can be private together.'

'You spent a goodly proportion of that time sailing the oceans to get as far away from me as possible,' she said coolly.

'What else could I do when you were going to be Magnus's wife?'

'Stay here and convince me not to be so silly, I suppose.'

'He's my brother.'

'True, but I'm your wife,' Isabella argued and the sound of that word, so new and precious she wanted to dance and do all sorts of other things not nearly as suitable for the outdoors at this time of year, made her forget to be angry with him for leaving.

'I know,' he said huskily.

'And you're my husband.'

'You talk too much, Wife,' he whispered against her lips.

'Silence me, then.'

'No, I like you noisy,' he said with a wolfish grin.

He tugged her closer and kissed her until her eyes crossed and her head was spinning as if he'd realigned the planets and even gravity couldn't be relied on any more. One of his hands was running over her neat derrière as if it had every right to be there. It did now and she didn't want it to stop. She wanted to be inside as fast as possible so that they could do all sorts of lovely things to each other as soon as possible behind closed doors.

'I love you, Wulf,' she said dreamily and the future she had secretly longed for looked back at her from his extraordinary silver-blue eyes, making her feel truly beautiful for the first time in her life.

'And I love you, Isabella,' he said as if they were making another set of vows. His voice had gone even more husky as she made a wickedly inquisitive exploration of his leanly muscular torso and it reminded her of the hot summer night when she met her fate on a shadowed terrace and nearly forgot herself in so many ways she ought to blush.

'Will it be dark soon?' she asked, the feeling she might melt from the inside out if they couldn't love one another making her long for the night ahead.

'Not soon enough,' he said, 'but you did say you were tired of lurking in the shadows with me, didn't you?'

'I did,' she whispered. 'I think it might rain,' she lied with a rapid glance at the clear blue sky.

'And it would never do for us to get wet on the first day of our honeymoon, would it?'

Isabella could feel shivers of pure need running through him as if he was a greyhound ready for the chase. He shaped her waist with broad, strong hands, bringing her hard up against his eager body, and she felt all her senses bloom and seek out every facet of him they could discover with all these finely made, wretchedly inconvenient clothes on. He felt hot and heady and totally male under her exploring hands and her knees were being unreliable again. She wanted these hotly passionate kisses more than ever, but the lovely, feverish delight of waiting for tonight, anticipating how it might feel or where they might go together before the night was done was something to savour, to feel her way through with his eager assistance because it mattered so much it shouldn't be rushed, especially on their wedding night.

'You're such a calm and peaceable man we'll never quarrel,' she lied with a witchy, knowing smile that invited him to share the joke as they hurried through the almost wild gardens towards the front door somebody had left invitingly open before tactfully disappearing.

'If you wanted one of those, you'd be on your way up the Great North Road with my brother bound for Gretna instead of married to me.'

'He's a true gentleman, but I do believe we can be silly and besotted and smug about each other without his help right now.'

'I wasn't raised to be such a gentleman as my brother, though, Isabella. I'll try to be better in future, but it's probably too late for gentility to take.'

'I love you as you are and you look like a perfect gentleman to me.'

'Then try behaving a bit more like a lady at least until we get upstairs,' he reproached her playfully, trying to put a little space between them so they didn't end up making love for the first time on the stairs.

'And I do like doing things I shouldn't with you,' she murmured provocatively as they had to stop and kiss each other again before they remembered to go up another step.

'We're married now,' he said sternly and he looked so manly and ruffled and trying not to be the wild lover under all that gentlemanly restraint that she laughed, causing him to look deeply offended and let her go.

'Then it's our duty to do all the things we weren't supposed to on the night we met, but with extra naughtiness added for interest. We can be lovers even if we are married, and if that doesn't work, we'll just pretend we're not.'

'Everything works with you,' he said shortly. 'A bit too well,' he added and she giggled because she was free to express all the emotions she'd had to keep bottled up for far too long. With him she could be the woman she was always meant to be, the one who'd stepped out from behind Miss Alstone's elegantly restrained protective cover the night they met and goaded her with wild fantasies of Wulf FitzDevelin as her lover from that moment on.

'Oh, my Wulf, you're such a good man, but could you stop being stern and gentlemanly and protective now and remember I'm your very willing wife?'

'Isn't that all the more reason to be most of those things now I'm your husband?' he said and the heat and hunger she could feel coming off him echoed the heat and hope inside her.

'No, not here and not now,' she said and shaped his tense jaw with tender urgency, hoping he'd lose that formidable control of his very soon and ravish her so thoroughly she forgot her own name and where she was.

'I am far less of gentleman than your husband ought to be,' he said far too seriously.

'You're the only one I want,' she said and stood on tiptoe against him so he could tell how much she did.

'You don't hold back when you give your everything, do you?'

'No, but I love you and you love me—that's the promise of a lifetime I believed I wasn't worthy of until I met you.'

'And you think I'm a wonder for you? What do you think you are for a mongrel wolf like me, love?'

'Oh, Wulf, I do love you,' she responded fatuously, but luckily he seemed to like it because he looked down at her and grinned as if he couldn't help himself.

'You do, don't you?' he said as if he'd only just let it truly sink in.

'I do; you are handsome and clever and creative and daring and I love you so much it almost hurts.'

'You are a dream I didn't dare dream and now I've got you chained to me for life I'm never going to stop having it, night after night.'

'Good, don't! And I think you're very good with words.'

'Words are the last thing on my mind right now,' he told her gruffly and gave up on getting her to their bedroom the usual way, lifting her off her feet, then impressing her mightily by running up the remainder of the stairs and into the charming old room she caught a glimpse of before he dropped her on the bed and joined her without even taking his elegant and gentlemanly wedding shoes off his feet.

'You'll get blacking on the sheets and Mrs Caudle will never forgive us.'

Wulf said something rude and toed the shoes off even as he did something very hasty to Isabella's elegant spencer jacket and let her up long enough to shrug that off before starting work on her fine silk gown himself.

'Careful, it's my wedding dress,' she chided breathlessly. 'Let me,' she urged and pushed his hands aside to undo the laces herself and push the fine fabric over her shoulders without ripping it because she knew she would treasure this gown all her life and she didn't want it damaged even though she wanted it gone as much as he did.

'Do I have to feel the same way about all this starch and silliness, love?'

'Not if you don't want to, but you look quite magnificent to me,' she said as she sat back on the wide old bed and admired him as he struggled with buttons and ties and she watched and appreciated the show from under heavy-lidded eyes.

'Did you know they make you wear a corset to get the right waist to fit this ridiculous nip-waisted coat and the right sort of trousers? The tailors call it a vest, but the damned thing has bones in it.'

'Now you know how we women feel, but it's all right; I can see from here you don't need one, so there's no need to convince me there isn't a spare inch on you anywhere, my Wulf. Thank you for enduring it for my sake, but we looked wonderful on our wedding day, didn't we?'

'We did, Belle, and now it's time for the best part of the whole day,' he told her huskily and ripped off the soft cravat that went with his fashionable finery before he knelt on the bed next to her and put all his best sensual efforts into getting her out of the rest of hers in the least possible time.

'It's a good job I didn't want to wear my underpinnings again,' she chided as he watched her with hungry, warm eyes and now it was her turn to feel a fine tremor run through her like wildfire.

'Your nether garments were quite charming, Mrs Haile, but right now I prefer you naked.'

'How are yours, Wulf?' she countered and tugged at the ties of his shirt to find out for herself.

'I'm not as pretty,' he told her.

'Let me see,' she said as she worried at the hem of his shirt until he gave in and pulled the thing over his head with a ragged sigh. 'More,' she ordered implacably and the silly, unnecessary 'vest' was soon gone and they were on to his undershirt. 'I preferred it when gentlemen like you wore those sleek cutaway coats and tight pantaloons, but I suppose it got ladies who couldn't have the likes of you in their beds too excited, so they invented trousers and nipped-in coats to stop them fainting with frustration.'

'You talk too much,' he murmured and she realised he could be right.

'That's because I want you too much,' she countered and then she was silenced and greedy and eager all in one incoherent package at the sight of him, all muscles and smooth male skin and tension. 'You're magnificent,' she said at last and breathed out because she was going to faint if she didn't.

'And you're simply breathtaking, my love,' he countered and took a ragged breath of his own as he ran his ravenous gaze over her softer curves and eagerly voluptuous breasts announcing she really did want him desperately with almost painful need.

'Touch me, Wulf. Kiss me,' she urged because she needed him to do something about this merciless hunger before it burnt her up completely.

'How can I not? I'll break if I don't have you now, my darling,' he breathed and now his hands were fire and power and gentle reverence all at once, and his mouth? Oh, as for his mouth... Isabella ran out of words and sank into a world of instinct and feeling and love with a delicious, delighted sigh.

'If I'd known love was like this, I would have tracked you down and badgered you to teach me everything about it a great deal sooner,' Isabella murmured as she lay back against her husband's shoulder, still learning every detail of him under her skin where it kissed against his and giving a delighted little wriggle at the idea of her best adventure yet.

'Be still, you wanton. We really ought to thank Magnus for getting me to Haile Carr and close enough to meet you for the first time. I wasn't exactly welcome in the best drawing rooms of the *ton* then, so we might never have met at all if not for him.'

'I hope you're not planning to lurk in the dark waiting for immodest ladies to fall on you like a she-wolf ever again,' she teased him, relishing how stunningly new and wondrous it felt to be his wife in every way. All the glorious days and weeks and years of learning even more about wedded bliss ahead of them left her utterly speechless and transported by sensual wonder, already anticipating the next time they could fly somewhere stunning and wordless together.

'Not unless it's with you,' he said and the intent heat in his ice-blue eyes said that could be arranged.

'Good,' she said militantly and rolled over to prop herself up on her elbows and stare down at him because why wouldn't she now she had the right to and he was so much worth the looking at. 'I hope you're not expecting any offspring of ours to be pattern cards because you're sure to be disappointed.'

'We're not exactly those ourselves, so it would be asking far too much,' he murmured and stopped her reply with fierce, joyous desire, then sat up and shifted in the wild nest they'd made out of the once-immaculate sheets and blankets. 'For the rest of tonight we'll have to pretend to be, though,' he added dourly and leapt out of bed to put more wood on the fire as if that was the only way he could keep his hands off her.

'Why?' she said as he leapt back into their joint warmth because this was April and an English spring and he was a human and not a wolf after all. She turned up her face for another kiss because whatever he was she loved him almost as desperately as she had before he showed her how much more there was to loving than she'd ever suspected.

'I want you...' he began, then raised his head.

She tried not to be disappointed he wasn't demonstrating how much at this very minute. She was greedy for her first and only lover now she'd finally got him into bed. 'I know,' she said smugly.

'Behave yourself, Mrs Haile. I'm not making love to you again tonight.'

'Why not?'

'Because it will hurt. No, stop that; you're not getting your own way this time.'

'I can't believe you're being so stuffy, and to think I believed you were so dark and dangerous when we first met and now you're being such a fine gentleman I could spit.'

'Put it this way, if we make love now, you won't want to do it again for days. Contain yourself and there's always tomorrow.'

'I suppose we could just cuddle, if it wasn't so cold.'

'Princess,' he accused her, then got out of bed again to snatch a shawl for her to wrap herself in. Isabella was glad Heloise had been over here to unpack her most treasured possessions before the maid enjoyed a nice little holiday at Develin House, ruthlessly reorganising the Haile ladies' wardrobes.

'With a body like that you can call me what you like, my Wulf,' she said with everything she wasn't supposed to want explicit in her heavy-lidded eyes as he slipped back into the warm nest of bedclothes beside her.

'And there I was, thinking you loved me for my mind,' he said easily and pulled her back into his arms, holding her wrapped in soft cashmere next to him to shield her from the arousal that had made her realise what a truly gentle man she'd married.

'I do, but it's not my fault if you come with added manliness, spice and sensuality. All that just makes me a very lucky woman, I suppose.'

'True,' he said modestly and reached for the finest wine and hothouse strawberries Magnus had somehow managed to present them with as a wedding-night luxury they hadn't had time to appreciate until now.

'What are we going to do about the girls?' Isabella whispered.

'Let them work out what they want, Belle. They have had too many years of being controlled and told what to do for us to start interfering now.'

'Then do you think Magnus would like to be my estate manager, since we're not going to be spending much time on them?'

'My wife the heiress,' he said with a wry smile of resignation.

'Just your wife, Wulf, that's all. We can put my fortune into trust for our children if you like because I'm a writer's wife now and we don't need it.'

'That depends how many you're planning to have, but I'd best get on and earn enough to keep you and them in style anyway, hadn't I?'

'You already do and we have a house I love in a place where we both want to live. I don't need any more.'

'Maybe an extra room or two for the babies when and if they happen to come along,' he suggested easily enough and she let out a quiet sigh of relief.

'Promise you'll never let my fortune come between us?' she said and twisted round to look at him with a plea to take her seriously.

'It's only money, love. I can manage on nothing much at all and Matty Caudle can turn a penny so many times I'm expecting the King to scream for mercy one day.'

'I really do wish I could have been with you when you first met her and her son, my darling,' she said truthfully and wriggled closer to show she meant it.

'I know you do and thank you, my love, but I never want you to find out at first-hand how hard life is for a girl on the streets.'

'Don't wrap me in cotton wool. You already know Ben's stepmama is Eiliane, Marchioness of Pemberley, and I'm sure you're aware she's set up an asylum for such children. I help out there when I can, so I'm quite aware of the things you're trying not to tell me. Those poor girls don't stand much chance of living long enough to become women at all, let alone happy ones, without the help of people like her.'

Wulf seemed to mull over the idea she knew a lot more than he thought she ought to about the darker side of London life. 'You Alstones and your web of powerful connections never fail to surprise me.'

'I'm a Haile now.'

'I'm not quite sure I am yet.'

'A Develin-Haile, then; it's a compromise I'm happy with.'

'If you are, then I shall have to learn to be, but I don't think I can ever be truly grateful the Earl of Carrowe was my father after all.'

'And why would you be when he treated you so harshly?'

'So our children don't have fingers pointed at them and other brats sniggering at them in corners. So you don't have to be married to a nameless man; so my mother isn't expected to be ashamed of me at every turn any more.'

'I don't think she ever was.'

'Then why did she let him get away with it, love? I know you would fight tooth and nail for our children if you had to, so why didn't she?'

'I can't answer that question, my darling, perhaps you should ask her.'

'I did and she palmed me off with some nonsense about him making such a mess of being a father to Gresley and Magnus she didn't want me to suffer it as well. Still, she's been hurt enough, and if believing that makes her feel better, so be it. At least she's not big or strong enough to kill a large and still-powerful man. So nobody can accuse her of making away with the Earl because it must have taken a man's strength to bludgeon and stab the old crow. It's only thanks to you that I'm not in Newgate awaiting trial for it right now myself.'

'I really am a paragon among wives, am I not?'

'Not if you don't stop doing that, no,' he told her shortly and removed her exploring hand from his intriguingly muscular belly.

'I've waited so long for you, Wulf. Even after I found you, you left me for what looked like for ever from this side of the Atlantic. So now I've finally got my hands on you I don't want to let you go.'

'It's your hands that are doing the damage right now, but I promise you I'm never going far without you again, love, if that will make you feel better and get them off me until you're more used to being my wife. I felt as if a vital part of me was being wrenched away when I sailed off to my new life swearing to forget you, but how could I stay here and long for you when you were going to marry my brother?'

'I lost faith in us before I even met you. I should have called off my betrothal to your brother the moment I set eyes on you, or at least I tried to set them on you, in the shadows—which was quite a challenge when all I wanted to do was feel what we could do to one another and never mind the rest of our senses.'

'I'm glad you didn't trust me that much then, love. I wasn't worth it.'

'You were always worth it,' Isabella said and told herself sternly not to turn into a watering pot because her failures had kept them so far apart for so long and he really thought he hadn't been worthy of her back then. 'And don't forget I learnt very young that Alstone women shouldn't trust devilishly handsome men and you're a devilishly handsome man, my darling. I suppose I had to find out for myself a deliciously desirable man like you doesn't have to have a devil living under his skin.'

'If your eldest brother-in-law hadn't dealt with him so effectively already, I'd castrate that piece of scum who pretended to marry your eldest sister all those years ago. His vicious misuse of an unfledged girl has made you distrust our whole sex ever since and I find that impossible to forgive.'

'Having to live openly with my cousin Celia is punishment enough for him.'

'Not for me it's not.'

'Miranda is worth a hundred of either of them and they did make her miserably unhappy, so I'm glad you hate them, too. But why are we talking about them when we could stare into each other's eyes and marvel at how we both finally managed to see sense at the same time, Wulf?'

'Distraction,' he said concisely.

'Oh, my love, I'm sorry. Let's go to sleep, then, so we can get to tomorrow and make love to one another again all the sooner,' she said and lay down on her side of the bed. She was going to have a lot to live up to, she decided as he reached for her hand and held it while they told each other silly stories to chase sleep so they could dream about the rest of their lives together.

* * * * *